the
further
adventures of

SHERLOCK HOLMES

THE MOONSTONE'S CURSE

THE MOONSTONE'S CURSE

SAM SICILIANO

TITAN BOOKS

THE FURTHER ADVENTURES OF SHERLOCK HOLMES:
THE MOONSTONE'S CURSE
PRINT EDITION ISBN: 9781785652523
E-BOOK EDITION ISBN: 9781785652530

Published by Titan Books
A division of Titan Publishing Group Ltd
144 Southwark Street, London SE1 0UP

First edition: February 2017
10 9 8 7 6 5 4 3 2 1

What did you think of this book? We love to hear from our readers.
Please email us at: readerfeedback@titanemail.com,
or write to Reader Feedback at the above address.

To receive advance information, news, competitions, and exclusive offers online, please sign up for the Titan newsletter on our website:
www.titanbooks.com

To Jeremy Brett,
for his unforgettable Sherlock Holmes

Author's Preface

M y last book was loosely inspired by Bram Stoker's *Lair of the White Worm*, a novel whose main interest today is as a bizarre curiosity piece. This time around, however, I can heartily recommend Wilkie Collins's *The Moonstone*. Published in 1868, it is generally acknowledged as the first mystery novel, and its detective, Sergeant Cuff of Scotland Yard, would have a prodigious number of twentieth-century descendants. The novel's ingenious plot has a clever twist worthy of Dorothy L. Sayers or Agatha Christie.

Collins's other early novels, *No Name* and *Armadale*, are also interesting, although something of a slog because of their length. Still, they are striking for their powerful and complicated female characters. Magdalen Vanstone and Lydia Gwilt are no shrinking Victorian violets! The two characters are like yin and yang, a flawed heroine and a sympathetic monster.

My novel is a sort of sequel to *The Moonstone*. Much of Collins's tale of the spectacular diamond and its vicissitudes provides a backstory set some fifty years in the past. Sherlock Holmes becomes involved with the jewel, and unlike Sergeant Cuff, he gets it right the first time. Like Holmes in my novel, I too must acknowledge an illustrious predecessor—two of them, in fact. All we modern mystery writers labor on under Wilkie Collins's and Conan Doyle's long shadows. I owe Collins a special debt for Murthwaite's final lengthy missive from India.

One

Mrs. Hudson had gone in to announce my arrival, but it was Holmes himself who opened the door on a Wednesday afternoon in July. That thin face with its predatory nose and intense gray eyes smiled at me. "Ah, Henry, excellent–excellent! Do come in. You were the only thing missing. Now this case must be promising indeed."

I followed him through the door. Mrs. Hudson curtsied and departed. A tall, slender man in his twenties with bushy brown hair and an equally prodigal mustache stood near the bow window. Like Holmes, he wore that ubiquitous uniform of an English gentleman: well-cut black frock coat, waistcoat with the gold Albert chain forming two loops between the pockets, and black-and-gray-striped trousers. Standing quietly nearby was a man, no doubt a servant, who seemed big because he was wide rather than tall. He wore a dark-gray suit, his arms extended, his large hands clutching a bowler hat.

"Mr. Charles Bromley," Holmes said, "may I present my cousin and my good friend, Dr. Henry Vernier."

Bromley had a relaxed, easy smile which wavered as his brow knotted. "Not Dr. W–?"

"No," Holmes and I exclaimed in unison. Holmes glanced at me, a brief smile pulling at his lips.

I drew in my breath wearily. "No. It is *Vernier.*"

Bromley's smile returned, and he extended his hand. "A pleasure, Dr. Vernier." His grip was firm but not fierce. He half turned toward the person in the dark suit. "This is Hodges, my man." Hodges nodded, his broad, rugged face remaining completely expressionless. The skin over his cheekbones was faintly pocked.

"Please take a seat." Holmes gestured. Bromley took one end of the settee, I the other, while Holmes took his battered favorite armchair. "Henry has been good luck to me, Mr. Bromley. His presence has always marked the beginning of some of my most interesting cases. It augurs well for your visit. You were about to tell me about your wife's diamond, sir. I take it this is no common gem."

Bromley laughed softly. "Good heavens, no! Hardly common. Have you heard of the fabled Moonstone?"

"Yes, certainly. The name comes from the diamond's appearance, does it not? And also because it was once part of a statue of an Indian moon deity."

"Very good, Mr. Holmes. It has been in the family for over ninety years. My wife's great-great-uncle John Herncastle took it at the storming of Srirangapatna, India, in 1799."

Holmes's eyes glowed. "And are there not stories about a curse?"

Bromley's melodious laugh repeated. "Exactly so, Mr. Holmes. Your reputation is well deserved, I see. I hope, however, that you do not give any credence to curses and maledictions?"

Holmes shook his head. "No, in general I do not." He extended his fingers and placed their tips together. "All the same, objects of great value have a way of leaving a bloody trail of crime and misery behind them. The cause is not supernatural force or demonic power, but human greed and iniquity. For example, I am certain the Indian inhabitants of the besieged Srirangapatna did not willingly hand over the diamond to their occupiers."

"No, indeed, and in fact, that was a source of some familial discord. One of Herncastle's cousins and a fellow officer claimed he had murdered the men guarding the diamond in cold blood, and Herncastle, as a result, was a rather despised outcast for his entire life. He died around 1840, leaving the diamond to his niece, Miss Rachel Verinder. There were some difficulties, but eventually…"

"Difficulties?" Holmes let his hands drop onto his knees. "Explain yourself, sir."

"Well, I'm not certain myself of all the details. The diamond disappeared, causing a great clamor, then reappeared, then disappeared again. Miss Verinder and her soon-to-be-husband, Mr. Franklin Blake, were called into question—unjustly I am sure. Another relation had actually stolen the diamond, I gather, and some Indians also became involved at one point. Regardless, the diamond was eventually restored to its rightful owners. A certain Sergeant Cuff of Scotland Yard was involved."

Holmes gave an appreciative nod. "My illustrious predecessor. Cuff was a giant amongst his kind, far beyond any of those mediocrities at Scotland Yard today. They are pygmies by comparison."

"Soon after, Miss Verinder became Mrs. Blake, and she left the diamond to her son Neville, my wife's late father, who left it in turn to Alice. 'Left' is perhaps an overstatement. Neville's will is complicated. My wife does not truly own the diamond. She has a life-interest, but it cannot be sold. It is to be passed on to our eldest child and remain in the family."

"Interesting. I have heard of similar arrangements before. And do you have any children, Mr. Bromley?"

Bromley's smile faded. "Not yet. Alice and I have only been married a little over two years."

"I see. And should your wife die childless, what then?"

"It would go to her younger sister, Lady Norah Bartram, who does have an infant son, James."

"I see. And the diamond... It must be worth a fortune."

"Its value is incalculable—incalculable." His eyes widened, emphasizing the clear blue circles of the irises. "Do you know much about diamonds, Mr. Holmes?"

"A fair amount. It is useful knowledge in my business."

"The diamond is a large one, but its clarity and color are without equal. It is curious. The story has it that the diamond's brightness waxes and wanes with the phases of the moon. On the surface of it, that would seem absurd, but if you study the diamond over time as I have, you cannot so simply dismiss the idea. I wonder if some curious tidal influence... And the diamond's color changes depending on the light. By day it is a clear yellow-white, while at night it gleams with a faint bluish tint. It also has one tiny flaw, an icy glint you can see only by turning it a certain way. The stone seems almost alive, taking on different hues according to its mood or fancy." He laughed. "I suppose that must sound incredible to one unfamiliar with the jewel."

Yes it does, I thought to myself, my smile forced.

"No," said Holmes. "That is a characteristic of remarkable gems: each seems to have a personality of its own."

"Exactly, Mr. Holmes, exactly. You do understand. I have come to the right man indeed!"

Holmes smiled politely. "And why have you come to me, Mr. Bromley?"

Bromley's smile faded, and he drew in his breath, releasing it in a great sigh. "A jewel of such splendor should be a source of joy. Unfortunately, that has never been the case for my Alice. She has always been obsessed with the stories about the curse, and over time, her fears have grown more and more morbid and obsessive. She has even…" He bit his lower lip, even as his right hand made a fist.

After a few seconds, Holmes said, "'She has…?'"

Bromley drew in his breath again. "This may sound extreme–it may sound almost as if I am–as if I am questioning my wife's sanity–but that is not the case! I assure you it is not. She is perfectly sane, but she is… Her health has always been fragile. Hers is a highly sensitive and overwrought nature. She worries too much, and her brooding gives these fears a sort of life, an actual embodiment. She claims, on more than one occasion, to have seen an Indian face at the window, a dark leering face with a white turban. We do have an Indian beggar in our neighborhood, and he may have even been at the window once, but I do not think there can really be anyone lurking about the house. No one else has seen anything at all. Surely skulking Indians seeking lost jewels are the stuff of some lurid melodrama, nothing more!"

Holmes smiled faintly. "I would tend to agree with that."

"And yet she is so fearful! It isn't just this supposed Indian. As long as I have known her, the diamond has made her nervous and uneasy."

"And how long would that be, Mr. Bromley?"

"As I said, we have been married two years, and the lightning struck, so to speak, almost exactly three years ago. That date is easy to remember: we share the same birthday, and by coincidence, it was on that very day. A lucky thing for me, that, since I'm dreadful with dates and numbers!"

"The same birthday, you say. Do you mean you were born the same year as well?"

"No. I am two years older than she."

"And what day did you meet, Mr. Bromley?"

"She had been a slight social acquaintance for some years, but I first realized I must marry her on the second of July, three years ago. It was shortly before her father's sudden and tragic death. Alice was wearing the diamond for the first time. She wore a gown of pale-blue silk, which matched her eyes—they are the delicate blue of cornflowers. She was tall and slender and beautiful, with the diamond resting on her lustrous white skin. I thought I had never seen so lovely a vision. I know it is ridiculous, but I think I fell in love with her at that very moment. She was awkward and uncomfortable: I could see that. I took her arm and tried to calm her. We danced the first dance together, and I stayed as close to her as I could that evening. Her eyes often seemed to seek out mine, and I tried to reassure her with my gaze that I would take care of her. Oh, this must sound like romantic nonsense, but it's true, you know."

Holmes's forehead had creased, and fingers began to drum at his knee. "How exactly did her father die?"

"Apoplexy, a sort of fit one evening. He was a hot-tempered man, and his doctor had warned him that he must better master his temper. Unfortunately, he did not take that advice to heart. Alice had tried to explain her fears about the diamond, but that would inevitably enrage him. He had forced her to wear it to that grand

soiree where I first fell in love with her, and it was shortly after that…
Poor Alice feels she is to blame, but I have told her that is nonsense."

Holmes nodded. "This is interesting, but so far it sounds
like you have more need of a physician or an alienist than a
consulting detective."

Bromley stared intently at him, then slowly rose to his feet.
"I'll not have my wife insulted—I'll not have her sanity called
into question!"

"Come, come, Mr. Bromley. I meant no offense. Do sit down.
Tell me what you want me to do."

Bromley gave him another hard look, then sank into the chair.
"Forgive me, Mr. Holmes. Things have been difficult lately. I love
my wife, and I cannot bear to see her suffer. I do so worry about
her. There is another thing I must relate. About two months ago,
we had a visit from a Mr. Tyabji, the son of an Indian who married
an Englishwoman. Tyabji attended Oxford, lives in London and
speaks English as well as you or I. He told us that the diamond is
still missed in his part of the country and that it did not belong to
us. He asked if we might do the right thing and give it back. The
maharajah could not pay its true worth, but he would give us a
thousand pounds for its return. I was polite, but I could not believe
what I was hearing! I told him the diamond had been in the family
for nearly a century and that returning it was out of the question.
'Regrettable,' was all he said, and he left shortly thereafter."

"And did you find this visit disquieting? Was he threatening?"

"In truth, Mr. Holmes, he was not. I quickly put it out of my mind,
but a few days later Alice asked me if we might take up Tyabji's offer.
I was even more dumbfounded than I had been when Tyabji made
his request. I did not dwell on the folly and imprudence of such a
course of action, I simply pointed out that legally the diamond is not

ours to give away. Again, she has only a life-interest. She can neither sell nor give it away. Her father's will is very clear on that point."

"I see."

"She acknowledged this at last, but she became more and more upset, and again about a month ago, she claimed to see a face at the window. Oh, I do not really believe there is anything to this, but I would like you to look into the matter, Mr. Holmes. Mr. Tyabji does not appear to be a scoundrel, but perhaps you could make certain he is not behind some attempt to frighten my wife. I must tell you, too, that I have resolved, if not to give away the jewel, to lock it up for good in a bank vault where it can no longer worry my Alice. There will be one last dinner party a week from Saturday, and then on the following Monday, it will be put away."

"There is a surer way, at least as legend has it, to break the curse on a large diamond."

"Yes—by having it cut up into smaller stones. That, however, is specifically forbidden in her father's will. It is to be kept intact. I must admit, too…" He shook his head. "It would seem a desecration to break apart such a beautiful thing."

Holmes shrugged. "Well then, hiding it away in a bank vault is wise. I have always thought that valuable jewelry is not worth all the trouble it entails."

Bromley smiled, something faintly ironic in the curve of his lips. "You will not feel that way once you see the diamond, Mr. Holmes."

Holmes's fingers began to drum at his knee again. "Jewels are only safe when they are secured out of harm's way. All too often… I recall a case where I warned a gentleman his wife's diamonds might have been replaced with fakes. He laughed at the notion, but the next day he came to see me in a frenzy of despair. He had discovered that the diamonds were fakes, and he had no idea when they might have been switched and stolen. A servant, a trusted housekeeper, was behind the theft."

The faint smile played about Bromley's lips again. "You said you knew something about diamonds, Mr. Holmes. Can you tell a real gem from an impostor?"

Holmes shrugged. "With my ocular glass I would have a pretty good idea, but I am not a jeweler, Mr. Bromley. If you want to be certain, you should see a professional."

"Perhaps, but might you give me an opinion, on say, a smaller diamond, like this one?" He reached inside his frock coat, withdrew a small black box and opened it. The light from the window sparkled off a diamond ring.

Holmes sighed. "I suppose you insist?"

"If you would humor me…"

"Very well." Holmes stood and went to his desk. He opened the second drawer, rummaged about and withdrew a small wooden box. He took out a square of glass and a black eyepiece about two inches long. He extended his arm toward Bromley, palm up. "If you please." He took the ring and held it up to the window, peering closely at the stone. He went to the desk, picked up the glass square and pressed the stone against it. He shook his head. "A very feeble imitation. It cannot even scratch glass, which a good fake will do." He gave the ring back to Bromley, whose melodic laugh rippled again.

"Very good, Mr. Holmes. Very good. Now let us try something a bit more formidable."

He turned to the man who had stood motionless behind him during the long conversation. "Hodges." The servant reached into his inner jacket pocket and removed a black velvet case about six inches square. Bromley's big hands were lightly freckled with reddish hair below his knuckles. He opened the case. "Behold, Mr. Holmes—behold the Moonstone!" He held up the silver chain and let the diamond hang a few inches below his fist.

I drew in my breath. "Good Lord," I murmured. The stone was enormous: it caught the sunlight and flashed yellow-white. I had never seen such a jewel in my life. It belonged in a museum under guard, and yet it was so remarkably beautiful you could see why someone would want to hold it up and dangle it before the light. The color and the intensity of the individual facets varied; some sparkled while others did not. The nearby bow window was open, and the gem swayed ever so slightly in the breeze, causing the facets to change in color and brilliance. It seemed to pulsate like a living thing, like the crystalline heart of some unimaginably beautiful being.

Holmes rose up ever so slightly on his toes, then sank back down. His eyes, like mine, were fixed on the diamond. He drew in a great breath, then the corners of his mouth rose slightly. "Nicely played, Mr. Bromley. A very dramatic entrance indeed." He extended his hand. "May I?" He took the diamond, stepped nearer to the window and held it up before him in the light, peering intently at its interior. Finally he nodded once, then went again to his desk. With a quick flip of his wrist, he drew the diamond across the glass. Next he fitted the eyepiece into his right eye and peered again closely at the depths of the jewel. At last he withdrew the eyepiece and nodded again, even as he drew in his breath and held the diamond up.

"I saw the slight flaw. Normally I do not find gems particularly tempting. However, this one is the exception that proves the rule. A remarkable specimen, Mr. Bromley. You were right about its being priceless. It is genuine, is it not?"

Bromley was still smiling. "It had better be. It was examined recently by Mr. Harter of the renowned jewelers Harter and

Benjamin. I have no doubt as to its authenticity."

Holmes stared again into the stone. He gave his head a quick shake. "Pity. I must admit it seems a shame to shut it away in the darkness. All the same... How many men—and women—have peered into its depths and been ensnared by its beauty? And how many have died for this piece of hard carbon, of coal, somehow heated and fused into this object of perfection and beauty?" He shook his head a last time, then turned to hand it back to Bromley.

I had stood up without even realizing it. "Might I have a look?"

Holmes glanced at Bromley, who nodded, and then he handed me the diamond by its chain. I hesitated, then touched its top face. The smooth surface felt faintly cold, which surprised me given the warmth of its color. I turned it slightly, noting how the facets would catch the light and sparkle. I thought of the jewel hanging just below the hollow of Michelle's slender white throat. It would be... a distraction. A woman's naked beauty was different. In the end, it would clash with that of a jewel. This might appear more spectacular, but after all, a diamond was a cold, dead thing, not a living, breathing being capable of love, warmth and passion. Still, its beauty could not be denied.

With a sigh, I gave it back to Bromley, who returned it to its case. He, in turn, gave the case to Hodges. We all sat again in our former places. "I trust you are wise enough to keep the jewel under lock and key at your home," Holmes said.

"Certainly, Mr. Holmes. Better yet, I have a well-made safe by the Withy Grove company. Perhaps you can have a look at the safe. I would like you to verify that the jewel is secure."

"If it is soon to reside in a bank vault..."

"In the meantime, if the safe were vulnerable, it would require only minutes to abscond with the diamond."

"A point well taken. I am at your disposal to examine the safe."

"Perhaps tomorrow, at say, ten in the morning? I'll give you our address near Kensington. You can also meet Alice."

"I shall want to speak with her about the diamond."

"And so you shall, Mr. Holmes."

"You said that you are having a final dinner party with the diamond on display. I think perhaps I should be there to ensure its safety."

Bromley's forehead scrunched up, his eyes troubled. "Do you think that is necessary, Mr. Holmes?"

"Better safe than sorry, as they say."

Bromley ran his tongue across his lower lip, then gave a thoughtful nod. "I suppose that makes sense. Yes, certainly you may come. A week from Saturday. I'll send you an invitation—and perhaps you as well, Dr. Vernier."

"Oh really, that is not necessary," I said.

"No, no, I insist. I am sure Mr. Holmes would like to have you there as well." He glanced at Holmes, who nodded.

"That's very kind of you, Mr. Bromley." I frowned slightly. "You said your wife was troubled by the diamond's alleged curse, and that her health had suffered as a result. Is she under a physician's care?"

Bromley's mouth straightened and stiffened briefly. "She is. Dr. David Cowen."

"Ah, I know Dr. Cowen. He knows his business."

"Do you think so?"

I stroked my chin. "You seem to have your doubts."

"No, no, it is only that nervous disorders are difficult to treat—you will grant me that?"

I smiled sadly. "They certainly are. There are no magic tonics or elixirs, despite what the patent-medicine sellers would have you believe."

"Cowen has been Alice's doctor for many years—since she was a girl, and yet her condition has not improved in the least. It has worsened over time, especially the last few weeks."

"Because of the diamond?" Holmes said.

"Yes—and its blasted curse." He laughed once. "I cannot understand how she can succumb to such superstition. Still, I must be fair. It cannot be denied that her family is unlucky. Her grandparents, the Blakes, were killed in a railway accident, and both her parents' deaths were untimely."

"What happened to her mother?" Holmes asked.

"A tragic accident some two years before her husband died."

Holmes's nostrils flared. "What type of accident?"

"An overdose of laudanum."

"But…" I began, then hesitated.

"Yes?" Two creases had appeared above Bromley's nose.

Holmes gave me a knowing look, and I only shrugged. Laudanum was an easily available tincture of opium, generally taken as a certain number of drops added to water or wine. Men might prefer to put a bullet through their brains, but an overdose of laudanum was a common method of suicide for women. It was also one of the most convenient ways to murder someone.

"Mrs. Blake was highly strung, like her daughter. She, too, feared the diamond and, before her death, she could no longer be persuaded to wear the jewel. It was the source of terrible arguments between her and her husband. Yes, little wonder this supposed curse weighs heavily upon Alice. She says that it is almost tangible, that she can sense an aura of evil hovering about the diamond. She has lost weight, and her sleep is even more troubled than usual."

"Has she tried vigorous exercise like long walks?" I asked. "Sometimes that helps."

"Her constitution is too frail. She suffers from heart palpitations and dizziness."

"Has she any hobbies or occupations to keep her busy?"

"Not really."

I shook my head. "That is not good. Has Cowen prescribed anything?"

"Yes." Bromley stared closely at me. "Laudanum."

I drew in my breath slowly.

"You do not approve?"

I shrugged. "It is one of the few effective medicines we have, but it is problematic. Has she taken it for a long time?"

"I believe so. I have suggested that she try another doctor, but she will not hear of it. She is generally very accommodating to my wishes, but Cowen is a subject upon which her opinion is absolutely fixed."

"I know Cowen quite well, Mr. Bromley. I worked with him in a hospital during my training. He is a good doctor and is as well reputed as anyone on Harley Street. Still, if your wife's condition has not improved, I would tend to agree with you. Medicine is as much an art as a science, and sometimes success is a question of personalities."

Bromley smiled. "Would you be willing to see her?"

"I was going to suggest she consult with my wife."

"Your wife?" Bromley laughed sharply.

"My wife is a physician, a very good one, and frequently women patients do better with a doctor of the same sex."

"You are not jesting, I see. I have heard of lady doctors. One of Alice's friends, Lady Jane Alexander, sees a Doctor Dudet something."

"Doudet Vernier. That would be my wife, Michelle Doudet Vernier."

"You surprise me, sir. Perhaps you could accompany Mr.

Holmes tomorrow and meet Alice. If you could tactfully suggest…"

"Let me meet with her and appraise the situation before I act."

"As you wish. By the way, you must bring your wife to the dinner party as well." He smiled at Holmes. "This visit has been a means of killing two birds with the proverbial one stone, it seems."

"I am glad you have found it helpful, sir. Before you leave, however, I have one or two other things to discuss."

Bromley smiled rather stiffly. "Your fee, I suppose. I fear that the Moonstone may have misled you. Alice has some income from her father, as do I from my family. We did also inherit her father's townhouse. However, we have no wealth commensurate with such an incredible jewel. The situation is ironic, since we cannot sell it or take advantage of its great worth in any way."

Holmes shrugged. "We can work something out. I am not unreasonable, and besides, your case interests me. We can discuss the fee later." Bromley looked relieved. "Oh. You have spoken about your wife a great deal, Mr. Bromley. Tell me something about yourself."

"Myself? There is little to tell, I fear."

"Come now, you needn't be so modest. I know you are a gentleman, most likely the younger son of a peer. Your tailor is among the top rank on Savile Row, probably Davies. Your cordwainer is equally preeminent, the Italian Scarpelli, I'd wager given the simple elegance of those boots and their slight reddish tint. I also know you have a large dog, most likely a black one, which you take for frequent walks. However, despite Watson's evocation of my quasi-magical powers, your occupation, if you have one, remains a mystery to me. Granted, one may distinguish certain coarser trades by the hands, but the hands of a banker, a bureaucrat and a teacher are much the same."

Bromley stared at him, then laughed. "Very good, Mr. Holmes!

Davies it is, and Scarpelli. But the dog? How did you know about Sally, my black Labrador?"

"Your stick, sir. Even the brass ferrule has been chewed. The teeth marks are broadly spaced and go quite high up. And black because I see no signs of hair on your trousers; it blends in."

He laughed again. "Very good! I have to replace my stick every few months. It is a game between the two of us. Your first surmise was also correct. My father, Lord Bromley, is a baron, and I am his second son. I was educated at Eton and Cambridge. As for my occupation…" He hesitated. "I have no regular occupation."

"An irregular one, then?"

Bromley shrugged. "Occasionally I am involved in certain business matters. On an informal basis." Holmes was watching him closely, but he did not elaborate.

"One last thing." Holmes stroked his chin with his fingertips. "Does your wife have light hair or dark?"

Bromley frowned slightly. "Light hair. She is blond."

Holmes nodded thoughtfully, even as his brow furrowed. "Very well, Mr. Bromley." His eye shifted toward Hodges, who had remained mute and still during the interview. "Perhaps also…" He shook his head. "No matter, sir. As I said, your case intrigues me, as does the jewel. Henry and I shall see you tomorrow at ten. You were going to give me your address."

"Oh yes. It's simple enough. Let me give you my card." As he stood, he reached inside his jacket pocket.

We all shook hands, and then the two men left. Holmes closed the door, then rubbed his long, thin hands together and smiled at me. "You are luck for me, Henry! This is a most promising case. Why don't we have a quick look at Debrett's?"

He walked to the bookcase, hunted about with a fingertip, then withdrew a thick volume in a red jacket with gold lettering. "Let's see." He set it onto the cluttered desktop, then flipped the pages. "Here we are. Lord Bromley, Robert was born 1839. Here's a son, Ronald, and another, Charles, born... Hmm. That makes Charles twenty-seven years old, so his wife is twenty-five. *Amor vincit omnia*–'love conquers all.'" He laughed softly. "Not a very original family motto, that."

He turned away from the book, put his left hand in his trouser pocket and stepped nearer the bow window. A gold chain hanging from a waistcoat button to its pocket, caught the light; light also showed on the broad expanse of his forehead beneath the shiny black hair. "What do you think of the Honorable Charles Bromley?"

"He certainly seems concerned about his wife, and he is rather charming."

"And charmed as well–did you notice how he regarded the diamond?"

"It is hard to resist."

"I wish there were some chronicle like Debrett's or Burke's which might trace the Moonstone's true history. There must be story after story wherein the diamond is lost and then gained, a grand series of thefts interspersed with murders, most likely between Hindus and Muslims. Enough to employ an army of consulting detectives."

"Do you really think someone is after the diamond? I'm afraid it sounds to me like another case of a neurasthenic young woman with a vivid imagination."

He shook his head. "No, no–it is much more than that. There are many interesting details that do not quite add up; there is little that can be taken at face value. I have high hopes, high hopes!"

I frowned. "What points?"

"His servant, for example."

"His servant? Hodges, you mean? But he didn't say a word."

"He didn't need to. His appearance told me everything. Why should the Honorable Mr. Bromley have hired a disgraced former soldier or policeman as his valet?"

"How on earth...?"

"Come, Henry, think it through! It should be obvious, even to you."

I frowned. "That kind of thing always gives me a headache—just tell me."

"His bearing—his bearing. He stood at absolute attention the entire time, his back ramrod straight! What valet has such posture? No, he was once either a policeman or a soldier, probably the army or marines, and why would an experienced soldier take a job as a valet? It would be quite a step down in life. It only makes sense if he was forced out of his earlier profession."

I was frowning. "Yes, that seems logical."

"Then, too, there was a large, distinctively angular lump in his right jacket pocket which caused the coat to sag on that side. Undoubtedly a revolver."

"A revolver?"

"Hardly extraordinary, given what he was carrying in his inside pocket. That would argue for the army—a service revolver, probably a short-barreled Webley. Yes, this case seems most promising. Oh, I would take it on just because of the diamond. I do not covet it as Bromley does, but it has a certain romantic allure, all the same."

I shook my head. "I have never seen such a stone. It makes me..."

"Yes?"

I stared past Holmes out the window. The breeze stirred the lace curtain. "Michelle has hardly any jewelry. I wish I could give her something worthy of her."

Now Holmes frowned. "She does not seem the sort of woman to be interested in such idle frivolities as jewelry. She has something far more valuable. She has you."

I saw that he was serious. "Thank you. That she does. For what it's worth."

"Come, Henry—you are worth a great deal to many people, including me."

"Thank you, Sherlock."

"Do you want to meet me at Bromley's tomorrow, or will you come here first?"

"I'll come here, and we can walk over together. I have nothing better to do. As usual, my practice is fitful to non-existent. It looks to be another fine day." I started for the door.

"One moment, Henry." Holmes had raised his long arm. "Would Michelle actually want some jewelry?"

I shrugged. "I think she might. I gave her some diamond earrings she cherishes. Rings, of course, are wasted on her given that her hands are bloodied up or in carbolic acid all through the day. Some sort of necklace would be nice for formal dinners or the opera, but it hardly matters, since I cannot begin to afford anything."

Holmes's right fingers drummed at his thigh. "I would think one hundred and fifty pounds would be sufficient for something simple yet elegant."

I laughed. "One hundred and fifty pounds! Yes, it would be more than enough, but I certainly do not have one hundred and fifty pounds to spare. Even Michelle, with her flourishing practice, does not earn that much in an entire year."

"That can be remedied." He turned and strode to his desk.

"Sherlock, what are you talking about?"

"This is overdue. It had skipped my mind. I shall write you a check." He sat down and pulled the cap off his fountain pen.

"For a hundred and fifty pounds? I cannot accept such a gift! Don't be ridiculous."

"It is not a gift—it is for payment earned. Adam Selton recently sent me a check for three hundred pounds for the successful conclusion of the affair of the White Worm. You well deserve half of that sum."

"Me? But you worked everything out, not I."

"No, Henry. Not everything. You determined just what was tormenting Adam Selton. You made his marriage to Diana possible. If he had thought of it, I am certain he would have sent you a check for an equal sum. The least I can do is split my compensation with you."

"I thought he was going to give you two hundred pounds, not three."

"So he was, but he was so pleased with the results that he added in another hundred." Holmes scribbled his name, then tore the check free. "Here you are."

I stared at it. "I really should not take that."

"You most certainly should! If not for yourself, then for Michelle. Spend it on that jewelry you were considering just now."

I slowly drew in my breath, then reached out to take the slip of paper. "Very well—but it is for Michelle and not myself."

Holmes nodded enthusiastically. "So be it!" He sat back and folded his arms. "There is one good thing to be said about a sum such as one hundred and fifty pounds."

"What might that be?"

"It is not sufficient to purchase a gem with a curse on it. Those cost far more."

Two

Holmes and I reached Bromley's home on Thursday morning just before ten. It sat amidst a row of townhouses on a quiet square. The narrow street was cobbled, and each four-story gray-brick façade had an ornate porch with two white columns and several chimneys above it.

Holmes sounded the bell, then managed to pull off his gloves without setting down his stick. I was carrying my medical bag at his urging. I would have felt half naked without it. The large oak door swung inward, revealing a tiny maid in the usual black dress, white apron and white lace cap.

"Mr. Sherlock Holmes, to see Mr. Bromley."

The maid stared up at him, her awe obvious, then curtsied quickly. "You're expected, sir. Come in while I fetch the master." Holmes and I took off our top hats and stepped into the cool, dim interior. "I'll just take those." She set our hats with our gloves inside on the small table, put Holmes's stick in a sculpted green ceramic umbrella stand, then raised her black skirts and swept away.

A short but broad-shouldered, big-boned woman soon appeared. Her face was rather plain, slightly ruddy. Her graying hair was parted down the middle and bound up into a compact bun. She wore a practical-looking black muslin dress with a lacy collar and a row of small black buttons which went down over her bosom to her waist. Her face formed a lopsided smile at the sight of Holmes. She gave a slight curtsey.

"Gentlemen, I am Mrs. Carlson, the housekeeper. I shall take you to the master, but I must admit I did so want to meet you, Mr. Holmes! I am one of your most faithful admirers. In fact, I think I was the first to mention your name to Mr. Bromley."

"Indeed, madam? I am grateful to you, then, for this most interesting case."

She gave a fierce nod. "I know that you can protect the mistress and the household from whatever deviltry is afoot!"

"I shall do my best, I promise you."

"This way, gentlemen."

But she had taken only a step or two when Bromley appeared before us. His curly brown hair looked freshly brushed, and over a white shirt and black cravat he wore a dark-red dressing gown with a black velvet collar, belted at the waist. His lips curled readily into a smile. "Ah, thank you, Mrs. Carlson. I shall take charge of them. Mr. Holmes, Dr. Vernier, it is a pleasure to welcome you to the old manor house, so to speak." He gave my hand and Holmes's a quick firm squeeze. "I hope you'll forgive my informal garb; I'm a trifle behind this morning."

Holmes nodded. "I have a favorite purple dressing gown I often wear into the afternoon."

"Ah, you understand, then. Which shall it be first, Alice or the safe?"

Holmes's black eyebrows rose slightly. "Mrs. Bromley, perhaps."

"Fine, she is eager to meet you." He took a step forward, but Holmes did not move.

"Mr. Bromley, I shall want to spend a few moments with her alone."

"Alone? We have no secrets, Alice and I."

"It is not a matter of secrets. We can begin with you present, but I should also like to talk with her in private."

"And what if she should have one of her spells?"

"Henry will remain with me. He is a physician and can attend to her."

Bromley shrugged, then touched the right side of his mustache. "As you wish, sir." He started forward. Holmes followed.

"Spells?" I murmured to myself.

We entered an overflowing sitting room. The chairs and the sofa were of dark wood and a paisley-patterned burgundy velvet; elaborate lace doilies and various knick-knacks covered the surfaces; etchings and painted landscapes hung on the walls. Two women sat at either end of the sofa, a brunette in black, obviously the maid, and a blond in white. Hodges was standing alongside the maid, his hand caressing her shoulder lightly even as he spoke softly to her. His familiarity was such that I wondered if they were either married or engaged. As we entered, he quickly lowered his hand and assumed his military posture. The two women both rose.

Alice Bromley forced a smile. She did look the part of a beautiful languishing female suffering from the vapors. She was thin and unnaturally pale with wan blue eyes, but each cheek had a rosy flush. Her ash-blond hair was bound up, but a few wisps showed about her small ear and another tendril drifted down round her cheek. She was tall for a woman, around five foot ten or so, about the same height as Bromley, and half a foot taller than her maid. Her ivory silk dress with its mutton sleeves was well cut and showed off her fashionably slim waist; elaborate lacework covered a bosom surprisingly abundant in one so slender. The maid was sullen-looking with pouting full lips, a mole near the right corner, and with eyes the same dark brown, nearly black, as her hair. She looked French.

"Hodges," Bromley said, "see that the trousers of my gray serge suit are well pressed. I want to wear it this afternoon."

"Certainly, sir." With a nod, he strode away. The maid's dark eyes followed him, the corners of her mouth rising slightly.

"Alice, this is Mr. Sherlock Holmes and his cousin Dr. Henry Vernier."

Mrs. Bromley clasped her hands together, even as Holmes and I bowed slightly. Her fingers were long, thin and shapely; the blue veins showed in the white skin below her bony knuckles. "Oh, I am so honored to meet you both! Who has not heard of you, Mr. Holmes? I have read all Dr. Watson's stories–read them many times, in fact. But I do not recall…" She frowned slightly at me.

"Henry is not in the stories, madam," Holmes said, "and you must not take them as gospel. Watson allowed himself great latitude. They are more fiction than history."

She squared her shoulders, thrusting her chin out slightly, which emphasized her long, slender neck. "Are they now? What of the hound? The incredible hound on the moors? Surely he was not mere invention?"

Holmes shrugged. "That one Watson did get mostly right."

She seemed to relax, and her smile was radiant. "I am delighted to hear it!" She appeared as guileless as a child. "Although the book did give me such a fright when I first read it. It was a dark, stormy evening and…"

Bromley had folded his arms, and he smiled. "Dear, I don't think Mr. Holmes wants to hear about your reading habits. He is here to help us determine if there is some conspiracy afoot involving the Moonstone."

She winced slightly, then drew in her breath. "The Moonstone." She shook her head. "Always the Moonstone—I would much rather talk about your adventures, Mr. Holmes." This last seemed almost a plea.

Holmes hesitated. "Perhaps later. If there is time." I knew there was nothing he loathed more than discussing Watson's stories. His eyes wandered about the room, came to a sudden halt. I turned and saw a violin resting on a nearby bookcase. "Do you or Mr. Bromley play the violin, Mrs. Bromley?"

"I play a little. A very little."

"Might I have a look?"

She nodded. "Oh yes, of course. It's hardly the equal of your Stradivarius, Mr. Holmes."

Holmes picked up the instrument and plucked the strings lightly. "From sometime around the turn of the century, fabricated in Venice. No, not a Stradivarius, but a respectable instrument all the same. The Italians are the masters."

"Play something for us, Alice," Bromley said. "I'm sure Mr. Holmes would like to hear it."

She seemed genuinely horrified. "Oh, I could not! Do try it, Mr. Holmes."

Holmes hesitated, then took up the violin and the bow. He spent some time tuning it, plucking, then tightening and loosening strings in turn. At last he drew in his breath resolutely, set the violin under his chin, and played a long soaring melody which I recognized as Bach. It was enough to show both his skill and his panache. He played for two or three minutes.

Mrs. Bromley clapped her hands together. "Oh bravo, Mr. Holmes, bravo!"

"Thank you." He nodded. "A very pleasant tone. This is a first-rate instrument."

Bromley set his hand on her shoulder. "Please, Alice. Play that tune from the opera, the one I like so well. Just a little of it."

She shook her head again. "Oh no, no, no."

"Please—just a little. For me."

Holmes took the violin by the neck and held it out to her. "You are not auditioning for an orchestra, madam. Play for us. I am not a music critic. No report of your abilities will appear in *The Times*."

She laughed. "I'd rather not."

"Alice…" Bromley made her name almost a sigh.

"Oh, very well. But just a little." She took the violin, set it on her shoulder, hesitated, then began.

The pitch wavered about as she found the melody, lost it, found it, lost it, found… I did vaguely recognize the piece. She was scowling as she played, her smooth white brow all knotted up with concentration. My eyes shifted to Holmes. His mouth remained fiercely neutral, but his gray eyes briefly showed his dismay. She was definitely not a musical prodigy like his former clients Rose Grimswell and Violet Wheelwright. She could not seem to keep either pitch or time.

The melody rose, faltered, quavered, then stopped abruptly. "Oh that is enough!"

Bromley gently clapped his hands together. "Bravo, my dear. I know you are nervous, but it was quite beautiful. Thank you."

Her mouth curved stiffly upward at the corners, and her blue eyes shifted to Holmes.

"The theme from Massenet's *Thaïs*," he said. "You play with great feeling, madam."

I quickly nodded. "You certainly do."

She was relieved, but not quite convinced. "Thank you." She quickly set the violin back on the bookcase, then turned to the woman in black standing nearby. "Oh, I haven't introduced you— this is my maid, Sabine Pascal."

The last name made it clear that the maid was not married to Hodges, not yet, anyway.

Sabine held her black skirts and curtsied slightly. "How do you do?" Her accent with just those four words revealed that she was indeed French. Alongside her mistress, the difference in their heights—and in their faces and noses—was striking. Sabine was dark-complexioned with a fleshy throat and rounded chin, and her prominent Gallic nose dominated her visage. Mrs. Bromley was pale and almost gaunt with high cheekbones and a thin, slight upturned nose. A rosy flush of embarrassment still showed. "Please sit down, Mr. Holmes, Dr. Vernier."

"Thank you, Mrs. Bromley." He stared at Bromley. "As I said, if you would allow us a few moments in private, sir."

Bromley drew in his breath resolutely. "Very well." He set his hand lightly on his wife's shoulder. "Answer any questions he may have. I shall be in the library should you need me."

Holmes glanced at Sabine. "Perhaps your maid would enjoy a few minutes of liberty?"

Mrs. Bromley looked puzzled for a second. "Oh yes. Sabine, you may leave us. I shall call for you if I need you."

"Very well, *madame*."

Holmes waited until Mrs. Bromley had sat, then swept back the tail of his frock coat and sat on the other end of the sofa. I took one of the chairs. "I fear the Moonstone is not an agreeable subject for you, Mrs. Bromley," Holmes said.

"No, it is not."

"Exactly what are you afraid of?"

She stared at him, her eyes opening very wide so you could see the pale-blue circles round her black pupils. Her mouth stiffened, then she put her hand over her mouth, even as a sharp laugh burst free. "What am I...?" She began to laugh in earnest, stopping to shake her head, and she again put her long slender hand over her mouth to try to block the sound.

Holmes's eyes were wary. "Madam?"

She drew in her breath deeply through her nose, raising her head very high. "Forgive me, sir. It is only... It is not truly funny, but..." Her mouth twitched into a grotesque smile, then recovered again. "Your question struck me as amusing, that is all. What am I afraid of? Sometimes it seems to me that I am afraid of *everything*. I know it is not reasonable–Dr. Cowen and I have often talked of it– but I am afraid of so many things. Afraid, for example, of germs. I wish I had lived in earlier times before Monsieur Louis Pasteur and Dr. Lister. Our forbearers did not know they were surrounded by thousands upon thousands of tiny unseen and malevolent creatures that could spread sickness and disease! They did not know that their food and water were crawling with microbes, that even a pure white linen pillowcase could be swarming with invisible creatures. How lucky for them! Truly, ignorance is bliss."

Holmes glanced at me, and I said, "Mrs. Bromley, microbes are not malevolent. They are just smaller forms of life. Many are harmless. They are not actively conspiring against us."

"No? Then how do you explain disease?"

"Some are harmful, that cannot be denied, but just as, in general, there are good and bad people, good and bad animals, so there are good and bad microbes." This idiocy was the best I could come up with. I looked at Holmes. His mouth twitched into a smile, which he fought to restrain.

"I suppose so, but..." She laughed. "Oh, I know I must seem quite ridiculous to you! Sometimes I seem ridiculous to myself—often, in fact. How can anyone possibly be afraid of so many things? It makes little sense. I am afraid of thunderstorms and dark cellars and fruit with bluish mold, and rats and insects—especially black beetles and spiders. That is not uncommon, is it, Dr. Vernier—to fear spiders, anyway? They can be poisonous, after all."

"Not at all. Most women seem to fear spiders." Except for Michelle. On one occasion, a throng of spiders hidden in a cake had terrified me but left her untroubled.

"But I'm afraid of cats, too, and most of the animals in the London Zoo, especially the snakes. And I'm afraid of tramps, gypsies, and men who speak loudly with deep guttural voices whom you cannot really understand because their English is so bad. And just lately I am afraid of Dr. Jekyll and Mr. Hyde. Have you read that, Dr. Vernier?"

I was still staring at her. "Read what?"

"*The Strange Case of Dr. Jekyll and Mr. Hyde*," Holmes said. "It is a short novel by Robert Louis Stevenson about a respectable English doctor who discovers a potion which releases his evil side and transforms him into the bestial Mr. Hyde."

"You have read it!" She was delighted.

"Yes. Most interesting, if quite fantastical. The idea that evil exists even in the best of men is hardly very original, but the story has rarely been told so well."

She nodded. "I think so, too."

Holmes's forehead had creased. "I think we are becoming somewhat distracted. I doubt it is useful for you to catalog all your fears, Mrs. Bromley."

I shook my head. "Most assuredly not."

"Let us return, briefly, to the Moonstone."

She sighed wearily, her smile fading away. "I suppose we must. I am afraid of it too, you know. Perhaps it was because my mother also feared it. My father would dangle it before me and say that someday it would be mine, and that would make me cry, and then he would be angry. In general, I don't like bright shiny things: I don't like jewels." She looked at me. "That, I realize, is very strange for a woman, but it is true. And I so much prefer a cloudy, rainy day to a sunny one. There is something so glary and false about the yellow sun shining everywhere and glowing off everything. It hurts my eyes. Yes, I much prefer the rain."

She raised her right hand apologetically. "Don't say it, Mr. Holmes. I am wandering again. Let me simply say that I am absolutely convinced the diamond is evil. That understanding came to me at a young age—the impression was seared into my consciousness. Grandiloquent language, perhaps, but the experience... The force of that impression has never left me.

"I was ten years old. I was staring into the diamond. Normally I would have looked away, but it hypnotized me, captured me. The sun caught it a certain way, and a red glint flashed. The spark came again and grew until it filled the diamond, setting it all aglow, a harsh and vivid scarlet. I realized it was the color of blood: that the diamond was swimming in blood—drowning in blood. I was so afraid I could not breathe. My mouth seemed filled with parched cotton. I wanted to look away, but I could not. I closed my eyes at last, but the red haze followed me into the darkness. I turned, staggered, and ran to my room. Alarmed, my mother followed me, but she could not comfort me. Do you understand now why I fear the Moonstone?"

Holmes gave a sharp nod. He glanced at me.

"Are you certain that was not a dream?" I asked.

She shook her head. "It was no dream. The Moonstone has always been a bane on our family, and I would be happy to be rid of it. I believe…" Her eyes filled with tears, and she lowered her gaze.

"Yes?" Holmes asked softly.

She did not look up. "If not for the Moonstone, my mother would still be alive." She bit her lip and fought to hold back the tears. "Oh how I wish… I would give it away in an instant if it were mine to give!"

"To Mr. Tyabji?"

"Yes."

"Your husband proposes to lock it away in a bank vault. Won't that make you feel better?"

She shrugged. "I suppose. A little, perhaps. But a curse is a curse, Mr. Holmes." She stared into his eyes. "It is there regardless of where you put the diamond. It does not go away."

One corner of Holmes's mouth rose, but not with amusement. "What is a curse, Mrs. Bromley?"

"What do you mean?"

"Explain to me exactly what a curse is."

Her eyes were still fixed on his. "It means bad luck and misfortune. It means suffering. It means death."

He shook his head. "All of that. Little wonder you want it gone."

Her eyes still glistened. "You are mocking me."

"I am not. I promise you that I am not. So you believe some

supernatural force is behind this curse, some non-human agency?"

She nodded once. Against the pure white of her silk dress with its lacy collar, you could see the subtle changes in skin color: her face had grown paler still.

"I do not believe in supernatural forces, Mrs. Bromley. But..."

"But what?"

"Human evil is sufficiently malevolent. It can hardly be outdone by ghosts or demons. Your husband, I think, does not share your views."

"No."

"But he is not so stern as your father?"

"Oh no. He never raises his voice to me. And he is going to lock the diamond away. That is... better than nothing." Her eyes turned downward, and she murmured, "One last time."

Holmes stared at her. "One last time?"

"I have to wear it one last time, and then I shall be done. After the dinner party next week, it will be over with. Just one last time– after all these years, certainly I can manage... one last time." She bit her lower lip.

Holmes looked at me, his concern obvious. "I do not like to distress you, but there is another subject we must discuss. Your husband said you have seen a face at the window, an Indian, you thought, in a white turban."

Her face stiffened slightly, even as she sat more upright in the chair. "I do not like to think about that."

Holmes, wisely, did not want to give her time to reflect. "When did you first see this Indian?"

"About six months ago. At our library window." She had begun to rub one hand against the other, her long white fingers moving rhythmically.

"And how many times have you seen him?"

"Three. The last was a month ago. Now I keep the curtains closed and try to remember never to look at the window." Her mouth pulled into a pained smile. "Charles thinks I imagined it, that I must have been dreaming or that it was only an idle fancy."

"And what do you think?"

"Oh, I don't know. I just don't know. It does not seem to make much sense. The jewel has been in the family for over ninety years. Why would the Indians reappear now? Surely after so much time–this is what I try to tell myself–they must have lost interest."

"Why do you say 'reappear'?"

"Because some Indians were supposed to be after the jewel when my grandmother first obtained it from her uncle around 1840. That was fifty years ago! And yet, Mr. Tyabji says the jewel's absence is still felt in his part of India. If it is felt, then perhaps…" Her voice shook.

"Besides the white turban, what distinguished this person as an Indian?"

"His skin was dark brown. And he had thick black eyebrows. And his upper lip… there was something odd about it." A slight note of hysteria had crept into her voice.

"Did he have any particular facial expression?"

"He smiled at me." She shuddered, then her shoulders stiffened even as her mouth twitched. "I screamed, of course. Rather loudly. I can really scream when I want to."

"I'm sure you can. And you are certain it was the same man each time?"

"Yes, I think so. I hadn't thought that it might be a different man."

"And what time of day was this?"

"It was in the morning the first time, and in the early evening the other two times."

"But not at night—or after you had been dozing?"

"No, not even the first time. I had been awake and out of bed for a few minutes."

"And other than this Indian, have you ever seen other strange faces at the window?"

"No."

"I see." He glanced at me. "This does not seem exactly like a hallucination to me."

I shook my head. "No." Granted Mrs. Bromley was excitable, anxious and overwrought, but she did not seem truly insane.

She let out her breath slowly. "I don't know if I should feel relieved or not. If I am not simply mad…"

I laughed. "There is no such thing as *simply* mad—madness, insanity, is complicated. There is often nothing simple about it."

"Charles seemed so sure, although Dr. Cowen was puzzled. If I simply made it up, then I would be safe, but if the Indian were real, then he would probably be dangerous. He might come back. He might be out there watching and waiting to strike. All the same, if I made it up, my safety would still be relative—I mean to say, I would obviously not be safe from my imagination, would I now?—and my imagination can be very frightening indeed."

"Regardless," said Holmes, "we need not automatically assume the worst. Your husband said that lurking Indians is the stuff of melodrama, and I tend to agree."

"But if the Indian was not interested in the diamond, why would he come to my window?"

"If he were interested, why would he appear at your library window? Thereby alerting you to a conspiracy. What could he possibly learn from peeking in your window? Besides, I am not at all convinced he was an Indian. Brown make-up and a turban are easily obtained."

She tilted her head slightly, her brow furrowing. "I had not thought of that. But why would someone–a white man–do such a thing?"

"It is too early to speculate." Holmes's thin lips formed an ironic smile. "But that is what I intend to find out, madam. Another question or two, and we can leave the painful subject of the Moonstone behind. Your husband has a dog, does he not?"

"Oh yes–Sally. Dogs often make me nervous, especially big barky dogs–my sister's husband has mastiffs, great slobbering beasts–but Sally is tolerable. She is very good-natured, and after all she is female, too."

"Did your husband think to turn the dog loose after the Indian appeared?"

Mrs. Bromley stared at him, frowned, then her brow cleared and she smiled. She had a slight gap between her upper front teeth, a minor imperfection that I found appealing. "The curious incident of the dog in the night-time, Mr. Holmes!"

Holmes gave a great sigh, then laughed once. "Touché, madam! You do know Watson's stories. And what happened with Sally?"

"Well, it was only the third time that Charles thought to let Sally loose. Nothing happened, but Charles didn't think to do it immediately, so the man probably had time to get away. Besides, I'm afraid Sally isn't much of a guard dog. Her barking is not consistent at all. Sometimes she barks just for the fun of it, other times, while James is running wildly about and shouting–James is my two-year-old nephew–Sally sits there, perfectly calm. She is not a young dog. She is perhaps five years old. She…"

Holmes raised his right hand, his long fingers outspread. "I see. And when this Indian appeared and you screamed, did your husband come immediately?"

"Oh yes, he…" She frowned and shook her head. "I know what you must be thinking—shame on you! Charles was not the Indian—certainly not. He was in the nearby sitting room, and he was there in an instant, within seconds."

Holmes shrugged. "It was necessary to be certain."

"Don't you trust anyone, Mr. Holmes?"

"If I have learned one thing in my profession, it is that trust must be earned and never given blindly. One must assume nothing."

"Yes, I suppose you have to suspect everyone. Still, wherever do you stop, then? If you question everything, then life is all a maze, and one soon becomes lost in one's doubts."

"You have a point, madam, but let us now drop all further philosophical discussions. We want to avoid becoming like a dog chasing its tail." He turned to me. "Henry, do you have any questions for Mrs. Bromley?"

We had agreed beforehand I would talk to her last to try to determine if a consultation with Michelle would be beneficial. "Your husband says Dr. Cowen has been your physician for many years."

She looked puzzled. "So he has. Since I was a girl of about twelve. He was also my mother and father's doctor. Do you know Dr. Cowen?"

"I do, and I respect his abilities." That made her smile. "All the same, sometimes another opinion can be valuable." This made her smile vanish.

"Charles has put you up to this, hasn't he? He's always asking me to see someone else—I know he doesn't like Dr. Cowen and wants me to give him up. But I will not—*I will not.*" Given her

44

flightiness, her resolution surprised me.

"It is not a question of giving him up—not at all. I would only suggest that you might see another doctor and…"

"I am sure you are quite competent, Dr. Vernier—otherwise Mr. Holmes would not have you as a friend. All the same…"

I laughed. "I am not talking about myself—I am talking about my wife."

"*Your wife?*" She was absolutely incredulous.

"She is a doctor, too, Dr. Michelle Doudet Vernier, and I believe your friend Lady Alexander is her patient."

Her brow had furrowed. "Jane has told me about her doctor, recommended her, even. All the same…"

"Many women find it very relieving to speak with a doctor of their own sex. They have certain questions or symptoms they could simply never discuss with a male doctor."

Mrs. Bromley opened her mouth, then closed it. For the first time, she seemed at a loss for words.

"Perhaps you have some such questions. It would not be giving up Dr. Cowen, not at all. She would merely meet with you and then discuss your condition with him. What harm could there be in a visit, testing the waters, so to speak? Some people actually have two doctors, you know, a regular doctor, and a specialist to deal with certain maladies. I am certain you would like Michelle."

She smiled faintly. "Would I?"

"I would let Dr. Cowen know before Michelle visits you. It would be done with his knowledge." I almost added "and with his consent", but reflected that was best not assumed.

She ran her tongue across her lips, then drew in her breath. "Very well. But only one trial visit—and I am not giving Dr. Cowen up."

"Certainly not."

Holmes nodded. "Excellent. I am glad that is resolved. I may have further questions for you later, Mrs. Bromley, but you have had enough unpleasantness for one day."

"Now might I ask a question or two of you, Mr. Holmes? It is only fair, after all."

He smiled. "Very well. I suppose you have earned the right."

Her right hand rested on top of her left, stroked it lightly. Michelle had big hands, too, but not so slender and thin as hers. "So often in the stories it seems that you meet people with a very dark secret in their past which comes back to haunt them. They are not so respectable as they seem."

"Certain of Watson's stories are fairly accurate, but often, probably to satisfy the public demand, he repeated them with slight variations. Many people have unpleasant secrets of one variety or another in their past, but rarely have they been convicts once transported to Australia."

"We spoke before of Dr. Jekyll and Mr. Hyde. Do you believe such a duality exists in everyone, good and evil counterbalanced, a raging beast lurking within the best of us?"

Holmes smiled faintly. "That, I think, is an exaggeration. The dark side of most people is more selfishness and unpleasantness than true wickedness. The boor is more typical than the fiend. And with the truly evil, it is not dualism—it is deceit, evil masquerading as good. It is men who may appear respectable and beneficent like Dr. Jekyll, but that is only a façade. Their private lives are dedicated to vice and crime."

Her slender face paled again, then her mouth pulled upward on one side in an ironic half-smile. "Like the Moonstone. It appears beautiful, radiant, but beneath its shining surface lies evil and darkness."

"Madam, such thoughts are hardly helpful. Try to strive for some objectivity. Try to look at the diamond as an attractive lump of valuable mineral dug up from the earth, and nothing more."

She sighed. "I shall try." She stroked her chin lightly. "But these deceitful persons who are villains inside... Beautiful outside, rotten within—is this common?"

"No. Most respectable-seeming people are indeed respectable, especially men when they reach a certain age and set aside the excesses of youth such as drinking, gambling and debauchery, excesses which are, by the way, the most common secrets we spoke of earlier. Yes, most are genuinely respectable. Boring perhaps, but respectable."

She laughed. "I probably fall into that category."

"Not at all—you are capable of an intelligent conversation. That puts you in the top tier of your sex."

I smiled. "You had better not say such a thing before Michelle."

He shrugged. "It is equally true of men."

"Ah yes," I said. "You can always argue that the misanthrope does not discriminate between the sexes." I looked at Mrs. Bromley. "Are you an avid reader, Mrs. Bromley?"

"Oh, I am! It is my one great avocation and consolation. It lets me forget my wearisome life and all my afflictions."

I stared curiously at her. She was young, attractive in a delicate sort of way, well off, and married to a man who loved her. Still, I had seen cases enough where a crippling mental pain tormented those who seemed to have everything. "Well, I hope you read other things than ghost stories or dark tales like the one about Dr. Jekyll."

"Oh, generally I avoid ghost stories and the like. I do enjoy novels of mystery and adventure. I have read much of Walter Scott, Robert Louis Stevenson, the Brontës and all of Dickens.

Wilkie Collins is a particular favorite. I'm especially fond of his *No Name*. The character Magdalen Vanstone is a wronged young woman determined to have her revenge, to turn the tables, upon her oppressors. One cannot possibly condone her conduct, nor should one admire her, but I do! She is so strong and determined, so full of life, so clever. I wish I had an iota of her fortitude. Have you read the novel, Dr. Vernier?"

I shook my head.

"I have," Holmes said. "Collins's early novels are favorites of mine as well."

A black dog with curly fur walked into the room, leaped up onto the sofa between Holmes and Mrs. Bromley, then curled up neatly beside the woman, draping its black paws over the edge of the velvet cushion. The large pink tongue hung out, and the dog panted lightly.

"Sally—there you are, girl." Mrs. Bromley stroked the dog's head, ruffled the fur slightly, then raised one large black ear and let it drop. "Such a good dog. Such a sweetheart." She stroked its head again, and Sally's brown eyes gave her that look of absolute canine adoration.

"Am I interrupting?" Bromley had appeared in the doorway. Gone was his red dressing grown, replaced with a dark tweed jacket.

"We were just finishing," Holmes said. "I was about to send for you."

"Ready for a look at the safe, then?"

"Certainly." Holmes stood. He nodded at Mrs. Bromley. "It has been a pleasure, madam."

She beamed and stood. "The pleasure is mine. If anyone can help us with the wretched Moonstone, it would be you, Mr. Holmes."

Bromley smiled slightly, then set his hand on his wife's shoulder.

They almost seemed posed for a family portrait. "Now, now, Alice, you mustn't be always thinking the worst of the jewel."

I had also stood. "We shall arrange a time for Michelle to visit you."

She smiled. "I look forward to it."

Bromley gave her shoulder a final squeeze, then started for the doorway. Sally jumped down from the sofa and followed. He led us down a hallway. "It's just in the library."

We went through the doorway. Walnut bookcases hid most of the walls, a table of the same dark wood was in the center, and at the far wall was a pair of tall windows.

"So this is the room where Mrs. Bromley thought she saw a face at the window?" Holmes asked. "Before I leave, I shall want to examine the back of the house."

"Certainly, Mr. Holmes. There is a terrace, then the empty stables."

"You do not keep a horse and carriage?"

"For us they are not worth the considerable expense." Sally had followed us into the library, and she stood beside her master.

"How many servants do you have, Mr. Bromley? We have met Hodges, Mrs. Carlson, Sabine and a housemaid.

"Not many, I'm afraid. The housemaid was Susan. There is another named Matilda, and the cook, Mrs. Bateson."

"Do they all live here with you?"

"Except for Mrs. Bateson. She lives close by."

"Their rooms are on the top floor, I suppose?"

"Yes, except for Hodges. He has a small room next to my dressing room." He gave Holmes a slightly puzzled look, then swept his arm about in the direction of the bookshelves. "I'm not much of a reader compared to Alice. She inherited most of these books from her mother and father. The situation was the same with them—Charlotte was the great reader, not Neville."

Before a section of bare wall, an elaborately framed painting rested on the floor, a pastoral tableau of sheep and a castle. Normally it must hide the black metal square of the safe with its circular combination dial in the center and to the side, a small silver knob. Bromley gestured with his freckled right hand. "After we were married, I had this put in and attached to the interior beams. You would have to tear the wall out now to remove it, and a stick or two of dynamite would hardly dent it. I didn't want to lie awake at night worrying about the safety of the Moonstone, and now I sleep quite soundly."

Holmes nodded. "Most impressive. Mr. Bromley, I must ask for a few minutes alone with the safe." Bromley looked surprised. "Professional secrets, you know. My examination procedure is unique and must remain confidential."

"Certainly, Mr. Holmes. As you wish. Take your time. I shall be in the sitting room with Alice. Come along, Sally." The dog looked up at Holmes and me, her tongue lolling out, her breath coming and going. "*Sally—come.*" The dog gave us a regretful look, then followed her master. He closed the door behind them.

"Have a seat, Henry. This may take a few minutes. Mr. Bromley has certainly spared no expense when it came to his safe—wisely so. If you are going to have a diamond like the Moonstone, you want to take the obvious precautions." He leaned closer and began to turn the dial lightly to and fro with his long fingers. "This is massive, massive."

There were sturdy wooden chairs at the table, but I sat in a comfortable leather armchair and crossed my legs. "I don't see quite why he wants you to look at it. Isn't it obvious that breaking into such a safe would be impossible?"

"Perhaps, but he is obviously very cautious in all matters concerning the Moonstone. It is his most prized possession." He went to the table, pulled out its single drawer, then rummaged about briefly before closing it. Next he picked up the painting and looked carefully at the back.

"What are you looking for?" I asked.

"Some people have an excellent safe, but are stupid enough to write down the combination and leave the paper close by where it can easily be discovered." He set down the painting, stroked his chin, then began to take books out of the bookcase and flip through them. "Ah, here is Wilkie Collins's *Armadale*, another novel with an interesting heroine—although that is definitely the wrong word for Miss Gwilt! You really should give Collins a try, Henry. *No Name* would be an interesting place to start."

"Perhaps I shall. I believe Michelle has a copy of the novel."

"Curious that Mrs. Bromley would find Magdalen Vanstone so appealing. She would seem to have more in common with the insipid sister. Magdalen was a born actress. A case of opposites attracting, or perhaps…" He shook his head as he returned a book to its shelf. "It would take some time to go through every book. I've done the ones close at hand. He might have put the combination in his billfold, which would be equally stupid, but I cannot check his billfold." He extended his fingers and tapped his hands lightly together. "I think before perusing more books, I shall have a look at the safe. This variety of Withy Grove generally has a combination of four double numbers in a left-right, left-right pattern, with an extra revolution in the middle."

"Eight numbers in total. How many random combinations does that make for?"

"I would say around half a million, Henry. Given eight digits, if you include the leading zeros, 99,999,999 numbers are possible. However, the dial only has the numbers from zero through fifty, so that means only half the numbers would be possible."

I laughed. "Not much chance of stumbling across it by luck!"

"No. Not by luck." He was turning the dial in both directions. "Sometimes people are clever in most respects, but even they can blunder."

I drummed lightly at the table, closed my eyes for a few seconds, then put my hand over my mouth to stifle a yawn. The dial made intermittent whirring, clicking noises as Holmes turned it to and fro. I could tell he was trying different combinations, then pausing a few seconds in between.

Finally I said, "How long are you going to fiddle with that? I think we agreed that you aren't going to find the combination by luck."

"So we did. Ah." Something clicked. He took the silver knob next to the combination dial, turned it, and swung open the safe door.

"*My God.*" I stood up to look inside. The black velvet case rested on the metal shelf.

Holmes gave me a conspiratorial smile. "Shall we have a quick look?" He hesitated, drawing back like an artist regarding his canvas, then he took the square case and opened it. The room was dim, muted and shadowy, but the diamond glowed faintly like some transparent sea creature, dormant but beautiful. Holmes closed the lid, then set the case back in exactly the same position. He swung shut the door, turned the knob, then spun the combination dial. "Very good."

I stared at him. "I never knew you were a cracksman!"

He gave a sharp laugh. "I am not."

"Then how did you do that? It was not luck."

"No. Our clever Mr. Bromley made one mistake."

"Which was?"

"He had the combination set to his birthday: the year, the month and the day. Thus he need not ever worry about remembering the combination." He laughed, then swept his hand round in a great arc. "A good thing I did not try to examine every one of these books!"

"But... how did you know the date of his birth?"

"The day is the same as for Mrs. Bromley, July second—remember? He told us. And the year came from Debrett's."

"I would have never thought of such a thing. You must tell him. He can have the combination changed."

Holmes's smile disappeared. "I think not, Henry. Not yet, at any rate."

"But should someone steal the diamond..."

"I do not believe the safe is in imminent danger from thieves. Besides, your common robber or cracksman prefers brute force and is incapable of deduction. We shall wait for a while."

I let out my breath. "I suppose you know best."

"You must not say a word of this. For now, we must let Mr. Bromley continue to sleep soundly at night." He began to hum something softly, even as he stepped around the table. "You might re-join the Bromleys while I have a look at the back of the house."

"Perhaps I shall."

A light rap sounded at the door, just as Holmes reached it. "Yes?"

The door swung open, revealing Hodges. His broad freckled hands rested lightly at his sides, and his forehead was slightly creased. "Mr. Bromley wondered, sir, if you were finished. He's engaged, but he thought you'd like me to show you round the back terrace and the stables."

"Indeed I would. You have arrived at exactly the right moment."

The big man half turned, but Holmes did not move. "Tell me, Hodges, that revolver you had in your coat pocket yesterday at Baker Street, do you know how to use it?"

Hodges did not move for a few seconds, then turned back toward us. In the dim light of the hallway his pupils were swollen black spots. Although he was not particularly tall, he had an enormously thick neck, mostly muscle. The wingtip white collar with its points folded down, must be the largest size available. His chin, on the other hand, did not amount to much. His big hand came up, briefly touched either side of his jaw, then fell again.

"Yes."

"I suppose being armed is a wise precaution when one is carrying a valuable jewel like the Moonstone."

Hodges nodded. "Exactly, sir."

"And have you any other hidden talents?"

"No. Not particularly."

Holmes smiled faintly at me. "I shan't be long, Henry."

I returned to the sitting room. The Bromleys had been joined by two other women. They all stood, and Bromley introduced me to Lady Jane Alexander and to his sister-in-law Lady Norah Bartram.

I would have never taken the two women for sisters. Norah was barely over five feet tall, plump rather than slender, bosomy, with chestnut hair bound up tightly. The firm set of her small mouth and the imperious glint in her brown eyes showed a self-assurance completely absent in her sister. Jane I had met before when she had come to see Michelle. A tall woman, almost brawny, a brunette with formidable black eyebrows, she always seemed self-confident to the point of haughtiness. Norah wore an elaborate striped green silk, while Jane had on a purple silk with the fashionable mutton sleeves tapering in at the forearms. The two women were each attractive in their own way and knew it. Pale Alice in her ivory dress resembled some dreamy wood nymph caught between two buxom Amazon warriors, a tall one and a short one, in their colorful battle garb.

Norah shook her head at Bromley. "So you actually went to see Mr. Sherlock Holmes? You have dragged him into this nonsense of Alice's?"

Jane's smile was faintly bitter. "Charles is always very thorough in his own way."

"Better safe than sorry," Bromley said. "We want to make sure the diamond remains secure and within the family."

Norah shook her head. "So you lock it in a bank vault where no one ever has the pleasure of seeing it again!" Norah said. "That's just lunacy. You know what I've always said: if you don't want the diamond, I'll be happy to take it off your hands. I'm not afraid of one of the most beautiful jewels in all of England. Give it to *me*."

"You know I cannot do that," Alice said.

Norah smiled sarcastically. "Because you care for me?"

"*Yes*. I would not wish its curse on anyone! Especially not my own sister."

"I'll be happy to take it, curse and all."

Alice had forced herself to smile, but her expression was pained. "Must you always joke about it?"

"What else am I supposed to do? Be terrified all the time like you? Afraid of every shadow?" She gave her head another fierce shake. "I would not live that way for anything."

"Come now, Norah." Jane's forehead was creased, and her lips pulled briefly outward and up. "Let your sister be. You know you will not change her. We are what we are. And where is Mr. Sherlock Holmes, Dr. Vernier?"

"Outside. He should be joining us momentarily."

"Excellent! I've always wanted to meet him. In the meantime, I must finish my story." She looked at Alice and Norah, her ironic smile returning even as she raised her large white hands. "You will not believe what Rose Chadwell did next."

Bromley looked at me and rolled his eyes upward.

Three

⟡

A light drizzle fell on Friday afternoon as Holmes and I took a hansom over Vauxhall Bridge to south London for a visit to Mr. Tyabji. Holmes had arranged to meet him around one o'clock. This was a rather ugly part of London, row after row of newly constructed plain brick homes as the metropolis threw its tendrils ever outward.

We went to the door, and Holmes rang the bell. A short Indian man neatly dressed in a black morning coat opened the door. "Mr. Tyabji?" Holmes said.

"No, sir. He is waiting for you. May I take your hats? This way please."

He led us down a dim hallway to a doorway that opened upon an oriental fantasyland. I drew in my breath in disbelief. Large tapestries of Indian scenes—men in turbans, exotic women in saris, elephants and tigers—hung on the walls, and a many-colored carpet from the *Arabian Nights* covered the wooden floor. In the corner a huge elaborate hookah of red glass with two long hoses gave off the smell of fragrant tobacco. Two men who appeared Indian stood up from amidst a pile of pillows with tassels and elaborate patchwork designs in red, yellow, green, azure or darker blue silk. One man was quite tall and wore a black waistcoat and black-and-gray trousers, the golden U of his watch chain showing. Upon a nearby chair lay a black coat. The smaller man wore light tan garments, a red turban and a red sash. He was obviously older with a thin brown face and a hooked nose.

Holmes looked between the two, then said to the man in the turban, "Mr. Tyabji?"

He laughed. "Sorry, old boy. Murthwaite is the name." His speech clearly established that he was English despite his dress.

The taller man took a step forward and extended his hand. "I am Geoffrey Tyabji, Mr. Holmes. It is a great pleasure to meet you." His English was almost perfect, with only a slight lilt. He was a very handsome young man with the straight nose and full lips of a classical Greek statue. Although he had the brown eyes and dark skin of an Indian, his curly hair was light brown, almost gold.

"The pleasure is mine, sir. This is my cousin and friend, Dr. Henry Vernier."

"Not Watson?" the two men said.

This required the usual tiresome explanation. The other man introduced himself as Jack Murthwaite, and we all took turns shaking hands. "Jack is my dearest English friend," Tyabji said, "and perhaps he should remain if you wish to discuss the Moonstone. He knows all about the jewel, and he has long been acquainted with the Blake family."

Murthwaite nodded, smiling. His white teeth stood out against his brown skin. He had a pair of dark brown eyes which went with his swarthy visage. "I have known Alice since she was a little girl. I used to entertain her with stories about my adventures in India. I'm afraid I stretched the truth a bit, especially when it came to tigers. My father knew the older Blakes well. He was at the birthday dinner where Rachel Verinder—soon to be Rachel Blake—first wore the diamond."

"Indeed?" Holmes said. "Yes, by all means, please stay."

"Very good," Tyabji nodded, then gestured about him. "Would you mind removing your shoes, gentlemen, and then take either a chair or some pillows on the floor, as you prefer."

Holmes and I both took off our shoes, and then I sat in a comfortable brown leather armchair. Holmes removed his coat and draped it over a chair, then drew together some cushions and sat cross-legged on them. Murthwaite was reclining, his chin propped upon his left hand, while Tyabji sat upright.

Tyabji leaned over and took one of the hoses from the hookah. "Would you mind if we smoke?" We shook our heads. Tyabji drew in deeply, making the charcoal atop the brass bowl glow, then released a cloud of fragrant smoke. Murthwaite sat up, took the other hose, then reclined again, even as he took in the water-cooled smoke. "I suppose you must have heard about my offer to the Bromleys," Tyabji said.

"So I have," Holmes said, "but before we discuss that, I am at a disadvantage. You and your friend know me from Watson's stories and my general reputation, but I know little about you. Tell me something about yourselves and your connection with the Moonstone."

Tyabji began. "I was born in the Indian state of Gujarat. My father, a Muslim, is now first minister and secretary to the Maharajah of Gondal, a Hindu. However, some twenty-four years ago my father married an Englishwoman. I am the only child of that union. My mother was the daughter of Christian missionaries.

Her parents were horrified at her marriage. Her father disinherited her and refuses to speak with her. My grandmother was more forgiving. I was raised in India, but my mother always spoke English with me, and I attended an English boarding school in Delhi. I came to England at the age of eighteen to pursue my education at Oxford. In my youth I was taught the rudiments of both the Christian and the Muslim faiths by my mother and my father. Theirs was a more tolerant variety than usual. Also, living where I did, the Hindus with their bewildering plethora of different gods and goddesses were everywhere around me. I learned to speak Gujarati and Hindi, as well as some Arabic.

"Recently the maharajah has begun plans for renovating the temple at Somanatha which was dedicated to the moon god Chandra. It was first home to the Moonstone centuries ago before it began its long exile and many journeys. The maharajah believes that the temple and its grand statue of Chandra will never be truly complete without the jewel. He gave my father the task of tracing the Moonstone's history since it was taken from the temple in the eleventh century. That is a long, complicated tale. I must let friend Jack have his turn."

Murthwaite released a cloud of smoke, then turned to Holmes, the hose end in hand. "Would you care for a draw, Mr. Holmes? It's an excellent tobacco; Indian, of course." He sat up and took the end of his shirt and wiped the tip vigorously. He wore no stockings, and his feet and toes were long and bony, the tendons pronounced.

Holmes smiled faintly. "Perhaps I shall." He took the mouthpiece, drew in a long slow breath even as his forehead creased in concentration, then eased out the smoke. "It is very good." He made to hand it back to Murthwaite, who shook his head.

"Take your time. No hurry. Can't really smoke and talk at the same time, can I? My name's Jack Murthwaite, and I'll have five decades under my belt come September. Most of them I've spent in India. My father Robert Murthwaite was an explorer who spent much of his life in the East—India, Afghanistan and Tibet. He took an English wife late in life, and I was born soon after. I grew up listening to his tales, and there was never any doubt in my mind that I'd follow in his footsteps. I'm afraid I was a rather wild youth, always fighting and getting in trouble at boarding school.

"Luckily I had a knack for languages, which was to serve me in good stead and make up for bad behavior. I threw myself into Greek because I wanted to read the *Iliad* and the *Odyssey*, and into Latin for the *Aeneid* and Caesar's commentaries. How I longed to become a wanderer like Odysseus! My father gave me a Hindi grammar and dictionary on my tenth birthday, and I perused it as if it were a novel. I practiced regularly with him, and every time I saw an Indian on the street, I would address him in Hindi. Often a conversation would ensue. Invariably the men were flabbergasted to meet an English boy who tried to speak their language.

"I started at Cambridge, but lasted only a term. I left for India with a pittance in my pockets, and when I first saw the Indian coast off Surat from the ship, I somehow felt as if I were coming home. The years since are something of a blur. A white man who speaks Hindi fluently will never lack for work in India, and within six months I had completely mastered the language. I learned several others as well. I had some respectable jobs working in the opium, silk and tea trades, but I could never bear to remain anywhere longer than a few months. The people of India, the diverse culture and the magnificent buildings and temples, all fascinated me, but I was especially captivated by the flora and fauna.

"Later, I joined expeditions into lesser known and little inhabited parts of the continent. I soon realized what had long been obvious: for some unknown reason, I was not born with a man's ordinary allotment of fear. I can take no credit for this or claim great bravery—I simply do not feel afraid as most men do, even in the most dire situations. My steady nerves and keen eyesight made me a formidable marksman with a rifle. Hearing of my prowess, the men of a village tormented by a man-eating tiger begged my assistance. I soon managed to bring down the beast, although it took a third bullet directly to the brain even as he charged me. I was knocked over, but by the time we hit the ground, he was dead." He grinned, showing his white teeth. His fluent British English and his appearance were certainly at odds: with that red turban and dark, weathered skin, he appeared more the Indian than Tyabji.

"After that, my reputation grew. I became a hunting guide, but this did not last long, because I could not bear to see leopards and tigers shot for mere trophies. It is different with confirmed man-killers, but such cats are rare!

"As for the Moonstone, my father had told me all about it. He knew Rachel and Franklin Blake well and was an occasional guest at their Yorkshire home and their townhouse in London. Their son Neville and I were close in age and became friends. When I returned home every two or three years to visit my mother and father, I would also see Neville and Charlotte Blake. Even as a small child, Alice could not hear enough stories about tigers, leopards, cobras, mongooses and the like. Over the years I watched her grow up. It was I who suggested to Geoffrey that he try reasoning with Alice about the Moonstone. She has always struck me as a clever and intelligent young woman, though highly strung."

Tyabji nodded. "I am most grateful for your suggestion, Jack, even if it did not bear fruit."

Holmes had been listening intently. After a final draw, he handed the hookah hose back to Murthwaite. "I heard you offered her a thousand pounds."

"Yes, a maharajah is not necessarily as wealthy as you might assume. Frankly, too, he tends to regard the Blakes and Bromleys as simple thieves of the usual English variety, but my father persuaded him that a thousand pounds was a small price to pay for the Moonstone. I argued for slightly more, but it would have made no difference. Mr. Bromley will never yield up the stone."

Holmes stared at him closely. "And Alice Bromley?"

"She was more sympathetic, capable of understanding our position. Her husband, not in the least."

Holmes had set his elbows on his knees and placed his fingertips together. "How exactly did you know who had the diamond?"

Tyabji laughed. "Come, sir, a valuable object like the Moonstone never disappears! It gives off far too much light for that—soon enough it flashes out in the darkness, making its presence known. Father did compile his complete history beginning in the eleventh century when the diamond was still upon the forehead of a great bronze statue of Chandra in the temple at Somanatha. It was removed and hidden before the Muslims overran and destroyed the temple, but much later, in the early eighteenth century, at Benares, it was finally taken by Muslims. The jewel was set in the hilt of an elaborate dagger, and towards the end of the century, the dagger ended up at the siege of Srirangapatna. When the city fell in 1799 and Tipu Sultan was killed, an Englishman took it, Alice Bromley's great-great-uncle. He murdered three priests, Brahmins who had been watching over the diamond even while it was in Muslim hands."

"But how did you learn of its whereabouts today?"

Tyabji laughed again. "Come, Mr. Holmes, surely you have heard of private detectives! At the time of the siege, there was much talk amongst the officers and the native soldiers about the uncle, Lieutenant John Herncastle. He was known to have come from Yorkshire. Given his name and a description of the diamond, it was trivial to discover the rest. After all, the diamond has stayed in the family for almost a century, and when Alice Bromley first wore it in society, that was in the newspapers."

"Now that your attempt at persuading her to give it up has failed..." Holmes's lips flickered briefly upward at the corners. "... will you hire a band of devoted Hindus to steal back the diamond?"

Tyabji had been smiling, but his smile vanished. "I presume–I hope–you are joking, Mr. Holmes?"

"Yes, I am."

"Good. We would do no such a thing. Unlike the English, we are not thieves."

Murthwaite coughed once, spluttered out tobacco smoke, then laughed in earnest. "Well put, Geoffrey–well put! We English with our precious moral superiority are always stealing from the Indians, aren't we now? Even the queen herself does it! We appropriated the Koh-i-Noor diamond when we took Punjab in 1849, and Prince Albert had it re-cut for her. Now the butchered stone is part of the royal treasury. It certainly doesn't make me proud to be an Englishman! The Moonstone belongs in India."

"Do you know of anyone else besides yourself who is interested in the diamond?" Holmes asked Tyabji.

"No. But that means nothing. An object like the Moonstone will always be coveted by many."

"This complete history of the Moonstone–would it be possible for me to have a look at it?"

Tyabji nodded. "Certainly, Mr. Holmes. I can lend you my copy of the manuscript."

"Excellent! And does the history discuss the idea of a curse?"

"Yes. It goes back to the earliest days. Those who would dare to pluck it from the head of the statue would be followed by misfortune and death. A dying Brahmin is also said to have warned Herncastle that the Moonstone would have its vengeance on him and his descendants."

Holmes stroked his chin thoughtfully. "You are obviously a well-educated and well-traveled young man, Mr. Tyabji. What do you think of this idea of a curse?"

The corners of Tyabji's mouth rose briefly, even as his dark eyebrows came together. "I believe in it absolutely."

I frowned. "But surely it is only superstition, nothing more!"

"I did not say the curse was supernatural, but any object of great value and great beauty like the Moonstone will always leave behind a trail of death and misfortune. Who knows how old it really is, or how many men have died because of it? Hindus, Muslims and Christians have all killed for it. So much for religion. Given all the blood spilled, how could the Moonstone not be cursed? I would like to see it returned to a statue in the temple, but I would never in a million years wish to keep it for myself! It would be like pinning one of those archery targets with the red bull's-eye upon your chest."

"You are wise, sir. Did you try to tell Mrs. Bromley that?"

"No. Jack had told me that she has a nervous disposition. I did not wish to take an unfair advantage by trying to frighten her."

Holmes clapped his hands lightly together. "Bravo, Mr. Tyabji! You are more the English gentleman than the vast majority of English gentlemen I have known."

Murthwaite laughed. "I'd remarked on that too. I am glad he didn't try to scare poor Alice. That would be like shooting fish in a barrel."

"What line of argument did you use?" Holmes asked.

"I appealed to the English sense of fair play, the idea that they possessed stolen goods which should be returned to the rightful owner. In doing so, I discovered that Mrs. Bromley has a well-developed moral sense while Mr. Bromley has none. He was quite charming, but told me returning the jewel was absolutely out of the question. Mrs. Bromley said nothing, but she seemed unhappy."

"Did they tell you they could not give up the jewel, even if they wanted to?" Holmes asked.

Tyabji let the hookah hose drop from his fingers. "What?"

"They could not give you the diamond because Alice Bromley has only a life-interest. Her father's will specifies that it is to be passed down to her children or to her sister and her children. She can neither sell it nor give it away."

Tyabji frowned sternly and turned to Murthwaite. "Jack, did you know this?"

His friend exhaled smoke. "I did not."

"Is this possible, Mr. Holmes? Does English law allow such a stipulation?"

"It is unusual, but it is possible. Neville Blake probably had only a life-interest in the diamond as well, and he wanted to ensure that it would remain in the family."

Murthwaite made a grotesque face, one side only rising up, which created many creases out of the corner of his eye. "Along with the damned curse. Poor Alice—stuck with the diamond and with that idiot of a husband."

"Idiot?" I said.

"I'm sorry—that's the wrong word. He's not stupid. He was smart enough to marry Alice, but he seems more in love with the diamond than with her."

"That is rather cruel," I said. "I thought him genuinely concerned about her well-being." I glanced at Holmes, but he appeared resolutely neutral.

Holmes turned to Murthwaite. "So you saw Alice through the years as she grew up? When exactly have you seen her in, say, the last five years?"

"Well, I saw her at the party where she first wore the Moonstone after her mother's death. That was about three years ago. Neville had always struck me as a little batty about the diamond, and that quirk was on full display. He was also one of those men who gets mean when they drink, and he drank far too much that night. Alice was obviously nervous and uncomfortable. Bromley was there staring continually at Alice's bosom and the diamond. I'm not sure which appealed to him most. I left for India shortly afterwards, and a couple of months later I heard about Neville's death. I didn't return until this spring, and I went to see Alice and her new—for me—husband. She greeted me warmly, and Bromley was friendly in his stuffed-shirt way. She and I talked a long while, mostly about old times. We didn't discuss the Moonstone."

"Did she tell either of you that she had seen an Indian man with a turban at her library window?"

Both Murthwaite and Tyabji stared incredulously at Holmes. Murthwaite snorted slightly, laughed once, then in earnest.

"What is the matter?" Tyabji asked sharply.

"It wasn't me, I promise you—it wasn't me!" His own quip set Murthwaite laughing again.

Holmes smiled. "I think you were probably out of the country

67

the first time. Besides, it was a white turban, not a red one."

Tyabji shook his head angrily. "This is nonsense, Mr. Holmes—just sheer nonsense! What possible sense does it make? I think only a Hindu would seek out the Moonstone in this way, because it belonged to their moon god—and Hindus do not usually wear turbans. And what possible advantage could there be in looking through her window?"

"The very same points that had occurred to me, sir. The answer, I think, is obvious."

Murthwaite had stopped laughing. "Someone wants to scare Alice."

"Exactly."

"Bloody bastards," Murthwaite muttered. He looked up at Holmes. "I forgot to tell you I'll be at that dinner next week, the last one before they lock the jewel away. No one will recognize me—I'll be wearing the requisite wretched and uncomfortable evening dress."

"Henry and I will be there as well," Holmes said, "in our own wretched and uncomfortable evening dress. You seem fond of Mrs. Bromley, Mr. Murthwaite."

"So I am. I have no daughters of my own."

"You have sons?" I asked politely.

He nodded enthusiastically. "I do indeed! Two young ones near Gondal, and two others on the other side of the continent near Benares."

Holmes and I exchanged a puzzled look. "Explain yourself, sir," he said.

"Oh, it's simple enough. I have two wives."

I stared at him. "Is that legal?"

"It is in India. Not very common, though, for Englishmen.

Many an English soldier takes an Indian woman for his wife, but they usually limit themselves to one. As you can imagine, my situation has given me something of a reputation as an odd duck among my compatriots. Most of them stay away from me. That's what drew me to Amelia and Ahmad Tyabji. There aren't many Englishwomen with Indian husbands. That is also unusual and much frowned upon by Mrs. Grundy." He glanced at Tyabji. "She's a remarkable woman, your mother, remarkable. As a general rule I don't much care for Englishwomen—hence, my two Indian wives."

"And do you support them both?" I asked.

"Oh yes. I've made enough money at my various trades, and it costs very little to keep up a household in India, if one lives out amongst the people and not in a separate English enclave. I see each family for a few weeks out of every year. A little domesticity goes a long way with me."

Holmes nodded. "Well, this has all been very interesting, gentlemen. I would enjoy whiling away the afternoon smoking with you, but I have other business."

Murthwaite sat upright. "A shame, Mr. Holmes! Are you sure you wouldn't like to stay? For our next smoke we are going to sample my own special blend of hashish, opium and tobacco. The proportions must be exactly right! And I have the finest ingredients, all of Indian origin."

I tried to keep my face neutral as my eyes shifted to Holmes. He smiled. "A very tempting offer indeed. Perhaps another time."

Murthwaite grinned at me. "Terrible vices, all three, Dr. Vernier! Although opium is indispensable for the Englishman in India. Dysentery would reduce you to skin and bones or kill you outright, otherwise. I could have never survived without it."

We all rose to our feet. Tyabji nodded graciously. "You would be most welcome anytime, Mr. Holmes. It was an honor to meet you." He gave me a slight bow. "And you, Dr. Vernier."

Holmes's fingers tapped briefly at his thigh. "I have one word of advice for you, Mr. Tyabji, and I hope you will take it in the right spirit. For the next week or so, until the diamond is locked away, do not go anywhere unaccompanied—not because of danger, but because you may need an alibi. Given your recent conversation with the Bromleys, if anything does happen to the Moonstone, the police will immediately come knocking at your door."

Tyabji opened his mouth angrily, then closed it. He drew in his breath slowly and nodded. "Wise counsel. Thank you, Mr. Holmes."

After another round of hand-shaking, Holmes and I put our shoes back on. Tyabji gave Holmes the manuscript on the diamond in a brown leather carrying case, then accompanied us to the door.

Outside, it was still raining, and the street was black and glossy. We hailed a cab, and Holmes gave the driver the address near Harley Street where Dr. Cowen lived. Holmes had arranged to meet him that same afternoon. He settled back in his seat and gazed out the window. The soft gray light illuminated his face, the aquiline nose, the prominent cheekbone and angular jaw.

"What an odd pair!" I exclaimed. "Especially Murthwaite. It's a lucky thing I came along. Otherwise I believe you might have stayed to sample his ghastly concoction."

Holmes smiled. "I fear I might have. I have not tried that particular mixture before."

I shook my head. "I don't suppose tobacco ever will be forbidden, but someday I think opium in the form of laudanum will no longer be easily available to the masses at the local chemist. Then, too, opium is the main ingredient, although not listed, in scores of patent medicines and tonics. I shudder to think how many people in London are addicted."

"You told Bromley yourself that it was one of the few effective medicines we have. And Murthwaite rightly said the Englishman in India would be crippled by dysentery without it."

"Yes, yes." I sighed softly. "It only goes to show how primitive medicine remains. And you—you must realize how dangerously addictive opium in all its myriad forms can be?"

He shrugged slightly. "I do. Oh, I have partaken occasionally, especially after a long and stimulating case. My mind, once truly active, races on, even when I am exhausted and there is no longer a need for urgency. A few puffs on the pipe brings welcome relief, a pleasantly relaxed and dreamy state. Still, I am hardly so blasé about drugs as Watson portrayed me. My analytical facilities—my mind, is my greatest power, and I would not dull it permanently with poppy smoke or drops."

"I hope not. At least you seem to understand the risk."

"I do, and yet sometimes..." He shrugged again. "It dulls the pain both physical and psychological. It is perhaps the only genuine remedy."

"I know so many doctors who have started up with ether, or morphine, or cocaine, or laudanum or... It ruins them. It destroys them. For God's sake, be careful."

"So I shall, Henry." He clasped his hands together, and his look told me the subject was finished. "I wonder if Dr. Cowen will be able to tell us much. I still think perhaps it might be better for you to see him alone first, to test the waters."

"Oh, it should be all right. He's a reasonable man, although his reply to my note was rather terse."

The cab wound its way through the late afternoon traffic, making its way across London in the rain. We passed Baker Street and Holmes's flat, then turned right onto Harley Street, then right again onto Queen Anne Street. Cowen's office was in his elegant home of red brick with white painted trim. The upstairs windows and the door had a half-circle of arced glass windows, and planters with pink geraniums were in front of the ground-floor windows. The rain poured down, but it hardly had time to touch us before we made it to the door. Just at eye-level was a bronze plate with *Dr. David Cowen, Physician & Surgeon* inscribed.

A young page wearing a dark tunic with a row of brass buttons let us in and took us to a luxurious waiting room with chairs of dark wood and red leather, the matching table covered with various publications. We were barely seated when he returned to tell us that Dr. Cowen would see us. The page opened the door to a small office illuminated by a tall window. Cowen sat behind a mahogany desk writing on a paper in a folder. Behind him was a bookcase filled with massive medical tomes.

"One moment, please," Cowen said.

He was one of those men with an abundance of hair everywhere except on his head. There, his black hair, cut quite short, had receded, emphasizing the expanse of light brown skin covering the massive cranium. His black full beard was thick and curly, grew almost to his bottom lip and well up his cheeks, and there was a distinct line along his neck below which he had shaved. His eyebrows were thick and dark, thinning only slightly above the bridge of his nose. I knew he must be under forty, but the partial baldness made him look older. His stern brown eyes rose briefly, regarding us, then he lowered his gaze and wrote something else.

"There."

He set down an intricately designed fountain pen of wood and silver, stood up and stepped round his desk. His was the usual professional attire: a well-cut black frock coat, black waistcoat, gray-and-black-striped trousers. He was shorter than Holmes and me, only a few inches over five feet, but rather brawny, barrel-chested almost, his hands large and graceful-looking. Fine black hair grew below the knuckles. His expression was carefully neutral.

I extended my hand. "How are you? It has been a long time."

"Yes, it has." He gave my hand a quick firm squeeze.

"This is my cousin, Sherlock Holmes. You will have heard of him."

"Certainly." They also shook hands.

"Do you have a few moments to discuss the Bromleys and their diamond?"

"Yes, if we must." He drew in his breath, then gestured at two armchairs. "Have a seat."

We sat down, but he sat back against his desk, folding his arms. "I suppose Bromley has put you up to this." He shook his head. "I must tell you I consider it ill-advised lunacy. You will only stoke Alice Bromley's anxiety and encourage her morbid obsession with the diamond."

"Do you think, then, that the Indian she saw in the window was imaginary?" Holmes asked.

He jerked his head resolutely downward. "Yes."

"Curious."

Cowen's black brows came together. "Why curious?"

"She said you were uncertain about the reality of the Indian."

"I didn't want to worry her."

I frowned slightly. "Then you think they were hallucinations?"

"Hallucination is a loaded word. Perhaps someone else really was passing by the window. The mind is capable of all sorts of tricks. It can manipulate and distort images. Sometimes we see what we want to see. I do not think she is insane, if that is what you are asking—and you can tell that to Bromley. He worries too much. She will never be a candidate for the madhouse."

"Just how often do you see Mrs. Bromley?" Holmes asked.

His arms still folded, he raised one shoulder. "Weekly, at least. Her symptoms of late have been exacerbated."

Holmes's eyes were fixed on him. "What exactly is wrong with her?"

Again one shoulder rose, then he lowered his arms as he stood, thrust his hands into his pockets and began to pace. "Occasional heart palpitations or tachycardia, attacks of faintness or anxiousness, difficulty sleeping, alternating bouts of diarrhea or constipation—all in all, a general overstimulation of the nervous system which could be classified as either neurasthenia or hysteria, both of which are common in women. There is, unfortunately, no easy cure." He stopped and stared sternly at us again. "But again, encouraging her flights of fantasy and her wild fears can only aggravate her condition."

"And I suppose, you dismiss the Moonstone curse out of hand."

He paused again mid-stride and clenched his fists. "Ah yes, the blasted Moonstone curse! Of all the superstitious ridiculous nonsense! You would think a grown woman in this day and age would be able to set aside, once and for all, such an utterly inane notion. A curse. A curse!" He began to pace again. "I have tried to reason with her, to make her see the absurdity of the whole thing, and she nods, and agrees, and then says she cannot help herself. I cannot understand it."

"Unfortunately, we cannot always reason ourselves out of our fears," I said.

"But we must try! It is the only tool at our disposal, the only thing that sets us above the beasts. To persist when it makes one physically ill…" He shook his head again. "No, no."

"Do you think locking up the diamond in a bank vault will help matters?" Holmes asked.

"I hope so—it cannot hurt. Still, she is so fixated on the idea of a curse… As long as the diamond is hers, she feels she is under its baleful influence. There, you see? Now I am doing it too. She talks about the diamond as if it were alive, as if it were some vengeful object pursuing her."

"Has this gone on a long time?" I asked.

"Oh yes. She was worrying about the diamond as a girl, when I first treated her. She complained of constant stomach aches."

"How long ago was that?"

"Let's see, she was about twelve, and she is twenty-five now, so a good dozen years, shortly after I began my practice. These stomach complaints were a problem throughout her youth."

"You were her mother's doctor, too, were you not?" Holmes asked.

He drew in his breath, stopped before his desk and sat back again on its edge. "Yes. And her father's."

"Her mother died of laudanum poisoning," Holmes said. "Do you think it was an accident?"

Cowen's lips were compressed as he drew in his breath through his nostrils. "No one knows the answer to that question."

"But you must have an opinion. You were her doctor, after all."

"Yes, very well, Mr. Holmes. I have an opinion. I do not think it was an accident."

"Why would she have wanted to kill herself?"

"I see you prefer blunt speech. Very good—because she was miserable. I doubt she and Neville were ever a good match, and as they grew older, the situation between them worsened. She..." A brief bitter smile pulled at his lips. "Alice is her mother's daughter. Charlotte Blake had the same morbid preoccupation with the diamond and a similar assortment of physical ailments. Neville Blake was ill-tempered and turned more and more to drink. When Charlotte finally refused to wear the diamond any longer, it enraged him."

"And so," Holmes said, "after her mother died, Mrs. Bromley became the target of her father's anger."

"Exactly."

"But what of Mr. Bromley? When her father died and she married, did her situation improve?"

"Yes."

"Your answer has a certain tentativeness, Dr. Cowen."

He stared at Holmes, breathing slowly through his nostrils. "He's not like her father. He doesn't drink or lose his temper. He is all sweetness and light." This last dripped sarcasm. "I wish I had a pound for each time he has said he only wants what is best for her."

"Do you think he is being hypocritical?" I asked.

"Damn it, how should I know? And how long must these questions continue? I have work to do."

Holmes gave me a cautious look. "Not long, Dr. Cowen. And I do appreciate you taking the time to speak with us. We all share a concern for Alice Bromley's well-being."

Cowen's face had flushed, but now the color slowly receded. "We do. We do. Forgive me, Mr. Holmes. It is only... the situation is frustrating."

"Does Mrs. Bromley take laudanum on a regular basis?" Holmes asked.

Cowen drew in his breath, then nodded. "Yes, between five and ten drops a night. It helps her sleep and keeps her calmer during the day. It is fairly standard in cases like this."

"Have you considered exercise like long walks and more fresh air, along with a possible stay by the ocean or in the mountains?" I asked.

He stared at me, then folded his arms resolutely. "I am not convinced that would help."

I hesitated. "It might be worth a try."

He said nothing, but his look was eloquent. I realized this was a bad way to ease into the next topic. "I know how difficult these cases can be. Mrs. Bromley says her husband has encouraged her to try another doctor."

"From the very beginning of their marriage."

"I told her—and Mr. Bromley—that you were a first-rate doctor, and I assured her, that we do not want her to give you up. There is no question of that. You know her better than anyone else, and she trusts you. On the other hand, sometimes a second opinion is useful. Two heads can be better than one, as they say."

"Oh, so now you want to have a go at it?"

"Actually... sometimes women have questions or problems they are only comfortable discussing with another woman. I was thinking of Michelle, my wife."

Cowen lowered his hands and slowly rose from the desk, shifting his weight to the balls of his feet. "Dr. Doudet Vernier?"

"Yes."

"Do you... do you have any idea how many patients she has stolen from me?" His voice, by an effort of will, was ominously soft.

"Stolen?"

"*Yes*. Stolen! I see them for years, and then one day they simply disappear, and later I hear they have gone to see the celebrated

Dr. Doudet Vernier, the lady doctor, the one who will understand them—who will coddle all their feminine whims and absurdities. 'Lady So-and-so has recommended her—you simply must see her—she is so wonderful!'" His falsetto was a poor mimicry of a woman. "I am sick and tired of it! And now you dare come before me, and to my face, ask if she can take away yet another of my patients!"

"I said nothing about taking away—nothing at all! I assured Mrs. Bromley—and I assure you—that it is only a consultation. No one is trying to steal your patient."

"So you say—and yet I know how these things turn out. One visit becomes two, and then she skillfully wheedles her way into their graces and…"

"Michelle is no wheedler! And she already has more patients than she can handle—she has no need to steal from other doctors!"

"Exactly! She has no need because she has already stolen so many! And what are her credentials, after all? She is a woman, nothing more and nothing less. As for her so-called education…"

"There was nothing wrong with her education—she is a good doctor, one of the best!"

"Is she now? Is she really?" His voice again dripped with sarcasm.

"Yes—and I should know—far better than you. I have seen her at work, and I am not blinded by prejudice."

"Oh, that is rich! No prejudice, I suppose? As if love has not utterly blinded you!"

"Love has not blinded me! You don't know what you are talking about!" I had risen to my feet, and Cowen and I both had clenched fists.

"Gentlemen—*please.*" Holmes had stood as well, and he stepped between us, a hand raised to each of us. "Dr. Cowen, you spoke earlier of reason. Be reasonable in this, and accept our assurances.

No one wants to steal your patient. Henry is sincere about that. Mrs. Bromley is dedicated to you, and you to her."

Cowen had compressed his lips, and you could see his nostrils swell and shrink as he breathed through his nose. Finally he nodded. "All right. Perhaps I was hasty." He looked at me again. "But I do not have to like this *consultation*."

I did not yet trust myself to speak.

Holmes lowered his hands. "I suppose you will be at the dinner party next week?"

"I certainly shall. And I am certain I will be needed. The situation seems perfectly designed to trigger a hysterical outburst: a large group of people all staring at her and the accursed diamond. She has told me she doesn't like to have it touch her skin."

"Henry and I will be there, too."

He looked at Holmes, his lips parting perhaps half an inch. "Oh Lord, are you serious?"

"And Michelle as well," I said.

He rolled his eyes upward, thrust his hands into his pockets and strode away. "Oh wonderful! Better and better!" He whirled about and yanked out his hands. "I don't suppose I could convince you that your presence would be counterproductive? Possibly quite harmful, in fact."

"Mr. Bromley wants to ensure that the diamond is safe," Holmes said.

"And Alice be damned! Bloody stupid idiot." He drew in his breath slowly, glaring at us. "Are we done? Are we finally done?"

"Yes, Dr. Cowen, we are done. Thank you for your time."

Cowen's breath slowed, and he nodded. His eyes caught mine, looked away at once. "I have paperwork to do." He looked at me again.

I was still seething, but I said, "No one wants to rob you of Mrs. Bromley, I promise you."

He was still scowling. "Good."

I stared at him and extended my hand. I thought he was going to ignore me, but he finally grasped it, gave it a quick jerk, then nodded again and started back round his desk.

"Good afternoon," Holmes said.

We closed the door behind us. The page looked worried. He led us back to the front door and gave us our hats. Outside, the rain had ended, and the air was cool and fresh. "Let's walk for a while, Sherlock. I need to cool down."

We started down Queen Anne Street. The traffic was lighter than on Baker Street or Harley Street, although this time of day plenty of carriages were about, and people had begun to leave their work. We walked for a while, passing the usual assortment: news boys hawking papers, men with signboards advertising various products, and carts overflowing with goods—flowers, sausages, eels, meat pies. Holmes remained silent.

Finally I slowed my pace. I turned to look at him. "Well, that went well, didn't it?"

He laughed. "I was wary of the interview, but I did not expect quite such a display of ill temper."

"I'm glad I told Mrs. Bromley that Michelle's visit would be with Cowen's knowledge and that I did not add the words 'with his consent.' He would never willingly allow the consultation. I was deluded about him. I forget how many physicians, including the very best, are still foolishly prejudiced against women in the profession. But he was irritable even before I brought up Michelle. He was never so touchy when we worked together before."

"Does Cowen have a wife?"

"I don't believe so. I recall him saying a dedicated doctor hasn't the time to spare for domestic attachments."

Holmes inhaled sharply, in what was almost a laugh. "A rather monastic notion of the practice of medicine, Henry. I doubt you would be capable of such devotion."

"No, I would not."

Four

Monday, as usual, was my day scheduled at a charity hospital. The work was a good remedy for my lackluster practice and my tendencies toward idleness and self-pity. There the wretchedness, the malnourishment and ill health of the London poor were on full display. Idle moments were few, and always I was left with the sense of how lucky my lot in life had been. Michelle was also going to be busy. Besides the usual throng of female patients, she was visiting Alice Bromley late in the afternoon. By way of a splurge, we agreed to meet around seven for dinner at Simpson's.

Around five o'clock a giant of a man arrived in agony, his foot crushed by the wheel of a heavy cart. Opium might be a curse for many, but at the hospital, its potent extracted alkaloid, morphine, was a blessing. An injection soon dulled his pain, and we managed to cut away the boot and stocking. The bruised misshapen foot with its swelling purple toes was a ghastly sight. There was little I could do besides cleaning the skin with an antiseptic. At best, I knew, he would be lame; at worst, infection or gangrene might set in, and the foot would need to be amputated.

His wife arrived just as I had finished, completely distraught, and I spent some time trying to gently calm her. When I finally finished, I hailed a hansom, then sank gratefully back into the seat. My legs and feet ached from standing all day. I could hear the clopping of the horse's hooves just in front of me, and a sort of muted rumble from other carriages, voices and all the sounds of the city. I felt too tired to even pull out my watch. What need? I knew I would be late, but there was nothing I could do about it. Hopefully Michelle was sitting at a quiet corner table sipping a glass of some fine claret.

I was soon to see my wish realized. George the waiter was a stout ruddy-faced man with a huge red-brown mustache who fitted well with the restaurant's overwhelming Britishness. He knew Michelle and me, and he smiled and led me upstairs to the main dining room. Overhead, elaborate cut-glass chandeliers hung from the ornate ceiling; in winter, at this hour, they would be lit by gas, but the long days of July made this unnecessary. The walls were of dark paneled wood, which along with the thick carpet helped dull the sound. Only the gentle murmur of voices and the click of cutlery could be heard.

My eyes went at once to the redhead in the electric-blue silk dress seated in the corner. A glass of dark red wine was before Michelle on the white linen table cloth, her big hands set on either side of the thin glass stem, her fingers spread apart. Her forehead was creased. She was obviously lost in thought, away in the clouds. In the morning, I had seen her bind up her long hair tightly. By now, the auburn strands had rebelled, loosening, shifting; some had escaped, one curled down over her ear and onto her collar.

The brilliant shimmering blue of the dress perfectly suited her. She had a slender neck and a large mouth which, to me, always seemed to call out for kissing. We had been married some three years. The first all-consuming explosions of passion might be done, but I loved her all the more. I was very happy that this beautiful woman seated in the corner was waiting for me.

"A penny for your thoughts."

She looked up and smiled. "Henry." She started to rise.

I leaned over to touch her shoulder. "Don't get up." I stroked her cheek lightly, and her hand came up and gave my wrist a squeeze. I went to the seat opposite her.

"Care for some claret, sir?" George asked.

"Nothing I would like better." The open bottle was on the table, and he poured some into my glass.

"And the usual, the prime rib roast?"

"Yes. No hurry, though. Let me settle a bit."

"Certainly." He nodded graciously and strode silently away.

I sipped the claret and stared at Michelle. "Quite a day. Sorry I'm late." I told her about the man with the crushed foot, and she asked a few questions. "And what of Alice Bromley? Did your meeting go well?"

Her forehead creased in a characteristic way, even as her mouth tightened. "Yes."

"That is a curious look. What do you make of her?"

She shook her head. "She is... odd."

"Did you hit it off?"

"Oh yes. I examined her briefly, and then we went for a stroll. She talked and talked. You were right in your supposition. She had many questions she would only feel comfortable asking another woman."

85

"Ah. Such as?"

The corners of Michelle's mouth rose, and her cheeks flushed ever so slightly. Her skin was very fair, and in summer she always had a few freckles scattered on her nose and cheeks.

"Oh my," I said, "are you blushing?"

She laughed. "I am."

"What did she ask you?"

"Well, among other things, she wanted to know how often we have 'relations.'"

"Relations?"

"Relations. You know."

"Oh yes. And you told her. What was her response?"

She laughed again. "She did not believe me. She thought I was joking and laughed. When I insisted, she told me she did not think that was possible."

I frowned. "I did not think we were that prodigal. You told her... two or three times a week, and she thought that impossible?"

"Exactly."

Michelle's left hand rested on the table, the blue cuff of her dress vivid against the white tablecloth. Her long fingers and her knuckles were faintly red from contact with carbolic acid and constant washing. I set my hand over hers. "Imagine what she would say if she knew of our most notable day, that time when I returned from a long trip with Sherlock."

"Oh, Henry."

"We must try for a repeat performance sometime before we get too old and decrepit."

"I don't think there is much chance of that, not with you."

"And did she say how often she has relations?"

Michelle's smile vanished. "She doesn't."

"What? Never?"

"Not any longer. They did a few times after they were first married, but since then…"

"Good Lord. They both seem young and healthy enough. Is there anything physically wrong or…?"

"She said her husband thought it would not be good for her health, that she was too frail or some such thing for the exertion."

"How strange. And how does she feel about the situation?"

"She said that, of course, he was right and that he was most considerate, that her nerves would probably not be up to such a trial on a regular basis, but when I probed a little, it seemed clear that she would welcome some renewed overtures on his part."

"Did she seem to have enjoyed the… relations, or did she find it painful or unpleasant?"

"She was ambivalent and embarrassed, especially initially. She had many questions about what was normal, what was to be expected. She had not thought it would be quite so physical, so overwhelming, and so pleasurable—although she would never use that word. It took some probing and questions to reveal that she had actually rather liked it. I had to reassure her that this was not perverse on her part."

I sipped at my wine and gave my head a slight shake. "Then perhaps all is not lost." I stroked her hand lightly.

"Oh, Henry, sometimes I want to throw up my hands in despair. I don't understand why it all has to be so complicated for so many men and women. It should not be *hard*, after all."

"Did you find any signs of an actual physical illness or any problem which might justify Bromley's concern?"

"No, not really, although she is a perfect example of one of those nervous high-strung women where it is difficult to tell how much is imaginary and how much is real. When I listened to her heart and lungs, they sounded perfectly normal, but she says her heart races at times and other times she can feel it pounding in her chest, especially at night. She also feels sometimes like she can't catch her breath, and when she stands up she feels dizzy."

"All of those are common enough, without any sort of underlying pathology."

"Exactly—it is difficult to say, but there is certainly nothing which would cause a reasonable physician like you or me to prescribe sexual abstinence."

"Did Dr. Cowen ever weigh in on this?"

"No. She has said nothing of it to him. The mere notion of talking about it with him had her blushing and stammering."

"Well this certainly justifies my suggestion of a consultation with a woman doctor. I wonder if I should try to talk with Bromley."

She frowned. "If you do, you mustn't directly tell him what I have told you. If the opportunity arises, you might broach the subject, and then let him know that his wife is not so fragile as he seems to think."

I shook my head. "This is a first. Usually it is the other way around, with the wife refusing because she is the one who feels too delicate. I cannot recall a man denying his wife, at least not a man in his twenties. But more generally, what were your impressions of Mrs. Bromley?"

"She is a conundrum, Henry, a strange mixture of the appealing and the repellant, clever and intelligent in some ways, child-like and simple-minded in others. She is one of those flighty women who don't quite seem to live in the real world."

George had quietly approached our table. "Are you ready for dinner, sir?"

I glanced at Michelle. "I'm ravenous," she said.

I smiled, then nodded at George. "Yes, please." I took a final swallow of claret, then took the bottle and poured more into Michelle's glass and then my own. "Did you talk about the Moonstone and the curse?"

"Oh yes. And there was the same dichotomy. One moment she was quite rational, quite sane, and then the next she was like some superstitious peasant fearful of someone putting a hex on her. She kept prefacing her remarks with 'I know it is foolish' and 'I know it is impossible.' However, her fear of the diamond was certainly clear. She hates it and thinks it killed her mother and father."

"Literally?"

She shrugged. "With her mother, that was her impression: that the jewel drove her to despair and suicide. With her father, it created an anger and a fury that eventually destroyed him. She didn't say it directly, but her mother's fate weighs most heavily on her. I think she is afraid that someday the diamond might make her so desperate that she too would kill herself."

"Lord–it is as bad as that?"

"I don't think she is suicidal, not now, but she is afraid of what might happen to her over time."

George pushed a massive cart up to our table, covered with a white cloth. "Here we are, sir." He lifted a gigantic silver dome off the serving dish, releasing a cloud of steam and the succulent odor of the slab of roasted beef. He took Michelle's plate, then used a long straight carving knife to slice off the end piece, which he set on the plate. "Here we are, ma'am."

"Oh thank you, George."

He took my plate and cut off a slab about half an inch thick. The meat was light gray and very juicy. Michelle and I had had too much experience with human anatomy, blood and wounds to be able to tolerate rare roast beef. He dished out some roasted potatoes and carrots from a silver bowl.

"Thank you," I said. He put the lid back on and wheeled away the cart. I glanced at Michelle, then took my glass by the stem and raised it high. She did the same, and we clinked the bowls together, sloshing the wine slightly. "To relations," I said.

She laughed. "To relations." She took a swallow. An older man with a bald speckled pate at a nearby table gave us an inquisitive stare.

We were briefly quiet while we had at the beef with our knives and forks. I picked up my napkin and dabbed at my mouth. "And what was your final diagnosis of Mrs. Bromley? Did you have any recommendations?"

"I definitely think she needs to get out more. Fresh air and exercise would do her a world of good. Unfortunately her husband and Dr. Cowen are always telling her how fragile she is and that she must rest."

"Cowen was not receptive to the idea of exercise when I spoke with him." I hadn't really told Michelle about the fiery words between Cowen and myself. I had only said tactfully that the doctor was not receptive to a second opinion, especially from a woman doctor.

"He wouldn't be. He is rather old school, I'm afraid. It ought to be obvious that a woman like Alice Bromley needs some outlet for all that nervous energy."

"She is devoted to Dr. Cowen, is she not?"

"Absolutely. She prefaced our conversation by reminding me that you had promised she was not to give him up. She said she would be glad to talk with me, but that she had her own doctor."

"I suppose such blind loyalty is common enough, inexplicable as it may be. Oh, did you question her about her use of laudanum?"

"Yes. She said she did not know how she could exist without it. That was not a promising start. I tried to tell her as gently as possible of the risks of dependency and that it would be well to try to wean herself off the drug. She was noncommittal, but said that after the diamond was gone, perhaps she might think of it."

"Gone? Oh, I suppose she meant once it is locked away."

"She is dreading that dinner party. She wasn't exactly glad to hear I was coming. 'There are too many people,' she said. 'Far too many.' But then she bolstered her resolve by saying, 'One last time.'"

I set down my fork and took my wine glass. "She said the same thing to Holmes and me. How did things end between you? Do you think you will see her again?"

"Yes, but not exactly as doctor and patient. She seemed to enjoy our stroll together and was forlorn at the idea of parting, so I suggested a regular walk might do us both good. She was delighted at the suggestion. I think she needs a friend. She certainly needs someone to talk to. She said as much. Jane Alexander and she have little in common. No one she knows reads books the way she does. When we got on the subject of novels, Wilkie Collins came up, and she became more enthusiastic and animated than I had hereto seen. We talked about Miss Gwilt in *Armadale* and Magdalen Vanstone in *No Name*. The two are opposites in some ways, alike in others."

"I suppose I should give Collins a try. Which book would you recommend?"

"Start with *No Name*. I think it is the better of the two, especially for a romantic like you."

"And do you think you can work these regular walks into your schedule?"

"I can find the time, and I also need more exercise to release my own nervous energy."

I smiled. "You always had a soft heart, especially for stray cats and dogs."

Michelle shook her head. "If only she had some real occupation, something worthwhile to do in life. One of the old maxims I believe in, is that an idle mind is the devil's workshop. It is not good for an intelligent, sensitive young woman like her to sit about brooding and noticing every minute change in her pulse or respiration."

"Did you also meet Mr. Bromley?"

"Yes, coming and going. He was very cordial, quite charming, almost excessively so. He is a handsome man." She smiled at me. "But not so handsome as my husband."

I smiled back, but then my smile faded away. "I wonder..."

"Yes?"

"I wonder if she really loves him."

Michelle's forehead creased. She picked up her napkin and dabbed at her lips. "She kept saying how good he was to her, how well he treated her, and yet... it was almost as if she needed to convince herself."

"He seems amiable enough. All the same..."

"Yes?"

"You'd have to truly be half dead before I could ever keep my hands off of you."

She smiled, set down her fork and leaned forward to grasp my hand with hers. "I feel the same way."

I raised her hand and kissed her fingertips. "Good."

* * *

Holmes had sent me a telegram asking me to stop by around ten on Tuesday morning. Unlike the day before, I had little to do, so I arrived exactly on time. Mrs. Hudson went up the stairs with me, her hand resting on the railing. "He seems in a fine mood the last few days, Dr. Vernier. You can always tell when he has an interesting case. It does his spirits a world of good."

"Yes, nothing like a good robbery, a mysterious poisoning or a corpse hauled from the Thames to cheer him up."

She gave me a conspiratorial smile. "What a wicked thing to say!" Every so often she showed unexpected flashes of irony given her conventional appearance as an elderly, respectable landlady.

I stepped into the flat, but no one was there. "Holmes?" I called.

"Give me a moment or two, Henry," came a voice from the bedroom. "Have a seat, and I shall join you soon."

I wandered over to the bow window and stared down at Baker Street. Nearby on Holmes's cluttered desk was a neat stack of papers. The title page had "History of the Moonstone Diamond" and "prepared for the Thakur Sahib Bhagwatsimhji Sagramsimhji by his servant Ahmad Tyabji." I found it difficult to imagine a typewriter in the midst of some exotic Indian palace, but it had obviously been typed.

At last I sat in Holmes's comfortable basket chair, crossed my legs and closed my eyes. After a while, I heard the door open. Before me stood an Indian in tan garments similar to Murthwaite's, but he wore a white turban. He was tall and thin, dark-skinned, with an odd nose. His upper lip also protruded strangely; he must have buck teeth. He raised two brown hands, put them together and bowed slightly. "Mr. Sherlock Holmes?" His voice was quite high, with the characteristic distinct and clipped speech of an Indian.

"He is in his bedroom. I'm just waiting for him."

"Perhaps I too shall wait for him."

I frowned. "Does this have something to do with the Moonstone?"

He lowered his gaze. "The Moonstone–I want nothing to do with it! Truly it has the curse of Kali upon it. Woe unto he who even views the wretched thing!" He spoke with great feeling.

"You do know about the Moonstone! Holmes will want to hear all about it."

He bowed to me again. "And so he shall, sahib. Pardon me for a moment." He went to the door to Holmes's bedroom and grasped the doorknob.

"What? Where do you think you are going? You cannot just walk into his bedroom!" I stood up at once and followed him. The Indian stood just before the bed, but no one else was there. "Wherever can he have gone? Sherlock... Sherlock, where are you?" I glanced at the wardrobe.

"No need to shout," the tall Indian said. The voice was transformed and completely unmistakable. The pitch had dropped, and the Indian accent was gone.

"I hate it when you do this! You know I am the least discerning of men. You could put on a funny hat and a clown wig and fool me. What did you do? Creep out while I had my eyes closed, then open the other door and pretend to enter?"

"Exactly."

"All right, but why are you disguised that way?"

"We need to visit Bromley's jeweler friend this morning, and I have had some dealings with him in the past. I don't want him to recognize me. However, the Bromley case–and Mr. Murthwaite– inspired me. This is an interesting addition to my repertoire, I think."

"You've done something to your nose. And your mouth. What's the matter with your lip?"

"It's theatrical putty. Nothing distorts the face like a wad of it under the upper lip. Remember that Mrs. Bromley said the Indian had an odd-looking lip? Probably the same technique. Well, should we be off?"

Mrs. Hudson was taking some air before the front door. "Good day, Dr. Vernier." She smiled. "And Mr. Holmes."

We both nodded. I shook my head. "No fooling her, I see."

"She is a most observant lady, and she has seen me in many different guises."

"Not so dense as me, is what you mean."

"Now, now, Henry, you mustn't take offense over a triviality. A fine day for a stroll. We have perhaps a half-hour walk before us."

We went through the busy London streets to a neighborhood that had gone downhill over the years. On our way several people gave Holmes and me odd looks. One little boy in particular opened his eyes very wide. Clearly he had never seen an Indian in a turban before. Holmes put his hands together and gave him a slight bow. His mother looked startled and grasped the child's hand tightly. We passed a wooden cart that stank of rancid fried fish. The vendor in his battered brown jacket and bowler frowned at us. We stopped before the corner building. Overhead was a large sign: MESSRS HARTER & BENJAMIN, JEWELERS.

"Are we seeing Mr. Harter or Mr. Benjamin?" I asked.

"Harter. Benjamin has been dead a good many years, but Harter never had the sign changed. I shall be questioning Mr. Harter about diamond rings. When I ask you who sent us, I want you to say 'Charles Bromley,' but no word of him until then."

"Perhaps I might look at something for Michelle while we are here."

He shrugged slightly. "As you wish, but don't commit to any

purchase until we have talked afterwards." He pressed a buzzer.

The door was a massive oaken slab with a solid front and a small peephole, and as it swung open, it showed itself a good two inches thick. A very broad man in a blue uniform, something akin to a policeman's with a row of brass buttons, stood before us. The jacket had a belt, and from it hung a thick black truncheon. His hands were at least six inches across, his fingers thick as sausages. His red-brown hair was thin on top, his nose slightly flattened with an enormous mustache sprouting below and hiding his upper lip. He frowned slightly at the sight of Holmes in his Indian garb. "Yes?"

"Two gentlemen to see Mr. Harter, if you please, sahib." Holmes had resumed the high-pitched staccato accent.

The main room had a large counter space in the middle lit from above by a big skylight. The thick carpet underfoot had an intricate pattern of red and gold. The small windows all had bars on them. Mr. Harter obviously didn't want his store to be robbed. The guard opened a side door and called out, "Company, sir." He went back to a chair near the entrance and took up a newspaper.

A man came through the door, fumbling at his frock coat to fasten the buttons. His gray hair was mostly gone, his scalp faintly pink under the light from above, but his eyebrows were bushy and black, each mustache-like. Two sharp blue eyes stared out from under them. Eyeglasses with thick rectangular lenses sat perched low on his bulbous ruddy nose. His lips were thin, colorless, and clamped tightly together.

"Good morning, gentlemen. I am Mr. Harter, and who may you be?"

"I am Mr. Ahmad Patel, and this is my very good friend, Mr. Henry Albert."

There was a round of polite nods. "Did you wish to purchase

jewelry? If so, I must tell you I only see people by appointment."

"Indeed, sahib?" Holmes said. "When is your next available appointment?"

Harter seized a small notebook on the counter and flipped through pages. He set it down, withdrew a gold watch from his waistcoat pocket and opened it. "I would have an opening in exactly three minutes at ten forty-five. Will that do, gentlemen?"

Holmes nodded gravely. "That would do nicely, Mr. Harter."

Harter scribbled on the page. "Mr. Patel and Mr. Albert. In the meantime, exactly what interests you?"

"I am considering the prospect of marriage," Holmes said, "and I am attempting to determine the precise expenses, so I certainly must know about the ring."

"And do you have some idea how much you wish to spend? Rings in general begin as low as five pounds, diamonds at more like ten pounds, but I should warn you, those are of a very low quality, and I carry very little of such stock. However, the sky is, as they say, the limit as far as the upper range."

"I was thinking of twenty-five pounds, sahib."

Harter shrugged, his face showing his distaste for such miserliness. He took another look at his watch, then extended his hand. "Well, it is time. Stand just there, gentlemen."

The counter was a huge slab of dark slate covered with thick glass. He stepped behind it, pulled open a drawer, withdrew one ring, set it before us, then another and another. "Time was when a diamond of any substantial weight for fifteen pounds would have been an impossibility, but since the mines in South Africa opened up in the seventies, the market has been flooded. However, the raw diamond is only the starting material. You can take the best grade in the world and botch the cutting, such that you end up with poor or mediocre results. This first one here is a commercial product, one carat set in silver. Not very impressive, but it only costs fifteen pounds. The second is also one carat, but notice the greater brilliance and the gold setting. I did this one myself. It is thirty-five pounds. This third one has a slight pinkish tinge that sets it apart and a more elaborate setting. It is fifty pounds."

Holmes examined each of the diamonds carefully, one by one, then handed them on to me. He made several variations of "ooh" and "ah," along with "exquisite," "formidable" and the like. The pink one was quite stunning, the slight tint evident under the natural light coming from overhead. Holmes seemed to settle on the second diamond. "Is the price of thirty-five pounds absolutely fixed, sir, or is there some room for negotiation?"

Harter gave a weary sigh. "And would you wish to negotiate with your beloved on the terms of your engagement? Of course you wouldn't! All the same… there is some flexibility. Limited flexibility."

"Such as thirty pounds?"

Harter looked even more pained. "If you wished to purchase it today, I could let you have it for thirty pounds."

"Indeed? Oh, I am almost forgetting, sir…" He turned to me. "Who is our gentleman friend who said we must mention his name?"

"Bromley," I said. "Charles Bromley."

Harter's enormous eyebrows came together, and he looked briefly as if he had a pang of dyspepsia. "Charles Bromley?"

"Yes, sir. He said you offered a special bargain for his friends."

"Yes, indeed, if Bromley sent you…" He pulled open another drawer and took out a fourth ring. "I can let you have this ring for thirty pounds, but there are to be no further negotiations." His voice was stern. "A fine diamond, not so ostentatious perhaps, but notice the two smaller stones."

Even to my eyes, the ring looked inferior to the other. The main stone was smaller and less brilliant in the light, the shine of the silver flatter, and the two minor stones seemed out of place. Holmes nodded appreciatively. "Most impress, sahib. And you cannot adjust the price of the other ring for a friend of Mr. Bromley's?"

"I cannot, but this is the better ring and a genuine bargain."

"I see. Well, unfortunately, the lady's inclinations are still unclear to me. She waxes hot and cold. One day she is all sweetness and admiration, the other she is stern and preoccupied. I must have a clearer understanding before I accost her, as they say. I will take your offerings under consideration, sahib. They are truly fabulous gems, worthy of the woman of a sultan or a rajah."

This last seemed a bit overdone to my taste, but Harter seemed to be taken in by the portrayal. He nodded politely. "As you wish." He took up the rings and began putting them back in the drawers.

"If you have a few minutes more," I said, "I wondered if you might show me something in a necklace with matching earrings for my wife."

"Certainly, sir. Did you have anything in mind? Diamonds, like your friend?"

"No, I was thinking of emeralds. My wife is a redhead, and I thought the emeralds would suit her fair complexion and hair."

"Indeed they would. I can show you some necklaces, and we could find or make matching earrings. And how much, sir, did you wish to spend?"

"Oh, perhaps one hundred pounds."

"A tidy sum, sir. One can get something of worth for a hundred pounds, especially in the wrongly called 'lesser stones.' Nothing lesser about emeralds in my opinion." He pulled open a drawer lower down and withdrew two necklaces. The first was a sort of emerald pendant with smaller emeralds in the silver chain; the other was a series of larger emeralds surrounded by smaller diamonds set in silver. The green and white of the gems was brilliant.

I took up the second one. "This is lovely. Are these real diamonds?"

"They are not, sir. They are what is broadly called 'paste,' but paste is not, despite what you may have heard, synonymous with trash. Paste well done by an expert is virtually indistinguishable from the real thing. I always say there is no shame in buying paste if you simply cannot afford a real diamond. No one will ever know the difference. This necklace is a high-quality item."

"It's certainly beautiful. How much is it?"

"Ninety pounds, sir. Another five for the earrings. However, might I say... It is true that emeralds suit a redhead very well, but almost too well–it verges on triteness. For something more unique you might consider sapphires. The contrast between red and blue is even more striking. Have a look at this."

The necklace had five blue sapphires set in silver, with a larger sapphire hanging below the others. Only the last was set with small white stones of what must be paste. The light caught the blue stones in a way that emphasized their color and slight differences in tone. Their blue color might be more muted than the green of the emeralds, but they had more brilliance. I drew in my breath slowly, closing my eyes. I saw Michelle on our bed, her red hair aswirl on the pillow, her palms with their faint orange flush up; she wore the sapphire necklace and nothing more. The image was so vivid I felt my face heat.

I shook my head. "This is lovely."

"It is one of my creations."

"What is the price?"

"One hundred and twenty-five pounds, sir, and for that, I would include the earrings. A trifle more than your one hundred, but well worth the extra expense."

I looked longingly at the necklace, then at Holmes. "It is difficult to decide. I must think about it."

Another long weary sigh from Harter. "Very well, sir." He took the necklaces from the counter top.

Holmes put his hands together and gave a slight bow. "We are most grateful for your time, sahib. By the way, I believe Mr. Bromley's wife has a celebrated diamond, does she not? The famous Moonstone."

Harter nodded. "Yes, indeed."

"And have you seen the famous stone, sir?"

"Oh yes. I have verified its authenticity on more than one occasion. Bromley was just in recently."

"And is the stone as magical as they say?"

Harter gave a slight shrug. "After so many years in the business, my sense of magic has greatly diminished, but the Moonstone is exceptional. When I gaze at it through my lens, an old sense of the shivers returns." His thin lips rose in a slight smile. "Not quite magical, but it is truly unique and beautiful. It has one really slight flaw, an interior sort of fleck that is visible in a certain light. That imperfection is what truly makes it perfect."

"And what of the curse of the Moonstone, sahib? Do you ever feel any fear before the diamond?"

Harter gave a sharp laugh. "Balderdash—sheer balderdash. One needn't fear gems—it's men you have to watch out for. Or rather… Most jewels go to women, after all, and that is where the curse generally lies."

I laughed. "You surely do not think women are a curse?"

"Not all of them, but enough to make many a man's life miserable. I should not say so, but much of my business consists of men buying jewelry they cannot afford for women who do not deserve it. The women run them into the ground and drive them to the poorhouse. However, it's different with the Moonstone. It has a history of its own, as do all famous gems. I've seen only a few of these stellar examples in my career, and it is the most illustrious of them all. They understand the true beauty of gems in the Orient. There, the jewels rise above the mundane. There, diamonds decorate statues of goddesses and gods in the temples rather than being flaunted by the empty-headed beauties of high society. And truly, nothing is more appalling than a beautiful gem necklace worn by some old hag with a wrinkled neck."

"You are a philosopher, sir," Holmes said.

"And an unmarried one, I suspect," I added.

"My work has always been my mistress, Mr. Albert. However, mark me well—I'm not saying anything against Alice Bromley. She's not one of the harridans. She is a beautiful woman, and the Moonstone suits her."

"But it might look better on the statue of Chandra at Somanatha under torchlight?" Holmes asked.

"Exactly, and especially since she is like a little child in her beliefs about the curse."

"But sometimes with great beauty comes great evil. Men have murdered for the Moonstone, sir, again and again. In my country the Muslim and the Hindu took turns trying to steal the diamond from each other. And an Englishman killed to steal the diamond and bring it back here. If that is not a curse, I do not know what is."

Harter shrugged. "I cannot argue with that, Mr. Patel. The Moonstone is truly a great beauty, one I have been privileged to see on several occasions." He stepped out from behind the counter and extended his hand, grasped each of ours in turn. "It has been a pleasure to meet you, gentlemen. I hope to see you again shortly. You, Mr. Patel, after you have better gauged the lady's intentions"– this to Holmes, and to me–"and you, Mr. Albert, after having pondered between the sapphire and the emerald."

The guard rose from his chair, slid back an enormous bolt and opened the door for us. While its exterior was wood, the inside was a thick layer of steel. It closed behind us with a slight rumbling sound.

"Not an easy place to burgle, I think."

"No. The windows were all barred, as was the skylight. The place is a miniature fortress, and Mr. Harter lives in some upper rooms further back from the storefront, I believe. Let us walk for a while, Henry. The weather is still very fine."

"As you wish. Sahib."

He laughed. "Perhaps I overdid that. It is easy to fall into."

We passed the fried fish cart. The vendor was handing a customer a greasy brown paper bag and gave us a curious look, faintly hostile.

"What was that business with Bromley's name and the second ring he showed you?"

"What did you notice about that second ring he produced for the same price of thirty pounds?"

"It seemed inferior."

"So it was–because for that one he was taking into account Mr. Bromley's commission. We threw him off by asking for a price on the others before we had mentioned Bromley. If we had, the first ring I selected would have cost more. I suspect Bromley gets at least ten percent, perhaps more."

"*A commission?* Is that kind of thing of done?"

"Of course it is. Bromley directs wealthy society clients to Harter, who gives him a percentage in return."

I shrugged. "It was obvious, now that you mention it. That doesn't seem exactly... above board."

"No, but that type of arrangement is common enough."

"I did think those necklaces were very fine."

"Harter is a skilled craftsman, and he has been in the jeweler's trade for over fifty years. His prices are not out of line. You could probably bargain him down at least ten percent. Tell him you don't really know Mr. Bromley, that I was the one who was acquainted with him."

"I hate haggling–and I am terrible at it."

"Have a look at some other jewelers as well."

"And I also hate shopping. I'm terrible at that, too."

Holmes laughed. "But is not Michelle worth it?"

I remembered my vision of her on the bed in the sapphire necklace. "I will do it for her."

Five

After our visit to Harter's, Holmes and I parted, but he told me to come by Baker Street later that afternoon. We were going to visit someone, of whom he would only say she was "*la crème de la crème* of society."

I returned home and had lunch with Michelle. At one point my brow creased as I stared at her and tried to imagine the sapphire necklace round her neck. "Why are you looking at me that way?" she asked. I lowered my gaze and made some feeble excuse.

Later I was in my consulting room reading a journal when there came a knock. When I opened the door, Charles Bromley stood before me, black top hat held in one gloved hand, his stick in the other. His dark chestnut hair was naturally curly, his grand mustache neatly trimmed just in line with his upper lip. If his wife was the archetypal languid blond female, he was the embodiment of male health and vigor. "Good afternoon, Dr. Vernier. Would you be free for a few moments?"

"Certainly. Have a seat."

I sat down behind my mahogany desk, and Bromley took the comfortable armchair. He unbuttoned his black frock coat and opened it up, then crossed his legs and tugged at the material over his upper knee. The red-brown leather of his stylish boot shone. Obviously Hodges kept his master's clothes and footgear in impeccable condition. Bromley had pulled off his gloves and held them loosely in his left hand.

"I wondered if you had talked with Dr. Doudet Vernier about her visit to Alice."

"I have."

"Did she have any thoughts about her condition, which you might share with me? I do worry so about Alice, Dr. Vernier." He gave a great sigh. "She is very precious to me. Her health has always been so precarious. Moreover, she has never, I think, been truly happy. I had hoped that our marriage might bring her round, and I think it has helped—and continues to help—but she is still a prey to so many dark thoughts."

"Michelle did examine her, and the results were ambivalent. It is hard to say if there is much physically wrong with her."

He stared at me. "You surprise me, sir. She seems so fragile. I had always assumed..."

"She enjoyed her walk with Michelle. If anything is wrong with her, I doubt it is serious. Her heart and lungs sounded all right, which is a good sign."

"Indeed? Dr. Cowen has always stressed she must rest and try to avoid too much excitement."

This last reminded me of what Michelle had said about their "relations." "I doubt she is as fragile as you and the doctor seem to think."

"No?"

"Things are improving nowadays, but during Victoria's long reign, there has been a certain cult of the valetudinarian, men and women morbidly obsessed with their health and convinced they suffer from a multitude of ailments. Often this leads to a self-fulfilling prophecy. Inactivity and worry make them sick. I cannot say for sure that Mrs. Bromley is one of those people, but it is certainly possible."

He nodded. "I see." He gave a deep sigh. "My greatest fear is... is..." His eyes would not meet mine.

"Yes? Tell me."

"Is for her sanity, Dr. Vernier! I worry that she may—that she may end up in a madhouse."

I shook my head. "I think that very unlikely."

"Do you really?"

"The madhouse is often a dumping ground for people who have no one to care for them. You are obviously willing to look after your wife, and you have some money. The only other real reason would be if you thought she might harm herself."

Bromley opened his mouth, but seemed briefly unable to speak. He let his gloves drop onto his leg, then ran his hand across his brow. "Exactly—*exactly*."

I stared at him. "You think she might try to hurt herself?"

A shiver seemed to work its way up to his shoulders. "Like her mother—like her mother."

I frowned. "Is it as bad as all that?"

"Oh no, not yet—not yet, but I worry about the future."

"Once the diamond is locked up, things should be better. Even she acknowledged that."

He nodded quickly. "Yes, that is what I am hoping for, too. Do you think all this reading she does is good for her? I sometimes think she should give it all up."

"No, no–it is her one avocation. She shouldn't perhaps read things like… *Dr. Jekyll,* I believe it was, but anything that keeps her mind occupied is worthwhile."

"Good, good. I would not want to deprive her of her one consolation."

I hesitated and took my lower lip between my teeth. Now it was Bromley's turn to say, "Yes?"

"Do you and your wife have sexual relations frequently?"

He gave me an incredulous stare. "Certainly not."

"Why do you say that?"

"Well, given her condition, I hardly think… I am not a mere animal, Dr. Vernier, to put my own unclean desires above my wife's health and well-being."

"I don't think her health and well-being would necessarily suffer."

"You do not?"

"No. It might actually help matters."

"Really?" He lowered his gaze. "If only it were possible… I cannot deny that it is difficult, but I would do anything for Alice–*anything.*"

"In this case following your natural inclinations may be helpful."

He nodded thoughtfully. "I must… think about this." He had a smile that might warm the chilliest room. "You have been very helpful, Dr. Vernier. Perhaps there is hope, after all."

"Of course there is. I cannot say for certain, but I doubt there is anything seriously wrong with her."

"If only I could get her out of Dr. Cowen's clutches! I do think he brings out the worst in her. Do you think you might talk with him?"

I shrugged. "We are not exactly on the best terms. Still, I do need to discuss the situation with him."

"Excellent." He beamed, then snatched up his gloves and

slapped his leg once with them. "It's odd, you know." He shook his head. "Sometimes loyalty seems so rare a virtue, especially among a certain class of men. However, I can tell, Henry, that you are absolutely devoted to your wife."

I shrugged slightly. "Yes, I am."

"And so it should be. They speak of the lower animals, and yet that little dog of mine, my Sally, has a truer heart than certain of my acquaintances. There is nothing I value more in a friend than loyalty." He was briefly silent, and a faint smile came and went. "Sometimes, however, there is a price to pay."

"How so?"

"Oh, I was recalling a time at school. There was a clever older boy we all liked, a very popular one with a certain mischievous streak. He poured out a bottle of India ink onto the Latin master's chair while the man was out of the room, and later the master sat in it!" He laughed. "His trousers were ruined, and he was furious. For some reason he chose me as a representative of our class. He must have suspected Huntley, and he knew I admired him. He gave me the choice of naming the guilty party or suffering his punishment in his stead. I refused to tell him. He had me drop my trousers, and he proceeded to angrily cane my bare bottom. Periodically he would pause and ask me again who had done it. I could not hold back the tears, but somehow I managed not to speak." He smiled, shaking his head. "Sitting was torture for the next week or two."

I also shook my head. "Our boys' boarding schools employ far too many sadists."

"Some good did come of it. Huntley and I became fast friends after that." He stood up. "I have taken enough of your time, Dr. Vernier. Thank you and your wife for all your assistance. I look forward to seeing you both at dinner on Saturday. The cook is preparing a feast."

I walked him to the front door. Michelle came out of her examining room with a patient. Soon Bromley and the patient had left. Another woman was waiting for Michelle, but she touched my hand lightly. "How did it go?" she asked.

"I hope I have done my good deed for the day."

She smiled and gave me a knowing look.

A couple of hours later I set out for Holmes's flat and arrived around three thirty. We went back down the stairs and stepped out onto Baker Street. A big four-wheeler, aptly nicknamed a growler, rumbled by. The sun was out, the light breeze pleasantly cool. We had both put on our top hats. "Still a fine day for a stroll." Holmes set off at a brisk pace, his stick swinging in time, and I followed.

"Where exactly are we going?" I asked.

"Remember our journey to the Underton rookery to visit Ratty and Moley?"

I came to an abrupt halt. "You do not propose to go there again!"

He smiled. "No, no–calm yourself. We are hardly dressed appropriately for a visit there. I only brought it up by way of contrast. That was our journey into the lowest depths of London society. Today, instead, we shall journey to a high-class street near Grosvenor Square and a representative of *la plus haute société*, a personage who is the counterpart of Ratty, the illustrious Dowager Viscountess Tigleywink."

"I have never heard of her."

"But you are not a frequenter of the highest circles, Henry. I helped her out with a difficult business involving her son, the Viscount Tigleywink, a few years ago. Since then... To put it bluntly, Henry, she is one of the biggest gossips in all of London. If I want to find out what is being said about anyone in society, she is the person I go to. She knows everyone, talks to everyone."

"What do you want to ask her about?"

He laughed. "Henry, do not be obtuse."

"Oh. The Bromleys, I suppose."

"Exactly. Bromley is the younger son of Lord Bromley. The Moonstone is a famous jewel. Lady Tigleywink will no doubt have some interesting tidbits of information."

"Gossip, you mean—that was the word you used."

"Yes. Although gossip is frequently fictitious, it is occasionally true, or, at least has some grounding in reality. We should be just in time for afternoon tea."

We came to Portman Square. The tall plane trees, with their pale blotchy trunks and abundant green canopy, shaded the expanse of lawn. A woman watched her two small boys running about in some chase game. Holmes shook his head. "Hard to imagine now that London is gray and miserable for so much of the year. In January, it grows dark at this time."

We walked on until we came to Grosvenor Square, then turned and went past it to a small side street. Holmes stopped before a red-brick townhouse with white columns and window trim, then went to the white door and used the knocker to rap loudly. A plump older parlor maid in her black dress and white apron soon appeared before us.

"Mr. Holmes, so good to see you! It has been a long time."

"It's good to see you, too, Nancy. How have you been?"

"I can't complain. I can't complain. Let me take your things. Just in time for tea, you are."

She led us through the grand parlor with an enormous cut-glass chandelier, several gold-framed paintings on the wall and a luxurious carpet to a smaller sitting room. A small woman in a dark silk sat in a chair with her tiny feet in their brown laced boots resting up on an embroidered ottoman. She swung her feet round and stood. "Ah, Mr. Sherlock Holmes, you wretch, where have you been keeping yourself?" She turned to me. "And who is this gentleman?"

"My cousin and friend, Dr. Henry Vernier."

She nodded. "Much better-looking than Dr. Watson. I approve. Vernier—let me think. Ah yes, you must be the husband of the lady doctor."

"Yes." I tried not to sound sour. Some days it seemed half the female population of London knew me only as the lady doctor's husband. "A pleasure, madam."

"Do sit down and make yourself comfortable, gentlemen." She turned to the maid. "Give us five or ten minutes, Nancy, and then you may bring the tea service." She sat again and put her feet on the ottoman. "My ankles tend to swell unless I keep my feet up." Holmes and I had sat on the purple velvet sofa, and she looked at me. "Some of my friends see your wife, Dr. Vernier. Myself, I am a traditionalist, and besides, I have always preferred the company of men—men, like Mr. Holmes, who has been sadly remiss in his visits.

"Duty has called, madam." Holmes's gravity was faintly ironic. "Nothing else could keep me away."

"How charming! Even though you don't mean a word of it. Well, what is it? About whom are we inquiring today?"

Lady Tigleywink had a round face with considerable flesh pouring forth below her small chin. Her hair was silver-white, bound up, her face pinkish with wrinkles radiating out from her eyes, which were a piercing blue at odds with the rest of her face. The navy silk was stylishly cut and looked new. She appeared to be in her seventies.

"The Honorable Charles Bromley and his wife, Mrs. Alice Bromley."

"Oh yes." She nodded enthusiastically. "Little Alice. I say little, even though she has grown into a giantess. How well I remember her and her mother Charlotte. Charlotte was so very refined, and Alice has turned out the same way, refined in a particularly pale, weak-blooded way. A thin line, Mr. Holmes, between being refined, and being a great ninny. Of course, one cannot mention Charlotte and Alice without bringing up the Moonstone."

Holmes smiled. "Certainly not."

"The Moonstone! What a wonder. I was there when Charlotte first wore it, and again, after her death when Alice first wore it. As I recall, neither of them looked very happy. In a way, who can blame them? What woman would not be eclipsed by a jewel of that magnitude?"

I smiled faintly.

"Out with it, Dr. Vernier."

"I know of one."

"Ah, a hopeless romantic, I see. Your wife is a redhead, I believe? That explains it—redheads are known for their lickerish dispositions. My friend Dorothea Dobson was a redhead, and she could never... Well, regardless, Dr. Vernier certainly comes from a different bloodline than yours, Mr. Holmes—he has none of your deliciously cynical streak. Yes, Alice and Charlotte with all their maladies, and the long suffering Dr. Cowen who has had to deal with them both. At my age, I have ailments aplenty, but the trick is never to let them take control of your life. Once that is done, you are lost." Her face showed a fleeting gravity. "But for a young woman, someone in her twenties—no, no, it will not do! And with a husband like Charles. Granted, he has his faults, but..."

"Such as?" Holmes asked.

"Well, certainly not a lack of charm—no, not that. He could

charm the dress off a virgin. Oh dear—I didn't quite mean that the way it sounds, although he always had something of a reputation as a lady's man—little wonder, given that head of hair, that mustache and those teeth. Interesting. His brother is something of a sullen lout. Perhaps Charles always tried harder because he knew he wouldn't get the title and the fortune."

"Do you know about his business activities?"

"I certainly do. Lady Margaret got an emerald necklace from his jeweler friend Harter. Over-priced, but she is convinced it was a bargain. Who am I to disillusion her? And Lord Frederick found a townhouse to let with Charles's help—it's only a block from here, very nice indeed. These second sons have to make a living some way, after all, and I don't find it reprehensible in the least."

I frowned slightly. "You don't think it is somewhat deceptive?"

She laughed. "Dear boy, surely it is deceptive! Deception is what makes the world go round. There is good deception and bad deception, and if people like Lady Margaret can afford the bracelet and are content, where's the harm? That's the good part of a charmer like Charles Bromley. All the same, I always feel the need to lock up the silver when he's to come calling. Either that, or have myself lashed to the mast like Ulysses did when he sailed past the singing sirens. One must protect oneself from oneself, if you know what I mean."

Holmes laughed. "You are in rare form today, madam."

"From Mr. Sherlock Holmes, that is true praise indeed. Ah, there you are, Nancy! Help yourself to tea, gentlemen." She sighed wearily as she contemplated leaving the chair again.

Holmes bounded to his feet. "Let me get you something, Lady Tigleywink."

"That is very kind of you, Mr. Holmes, very kind."

Nancy had wheeled in a cart. On it was a beautiful tea kettle and matching cups of white china with gold trim and a few red and yellow roses with green leaves. A pyramid was formed of three plates on a wire rack, the higher ones slightly smaller. On the plates were scones, tiny quartered sandwiches and biscuits. Holmes took the tea kettle and poured into a cup. "Milk or lemon, madam?"

"Milk, please."

"And anything to eat?"

"One of the raisin scones, if you please." Holmes set a small plate and the tea cup and saucer on a small table next to the chair. She reached over and sipped at the tea, almost but not quite slurping. "Oh very good, just the right amount of milk."

Holmes took tea, a scone, a biscuit and a quarter of cucumber sandwich. I was content with tea and a slice of lemon. We sat, and I squeezed the lemon into the liquid, then stirred it.

"So civilized, tea time, and such a pleasure to have gentlemen callers! You must come again, Mr. Holmes. The fate of the British Empire can be set aside for a few moments while you join me for tea. Cook makes such excellent scones, you know."

"They are delicious," Holmes said.

"Where were we now?" she said.

Holmes sipped at his tea, then said, perhaps too innocently, "Did you say something about Charles Bromley being a lady's man?"

"Oh my, yes. Before his marriage, he had something of a reputation. Well, not exactly a reputation, because it was hushed up. There were one or two young ladies of the most impeccable breeding—one especially—and Charles forgot himself on the divan one evening when the elderly aunt who acted as chaperone had wandered off. When her father appeared... He was a big man, Sir John, stout but strong, if you know what I mean. Luckily he could not run very fast. Charles was not allowed to see her again. They were still fully clothed when apprehended–that must be said. Georgiana went on to marry a clergyman, I believe. Yes, the Reverend Wrangles, and they have had a child nearly every year like clockwork. Clearly she wishes to emulate the old woman who lived in the shoe."

"Who was the other young lady?"

"Let me see." She sipped at her tea, again with a faint hint of a slurp. "Ah yes, Lady Alexander, I believe, although she wasn't Alexander or Lady then but only Miss Jane Huntley."

I frowned. "Alice Bromley's friend?"

"Yes. I'm sure she never said anything to Alice about Charles. Too embarrassing, after all, and she was frightfully young."

Holmes was watching her very closely. "And have you heard of anything more recently?"

"No, no, he's supposedly above reproach, turned over a new leaf, and all that, but I'll wager he's just like all the others. There is always a mistress hidden away on the side. Can't be a gentleman without some dainty little thing kept in her own quaint villa."

"That is truly cynical."

She smiled. "Ever the romantic, aren't you, Dr. Vernier? Most men would assume that lady doctors must be very plain things, but I hear your wife is quite pretty. That certainly helps. Well, I hope your feelings will last. One can always hope."

"My feelings will *definitely* last."

"Again, let us hope so. Mine lasted about five years, and then I found out about the dainty little creature–an actress, of course–and the villa. Still, I made the best of the situation. I never expected much from Edward after that, and I was never disappointed again."

"But in Bromley's case, this mistress and the villa are only supposition on your part?" Holmes asked.

"They are. I could be wrong. Alice is not unattractive, which helps matters. Still, she is a great ninny."

Lady Tigleywink had begun to grate on me. "Why do you say that? What exactly do you mean?"

"All these ailments and palpitations and faintness! I have no patience for it. I know so many women who have adopted a valetudinarian outlook early in life. They are always worried about one thing or another. A pang in their stomach may indicate a fatal illness, or someone who snaps at them may set their heart all aflutter and make them nearly faint, or the death of a young poet demonstrates the deep and abiding sadness of life! It is all such nonsense. Life is what you make of it. One should not allow oneself the luxury of all this histrionic misery."

My lips were pressed tightly together, but I said nothing.

"You do not agree, I see, Dr. Vernier."

"I don't think it is merely a matter of willpower. I've seen too many people, men and women alike, who were terribly unhappy even though they seemed to have everything."

"Yes, and often they have to work very hard indeed to make themselves so unhappy."

"Do you think Charlotte Blake's death was suicide or an accident?" Holmes asked.

Mrs. Tigleywink didn't hesitate for an instant. "Suicide. Her husband had become a terrible bully. Anyone could see that. She was a sensitive woman, as I said. And she was afraid of the Moonstone. Anyone could see that, too. Little wonder she killed herself." She sipped at her tea.

I said nothing, but my good mood inspired by the fine weather and the walk was gone.

"Do you also know Alice Bromley's younger sister, Lady

Bartram?" Holmes asked.

"Oh yes. Have you met her? She is the opposite of her sister in every way, physically and mentally. She also reigns supreme in her household. James Bartram was always a shy and lanky sort of milksop, nothing like his iron-willed father, but in a remarkable feat of legerdemain, Norah managed to convince James he was in love with her and to propose marriage. He has been rewarded with a James Junior. Norah would love to get her hands on the Moonstone. She thinks her sister is an idiot about the diamond."

I frowned. "I wish Mrs. Bromley would just give the diamond to Norah."

Holmes shook his head. "She would never do that—it would mean passing the curse on to her sister."

Mrs. Tigleywink took a bite out of the scone. "Fiddlesticks! These foolish curses! Why invent such nonsense?"

"Many people have been murdered over the centuries for the diamond," I said. "Her great-great-uncle is reputed to have killed three men in the taking of it."

"I don't believe in clean money, Dr. Vernier. Wealth of any variety always comes a bit soiled—all that varies is the degree. It never comes all clean and sparkling white."

In spite of myself, I laughed. Holmes and Lady Tigleywink moved on to discuss some mutual acquaintances and the latest scandals in London society. A duke's son had taken up with a parlor maid—"Little wonder there," Lady Tigleywink said—but incredibly, he had actually run off and *married her*. That was unusual. She gave me an amused glance. "Another romantic, Dr. Vernier."

A clock on the mantelpiece chimed once to mark five thirty.

Holmes stood and said we must be running along. Lady Tigleywink managed to haul herself out of her chair. She took up a cane and accompanied us to the door. "Do not make yourself such a stranger, Mr. Holmes," she chided. She glanced up at me, a lopsided smile pulling at her mouth, her blue eyes faintly gleeful. "I hope I have not distressed you too much, Dr. Vernier?"

"Not at all," I said stiffly.

"I know I often sound horrible—so frightfully cynical, such a vicious old harridan!—but I cannot help the way things are. Believe me, at least once in a while, I would like to be proven wrong in my appalling view of human nature. I don't exactly enjoy it, you know. However, people always seem to live down to my expectations. Perhaps someone like yourself will become the exception that proves the rule."

I laughed softly. "I hope so. Good afternoon, madam."

Holmes and I stepped outside. His gray-blue eyes peered at me from under the brim of his black top hat, his thin lips forming an ironic smile. "I fear she did distress you."

"She did. What an old dragon! All the same…" My brow knitted up. "She was curiously appealing at times. She is wickedly funny, but sometimes rather sad as well. Did you find the visit helpful?"

Holmes nodded. "Oh yes."

"That business about Bromley being a lady's man seemed particularly cruel. He came to see me today to ask about Alice Bromley's visit to Michelle. He obviously cares deeply about his wife."

"Do you think so?"

"Certainly. You do not?"

Holmes shrugged. "I must admit that my general sentiments about typical masculine behavior are closer to Lady Tigleywink's than to yours, but I am reserving judgment." He stared more closely at me. "Out with it, Henry."

"I am not sure this has any bearing on the case."

"Let me be the judge of that."

"Michelle found out from Alice Bromley that she and her husband have not been having relations."

"Relations?" His eyes narrowed. "Oh yes, relations. And why not?"

"I spoke with him, and he was concerned for her well-being. He thought her too physically fragile."

"An impression I suspect you and Michelle do not share."

"No. I told him as much. However, I was impressed by his willingness to do what he thought was best for her."

Holmes's mouth again formed an ironic smile. "Some wag once remarked that abstinence makes the heart grow fonder."

I groaned. "He is obviously very worried about her. He fears she might go mad or try to kill herself. I tried to reassure him that both seemed unlikely to me."

"Interesting. I am not a physician, but that was my impression as well. She is a very rational sort of woman, despite all her worries. As for Charles Bromley, you find him a model husband... the very model, the very model..." He laughed, then began to softly sing the song from *The Pirates of Penzance*, "I Am the Very Model of a Modern Major General."

I could not help laughing.

Two days later, on Thursday morning, I received a telegram from Holmes. *Look at page 5 of* The Times, *then meet me at New Scotland Yard at one if possible.* I found my newspaper, then folded it open on page five. A heading leaped out: *Prominent Jeweler Found Murdered.*

"Good Lord," I murmured. A brief paragraph told how the guard had found the proprietor Bartholomew Harter dead. I shook my head. It is always a shock when someone you have recently seen alive and well is suddenly dead and gone. "Who would have done such a thing?" I could not believe the old jeweler could have any enemies. It must have been robbery, but the place was a fortress. How could someone have ever broken in—and why commit murder?

Just before one, I reached New Scotland Yard and found Holmes sitting on a bench on the Embankment staring out at the river traffic on the Thames. A massive barge was just passing by piled high with boxes and barrels, leaving a wake in the gray-green water, its stack belching smoke. Holmes withdrew his watch from his vest and popped open the cover.

"Almost exactly on time, Henry." He returned the watch to his pocket, even as he stood.

"It has only been two days since we saw Harter. Could his death possibly have anything to do with the Moonstone?"

"It seems unlikely, but one must assume nothing. Lestrade has this case. I sent him a telegram asking if I might see him at one. Let's go. And by the way, Henry, not a word of our visit to Mr. Harter."

The police had moved to "New" Scotland Yard only a year or two before. The ornate red-brick building was six stories tall, with round turrets at the four corners, and with four large square brick chimneys and four imposing spires rising equally high. The policeman at the front desk nodded at Holmes, and we went up the stairs to the second floor and then down a long corridor. Holmes obviously knew his way around.

We passed a section of wall covered with framed photographs. Holmes glanced at them, then came to an abrupt halt. "Henry, have a look here." He pointed with a gloved finger at one of the portraits.

A grotesquely thin face with dark eyes stared fiercely at the camera, an odd forced smile contorting the lips. The eyes seemed somehow to be casting some curious judgment upon the entire world. The man wore not a uniform, but a dark suit and cravat, his thin neck thrusting out from the white curving collar. All in all, he conveyed much the same intensity and energy which I had often seen in my cousin.

"Who is this?"

"Sergeant Cuff. Remember? He was involved in the original case with the Moonstone in Yorkshire earlier in the century. I have studied several of his cases. He is the only one who has ever worked at Scotland Yard to whom I can give my unreserved admiration. Tyabji Senior mentions Cuff in his history of the Moonstone. Cuff initially got things wrong, understandably so, but he went on to redeem himself." He shook his head. "A pity he is not better known. Or, perhaps not—I could gladly dispense with the notoriety Watson has given me, most gladly. It is a hindrance in my work. Ah well, I suppose a few years after I am gone, I too shall be forgotten."

"Somehow I doubt that."

We continued down the hall, and Holmes rapped on a door near the end.

"Come in."

Seated before a cluttered desk with an ashtray full of twisted, crumpled cigarette butts, a small man sat leaning back in his chair with his hands behind his head. His face was thin, his skin unnaturally pale, his hair and eyes dark, and black sideburns came down to the bottom of his outspread ears. There was something feral in his look, something about the shape and prominence of his long nose, their large black nostrils, and his dark, keen eyes. His waistcoat was a brown wool tweed, the matching jacket hung over his chair back. He lowered his hands and gestured at the chairs before his desk. "Mr. Holmes, Dr. Vernier, have a seat." He picked up a half-smoked cigarette and drew on it deeply.

"Thank you."

"Care for a smoke?"

I frowned slightly. Holmes gave me a wary look. "Yes. I have my own." He withdrew a silver case from his jacket even as Lestrade pushed forward another smaller ashtray. The room had a stale, saturated smell of smoke, but at least the window was open.

"So you want to know about the Harter case? Nasty business that. Someone bashed in the old man's head, probably with a cosh. He knew what he was doing, and he must have hit him a couple more times once he was down, just to make sure. You could tell merely from the shape of his head that he was a goner, and the blood has certainly ruined the fine carpet. The guard had left at six the night before, then arrived the usual time the next morning, shortly after nine. The front door was locked, but the big bolt wasn't thrown. The guard had a key to the lock, but Harter always had to throw the bolt. The guard would buzz for him. He tried that several times, but discovered at last that he could unlock the door and simply open it. He found the body on the floor about six feet from the front door, face down."

Holmes exhaled a cloud of smoke. "A cosh, you say? An odd weapon for a jewelry customer to wield. Obviously it was someone Harter knew, someone he trusted. The person came after the regular store hours. Harter must have let him in, done some bit of business, then started for the front door."

Lestrade's mouth pulled back into a grimace of a smile. "That much I figured out, Mr. Sherlock Holmes." His voice was ironic. Holmes had little love for Watson's stories, but the one who had suffered the most from them was Lestrade.

"Tell me, did you happen to find a small notebook with a brown cover? That was Harter's appointment book in which he wrote down every visit."

Lestrade shrugged. "No, and little wonder. The murderer must have taken it."

"Yes, I suppose so. Was much stolen?"

"One would think so, but nothing is obviously missing. The place was not ransacked, as I would have expected. The inventory must have been in the old man's head, and the drawers were all neatly in place and filled with an Ali Baba's treasure of rings, bracelets and necklaces of diamonds, rubies, emeralds and the like."

Holmes frowned. "In his head? I doubt that. Harter was meticulous. I suspect the inventory book was taken too."

Lestrade slowly nodded. "Makes sense. We did find something unusual. Nonsensical, really."

Holmes's long fingers holding the cigarette momentarily froze. "Yes?"

Lestrade snubbed out the last of his cigarette, then dug around in some folders, pulled out one, and gave Holmes a small piece of paper. On it, written in block letters, was WOE UNTO HIM WHO TOUCHES THE DIAMOND. Holmes laughed softly. "A nice touch, that."

"Do you have any idea what it means?"

Holmes hesitated. "No."

"Such a warning hardly makes sense for a man who touches diamonds all the day long."

"Do you have any suspects?"

Lestrade skillfully struck a match on the bottom of his shoe, then lit another cigarette. "Yes, as a matter of fact." The words came out garbled because he had the cigarette between his lips. He took it out. "The guard and the fried fish man out front noticed an odd pair coming in the day before. Two tall men, one with a mustache dressed like a gentleman in a frock coat, top hat and striped trousers. The other–an Indian."

"An Indian!" I exclaimed. Holmes gave me a warning look. "That is… odd."

"That's what I thought. The guard said he'd never before seen a man dressed that way come into the store. He had on tan linen trousers, a sash and a shirt, as well as a turban. His face was nut brown, and his nose and mouth were somehow twisted. That's what both witnesses told us. It can't be a coincidence: the Indian comes into the store, and that night the old man is murdered."

By then, I had realized exactly who this mysterious Indian and his companion were and what their connection with the Moonstone was. I glanced at Holmes, who smiled faintly. He knocked his cigarette ash into the ashtray. "That may just be a coincidence. If Harter had just met them, he would hardly be likely to open up his store to them in the evening when the guard was gone."

Lestrade frowned. "I hadn't thought of that. All the same, we'll be on the lookout for that Indian. I want to bring him in for questioning."

"A cosh isn't a particularly Indian sort of weapon either. Their preferred method is strangulation with a garrote or scarf. That was the famed technique of thuggee."

"As ever, you are a bountiful font of information, Mr. Holmes."

"You must have questioned the guard. Did he say anything about Mr. Harter's recent work or his clients?"

Lestrade leaned back in the chair and exhaled smoke. "Nothing particularly interesting. Business had been slow for several months. He had worked for Harter for a dozen years, but they hardly spoke to one another and were very formal in their dealings. He did say Harter had been working on some job, some commission, but that's hardly unusual."

"But he knew nothing about it?" Holmes asked. Lestrade shook his head. "And did you find anything of interest in Harter's workshop?"

"No, just more jewelry, mostly small stuff. There was an emerald necklace which seemed half done."

"No diamonds?"

"Only two small rings."

Holmes had finished his cigarette and snubbed it out in the ashtray. "A puzzling case."

"Unless we can find that Indian and get something from him, it will probably go into the file of unsolved cases. This is a bizarre one. Why murder a jeweler and leave all his stock untouched? I'd have expected the store to be cleaned out."

"Robbery was obviously not the motive."

"But who would have wanted to kill the old man? He was an odd duck and a recluse—he hardly ever left the store. He had his rooms on the top floor in the back. Had a maid come daily to do the cleaning, but he did all his own cooking."

"You did search the rooms?"

"Mr. Holmes, I am not an utter idiot, regardless of what Watson seems to think. I know my job. We searched them very thoroughly and found nothing out of the ordinary." His mouth pulled outward again into a pained smile, then a sharp laugh escaped him. "I take that back. There was an unusual picture book by the bed, the pages well worn. Photographs of French ladies. Cavorting. The kind you buy at the back of certain stores."

"I doubt some outraged Frenchman killed him."

Lestrade laughed again. "No."

Holmes sat upright, then picked up his stick from the floor. "Thank you, Lestrade. If you do find out anything more, let me know."

"Not much chance of that unless I find that Indian." His dark eyes stared intently at Holmes. "You wouldn't know anything about him, would you?" Holmes shook his head. "Plenty of people are murdered all the time in London, but you haven't graced my humble office with your presence in some time. Why the interest in Mr. Harter?"

"We have had some dealings in the past. He was an acquaintance. His name seemed to leap out at me from the newspaper." He stood.

Lestrade also stood and came around his desk. "Well, if anything else should leap out at you, be sure to let me know about it."

"So I shall. Thank you, Inspector Lestrade." They shook hands, and then Holmes pulled on his gloves.

"Always a pleasure, Mr. Holmes." Lestrade also shook my hand.

Holmes and I soon stepped back out into the afternoon sunshine. He smiled at me. "See, you are not completely obtuse—you did know who the tall Indian and his friend were."

"It took me a moment. Shouldn't you...? Why not tell Lestrade the truth?"

"Then he would have been even more insistent in his questions about my connection with Harter. I didn't want to tell him about the Bromleys and the Moonstone, not yet, anyway."

"You do think there is a connection, then?"

"I told you, one should assume nothing, but I think I shall know, one way or another, soon. Are you free for the rest of the afternoon? Excellent, then perhaps you could accompany me to the Bromleys. I am certain Harter's death will not have gone unnoticed."

Six

Holmes used the ornate brass doorknocker. This time the housekeeper, Mrs. Carlson, answered the door instead of the little parlor maid. Her sturdy frame was clad in the same sort of practical black muslin dress with a row of black buttons down the front. Her brow was creased.

"Good afternoon, gentlemen. Do come in."

"Has Mr. Bromley heard about Mr. Harter?" Holmes asked.

"Indeed he has—and so has the mistress. She's most dreadfully upset." She took our hats and gloves. "You can wait in the sitting room, if you please, while I fetch the master." As she turned, her voluminous black skirts made a swishing sound.

"One moment, madam—a quick word, if you please."

Mrs. Carlson turned to look back at us.

"Was your master at home on Tuesday evening?"

"Tuesday." Her brow knotted up. "Yes, I believe so."

"You believe so, or you are certain?"

She gave an emphatic nod. "Certain. He played whist with the mistress in the library, and then afterwards he and I went over some accounts together until bedtime."

"Does he often play whist with the mistress?"

"Often?" She shrugged. "Not often. He thought it might lift her spirits."

"Thank you, Mrs. Carlson."

As we started for the sitting room, I shook my head. "Surely you cannot suspect Bromley of having anything to do with Harter's death. You said yourself that he profited from the relationship."

Holmes made an exasperated sound. "Have you learned so little of my methods after all this time, Henry? In my entire life I have passed some two or three hours in Mr. Bromley's company. Would you have me automatically trust every charming, handsome gentleman who dresses well and wishes to hire me? It is as I told Mrs. Bromley—my trust must be earned. I do not give it to every stranger I meet."

"Well, you must admit he has an alibi for Tuesday evening."

"Ah yes, an alibi." Holmes stroked his chin, then glanced at the violin sitting on the bookcase. He took it up and lightly plucked out some melody, as if it were a guitar or mandolin. Bromley swept into the room, and Holmes set down the violin.

"Thank God you've come, Mr. Holmes!" He shook his head. "I still cannot believe it. I saw him only a few days ago. I had known him for so many years. I…" His voice broke, and he struggled to master himself.

"How did you find out?"

"The newspapers—and Alice, poor Alice—she was the one who first saw it. She enjoys reading a newspaper at breakfast, a habit I have never condoned. She dropped her coffee cup, actually shattering it. She snatched up the paper and brought it to me.

'The Moonstone!' she exclaimed. 'The Moonstone!' I tried to tell her it was only thieves and had absolutely nothing to do with the Moonstone, but she wouldn't listen to me. She has been in a state all day long."

"Where is she now?"

"Resting in her room."

Holmes's sharp laugh was almost a bark. "Resting? Somehow I doubt that."

"Well, trying to rest, anyway. Perhaps you can convince her, Mr. Holmes, Dr. Vernier. Perhaps you can get her to see reason."

"I can certainly try," Holmes said.

"I'll see if I can fetch her." He turned and strode away.

Holmes had unbuttoned his frock coat, and he thrust his left hand into his pocket. The fingers of his other hand gently stroked the curving side of the violin.

I shook my head. "She would naturally assume the worst. Could the Moonstone possibly…?"

"See, they have come to see you, to comfort you, darling. You must not let yourself be so carried away. You will only make yourself sick." Bromley's voice was soft, and he had his hand round Alice's left arm just above the elbow.

She gave us a ghastly smile. Her face was incredibly pale, but with a bright pink flush at each cheek. Her hair had been bound up, but was something of a mess, pale blond tendrils curling down everywhere, even in front of her eye. She wore a pale-blue silk that emphasized the deeper blue of her eyes.

"Tell me the truth, Mr. Holmes—was it the Moonstone? Did he die because of the Moonstone—because of the curse?"

Bromley groaned. "There is no curse."

Holmes stared at her. "I do not know, madam."

She eased her breath slowly out, and her face relaxed somewhat. "You don't?"

"No."

"It's unlikely," I said.

"But not impossible," Holmes added.

I frowned, and Bromley's eyes widened. Alice could not see his face, and he quickly shook his head. "It was robbery, Alice, nothing more."

She was staring at Holmes. "Was it robbery?"

He shrugged one shoulder. "The police are not sure. The store was certainly not emptied. The drawers were still full of jewelry."

She laughed once and smiled fiercely even as she clenched her teeth. "Then I'm not simply crazy–I'm not!" She laughed again, a dreadful sound.

Bromley groaned again. "*Alice.*"

Her eyes suddenly filled with tears. "Oh, I do not want to die–I do not!" She laughed. "It is so odd. My life is a nightmare, I am often miserable, but I am so afraid of dying. What sense does that make? Why should it torment me so? I'm next, aren't I, Mr. Holmes? The Moonstone will kill me, too. It wants me dead. Just like my mother and father. Well, foolish as it is, I do not want to die."

Her fear was obvious, and very disturbing. For the first time I began to question her sanity; this had clearly become a form of paranoia. "No one wants to hurt you, Mrs. Bromley," I said. "Mr. Harter had many clients. The Moonstone most likely had nothing to do with his death, nothing at all."

"Listen to him, Alice!" Bromley gave her arm a squeeze. "Listen."

She took a step forward and touched Holmes's arm just below the shoulder. He drew himself up, but did not step back, which I knew would have been his first impulse. He was not comfortable being too close to a woman. "Tell me, Mr. Holmes, will they murder me next?"

"You ask me questions which I cannot answer, not yet."

"For God's sake, Mr. Holmes!" Bromley exclaimed.

Holmes turned to him. "Will you give Dr. Vernier and me a few minutes alone with your wife?"

"I cannot leave her alone—not when she is like this."

"She will most certainly not be alone. Please, Mr. Bromley—I insist."

He nodded. "All right, but I hope you know what you are doing. I shall be in the library if you need me." He glanced at me, then left the room.

I stared at Holmes. "Sherlock?"

Alice had let her hand drop, and an odd smile pulled at the right side of her mouth. "You will not lie to me, Mr. Holmes. You will not lie. I know it."

"No. I shall not."

She bit at her lip, laughed once, her eyes opening wide. "I'm afraid. I'm so afraid."

I put my hand on her arm. "Don't be afraid."

Holmes was still staring at her. "I cannot tell you for certain what will happen, but I will not let anyone harm you. That I can promise you."

Again her breath came out in a long sigh, and I felt some of the tension go out of her. "Can you really?"

"That is my business, madam. People come to me because they are afraid, and I protect them. I find out who the culprits are and have them put away where they can never hurt anyone again." The familiar sardonic smile appeared. "You have read the stories. Isn't that what usually happens?"

"And you will do that for me?"

"I shall do my best."

She laughed once, and then her eyes seemed to overflow, tears running out. "I need to sit down for a moment." Still holding her arm, I directed her to a chair. She pulled a handkerchief out of a pocket and wiped at her eyes. "Nothing worse than a hysterical female. I wish I wasn't hysterical–I wish that more than anything. It is all so tiresome. Life is very strange. I just wish I didn't feel so... alone."

"You are not alone. You have a husband who loves you very much."

She looked up at me. Her eyelids were puffy and her eyes red. She brushed some hair out of the way. "Does he really?"

"Of course he does."

"I don't know," she whispered. She covered her mouth with her hand, then let it drop. "I wish my heart would stop beating so hard."

"Let me have a listen." I took up my bag, pulled out the stethoscope and put the ends in my ears. I set the bell on the silk near the curve between her breasts. The heartbeat did sound a little more forceful and rapid than normal, but nothing unusual for someone emotionally upset. "Nothing out of the ordinary," I said.

The muscles to the right side seemed to pull unconsciously at her mouth, forming a half smile. "Sometimes I feel like I could jump out of my skin." She took a long deep breath. "But I'm so tired."

"I think a walk would do you some good."

"Do you?"

"Yes."

Holmes nodded. "An excellent idea, Henry. The day is a fine one, and we might walk to Kensington Gardens. Why don't you tell Mr. Bromley that we shall be back in about an hour and that

I shall want to talk with him briefly when we return." I felt my forehead crease. "Please, Henry."

I went down the hall to the library door, rapped once, and opened the door. Bromley sprang up from his chair. "Is she any better?"

"Yes. We're just going to take a brief walk. When we get back Sherlock wants to talk with you."

He frowned. "Can't I join you?"

"I think he still wants to be alone with her. He…" I tried to think of some excuse. "I think the fewer people with her at this point, the better."

He nodded gravely. "I see."

"We won't be longer than an hour, at the very most."

Holmes and Alice were waiting for me in the entranceway. She had put on a blue hat with a broad brim and an enormous plume. Her eyes were still red and puffy, but she did seem better. She smiled at me. I took my hat as Holmes opened the door.

A face in shadow framed by sunlight: two dark brown eyes under the brim of the black top hat, a broad nose, the curly black hairs of that thick beard and mustache set against somewhat olive skin–"Alice"–he said softly, and then the brown eyes shifted minutely, saw me, and his lower jaw thrust forward as his expression changed.

"Dr. Cowen." She sounded happy to see him.

"I came as quickly as I could. It has been a busy day, and I had a hard time getting away." His stare made his disapproval obvious enough.

"We were just going for a walk," I said.

He looked at me, then at Holmes, and he stepped back so we could come outside. Even with a top hat on, he looked short next to Alice.

"I feel so much better," she said. "Thank you for coming."

I hesitated. "I listened to her heart. Nothing out of the ordinary."
I realized I had been right to hesitate.

He gave me a black look, even as he nodded. "It sounded
urgent. Are you certain you are up to a walk?"

"Oh yes–I just want to get out–I want some air."

"Very good. If you like, Mrs. Bromley, I can stop by later and
check on you after my appointments are done for the day."

She smiled at him. "That would be very kind."

He nodded at Holmes and me, his lips set as if they had frozen
together. "Good afternoon, Vernier, Mr. Holmes. I shall see
you Saturday evening, I suppose." He turned and walked away,
swinging the stick in his right hand, while his left held the medical
bag of black leather. His driver hopped down to open the carriage
door for him.

Alice took a deep breath and looked up at the blue sky. "There
are at least a few clouds. One can always hope for rain."

"What?" I exclaimed.

She laughed. We had come to the sidewalk and turned right. "I
told you how I hated sunny weather, remember? I much prefer
the rain. Too much light, too much yellow, too cheery altogether.
To live in London one should love fog, drizzle and rain, and I
surely do."

Holmes smiled faintly. "I also have a certain partiality for the
rain."

"Well, I don't!" I exclaimed.

"That is your French upbringing," he said. "Let us walk toward
Kensington Gardens. I hope, Mrs. Bromley, that you do not feel
the same way about trees and lawns as you do about sunshine."

"No, I like trees and flowers–especially rhododendrons." She laughed. "But then, I always associate them with wet, cloudy spring weather. Their blossoms are so exuberant, so extravagant."

She and Holmes walked side by side, he swinging his stick, while I followed just behind them. I felt a slight breeze on my face. The temperature was probably around seventy degrees, a perfect summer day—perfect, to my mind, regardless of what Alice thought.

"Mr. Holmes," she said, "do you think I am wrong to fear the Moonstone so?"

He did not hesitate. "No."

"No?" She was surprised. Like Bromley, I hoped he knew what he was doing.

"A jewel with a history like that of the Moonstone should be at least respected, if not feared."

I saw her shoulders move upward. "And am I wrong to think of it as almost alive?"

"That, I think, is an exaggeration. It is a lump of compressed carbon, a hunk of mineral. It may glow and shimmer in the light and change color, but it is not alive. That is only an illusion."

"Only an illusion. I am glad to hear it."

Holmes had hold of the stick in his right hand, but even as he walked, he brought that hand round and grasped his wrist with his left hand. Ahead of us at the end of the street, we saw the greenery of Kensington Gardens. Kensington Road, which fronted the gardens, was a busy street with much carriage traffic, but we crossed it and took the less busy path through the park. A few pedestrians passed us by. Because of the weather, some of the men wore lightweight suits and straw boaters rather than the usual frock coat and top hat. A tall woman wearing an elaborate hat with plumes, flowers and fake birds loitered behind two small boys who ran in a zig-zag, chasing one another. Ahead of us on the left we could see the spire of the Albert Memorial.

"It is good to be out of doors," Alice said. "Thank you for taking me. Sometimes when I am in my room... I grow tired of it, that is all."

"Walking may not cure melancholy," Holmes said, "but it is a distraction."

We came nearer to the Albert Memorial, a towering structure of bronze, gold and marble, evoking Gothic cathedrals and spires with a cross at its top. Below the flèche's arched interior and above the elaborate bas-relief along the bottom, was a glimmering gilt-bronze statue of the seated Prince Albert, Queen Victoria's husband, who had died in 1861. To my mind the memorial was hideously ostentatious and overblown, a Gothic concoction out of place among the spacious green lawns and tall trees. We slowed as we approached it, then paused before a sweeping rise of steps.

"The Queen must certainly have loved her Albert," Alice murmured. "I wonder what that structure cost."

"About one hundred and twenty thousand pounds," Holmes said.

"My goodness," she exclaimed. "I never knew it was quite so much. He died before I was born. How old was he, Mr. Holmes?"

"His early forties, I believe."

"Oh, so rather old, after all."

Holmes laughed. "That does not seem so old to me, madam."

"And I suppose you must know how many children he and the queen had?"

"I think it was nine, many of them becoming queens or princes in their own right."

"Nine! So many. I wonder..."

"What do you wonder?"

"Nothing–nothing at all."

"I think the children are a more fitting memorial than that thing," I said.

Holmes laughed. "You do not approve of such extravaganzas, Henry?" He raised his stick, turned and pointed in the other direction. "There is perhaps a more fitting memorial–the Royal Albert Hall." In a gap between the trees we saw the domed building of red brick. It also had a frieze of bas-relief Grecian-style figures just below its dome, then a series of tall, arched windows; the main entrance had a grander arch still. "The memorial is for the dead, but the hall is very much for the living. Do you go there often for concerts, Mrs. Bromley?"

"I have never been inside the Royal Albert Hall."

"What? You must go sometime–you should try a performance of Handel's Messiah on Good Friday. The music is sublime, even if the acoustics are not truly ideal."

She was staring at the Hall, and her lips rose at the corners. "I don't like crowds. Which should hardly come as a surprise."

"They scare you, I suppose," Holmes said.

She laughed. "You are truly coming to know me, Mr. Holmes."

"Sometimes a little fear is the price we have to pay for a good time," I said. "Generally it is the anticipation that worries us most."

She shrugged. "Yes, I suppose that's true."

"Once the music begins, I always forget the crowd." Holmes pulled his watch out from his waistcoat pocket. "I suppose we had best start back. I need to talk to your husband."

Alice sighed. "I must come here again. I must walk in the gardens all day."

"Michelle will be happy to join you," I said.

She smiled and then grew thoughtful. "One more day, and then it will be gone—locked away forever." A sudden shiver seemed to overcome her. She turned round, paused, facing the memorial again. "How she must have loved him." We began to walk again, back toward the house. "I really loved my mother. She has been gone over four years. I miss her so."

"I'm sorry," I said.

She shook her head. "The memorial doesn't belong here, after all—it does not. What's the point of always reminding us of death? It's hard enough to forget about it as it is."

I frowned. "But we are alive. We can breathe in the air and walk and feel the breeze on our face."

She drew in her breath deeply. "Yes, I suppose we can." She smiled, then laughed softly. "But I still wish it wasn't so sunny." In spite of myself, I laughed too. Holmes and I were walking on either side of her now. "You and your wife love each other deeply, Dr. Vernier. I could tell that from the way she spoke of you. It's obvious. Has it always been that way?"

"Yes."

"And how long have you been married?"

"About three years."

"So little? That's not much more than Charles and I. I wonder… I wonder…"

"What is it?" I asked.

She turned toward me, the enormous brim of her blue hat shading her thin face. "Sometimes I wonder if Charles really loves me—"

"Of course he does."

"—and if I really love him." She stared at me. "Can you really be so certain? Can you see inside his head?"

"No, but it seems obvious." She paused for a second, turning her head back toward Holmes. "And you, Mr. Holmes, do you think he loves me?"

"I could not begin to say. I hesitate to judge the interior emotions. Henry may be able to see inside people's heads, but I surely cannot."

She laughed at this. "I cannot deny that he has been kind. He never shouts at me like father did. Although sometimes it can be difficult."

"Why is it difficult?" I asked.

"If someone is always the same, even if you are upset or angry... it is confusing."

"He likes it when you wear the diamond, doesn't he?" Holmes asked.

"Oh yes. He says it makes me appear even more beautiful. That's how I know he must care for me–I mean to say, he wouldn't be willing to lock it up in a bank vault if he didn't care for me. Father would never have done such a thing."

"There, you see," I said.

"I suppose I expected too much. When I was a young girl, I always thought that once I was married, everything would change, that my melancholy would go away and I would be happy. That was like believing in fairy stories."

"We are born with a certain fixed temperament," Holmes said. "Come what may, that never truly changes."

I shook my head. "If I listen to you two much longer, I shall go hurl myself into the Thames!" They both laughed.

"Well put, Henry," Holmes said. "Well put."

Alice smiled at me. "Let us enjoy this beautiful–if not perhaps, perfect–weather."

We remained quiet most of the way back. I glanced at Alice. She seemed to grow more pensive as we approached her house.

The bright sunlight emphasized her pallor. With her fair skin, pale-blue eyes and blue-gray silk dress she seemed rather washed out–faded–halfway toward becoming a wraith. In spite of the sun's warmth, I felt a sudden shivery sensation at the back of my neck.

"Walking with you two gentlemen has been a delight," she said.

"The pleasure was mine," said Holmes.

"Perhaps after Saturday, I might hire the famous consulting detective for regular walks."

"You tempt me, madam." He opened the door and waited for Alice and me to go through first. We all removed our hats, and Holmes set his stick in the umbrella stand.

In the parlor Sabine sat on the sofa working a large circular embroidery hoop. Hodges was sitting very close to her and speaking softly. Bromley had a newspaper open before him, but he bounded up from an armchair and smiled. "You look much better, Alice. A pleasant walk, I take it?"

"I need to talk with you," Holmes said. "Perhaps in the library."

"Very well."

We followed him down the hallway. There was a door to the left just before that of the library. "What room is this, Mr. Bromley?" Holmes asked.

"That?" He pushed open the door, revealing another smaller, slightly less ornate room. "It is another drawing room, a smaller one."

Holmes nodded, then we followed Bromley into the library. The curtains were drawn over the two tall windows, making the room with its dark wood and rows of books shadowy. "It is rather dreary in here," Bromley said. "We keep the drapes drawn because... The Indian, you know. Perhaps we should try the drawing room."

"As you wish," Holmes said.

We followed him back into the other room. I caught a glimpse of the three of us in a large gold-framed mirror, all rather grave, two men with mustaches and Holmes's slender face. Holmes closed the door behind us. He and I sat on an ornate wooden-framed sofa, while Bromley took an armchair.

Holmes set his hands on his trouser legs just above the knees. "Mr. Bromley, even before reading about Mr. Harter's demise, I had planned on visiting you today. I wanted to ask you a few questions about your servants."

"My servants? Why are you so interested in them?"

"You must understand that frequently when jewelry is stolen, the theft is what is referred to as an 'inside job,' and the inside persons referred to are most often servants."

Bromley sat straight up. "None of ours would be involved in such a thing! They are all honest and trustworthy. I have seen to that. I hired them all myself."

"Perhaps, perhaps. First of all, let me ask you a related question. Have any servants left your service within the last year or so?"

Bromley frowned. "Well, yes, one of the housemaids, Amy, a very sweet girl."

"How long ago was this?"

"About six months. She met a young man with prospects in Bristol. She left to marry him."

"Did she leave a forwarding address?"

"No. Why would she?"

"She might want you to forward some references."

"I told you—her young man had money. Once they were married, she wouldn't have to work again. She was looking forward to that."

"What was her young man's name?"

"William."

"What was his surname?"

Bromley pulled at his chin. "I... I don't know. He was always just William."

"I see. Regrettable. I believe you told me that you have six servants: Matilda and Susan the housemaids, Hodges, Sabine, Mrs. Carlson, and the cook."

Bromley nodded. "Yes, exactly. Susan replaced Amy. As I've told you before, Alice and I are not so wealthy as the Moonstone might lead you to believe. We cannot afford the full retinue of servants, a butler or steward, a coachman, and the like. For that same reason, the servants we have share certain duties. Matilda and Susan both do the general house cleaning, and Mrs. Carlson helps prepare the table for formal dinners, where Hodges also helps serve."

"And you say you hired them all? Even your wife's own maid? That is rather unusual."

Bromley tapped at his knee with his knuckles. "Alice did not feel up to it, and she had little experience with such matters. I was happy to help out. She was rather shy and awkward. I wanted someone with an eye for style who could help bring out her natural beauty. The French are the masters of that."

"And who recommended Sabine?"

"Alice's friend, Lady Alexander, among others. She knew she was looking for a better situation."

"Indeed? And what about Hodges? Did you hire him when you married or did he come with you from before?"

"He came with me. I hired him when I was only about twenty."

"And what can you tell me about Hodges?"

"What can I tell you? What is it you want to know?"

"He was either a policeman or a soldier. If so, why would he want to become a valet?"

Bromley's eyes widened, then he laughed. "I forget there is no keeping secrets from you, Mr. Holmes! By now I should know better than to try. Very well, Hodges was a soldier. He served both in India and here at home for some years. He had an altercation with an officer that ended badly, and things went downhill after that. I first saw him lying in a drunken stupor before a public house. My friend wanted to leave him there, but it was frightfully cold and pouring rain. You wouldn't leave a dog out in such filthy weather! I didn't want the poor devil to catch pneumonia and die, so we hauled him into a cab, and I took him home. When he sobered up the next morning, he was very grateful. We talked a bit, and as a soldier, he knew all about polishing boots and keeping uniforms clean and pressed. I was looking for a valet, and he seemed made for the job, so I gave him a try. I've never had any regrets."

I smiled faintly. Michelle also had great sympathy for stray cats and dogs of every sort.

"There is clearly an attachment between him and Sabine."

"Yes. I suppose it's rather hard to miss. It happened quickly and has only deepened over time. They are engaged to be married."

"Indeed? And have they set a date?"

"They hope it will be sometime in the next year or two."

"But they have no definite date?"

"No, they are saving up their money, you see."

Holmes regarded him closely, his gray eyes thoughtful. "Are you quite certain Hodges's intentions are honorable?"

Bromley's smile vanished. "Certainly! Do you think I would allow anything dishonorable under my own roof—in my wife's presence? Granted... perhaps they are sometimes overly familiar. Even so, Hodges respects her too much to abuse her honor."

"I see." Holmes's faint smile seemed, to my knowing eyes,

somewhat ironical. "I believe you told me before that Hodges's room is next to your own."

"More or less. There is my dressing room between us. Very convenient to have him so close at hand, so readily at my beck and call."

"Could you tell me how much you pay your servants?"

Bromley shook his head. "Why on earth...? Ah. I understand. As you please: Hodges and Mrs. Carlson get sixty pounds a year, cook and Sabine forty-five, Matilda gets thirty and Susan twenty-five."

Holmes gave an appreciative nod. "Very generous, sir."

Bromley smiled. "As I think you know, servants are much less likely to steal from a generous master than from a stingy one."

"Exactly so. You would be surprised, however, how many gentlemen are ignorant of that fact, which would seem so obvious. Often the very wealthiest are the most reluctant to pay decent wages."

"Perhaps because they no longer have a real sense of the value of money."

"Perhaps. And I suspect all the servants must know that the diamond is kept in a safe in the library?"

Bromley shrugged. "I suppose they do."

"But you never open the safe when anyone is present?"

Again, he smiled and shook his head. "*Never.* I always make certain the door is closed."

"Very sensible, Mr. Bromley. That is all I need to know. For now."

"May I ask a question? You have met Mr. Tyabji, have you not? What was your impression? Do you think he is plotting to steal the diamond?"

Holmes slowly drew in his breath. "I doubt it. Murthwaite would be a likelier suspect."

"Murthwaite? But he was a friend of Alice's father!"

"I said 'likelier,' which does not necessarily mean 'probable.'"

"Could there be Indians other than Tyabji plotting to steal the diamond?"

"Of course there could—or Englishmen, or Welshmen, or Irishmen, or Frenchmen. That is why you hired me, as you know. Oh, one other thing. Who exactly is coming to the dinner on Saturday?"

"The Bartrams, the Alexanders, my friend Harrison and his wife, Cowen, and Murthwaite."

"And they all know that this will be the last appearance of the diamond for some time?"

"Yes. I did tell them to keep that information confidential."

A short sharp laugh burst from Holmes's lips. "As if that many people could ever keep a secret."

"It will not be in the newspapers as her coming-out soiree was."

Holmes nodded, his forehead creased. "You do not seem to have invited anyone from your own family, neither your parents or your brother. Why is that?"

Bromley drew in his breath, then slowly eased it out. "You have put your finger upon a sore spot, Mr. Holmes. My family did not exactly approve of my marriage to Alice. They thought her unworthy of my affections. They would have preferred a woman from a wealthy, titled family; someone without Alice's ailments and eccentricities—they could not acknowledge her many better qualities or her beauty. Because she has only a life-interest, the Moonstone did not count for them as anything of value. Their objections to her bloodline were particularly ridiculous—Alice's great-grandmother Lady Verinder, was married to a knight, and Alice's great-grandfather was denied a dukedom that should have been his. Her grandfather Franklin Blake should, by all rights, have been a duke. I had hoped things might change after my marriage, but my family has still not come round and learned to appreciate Alice as I do." He lowered his gaze and shook his head.

Holmes nodded. "This has been most helpful, Mr. Bromley. I shall not take up any more of your time. By the way, your invitation was for seven o'clock. When exactly will you be taking the Moonstone out of the safe?"

Bromley frowned. "I had not thought about that. I should probably wait as late as possible. No need to take it out until Alice is all dressed and done up, probably six thirty."

"I shall want to be here when you open the safe."

"A wise precaution, Mr. Holmes!"

"I promise I shall stay out of the way and not impede the preparations." Holmes turned to me. "You and Michelle can come at the usual time."

We all stood up. Bromley shook Holmes's hand, his other hand grasping Holmes's wrist eagerly. "Thank you so much, Mr. Holmes, for looking after Alice. I had my misgivings, but I saw from her looks when she came in that the walk and her time with you seem to have done wonders. As for Saturday, come what may, I promise you will dine well!"

Holmes and I soon stepped back outside. After the dark interior, the bright sunlight made me blink, but then a cloud passed before the sun. I smiled, thinking of Alice. Holmes and I started down the street toward Kensington.

"Maybe we have all become alarmed over nothing," I said. "Perhaps the dinner will be uneventful, and the diamond will go into the vault on Monday."

Holmes laughed softly. "Perhaps. One way or another, we shall soon know."

"This brouhaha over the diamond may amount to nothing."

"It may—or it may not."

"Must you always be so pessimistic?"

His gray eyes peered at me from under the brim of his top hat, his eyebrows coming together. "People do not hire Sherlock Holmes to be an optimist, Henry. Like Lady Tigleywink, I too would like to be proven wrong in my cynical views about human nature. However, once and for all, it is too early to assume much of anything. There is insignificant evidence to theorize." He set the ferrule of his stick on the sidewalk, then paused for only an instant. "All the same…"

"All the same?" I asked.

He walked without speaking for a few steps, then stopped and turned to me. "All the same, there are too many details which do not add up, too many little complexities. Somehow, no one is… exactly as they seem. And the Moonstone may not be cursed, but despite its brightness, it casts a dark shadow. No, until I see it locked in that vault, I shall not be at ease."

"It is as bad as all that?"

He smiled and resumed walking. "Ask me that again in another week."

Seven

Michelle and I sat close together in the carriage staring out at the streets of London. My gloved hand rested on top of her gloved hand. She sighed, and I glanced at the white expanse of her chest above the fine blue lacework of her evening dress and at the slight hollow showing between her breasts. Women were usually so covered up, but ball gowns and evening dresses were the exception, showing off their décolletage and their bare arms. I stared at her profile, her slightly upturned nose, the strong jaw and chin, the full lips, her long neck, and then I turned and leaned over to kiss her chest just above the lace.

Her fingers thrust themselves into my hair. "What do you think you are doing, forward man?"

I backed away an inch or so. "Kissing your lovely chest. I wish this dress wasn't in the way." I kissed her again and set my hand on the skirts over her thigh, making the silk and petticoats rustle.

"Henry, don't do that." Her fingers caressed the back of my neck, contradicting her words.

I sat up and drew in my breath. "I suppose I shouldn't start anything. We're almost there. All the same…" I leaned over to kiss her on the lips. I drew back, and her blue eyes stared back at me from under her thick red-brown eyebrows.

"So much trouble getting all dressed up, all bejeweled and decked out, and you make me want to tear off all of my clothes and all of your clothes."

"I suppose we have to eat dinner first, then we might rush home and try that. I wonder exactly how long it would take to tear the clothes off one another."

She touched my cheek with her fingertips. "Not long, I suspect. That would be an interesting experiment. Shall we find out? But you must promise to be careful with my new dress and take a few seconds to undo all the little hooks from the eyes. My underwear you can simply rip to pieces."

I gave her hand a squeeze. "Something to look forward to, anyway. This dinner party makes me uneasy. At least you will have a chance to see the Moonstone. It is a remarkable gem." I hesitated. "Do you ever wish you had some spectacular jewelry yourself?"

"Oh yes—what I really want is a tiara, one with a huge ruby flashing red at the center so I can stand in the sun and pretend to be a lighthouse."

I laughed, and then my hand tightened again about hers. "No, seriously, if we ever came into some money, would you want something?"

She shrugged. "I don't know. Since it seems outside the realm of possibility, I haven't given it much thought. I doubt it."

Her reply didn't surprise me. I had not ventured upon the dreaded shopping trip because I was afraid that even if I bought her an emerald or sapphire necklace, she would not wear it.

Outside, I recognized the townhouses along the Bromleys' street, and the carriage soon pulled to a stop. The driver opened the door and helped Michelle out. He wore a battered brown bowler hat a size or two too large. I handed him the fare and a tip, and he nodded gratefully.

I took Michelle's arm above the elbow. "Well, here we are. Once more unto the breach, dear friends." We started toward the porch.

"Oh, Henry, it can't be that bad, can it?"

"We shall see."

Hodges opened the door and greeted us, bowing slightly. His broad frame and ramrod posture went well with his formal attire, the black tailcoat, bow tie and waistcoat. We found the others all gathered in the parlor.

Holmes's tall, thin figure was perched near the far window like some dark predatory bird coolly appraising the party for its prey. His thin face with the swept-back black hair, with that hawk nose and those staring gray eyes, stood out against the vivid white collar and the white bow tie. He also wore a white silk waistcoat with white buttons and a black tailcoat with black satin lapels. His right arm was bent, his right hand loosely grasping his left arm just above the wrist. He gave me a slight nod of acknowledgment. A few feet away from Holmes stood another solitary figure in formal dress, Dr. Cowen. His arms were folded, and he stared sternly downward.

Bromley smiled, his white teeth showing under the thick brown mustache as he swept toward us. He shook my hand enthusiastically, also grasping my forearm with his other hand.

Alice smiled and came forward. At her throat hung the Moonstone in all its splendor. As she moved across the room, the diamond glittered and sparkled as if it were alive and trying to signal something. *What might it have to say?* I wondered. Alice wore a simple pale-blue silk evening gown with darker blue lacework at the bodice. Her ash-blond hair was braided tightly and fastened up at the back. Her long, thin arms, mostly hidden now by elbow-length white gloves, contrasted with the short puffy blue sleeves ballooning out over her shoulders.

A shorter man turned toward me. He had an amazing tan that darkened the bottom of his face and went up about an inch above his black eyebrows and dark eyes, leaving his pale, balding crown almost glowing in comparison. What gray hair remained was cut very short. "Dr. Vernier!" He smiled at me and, in the shape of his mouth and jaw, I finally recognized him.

"Mr. Murthwaite!"

"It's Jack," he said. "Remember?"

His wretched and uncomfortable evening wear, as he had called it, had an antique flavor. The other men, including me, all wore white shirts, bow ties and waistcoats, but his waistcoat was a black double-breasted one with two rows of buttons, and his bow tie was a brilliant scarlet. He looked so different without his turban! His eyes swept over Michelle in a quick, appreciative appraisal, lingering upon her white shoulders and her bosom. "And who is this spectacular lady?"

Bromley proceeded with a round of introductions, taking us around the room. Midway through it, Hodges appeared with a silver tray bearing small glasses of pale, amber-colored sherry. Alice quickly seized one and drank eagerly. Something seemed slightly off in her pale-blue eyes with their swollen black pupils. Those eyes caught my gaze, and her mouth scrunched up on one side in an ironic half-smile. Clearly she was on edge. I would have to keep an eye on her: laudanum and alcohol could be a deadly combination.

Norah, all in green, clung in a proprietary way to a tall man with a blond cowlick which stood exuberantly upright above his broad forehead. She and her James were a study in contrasts: she–short, plump, proud, rounded, self-assured; he–long, thin, awkward, slack, timid, reluctant. Jane wore a pink-and-red extravaganza, the bodice a thick velvet, the skirts and short sleeves covered with silken ruffles gushing forth like miniature pink waterfalls. The dress made her look even larger and more imposing, but since her husband, Lord Franklin Alexander, was tall and stout, his chest and belly under the white starched shirtfront proudly puffing out, the two were a good match. They recalled two large, proud, stout pigeons. Bromley's friend Jasper Harrison had the same easy charm as his friend, and his wife Florence was a voluptuous blonde with a purple silken gown that took the prize for showing the most bare shoulders, chest and cleavage.

Drawing in my breath resolutely, I took Michelle by the hand and led her to Cowen for a formal introduction. His mouth went from a scowl to a straight, neutral line, even as the lines in his forehead decreased ever so slightly. He bowed his head in greeting. "We have met before," he said. Michelle and I tried briefly to talk to him, but the futility soon became obvious. Despite his black beard and his black formal garb, he most resembled some miniature blue-white glacier radiating forth waves of frigid air. Michelle retreated to talk with Jane, while I approached Holmes.

He nodded toward the others. "Michelle looks splendid tonight. If anything, maturity has improved her beauty."

"Yes, I think so too. Tonight will be no different than usual. It will be my privilege to leave with the most beautiful woman in the room."

"Let us hope so."

I frowned. "What is that supposed to mean?"

"Nothing in particular—certainly nothing concerning Michelle. I am only being cautious. We have a long evening ahead of us. Also…" The corners of his mouth briefly rose. "A good thing we are not superstitious. There will be thirteen at the dinner table."

"Thirteen?" I looked around the room and did a quick mental calculation. "Bromley cannot have noticed that! I hope Alice has not either."

A few minutes later, Bromley announced that dinner was ready. He led the way with Holmes, while Alice took Murthwaite and Cowen's arms. We married couples followed them up the stairs.

All the servants except the cook were present in the dining room. Mrs. Carlson was the mother hen, large and sturdy; Matilda and Susan were the two small chicks, while Sabine was another more mature fowl. The women wore black dresses with white aprons and white lace caps. Hodges stood beside them in his formal wear, his right arm neatly bent, his gloved hand resting before his stomach.

The tall open windows beyond the table let in some cooler air. Overhead a cut-glass chandelier shone down on the spectacular table. Red, white and gold roses in full bloom were in bowls set alongside ornate silver candelabras with their tall white unlit candles. Each place setting had a bewildering variety of tableware: multiple silver forks, spoons and knives; four glasses of various sizes, each with a thin gold rim round the top, the largest of which had a cream-colored linen napkin fanning out from its interior; the two plates, one large and one small, were pale ivory with an ornate circular design half an inch thick round the outer edge. Small folded placeholder cards rested on each plate, next to another card, the menu. The thick Persian carpet deadened the sound of our footsteps, and along one wall, a gold-framed mirror hung over a massive sideboard covered with wine bottles and various liqueurs, many in rectangular or other oddly shaped receptacles.

Michelle sighed softly. "How lovely. It always seems a shame to me that we have to actually eat in such a beautiful room and mess everything up."

"Not me," I said. "Eating is a serious business which takes precedence over aesthetics."

We wandered around the table, finding our places, the gentlemen pulling out the curved-back chairs for their wives. Normally you would strictly alternate men and women, but we were an odd party with the men clearly dominant, so exceptions had to be made. Alice sat at the far end of the table, Charles at the other end. To Alice's right were Murthwaite, Lady Alexander, Lord Alexander, Dr. Cowen, Florence Harrison and Jasper Harrison. To her left were Lord Bartram, Lady Bartram, Holmes, me and Michelle. Thus, despite being the majority, each man had at least one woman at his side.

We all plucked out our napkins and arranged them on our laps. At a small serving table Mrs. Carlson began ladling out soup from a large porcelain tureen. The maids set the bowls before us, starting with the ladies. The thick yellow stock had a fragrant curry smell. Michelle smiled at me. "Mulligatawny soup—my favorite!"

She was seated next to Bromley, who frowned slightly. "I hope you are not too disappointed that it is not turtle soup. This is a specialty of cook's."

"Disappointed?" she exclaimed. "I loathe turtle soup!" Bromley gave her an incredulous look, and some of the others stared at her. She blushed ever so slightly. "I mean to say, I do not much care for turtle soup." I could hear the faint irony in her voice. "I had a pet turtle when I was a girl, and I always feel like it is a betrayal to eat turtle soup."

Bromley nodded. "Very good. I should warn you this will not perhaps be the most extravagant of dinners, but we have done our best. No elaborate French dishes tonight. Our cook is very good, but English and down to earth. There will only be three courses besides soup and dessert, and not several choices for each course."

Michelle looked grave. "Somehow we will manage." She smiled.

"I see you are somewhat ironical, Dr. Doudet Vernier."

The thick soup tasted pungent and peppery. It contained rice, chicken, bacon, apples and onion. "This is superb," I said. "I must agree with Michelle—I prefer it to turtle soup."

Across the table, Harrison nodded enthusiastically. "Righto! Better to spare the poor creatures. And such a dreadful color turtle soup is. Always looks like it has been left out for days."

His wife Florence smiled. "Come now, Jasper, you know it's my favorite."

Beside her Dr. Cowen stared at his bowl and mechanically spooned soup into his mouth. Alice was talking to Murthwaite. She raised a spoonful of soup, but her hand was shaking so that she hardly managed to get it to her mouth. She swallowed, then set down the spoon and put both hands beneath the table. She did not touch the soup again.

Next we were served cold salmon with a dollop of mayonnaise, lemon wedges and a sprig of dill. A glum-looking Sabine set a plate before Harrison and another before Florence. Her broad mouth curved down at the corners, and again I was struck by how her hair and eyes were the same dark brown, nearly black. Her expression was faintly irritated, as if she wished she were elsewhere. Certainly in a wealthier household with the full complement of servants, the mistress's personal maid would never have to put up with the indignity of serving at the table.

Hodges and Mrs. Carlson began pouring wine, the choice being champagne or white wine. Michelle and I both chose champagne. She smiled at me as she sipped hers. Recalling our earlier conversation, I decided it would be amusing to actually try ripping her underwear to shreds. Alice also took champagne, and gulped it down. Sure enough, Murthwaite was loudly telling her some story which involved not just one tiger, but two, a male and a female. Norah and Jane listened for a while, then started talking to one another across the table. Beside me, Holmes took bites from his salmon and small sips of white wine even as his gray eyes looked round the table. The wine soon had the desired effect of lubricating the conversation and stimulating laughter. The only one abstaining from drink or jollity was Dr. Cowen; he seemed determined not to participate in the festive mood.

Bromley turned to Michelle. "I see you like the champagne."

She nodded enthusiastically. "Indeed I do."

Bromley's gaze shifted from her to me, then back again. "Have you and Dr. Vernier actually spent time in France?"

"Certainly. We were both raised there. Our mothers were English, our fathers French."

"Really? Oh yes, that makes perfect sense: Doudet and Vernier." He did pronounce our names correctly, dropping the final consonant and pronouncing the e like the letter a. "I suppose you both must be fluent in the language. How I envy you! I'm very fond of France myself. Harrison and I spent some time there before our marriages, didn't we?" He turned to his friend.

Harrison swallowed a mouthful of salmon, a bit of bone going last. "Oh yes. Wonderful people, the French. Especially the women." His wife scowled, then made a fist and playfully punched him on the shoulder.

Bromley turned away, ignoring Harrison's last observation. "I wish I had some aptitude for languages, but I'm dreadful at them. Still, I enjoyed my time in Paris. All the wonderful museums and the great boulevards, the walks along the Seine, and the food—such food! I suppose you both must like escargots?"

Michelle shook her head. "Not me."

"No? And you, Dr. Vernier?"

"I eat them, but I'm not terribly fond of them. Sherlock, on the other hand, is a connoisseur of escargots."

"Can this be true?" Bromley asked.

Holmes sipped at his white wine. "Henry exaggerates somewhat, although I do generally order a plate of escargots as part of my first meal upon arriving in Paris."

"And I suppose you also speak the language, Mr. Holmes." Bromley shook his head. "Perhaps I should try to study it again." He glanced down the table to where Alice was still talking to Murthwaite. "Someday I hope to take Alice to Paris. When her health improves."

"Why not take her now?" Michelle said. "It would do her good."

Bromley's eyebrows came together. "Do you really think so?" He glanced at Cowen, who had been listening silently. "What do you think, Dr. Cowen?"

Cowen dabbed at his mouth with his napkin. "I would not recommend it." His voice was grave, as if proclaiming some fearful diagnosis.

A playful glint showed in Bromley's eyes. "We seem to have a tie. Perhaps we could ask the third physician to cast the deciding vote."

"Oh no!" I said. "This is hardly the time or place to discuss medical matters."

Bromley nodded. "Well put, Dr. Vernier. All the same, I hope to revisit France someday soon. The French certainly know how to live. They have such—oh dear, I know I'll massacre this—but they have such *joie de vivre*—joy in life. They are not so stuffy and reserved as we English."

Harrison nodded enthusiastically. "Especially the women."

"Jasper, will you stop that!" Florence punched his shoulder again. "You would think you were half starved or neglected. It's not as if..." She winked at him.

Bromley's eyes were fixed on Michelle. "Tell me what it was like growing up in France."

Bromley was a willing listener as Michelle and I talked about France. After the fish came the meat course, a saddle of mutton. Hodges carved at the serving table, and then the slices were passed around by the maids. Mrs. Carlson followed with the gravy pitcher and a bowl of potatoes. I took some meat, then let Hodges fill another of my glasses with a beautiful red claret.

Alice had taken only a morsel of mutton and one potato, but she nodded eagerly to claret. Her smile was too extreme, and her eyes had a slightly glazed look as she glanced round the table. Murthwaite was obviously doing his best to keep her entertained, while Jane and Norah conversed loudly about the stupidity of some mutual friend. *With friends like these*, I thought to myself. Somehow amidst all the splendor of the table and everything, the Moonstone seemed to have dwindled, one other object of luxury lost amongst so many others.

Despite her exaggerated animation, Alice did look fragile, and she was so thin. Her arms and throat were well formed and beautiful, but underneath the diamond, I saw the outline of each rib joining to the sternum. Her collar bones also stood out starkly. Michelle was certainly not fat, but she was... all curved and abundant. Her arms were rounded but firm and muscular, her face and bosom full and healthy. Alice had drunk half a glass of claret, but she had Hodges pour her more champagne. She had not touched her meat or the lone potato.

Michelle touched my shoulder, then leaned closer and said softly in my ear, "Have you noticed how much she has had to drink?"

"Yes."

"If she is taking laudanum… It worries me."

"I know. I shall do something." I wiped at my mouth with the napkin, then set it on the table. "Dr. Cowen, can I have a word with you in private for just a moment?"

His thick black eyebrows made for a formidable frown, and he nodded. Bromley also frowned. "Is anything the matter?"

"No, no." I stood, then walked over to the corner of the room. Cowen followed, then folded his arms. "Have you noticed how much wine Alice has had to drink? If she took her usual dose of laudanum last night…"

"She did not. I warned her that if she wished to drink wine at dinner this evening, she must abstain from her usual dosage the night before. She told me she has done so."

"Ah. That is a relief."

A familiar anger showed in his eyes. "Do you really think I would be so remiss?"

"I'm sorry. I just wanted to be certain." We both returned to the table. Michelle leaned toward me. "It's all right," I whispered.

Holmes tapped my other shoulder. I quietly explained the situation. He gave an appreciative nod. "Well done, Henry. I know enough of laudanum to have been worried too." He joined in our conversation with Bromley, which turned into one of those comical quasi-philosophical discussions about the British versus the Gallic temperament.

Next came the rôti course, roasted capon. I took from Mrs. Carlson only a drumstick, while Michelle took an ample breast and wing. "I sometimes forget how much you can eat," I said to her.

Bromley smiled. "It is most impressive."

Michelle flushed slightly and laughed. "My appetite has never been a problem."

Bromley shook his head and stared down the table at his wife. "I wish Alice had such an appetite."

The light coming in from the windows had dimmed and had a reddish-yellow cast. Hodges used a long wand with an adjustable wick to light the candles set in the large candelabras at the table. After the capon came the dessert course, a macédoine: lemon jelly containing various fresh summer fruits, accompanied by a crusty chocolate biscuit. Holmes was talking with Jane and Norah. Bartram, as had been the case all through dinner, remained a silent auditor. Alexander had tried earlier to chat with Cowen, but he had given up and also listened silently to Holmes. Given that Alexander was the only one at the table who had eagerly consumed a full allotment of each course, his great belly and that second chin resting upon his collar were certainly understandable.

Holmes set his napkin on the table and leaned back in his chair. Norah had a small, plump, white hand, very different from her sister's. She wore a gold necklace with many small diamonds and a big green emerald; her fingers toyed with the emerald as she listened thoughtfully to Holmes. The necklace was impressive but could not compare with the less ostentatious splendor of the Moonstone and its simple setting in the silver chain. Unlike her sister, Alice never touched the gem.

The Further Adventures of Sherlock Holmes

At last Bromley set down his napkin and rose to his feet. "Before we leave the table, I would like to propose a toast." Hodges and Mrs. Carlson hovered nearby with champagne and wine, filling any empty glasses which were then raised. Bromley extended his own glass. "To the precious Moonstone and to my even more precious treasure, my dearest Alice." Alice gave a loud laugh, then smiled and nodded. Her blue eyes had a strange expression.

"Hear, hear," Alexander said, and we all raised our glasses, clinked them, then sipped at the wine.

Bromley sat, but Murthwaite set one hand on the table and, with some difficulty, rose to his feet. "Yes, yes, to dear Alice, Alice whom I knew as a little girl, and to the Moonstone—yes, the Moonstone! May it someday shine again on Chandra's head back home in Somanatha where it belongs!" He collapsed back into his chair. Alice smiled fiercely and extended her long, thin arm to clink his glass.

The rest of the table was briefly quiet. Alexander looked puzzled, Norah angry. Bromley's lips pressed together, even as he gave his head a slight shake. A few people half-heartedly raised their glasses and drank. Bromley did not participate. Murthwaite looked like he was going to try to get up for another toast, but Bromley shot to his feet first. "I'm afraid we don't have a smoking room for the men, but we can all adjourn again to the drawing room for some port, tea or coffee."

Everyone set down their napkins and rose. Alice stood, then lurched forward against the table, her hand clutching for the table cloth. Murthwaite grabbed her arm, but he looked ready to topple himself. Bartram stepped forward and seized Alice's other arm, steadying her. She smiled and nodded, thanking him.

I exchanged a look with Michelle, then stared for the last time at the long table, all the silverware soiled, the small plates with half-eaten morsels or debris, the linen napkins crumpled up. Beyond the table, the tall rectangles of the windows were dark, the only light coming from the chandelier and the candles. We followed Bromley and Holmes down the dim hallway to the stairs.

Michelle grasped my arm with both of her large, strong hands. "I am so full."

"You did well," I said. "The dinner went better than I expected, although Murthwaite's toast provided some unexpected excitement." When we reached the sitting room, Michelle pulled her long white gloves back on. I slipped my forefinger underneath one glove, tickling the crook of her arm. "Do I get to tear these apart too?" I murmured.

One side of her mouth rose. "They are made of a tough material. Pulling them off will probably be faster and simpler."

I glanced at the sideboard. "Would you like coffee or port? I would suggest coffee. We don't want you to fall asleep on the way home."

"No. Coffee it is, if you please."

I took a cup of coffee from Sabine, added a bit of cream, then took it to Michelle. I returned for another cup for myself. Holmes sipped from his own.

"You finally escaped from your admirers?" I asked.

He winced slightly. "I thought it would never end. Lady Alexander seems to have memorized all the stories. She particularly wanted to know about the speckled band." He was staring across the room at Jane, Norah and Alice. As before, the darker Norah and Jane in their extravagant overblown gowns, the one of patterned green silk, the other of dazzling red and pink, appeared to be members of a different species to the tall, wraith-like Alice in pale blue. Alice held a tiny glass of port, her teeth clenched together in a frozen smile. More wine was the last thing she needed.

Norah's sharp voice rose; it cut through the room. "So you really are just going to lock it away? You will actually let such a diamond go to waste. Father must be turning in his grave. Lord, I cannot believe how absolutely stupid..."

Alice's lips pursed together, spread apart again revealing her teeth, and then she hurled her glass of port into Norah's face. Norah shrieked and let her cup and saucer fall, spilling coffee and breaking the china to pieces. "What do you think you are doing!" The dark scarlet liquid had splattered her face and her bosom, stained the dark green silk black.

"Lord, I am sick of you–sick to death of you!" Alice hurled her empty glass against the wall, shattering it, then clenched her fists and half turned to Jane. "And you as well." She laughed. "My sister and my best friend–what a joke, what a farce! You hate me, and I hate you. Always cutting at me, nibbling away, gnawing at me like filthy mice or rodents. You disgust me, the two of you! And Father– you dare mention him to me? God, how I hated him!"

The room had grown absolutely quiet. Bromley and Cowen quickly walked toward Alice. Holmes slowly raised his right hand, then rubbed with his thumb and fingers at his chin.

"Alice..." Bromley raised his hand as he came closer.

Alice turned and backed away. "Stay away–don't touch me!"

"Please, darling. I can see that you don't feel well. Perhaps..."

"There is nothing wrong with me–nothing at all! It is... it is the people around me, all of you, only..." She laughed once and smiled at Murthwaite. "Jack is my only friend, the only one. At least he has a reason for..."

Cowen had come forward too. "That's enough, Alice."

"Don't you tell me what to do!" She glared at the two men. "I'm sick and tired to death of you both! You treat me like a child, like a baby! I'm not a child–I'm a woman."

"Then act like one!" Cowen exclaimed.

Alice stepped forward, pulled her glove off her right hand, and slapped him hard. He blinked wildly and took a step back. "Alice!" Bromley shouted.

Alice's wild glee was fading, but she smiled fiercely all the same. "I told you to stay away. I told you." She blinked once. "Where's my glass?" She seemed to notice the pieces on the floor. "Oh. I need another glass. I need more port. I need..."

"Please, Alice!" Bromley moaned.

She made it to the sideboard where Hodges and Sabine in their formal black-and-white seemed frozen in place. Alice reached out for the bottle of port, her hand trembling wildly. "Damn it." She winced, made a face, then clutched at her stomach. "I don't... I don't feel well."

Michelle started forward. "Alice, let me help you."

She shook her head wildly. "No, no–you stay away. You're like all the others! Don't come near me." She swallowed once. "Oh God, I think I'm going to be sick."

Cowen took two steps and grasped her right arm. "That's quite enough, Alice. You need to rest now."

"You cannot tell me what to do." Her sudden fury seemed to have drained away.

Cowen looked at Sabine. "Come with me, Sabine. Help get her ready for bed, and then I shall give her a sedative. My bag is in the hall."

"I'm not sleepy. I don't think. Maybe I am. Maybe..."

Still grasping her arm tightly, Cowen turned her toward the

doorway and steered her forward. Alice didn't seem to see any of us. "Can I help?" Michelle asked.

Cowen didn't look back. "No. All of you just stay here." Sabine followed them through the doorway.

Bromley sighed softly. "Dear God." He looked round the room and smiled weakly. "Friends, I must apologize for Alice. She was not herself tonight—she was not. She…" He fought briefly to control himself. "I should never have… The cursed Moonstone—always the Moonstone!" He drew in his breath. "Forgive me, my friends. Finish your coffee or tea, or have a glass of port. Don't let this unfortunate event spoil what has been a wonderful evening!"

Michelle, Holmes and I approached Jane and Norah. Murthwaite was shaking his head sadly. "Poor Alice, poor girl."

Bartram had given Norah a handkerchief, and she was wiping port from her face and chest. "Well, it has finally happened. She has finally gone mad." The white cloth was stained with dark red splotches. She pushed at a large piece of broken cup with her toe.

Jane laughed harshly. "You give her too much credit. She never could handle drink. It is a good thing she did not try any such thing with me—I would not have abided it. I have had enough. Franklin, let's go."

"Certainly, my dear."

Bromley had been talking with Hodges, asking him to clean up the mess. He came back to us, his smile forced. "Goodnight, Jane, Franklin. Thank you for coming."

Jane smiled back, then raised her gloved hand and patted his chin with her fingertips. "Always the gentleman, Charles. Gentleman and long-suffering husband. How well you play your part." Her lips parted ever so slightly. Bromley stiffened, his mouth clamped together tightly, but he did not speak. "Goodnight and thank you for a wonderful evening," Jane said. Alexander nodded once at Bromley, making his second chin thicken, then followed his wife.

Norah gave Bartram back the stained handkerchief. He hesitated, then stuffed it in his trouser pocket. "We're going too," she said.

"I'm sorry," Bromley said. "I know Alice will be sorry too. She was not herself."

Norah smiled briefly. "Wasn't she? I think perhaps she was." She and Bartram left.

Harrison grinned. He and Florence were the only ones who seemed to have taken Alice's behavior as a lark. "Well, old chap, I think we'll be shoving off too. Excellent dinner and all that. Our regards to the cook."

Florence was also smiling. "Delicious it was, most truly delicious!" They followed the others out.

Bromley gave Holmes a pained smile. "Well, Mr. Holmes, do you and Dr. Vernier also wish to abandon the sinking ship?"

Holmes finished his coffee and set down the cup and saucer. "I shall wait to see the Moonstone safely locked away."

"Thank you. Would you care for port or a brandy? I think I could do with a brandy myself."

Holmes refused, as did I, but Murthwaite grinned happily. "I would love a brandy!" Bromley's eyes rolled upward, then he poured out two into amber-colored snifters. Hodges was busy with a broom and dustpan sweeping up the broken glass and china. Bromley gave Murthwaite one of the snifters, then sipped from his own and sighed deeply. He gestured at the sofa and the chairs. "Why don't we sit down?"

Michelle glanced at me. "We cannot make our escape yet?" she said softly. I shook my head. We sat together on the sofa and drank our coffee. Holmes sat at the far end. He had made it through dinner without a single spot on his white shirt front or silk vest, no small achievement. I had a bit of gravy on my shirt.

Bromley took a swallow of brandy, then sank back into the armchair. "I should have known this dinner was a bad idea."

"No, no," Murthwaite said, "I had a wonderful time, and I think Alice did, too, until the very end. You mustn't let that one little scene spoil everything."

Bromley stared thoughtfully at him. "I hope you are right."

"Of course I am. Poor Alice. She is a troubled soul. And Norah never was nice to her—never. I knew Norah when she was little, too, and she was always teasing and tormenting her sister. Just like her father, while Alice favored poor Charlotte. Oh, what's the sense of it all, anyway? This is very good, you know." He took another big swallow of brandy.

"I never know quite what to do. At least... Soon now the diamond will be locked away and forgotten. We can get on with our lives."

We were all content to sit and savor the silence after the evening's excitement.

Sabine stepped into the room. "Dr. Cowen will be down soon. He said no one is to disturb them."

Bromley nodded. "Thank you, Sabine. Can you help Hodges, and then why don't the two of you have a brandy as well? You have earned it." Bromley turned again to Murthwaite. "How long before you return to India, Mr. Murthwaite?"

"Not long, sir, thank God. I'll wait until September, though. The heat is fearful in August."

"Is India as romantic and fantastical as they say?" Michelle asked.

Murthwaite grinned, his teeth contrasting with his bronzed skin.

"It is truly a land of magic and splendor, even if it has more than its share of heat, squalor and bugs."

We talked for a while. Hodges and Sabine finished cleaning up, and then Hodges poured their brandies. They stood by the sideboard. He put his hand on her shoulder, said something, and she laughed softly. When Cowen came into the room, his medical bag clasped in his left hand, we all fell silent. "I gave her something that should put her right to sleep. I have another patient I must check on this evening before it gets too late, or I would stay longer."

"And where is the Moonstone?" Holmes asked.

Cowen frowned. "The Moonstone? Oh yes, the precious damned necklace. She put it on her dresser. You can fetch it, but give her a few minutes to fall asleep. Whatever you do, don't go barging in and waking her."

"What exactly did you give her?" Michelle asked.

Cowen stiffened, his black eyebrows coming together. With his full black curly beard he looked like some wrathful, slightly aged Grecian warrior in formal dress. *Oh Lord,* I thought, waiting for the lightning to strike, but he said mechanically, "A few drops of chloral hydrate. Does that meet with your approval, *Doctor?*" The last word dripped with sarcasm.

Michelle did not rise to the bait. "Yes." Chloral hydrate was a sedative given alone or with opium, which rendered people unconscious. It had something of a notorious reputation because some men had been known to slip it into a woman's drink and, later, sexually abuse their insensate victims.

"I shall try to drop by in the morning if I can. Given all that she drank and a second night without laudanum, she will feel dreadful." He turned to Bromley. "If I cannot make it here in the morning, give her five drops of laudanum in water around eight or nine o'clock. That is half her usual dose."

Bromley nodded. "So I shall. Are you certain you don't have time for a brandy, Doctor?"

"No, I do not. As I said, I have a patient to see. And again—leave Alice alone for a few minutes so she can get to sleep." He glanced suspiciously round the room, then nodded. "Good evening."

As soon as he left, the level of the tension in the room dropped dramatically. Murthwaite stared at his glass, took a final swallow, then slowly stood. "I must be going too." We all rose to say our farewells. Murthwaite smiled up at Michelle, who was a few inches taller, then glanced appreciatively at her throat and the white skin above the elaborate blue lace covering her bosom. His eyes met mine; he was not embarrassed but amused. "You're a lucky devil, Dr. Vernier."

I smiled. "Yes, I know."

After Murthwaite had left, Bromley glanced at Sabine and Hodges who were still talking quietly in the corner. Bromley walked over to the sideboard, poured himself more brandy, then returned to the chair. He gave his head a shake, then laughed softly. "Thank God, it is finally over."

I glanced at Michelle, thinking the same thing. Her gloved hand gave mine a furtive squeeze. Three lamps in the room had been lit, and the lighting was pleasantly subdued. Bromley looked the very model of an English gentleman in his white bow tie, vest and shirt. His hand was large and well shaped; alongside it was an inch of white cuff, then the black sleeve of his jacket. His long curly brown hair had become more tousled as the evening wore on. Sabine laughed softly, and Hodges murmured something.

Holmes raised his hands and placed his fingertips together. "I believe you said you inherited this townhouse from your father-in-law. How enviable. This is an agreeable neighborhood."

Bromley nodded. "It is, Mr. Holmes. A lucky thing for us—we could never afford such a house, and I'd not live elsewhere in all of London."

"You have some dealings in property, I believe. You must know London well."

"Indeed I do, Mr. Holmes."

"And do you think the area around Grosvenor Square is overrated?"

He and Holmes launched into a full-blown discussion of various London neighborhoods, their advantages and disadvantages, the prices to buy or let. After a few minutes of this, Michelle squeezed my hand again and gave me a desperate look. I withdrew my watch and opened it, hoping they might take the hint. It was after ten, and it had been at least fifteen minutes since Cowen had left. Michelle put her hand over her mouth to stifle a yawn.

"You must stay awake," I said softly.

"I'm very tired. Perhaps if I just close my eyes. I need to rest a bit, so as to conserve my strength for later."

"As long as it is to conserve your strength."

She shut her eyes and settled into the sofa. I admired her features for a while, then glanced around the room. Finally I pulled out my watch again. It had been a good half-hour. Bromley was describing the qualities of an admirable townhouse close by which his friend had just bought.

Enough is enough, I thought. "Pardon me, but hadn't we better check on Alice? It is getting late. It is nearly ten thirty."

Bromley shook his head. "Heavens, I had no idea! Yes, by all means. We must put away the necklace, and then you can all be on your way." He and Holmes rose to their feet.

Michelle opened her eyes and sighed softly. I gave her hand a squeeze. "Keep resting–and conserving your strength. I shall be right back."

Bromley used a match to light a short candle set in an elaborate silver holder. He turned to Hodges and Sabine. "You can turn in anytime." They nodded. We followed him to the stairs, then went up two flights and down a dark hallway. Bromley stopped before the door, then raised a forefinger to his mouth as a warning to be quiet. He turned the knob slowly, then gently pushed open the door.

A lamp with a sculpted bronze base and fluted green glass shade sat on a walnut nightstand beside the bed. The lamp was set very low. Alice lay sprawled in shadow across the quilted blue and white bedspread, her head thrown back, her long ash-blond hair all astray across the pillow. She wore a long white lace nightgown and matching robe. Her bony ankles and thin white feet stuck out, her feet flopping slightly to each side. She looked half dead, but her breathing was loud, slow, and faintly hoarse. Bromley stepped silently into the room, approaching the bed. Holmes followed, equally silent. I remained in the doorway. A cool gentle breeze touched my face, and I looked across the room and saw one of the windows was opened very wide. The other window was closed.

"Poor darling," Bromley whispered softly.

Holmes's back was to me. He had remained where he was, but his head had turned slowly to and fro as he surveyed the room. "Well," he said softly. "The diamond is gone."

Bromley froze, even as I came into the room. "*What?*" he said.

There was a single tall dresser, another ornate walnut creation with many carvings. On top was a spectacular circular beige doily; on it was a metal tray with a glass, a pitcher of water, and a small blue-green bottle with LAUDANUM and POISON on the label. The necklace with the Moonstone was not there. Bromley's eyes opened so wide you could see the white part round the irises, then he rushed to the dresser and fell to his knees to look underneath. He stood quickly and looked behind it as well. He shook his head wildly. "*No, no!*" His whisper was fierce.

"Oh, it is gone," Holmes said. He turned to me. "Have a look at this, Henry."

He started around the bed toward the window, and I followed him as quietly as I could. The window to the right was fastened shut. Holmes gestured with his hand at the open one to the left. Just above the bottom of the lower wooden sash, a six-inch hole had been cut in the glass pane. I glanced down at the floor. A glimmer of light from the lamp caught the edge of a matching glass circle.

Holmes smiled faintly at me. "Neatly done," he said.

Bromley gripped Holmes's arm tightly, his eyes wild. "Both windows were locked–I know they were!–ever since she saw the Indian we have kept her windows closed, even though we are two floors up. They must have had a ladder! What are we to do, Mr. Holmes? What are we to do?"

"You must send for the police, at once."

"The police!" He spoke loudly, winced at his lapse, then glanced back toward Alice. "Is that really necessary? Must we involve the police?"

"Yes, we must."

Bromley drew in his breath, struggling to control himself. "Yes, certainly we must."

Eight

Inspector Lestrade came into the sitting room accompanied by three other policemen. He wore a dark suit and bowler hat, while the others all wore the standard uniform, a navy jacket with a row of brass buttons and a navy helmet with the silver insignia over the brims. All the servants were waiting there, along with Holmes, me and Bromley. I had sent Michelle home earlier. She had left muttering about injustice, and said she would try to wait up for me.

Holmes introduced Bromley to Lestrade. The inspector nodded severely, then pulled off his glove and ran the fingertips of his right hand along the V of his narrow jawbone. He smiled at Holmes. "You were in luck. There was no need to send for me. I was already working at my desk. And what a remarkable coincidence! The jeweler Mr. Harter is murdered, you come to visit me the next day, and three days later, one of the most valuable and celebrated diamonds in the country is stolen. Surely there can be no relation between these events, can there?" The final question dripped with irony.

"I shall tell you everything I know," Holmes said. "But first you might have your men search of the house and grounds. They can begin with the servants' quarters on the top floor. That way, the servants can retire for the night."

Lestrade turned to Bromley. "Have we your permission to search the house, sir?"

Bromley nodded eagerly. "Certainly! Although I fear it will be of little use. The hole in the window makes it obvious enough. The thief must have used a ladder. Once he had the window open, he snatched the necklace and fled with it."

"Hole in the window?" He glanced at Holmes.

"A glass cutter was used," said Holmes. "Undoubtedly the variety with a suction cup in the center. A very neat job."

Lestrade turned to his men. "Reynolds, Brown, have a look about, starting with the top floor. Stevens, get a lantern out of the van and check the grounds."

Holmes raised his slender hand, his fingers spread apart. "Might I first examine the back terrace before anyone disturbs anything?"

Lestrade smiled. "No elephants stampeding about, obscuring the trail? Very well. Stevens, get the lantern, come back here, and wait for Mr. Holmes."

Holmes gestured with his hand in the direction of the seated servants. "I already spoke briefly with the servants. Mr. Bromley, Henry, Dr. Doudet Vernier, Mrs. Bromley's maid Sabine and Mr. Bromley's valet Hodges were all here in this room with me during the time when the diamond was stolen. None of the other four servants was alone during that same time. The two maids, Matilda and Susan, carried the dishes downstairs together, then begun washing them. Mrs. Carlson the housekeeper was talking with the cook, and then joined in the washing and drying."

Lestrade shook his head. "Better and better! Alibis for all." His smile vanished, and he said softly, to Holmes and me alone: "But they could all be in on it together." Holmes only shrugged. "And the guests—what about them?"

"They had all departed before the diamond was stolen."

Lestrade nodded. "Some suspects at last!" He turned to Bromley. "I shall need all their names."

Bromley frowned. "Certainly, although it is out of the question that any of them might have been involved in the theft—two of our party, in fact, are members of the peerage."

Lestrade's eyebrows rose briefly, but he said nothing. He turned again to Holmes. "I want to speak with you. In private."

"Certainly, although, might Henry accompany us?"

"I suppose so."

"You can use the library," Bromley said.

Holmes nodded. "Very good." He took a candle, and we went down the hallway. He set down the candle, then used a match to light one of the lamps.

Lestrade had crossed his arms. "Tell me everything—and this time, don't leave anything out, not a blasted thing, all right?"

"Certainly," Holmes said.

I pulled out a chair and collapsed into it, putting my hand over my mouth to suppress a yawn. I reflected that I should be home lying in bed with Michelle now, both of us completely exhausted, our underwear torn to shreds.

"Would you mind, Inspector, if I have a look around the library while we talk?" Holmes asked. "It also should be searched, and I might as well be employed while we talk."

"As you please, Mr. Holmes."

Holmes did tell him truly everything this time, beginning with

Bromley's first call at Baker Street, the Indian apparitions that Alice had seen, and their visit to Mr. Tyabji. At the same time he was removing books and searching the shelves of the bookcases. He finally came to our meeting with Harter, admitting that he had made himself into an Indian to test out the disguise.

Lestrade scowled and shook his head. "Badly done, Mr. Holmes—badly done! You should have told me that before. That is withholding critical evidence."

"I still do not know if Harter's death was related to the diamond. Nor was I certain that the diamond was about to be stolen."

"But you had your suspicions?"

"Certainly I had my suspicions. That is my profession."

"You take your profession more seriously than you take mine—how am I to figure out anything when you masquerade as fantastical Indians and tell me nothing! It is outrageous."

Holmes hesitated. "You have my apologies."

Lestrade stared incredulously. "I do believe you mean it."

Holmes pulled open a drawer to a small bureau. "Well, what have we here?" He held up a stethoscope. "Henry, could this be yours?"

"Absolutely not. Mine is at home in my bag."

"It seems unlikely that it could be Dr. Cowen's either. I must ask Mr. Bromley about this."

"Forget the stethoscope," Lestrade said. "Tell me more about Murthwaite and this Tibji."

"Tyabji," Holmes said.

"As you will—tell me more."

Holmes related their histories. He then proceeded to a brief account of all that had happened earlier in the evening."

Lestrade stopped him at one point. "She actually threw her port at her sister?"

"She did." Holmes told him, complete with approximate times, all that had happened after Alice went upstairs with Dr. Cowen. By the time he had finished, he had also completed his search of the library.

Lestrade had begun to pace about. "So there was about a forty-five-minute period when someone could have come through the window and stolen the diamond. An experienced thief could easily cut a hole in the glass in only a minute or two. More than enough time. They could have somehow been watching the window, waiting until she was left alone and had fallen asleep. But how would they know the diamond would be by her bed? Any of the guests might have alerted the thief, but all of them were respectable members of society except possibly this friend of Mr. Bromley."

Holmes had crossed his arms. "May I have a look outside now?"

Lestrade nodded brusquely. "Yes, you may, but, Mr. Holmes, do not withhold critical information from me again–do you understand? It is very... tiresome. And frustrating."

The flicker of a smile pulled at Holmes's mouth. "I always tell you everything in the end, do I not?"

"Yes–and that is the problem! Next time, tell me something in the beginning."

We returned to the drawing room. Bromley leaped up from a chair when he saw us. "Have you found anything?"

Lestrade hesitated, then said, "We are not miracle workers, Mr. Bromley."

Holmes stared at Bromley. "What do you know about a stethoscope in the desk drawer of the library?"

Bromley opened his mouth, then briefly seemed to freeze. "A what?"

"A stethoscope. You must have seen Dr. Cowen use one to listen to Mrs. Bromley's heart."

"A stethoscope—oh, certainly. Yes, indeed. It is mine. The stethoscope, that is."

"*Yours?*" I said.

He nodded eagerly. "Yes, you see—I know it's presumptuous, perhaps, but with Alice always complaining about her heart... I happened upon one at a market, a used one, and I bought it thinking I might learn to use it, so I could check on her heart myself someday. I did listen to my own heart a few times. Fascinating. Perhaps at some point you might instruct me in its use, Dr. Vernier."

I shrugged. "Perhaps."

Lestrade's right hand tapped involuntarily at his side. "Mr. Bromley, would it be possible to wake your wife?"

"Absolutely not—she was most upset. She must be left alone."

"I would not recommend it either," I said. "It may not even be possible. She was given a fairly strong sleeping draft. She should not be disturbed."

"Very well, my interview can wait until morning, but I will want to have a look around the bedroom. First, I wish to speak with you in the library, Mr. Bromley, and then the servants, one by one."

Bromley nodded. "Certainly."

The servants—the five women and Hodges—all looked rather grim. I reflected that no one had asked their permission to search their rooms, but of course, the house belonged to Bromley. He followed Lestrade.

Holmes turned to Stevens, a tall, lean man with the sort of impassive expression desirable in a constable. "Let us go out the back way. Might I borrow your lantern?" Holmes took the dark lantern and slid open the cover. We followed the bobbing yellow beam down the hallway, then Holmes stopped with his hand on the doorknob. "Please, do not come out until I have had a quick look around." He opened the door, shone the light on the ground, then advanced, taking huge steps in slow motion like some gigantic predatory insect.

I hesitated, then stepped into the doorway. Stevens was a tall, looming presence behind me. There was an almost full moon, which had lit up the terrace's large square flagstones. On either side stood a wooden fence about six feet high, and about thirty feet back was a dark brick-and-wood structure, the two-story stables and coach house. Since the Bromleys did not keep horses or carriages, it was vacant. The light breeze on my face felt pleasantly cool after the warmth of the house. I glanced up and could see stars in the swath of sky overhead. It was a lovely London summer evening, the kind you dreamed about during the long, cold, gray, wet winters.

Holmes was methodically sweeping the light back and forth as he advanced, then he turned to look up at the house, most likely at Alice's bedroom window. He lowered his gaze, then made further sweeps across the terrace with the lamp. Green grass grew in the narrow gaps between the stones.

"Ah," Holmes exclaimed. He stepped back, then shone the light very carefully on the terrace where it met the brick wall of the house. "Pity it didn't rain. One might hope for muddy footprints, or at least some sign... But this is hopeless, hopeless. The grass could have been flattened by the ladder ends, but of course, those ends might simply have been resting on the stones." He shook his head. "Oh, very well, you might as well come on out, gentlemen." He walked toward the house as we came outside, then he bent over to pick something up. "Recognize this, Henry?" With one hand he turned the light upon a thin silver chain which dangled from his other hand.

"Good Lord," I murmured. "That's from the necklace, isn't it?"

"Yes." He turned his hand, letting the chain slip to one side. "It has been broken."

I stared up at the dimly lit orange rectangles of the two bedroom windows. The top-floor windows where the police were searching were also illuminated. "The thief must have torn the Moonstone off before he made his escape."

Holmes laughed softly. "So you might think."

Tired and slightly annoyed, I refused to take the bait and did not ask for an explanation. My hand went unconsciously to my mouth as I yawned deeply, suddenly aware of how exhausted I was. It must be close to midnight.

Holmes crossed the yard to a wooden gate next to the coach house, and I followed. He flipped up the latch, then pulled it open. "Not even locked. How convenient." He looked around, then bent over and picked something up.

"What is it?" I asked.

"A padlock. An unlocked padlock. This is a very cheap simple device. A child could pick the lock. All the same…"

"It must have taken two men to manipulate a ladder so long it could reach the window."

"Yes." Holmes nodded, then turned back to stare at the house. "If there was a ladder."

"You think we are dealing with a human fly, then?" A prodigious yawn escaped me.

"Go on back inside, Henry, and have a rest in one of the comfortable chairs. I won't be long."

"Very well. I am tired."

I managed to make my way down the darkened hallway to the sitting room. Bromley had returned, but Mrs. Carlson was missing.

I sank into a chair, yawned again, then pulled at my bow tie, loosening it slightly. I closed my eyes and immediately fell asleep. Occasionally I heard the murmur of voices, but I responded by drifting deeper into the warm, dark depths.

"Obvious, isn't it?"

I sat up abruptly. Lestrade had spoken very loudly. Holmes had raised one finger to his lips, but too late. Bromley and the servants were all gone, and the clock on the mantel showed twelve thirty, which meant I had slept for nearly half an hour.

Lestrade went on. "There must have been two of them. The padlock was child's play. One held the ladder while the other climbed up, cut the hole in the window, took the necklace, and quickly descended. He tore free the chain, which is of little value, and pocketed the diamond. Then they fled with the ladder."

Holmes's thick black eyebrows came together over his raptor's nose, and a small muscle to the left side of his mouth tightened. "Perhaps."

"*Perhaps.* Sometimes you carry caution too far. Sometimes the obvious is the obvious. The only real mystery here is how the thief knew when he would have his opportunity. If you want to join me for my interview with Mrs. Bromley and further interrogation of the servants, be here at nine in the morning."

"So I shall."

"Good night, then." He turned and left.

"Sorry, Henry," Holmes said. "I would have wakened you more gradually."

I raised my arms, stretching them. "Did you find anything else?"

"Nothing."

I stifled a yawn, then slowly rose to my feet. "Can we go home? Have the police finished their search?"

"Three are still working on the search. They finished the top floor so the servants have gone to bed. The men will probably be done in an hour or two. I shall have a look about myself–although I would wager that we find nothing."

"And you will be back at nine tomorrow morning?"

He nodded.

"Oh Lord, I suppose I shall try to be here too–I started this business with you, and I shall finish it."

He laughed. "Poor Henry! I know how you hate getting up in the morning."

I walked down to Kensington Road, but at such a late hour, it was half an hour before I managed to hail a cab. When I finally got home, I unlocked our front door and went quietly up the two flights of stairs. The lamp on the bureau was set very low. The upstairs rooms tended to get warm in the summer, but the two windows were each open about a foot, letting a breeze waft in. Michelle lay sprawled across the bed, fast asleep, stomach down, one hand spread out just before her face. Her long red hair was swept to the side and spilled across the dimpled fabric of the bedspread. She was wearing only her plain white cotton drawers and chemise, so her arms and her calves were left bare. The thin fabric revealed the curved shape of her body. Her blue silk dress was thrown across a nearby chair, the seat itself heaped with various petticoats, a shift and her gloves.

I followed the shape of her white calf as it tapered to her ankle, then came the pale-orangish sole of her foot and the small circles formed by the ends of her toes. A weary pang of longing stirred in my chest. However, I didn't want to wake her, and I truly was tired. I set one hand on the bed, leaned over and gently kissed the knuckles of the hand resting before her face. She did not stir. As

I stood, I drew in my breath, then picked up my alarm clock and set it for eight.

As a physician, I was the first to visit Mrs. Bromley the next morning. I was to judge if she was fit to see Inspector Lestrade. Sabine dressed in her usual stylish black dress, but without the white apron or cap, led the way. I found that my eyes had fixed themselves on her rather voluptuously abundant, swaying hips, their shape obvious under the dress (another woman who did not believe in corsets!), and then I guiltily looked away. This was what came of an evening culminating only in unfulfilled longings. I had left Michelle still fast asleep. She worked so hard all week long, and Sunday morning was her only opportunity to catch up on her sleep.

Sabine opened the door, and I followed her into the bedroom. Alice was sitting in a chair by the window. She turned to stare at me with half-open eyes. Someone, probably Sabine, had brushed out her hair, which hung about her thin face and slender neck. Shadows showed under her eyes and in the hollows under her cheekbones. She wore an elaborate white silk robe, layers of lace forming the collar which fell to her waist, with more lace cascading forth from the sleeves. All the puffy frills emphasized her long, thin hands and bare feet all the more. She did look dreadful. Some faintly crusty substance adhered to the corners of her mouth, and her lower lip was cracked. Her skin was even paler than usual with an almost bluish tinge.

"How do you feel?" I asked, although the answer was obvious.

She winced slightly. "I have a terrible headache."

I could sympathize: I had drunk enough the night before, that I had a mild headache myself. "Did you take some laudanum drops?"

"Yes. I've been up for a few hours, since five or so. I felt for the longest time as if I might vomit. Charles gave me the drops around six. He told me about the necklace and wanted to talk, but I could not bear the sound of his voice. I begged him to leave me in peace, and he did. I dozed in my chair after that."

I frowned. "Your mouth looks very dry. I think you need to drink some water." I went to the dresser where a pitcher of water and a glass sat, as well as the laudanum bottle.

"I'm not thirsty."

"Drink it down anyway–doctor's orders." I handed her the glass, and she took a big swallow. The muscles in her long, slender throat rippled. "Again. It will make you feel better."

She finished the glass, then handed it to me. "Thank you." Her eyes stared up at me, their blue color somehow as wan as her face, and tears suddenly formed a film along the lower lids. "I'm so ashamed–not because of the others–not exactly–but you and Dr. Doudet Vernier... How I wish you had not been there! Especially your wife. She was so kind to me. Now she will never want to see me again."

"No, no, I assure you, you are wrong. She is made of stronger stuff than that."

"I was so rude to her."

"You were not yourself. You had too much to drink."

"I certainly did. I hope you do not think... I never drank so much in my life. At least now I know I was not missing anything." A smile pulled at one corner of her mouth. "Henceforth I shall stick to my laudanum and do without wine and champagne."

I shrugged. "You would be better to do without the laudanum and take an occasional glass of wine. Regardless, would you feel up to seeing Inspector Lestrade of Scotland Yard and Mr. Holmes?"

"Mr. Holmes, yes, certainly–but a policeman? Must I?"

"A valuable jewel has been stolen. You must see him, either now, or later."

She drew in her breath slowly, then brushed a long strand of hair back from her face. "Best, I suppose, to get it over with."

"I think so, too."

"Very well." She nodded resolutely. "But they must not stay too long. I don't feel very well."

"I shall tell them that." I turned. Sabine stood listening, her right hand grasping her left wrist. Her faintly bored expression seemed typical.

I went downstairs and soon returned with Lestrade and Holmes. Both men looked none the worse for wear. Holmes's ability to go with minimal sleep for long periods of time had always impressed me, and that capability must also be necessary for a Scotland Yard detective.

After the introductions, Lestrade asked her about the necklace. "I took it off before I got into my night things and set it just there." She pointed at the walnut dresser.

Lestrade watched her carefully, his dark eyes intense under the black eyebrows. "And you are absolutely certain it was there before you went to sleep? After the doctor left?"

"Oh yes. Before he stepped outside, I remembered the diamond, for some reason, and sat up suddenly in bed. 'Where is the necklace?' I asked. And he said–begging your pardon–'The damned thing is there where you left it, on the dresser.' I saw it was so. He closed the door behind him, and then I lay down."

"Did it take you long to fall asleep?"

"Oh no, not at all. He had given me some drops, and I was asleep almost at once."

"And the windows were closed?"

"Yes." She laughed nervously. "Ever since I saw—or imagined I saw—an Indian at the library window, I've kept my windows closed at night. I know it is superstitious nonsense—and it does get warm—but..."

"Hardly nonsense," Lestrade said. "Someone came through that window last night to steal your necklace. I don't suppose you heard anything?"

"Not at all. I was fast asleep for a few hours. I did not wake until about five."

"Do you have any idea at all about who might have taken the diamond? Could it have been this Mr. Tyabji?"

She gave her head a quick shake. "I doubt it. He struck me as a very honorable gentleman. I cannot believe he would have been involved, although perhaps some other Indians might have taken it, some dark cult or some such thing."

"And how do you feel about the loss of this incomparable diamond? I must say, you seem remarkably composed."

"It is because of my laudanum drops, I believe, but all the same, I have never exactly felt that the diamond truly belonged to me. Have Mr. Holmes or Charles explained to you that I have only a life-interest? Well, the diamond was a part of our family inheritance, and as such, its loss is a blow. I do feel bad, too, for Charles, but all the same, all the same..." She clenched her teeth, her mouth forming a grotesque smile. "I am glad to be rid of the 'damned thing.'" She laughed once, then covered her mouth with her long, slender hand. "Forgive me, but I truly believe it was cursed. It had—it looked beautiful—but it had blood all over it." She blinked twice. "My head hurts so. Could you leave me alone now, please?"

Lestrade stared curiously at her, his brow furrowed, and he

ran the fingers of his left hand along the right side of his jaw. "Certainly. I'm sorry to have disturbed you. Do you have any questions, Mr. Holmes?"

"Only one, and then we can leave you in peace, madam. Dr. Cowen said you did not take your laudanum drops the night before last, so that you might drink wine during the party. What made you decide to do that?"

Her blue eyes were the palest hue I had ever seen, washed out in a way that matched the pallor of her face. "I…" She swallowed once. "I think you must know that I was dreading the party. I have never liked wearing the diamond—nor have I ever really liked high society. I thought some champagne might make the whole ordeal easier to bear."

Holmes smiled briefly. "And did it help?"

"Yes." Her lips squeezed together into a brief ironic smile. "But there was a price to pay, then and now, as you can see."

"Thank you, madam." He and Lestrade exchanged a look, and then they turned to leave.

"Oh, wait," Alice said. Some slight color appeared in her cheeks. "Please pardon my outburst last night, Mr. Holmes. It was unforgivable."

"It was… understandable." With a parting nod, Holmes turned again.

I touched Alice lightly on the shoulder. "I would suggest you try some dry toast along with hot tea. The tea may help with your headache."

"Thank you, Dr. Vernier. So I shall."

On the stairway, Lestrade shook his head. "A lady who doesn't care for diamonds. Will wonders never cease! I would never have believed it if I hadn't seen it." He stopped at the bottom of the stairs to speak to Holmes. "By the way, I saw Dr. Cowen briefly this morning before I came here, and his story matches hers. He said she asked about the diamond just before he left the room. And he had a last look at the necklace before he closed the door." Holmes gave an almost imperceptible nod. "The doctor wanted to rush over here, but I told him he would only be in the way and to remain at home until noon or so."

Lestrade had arranged with Bromley to conduct interviews with the servants again in the library. He sat at the end of the large table, Holmes and I to one side, one of his men with notebook on the other. The servants entered, one by one, and stood at the far end of the table. Lestrade's questions were always the same: how long had they worked for the Bromleys, what did they think of their master and mistress, what did they know of the diamond, when had they last seen it, what exactly were they doing while it went missing, who did they think might have taken it?

Holmes, on the other hand, asked if they had noticed anything unusual in the house in the last few weeks, absolutely anything the least bit out of the ordinary. That question generally drew blank looks, although everyone except Sabine came up with something. Mrs. Bateson the cook, who came first, mentioned that the butcher had delivered some dreadfully "off" mutton three weeks ago on Monday. She had had to return it along with a stern warning never to send such deficient meat again.

When he asked Susan that question, she grew very grave. She was one of those tiny, thin, pale women who looked weak, but somehow managed to do much of the cleaning and housework in upper-class townhouses around London. Her white lace cap sat slightly to the side, as if to emphasize her small, perfectly shaped ear with blond hair swirling back over it. "Anything, sir?" she asked.

"Yes," Holmes said, "anything in the least bit unusual."

"Well, the master was struck ill one day, most powerfully so."

Holmes set both of his long hands on the table surface and leaned forward slightly. "When was this? Please explain yourself."

"Well, I was coming down the hall near the library door about a month ago, and I heard a groan. I came closer, and the groan came again, longer than before. I rapped at the door. 'Who's there?' I asked. 'Are you all right?' No one answered. 'Hello,' I said. 'Please?' Then the door opened and the master was there. He told me he had had a bad stomach ache, that it had momentarily got the best of him, but that he had just taken some medicine and felt better already."

Lestrade eased his breath out, his impatience obvious, but Holmes tapped at the table with his fingertips. "And did the master look sick to you?"

"Certainly."

"Was he… was his face pale or ruddy–red?"

She stared curiously at Holmes. "I can't remember."

"Try to remember. Think carefully. You opened the library door, and there he was. Perhaps if you think of his face set against the white of his collar."

She frowned, then closed her eyes tightly for a second or two. "Red, I suppose."

"And there were no reoccurrences of this stomach ache that you can recall?"

"No. That's why I said it was unusual. He sounded in most dreadful pain. It frightened me some, that sound, it did."

Holmes smiled graciously. "Thank you, Susan."

Matilda was older than Susan, taller and plumper, with bad teeth. She had been with the Bromleys for two years. When

Holmes asked his question, she also had to think for a while. "The missus had considerable wine to drink with dinner last night. I never seen her do that before."

Holmes smiled. "Very observant. She admitted as much. Anything else?"

She screwed up her face in a pained expression. "Well, Sabine actually helped us serve the dinner last night." A brusque laugh escaped her. "I never seen that before either!"

"Ah. And what do you think of Sabine?"

The pained expression returned. "Think of 'er? I don't. I don't think of 'er." Her distaste was obvious enough, and indeed the two women were certainly a study in contrasts.

"Did you have much to do with Amy?" Holmes asked.

"Amy? No."

"Who is Amy?" asked Lestrade.

"A former maid whom Susan replaced six months ago," Holmes said. "She supposedly left to be married."

Matilda was frowning. "Amy was… Amy was not a good girl."

Holmes's eyes opened ever so slightly. "Why do you say that?"

Matilda suddenly blushed. "Not nothing too terribly bad—I don't mean to say… She was not a fast girl. But she was always joking about, and being disrespectful, and all. She didn't go to church either. I offered to take her along myself, but she wouldn't go."

"And is Susan more to your liking?"

She nodded eagerly. "Oh yes! They're like night and day. Susan is a very good girl."

"And did you know this William with whom Amy went off?"

"No, sir."

"She had never spoken of him to you?"

"No, sir."

"Did Amy say much to any of you before she departed?"

"No. She was here one day, gone the next, so to speak. She did say she wouldn't have to dirty her hands again anytime soon. She was done with all that."

"Very well. Thank you, Matilda."

Sabine was clearly on her best behavior, but something about the set of those full lips conveyed a mild disdain. The constable taking notes glanced at her as she walked in, lowered his eyes, then sat up straight and gave her an appraising look, his eyes clearly fixed on the area just below her neck. Her black dress was stylish and tight enough that it showed off her bosom to good effect. I knew I had a tendency myself to stare at women, but I hoped I was not quite so obvious as this man. Lestrade gave him a dark, chiding look, and he quickly busied himself with his pencil and notebook.

Lestrade went through his questions, and she answered them briefly and mechanically. Holmes's question about anything unusual made her simply shake her head. "Nothing at all?" he asked, and she shook her head again immediately.

Holmes sat back in his chair and briefly massaged his thin jaw. "Do you like your mistress?"

"Like her? It is not my job to like her, but to serve her. For that, I do my best." She spoke with a strong accent, and her dark eyes smoldered.

"And does she follow your recommendations concerning dress and style?"

She shrugged. "Sometimes. Not always. We have some different tastes. Occasionally I succeed."

"Ah. Perhaps that lacy silk robe she was wearing this morning was one of your suggestions?"

She gave Holmes an inquisitive look. "Yes."

"But she does not share that love of fashion and meticulous devotion to dress which many society women do?"

Sabine's eyebrows came together. "No."

"I suppose that must be a disappointment." She did not respond to his observation. "And is it true that you are engaged to Hodges?"

Her hands curled into fists even as she seemed to stand taller. "What?"

"I did not think it was supposed to be a secret. Mr. Bromley said that you and Hodges are engaged to be married."

"We are—but that is none of your business."

Holmes smiled faintly. "No, I suppose not. Thank you, mademoiselle."

Hodges was also uncommunicative. A certain wariness, perhaps of the police, seemed to show itself in his eyes. If the blue of Alice's eyes recalled some muted lake or sea, his had more in common with crags of ice. His broad face was carefully neutral. His complexion was pale, his cheeks pocked. His sandy-colored hair was parted to the right side and cut short more in the Prussian than the English style. He was not quite so laconic in his responses to the inspector as Sabine had been. When Holmes asked his usual question, he was silent for a moment.

"Mr. Murthwaite came to visit a few weeks ago. He was someone new, not one of the master or mistress's usual visitors." He shrugged. "Not terribly unusual, but it's all that comes to mind."

"Yes, and it was out of the ordinary. Were you present during his visit?"

"No, sir."

Holmes nodded rather mechanically. "I see. And I have heard that there is an attachment between you and Mademoiselle Pascal. Is that so?"

His reaction was not so extreme as hers, was instead a studied indifference. "Yes, sir."

"And you are engaged to be married?"

"Yes."

Holmes's fingers drummed briefly at the table. "I suppose you take her to the music hall and that sort of thing?"

"No, sir—a music hall is hardly the place for a respectable woman."

"Perhaps not. And have you set a wedding date?"

"More or less. We hope to be married next year in June."

"That seems a long time to wait."

"So it is." He eased out his breath in a strangely long sigh. "But our love sustains us. She is truly the woman for whom I have been searching all my life." His impassive face was at odds with the flowery declamation.

"Mr. Bromley pays you well and provides for your needs. Given your passionate sentiments, why must you wait?"

Hodges's face remained impassive. "I have some debts to pay off, and I'm saving to buy her a fine ring and a wedding dress worthy of her."

Holmes nodded. "I see. You said earlier that you have been with Mr. Bromley for about four years, so nearly two years before his marriage. And he told me that before you worked for him, you were a soldier. He said you had some difficulties with an officer which led to your dismissal."

"That was a long time ago now, Mr. Holmes. I drank too much, and when I drank too much I was ill-tempered and insubordinate. Mr. Bromley took me in, and I haven't touched a drop since then. I owe him everything, and I have never betrayed his trust in me." His look at Holmes was faintly antagonistic.

"I am happy to hear it. That will be all."

Last was Mrs. Carlson. She had worked for Alice's father as housekeeper, and Bromley had kept her on after his marriage. When Holmes asked if she had noticed anything unusual happening recently, she scowled horribly. "Just over two weeks ago there came from the butcher's a joint of mutton with a smell which can only…"

Holmes raised his hand, his long fingers spread wide. "Yes, we know—Mrs. Bateson already told us." He looked ironically grim, then shook his head. "Most unfortunate. Do sit down for a moment, madam."

She pulled out the chair and sat. Her face was full, almost square. Above her broad forehead, her graying hair was parted in the middle, just beneath the lacy border of her cap. She wore a black dress, but nothing so stylish or expensive as Sabine's.

"Tell me, Mrs. Carlson, when did you learn of the engagement between Hodges and Sabine?"

She gave me a puzzled look. "About a year ago."

"And did it surprise you?"

She opened her mouth, then closed it. "No. They did seem most friendly right from the start, but it's hard to tell anything with her, isn't it? Maybe it's a French thing. She's a very quiet, shut-up sort of person."

"Yes, I had noticed that."

"More obvious with him, perhaps, although he's the quiet type as well."

"And do you see any problem with having a romantically inclined couple under your roof, Mrs. Carlson?"

She stared at him. "What do you mean?"

"Well, it complicates things, does it not? There could be inappropriate behavior."

A slow flush began to appear on her cheeks.

"I suppose in certain circumstances you might even feel compelled to talk to your master."

She nodded.

"And have you done that—spoken to your master?"

"I meant no harm—but something needed to be said."

Holmes's calm gray eyes were fixed on her. "Did you happen to notice her going into his room?"

Her flush had deepened. "How… how could you know that?"

He shrugged. "Did you notice it more than once?"

"Yes."

"And what did your master say?"

"That he would speak to them, and he did. Hodges told him they just wanted to chat, that they had little time for one another, and that while he was polishing or pressing in the dressing room, they could be together."

"And did this explanation satisfy you?"

"Yes." Her pained expression belied her affirmation. "But he did tell them it could give people the wrong impression, and that they'd best avoid it! And I think it has helped. Oh, I don't want to be considered an old busy-body! Live and let live is my motto."

"You seem very broad-minded, madam. One final question, and then we can drop the subject. Have you ever seen Hodges kiss Sabine?"

Lestrade drew back slightly in his chair, letting out his breath sharply. Mrs. Carlson thrust her jaw forward and shook her head. "No."

Lestrade made an exasperated noise. "Mr. Holmes, must we lose ourselves in such sensational distractions? The issue at hand is the loss of the diamond."

Holmes nodded. "Moving on then, Mrs. Carlson, when Amy decided to leave your service, did she speak to you or to Mr. Bromley first?"

"To him. I would have let her know what I thought of her—telling us she must leave with only a day or two's notice! I'm sure she's smart enough never to ask me for a reference. They'd get a mouthful from me!"

"And exactly what did you think of her?"

"That although much of the time she could work hard and do her chores, she had a saucy tongue and was trouble for others in the household. Matilda could hardly bear her company. When I told her to mend her ways, she had a nasty sort of smirking smile that made me want to slap her."

"So, I take it, you are happy to have Susan here as a replacement."

"That I am. Susan is all sweetness compared to Amy."

Holmes nodded. "I see. And I have heard that Amy left no forwarding address?"

"No. She seemed all too happy at the prospect of not seeing us again, and we felt the same."

"Could you describe her physical appearance for me, please? Constable, do write down these details. Also, did she have any distinguishing marks: a mole, a birthmark, scars?"

"She did have a birthmark. It was just under her right ear, a reddish purple blotch about an inch or so across. Strawberry mark, they call them, although this one was more the shape of a mushroom. Let's see, she was tiny, but not so tiny as Susan. About five foot two or so, with curly black hair. Brown eyes. Her upper lip much fatter than the lower, almost sticking out some. Her teeth were none too good. She was missing one on the lower left side."

"Thank you, Mrs. Carlson. Would you please close the door on the way out?"

Once the door was closed, Lestrade leaned back in his chair, brought his arms forward to stretch, and then clasped his hands behind his head. "All right, Mr. Holmes, why this bizarre fascination with Mademoiselle Pascal and Hodges? Can you possibly believe they are somehow behind the robbery?"

"No, I do not think so. Again, they were both present in the drawing room with me while the theft took place."

"She could have signaled to someone outside before she came down."

"But the doctor was with Mrs. Bromley, so she could not have known how long he would be with her."

"Blast it! Then why all these questions about the two of them?"

Holmes smiled and set his left hand onto the palm of his right. "I'm merely trying to understand all the various tangled relationships within this little household."

"And this girl, Amy—obviously she knew about the diamond and the layout of the house. She could have conspired with someone else, possibly someone still in the house. True, she doesn't seem to have left a very good impression on the other servants, but that could be an act on the part of one of them."

"That is possible, although none of them strike me as having hidden thespian abilities. There is another alternative. Could you have one of your men look at the files and photographs for all unidentified young women either found dead on the streets or exhumed from the Thames during the last six months? See if anyone matches Amy's description. The birthmark should be the giveaway."

This last request made me feel a sudden queasy sensation low in the belly. Holmes's questions had not prepared me for such a possibility.

"We are finished, are we not?" Holmes asked. Lestrade nodded brusquely, and Holmes stood. "Well, Henry, I think we have earned a good lunch, and then if you wish, you may join me in another visit."

"Where?" I asked.

"We must drop in on Mr. Tyabji."

Lestrade laughed. "You will find that he has already had visitors today."

Nine

We arrived at Tyabji's house shortly after one that afternoon and were again ushered into the main sitting room with its exotic and colorful tapestries, carpets, pillows and statuary. This time I noticed the fantastical three-foot bronze in the shadowy corner. The rotund deity had an elephant head and four arms; it sat cross-legged, its elephantine ears outspread, an elaborate crown or headpiece up top. The beautiful red-glass hookah sat in another corner, unlit and silent this time.

Tyabji rose to meet us, dressed again formally in striped trousers, white shirt with black cravat and black vest. However, over this he wore a spectacular dressing gown partaking of both East and West, a paisley print of blue and green on silk. His smile set off his brilliant white teeth against his dark skin, and his abundantly curling brown hair had highlights of gold.

Sprawled across an armchair with his bony white feet perched on the ottoman, lay a more earthbound figure: Murthwaite, still dressed in remnants of the prior evening's formal wear, the black trousers and white, long-sleeved shirt. The red bow tie was undone, its ends dangling from the open collar, and his black braces had slipped off his arms and lay drooping at the sides of his trousers. His eyes struggled to open more than halfway in acknowledgment of our presence. Despite his tanned skin, he looked pale. One hand, its bony fingers curved like claws, rose from the chair arm in a feeble greeting, accompanied by an equally feeble sort of croak.

"Good afternoon, gentlemen." Tyabji's voice was hale and hearty.

It triggered another croak from Murthwaite, along with head shaking. "No, no—easy now—easy. Not loud. Not loud."

"I'm sorry," Tyabji said more softly. "You gave me very sound advice, Mr. Holmes. I had an alibi for the time of the theft. My two servants and I were playing cards all evening long. I allowed the police to search the house this morning."

"Inspector Lestrade told us his men visited," Holmes said.

Tyabji shook his head. "Very sloppy and careless they were in all their rummaging about! It will take my servants the rest of the afternoon to completely restore order."

"They did not, of course, find anything?"

"No, as I could have—and did—tell them."

Holmes glanced at Murthwaite whose half-open eyes were vaguely focused on some spot about two feet in the air before him. "And did they also question Mr. Murthwaite?"

Tyabji smiled. "They tried to. They had little success."

Murthwaite made a labored sound, shifted in the chair and managed to rise some six inches upward. He raised his clawed hand again as he turned to Tyabji's servant. "Sunil, please, coffee now—with brandy, a big dose of brandy." Sunil nodded and slipped quietly away. Instead of shoes he wore red slippers with his black trousers and morning coat.

Tyabji smiled down at Murthwaite. "How good to see you returning to the living again, Jack."

Murthwaite winced and waved his hand. "Softly, please."

Tyabji folded his arms. "So the diamond is gone, Mr. Holmes?"

"It is."

He shook his head. "You are lucky to have seen it. No doubt the thieves will have it hacked to pieces, and the fragments will be sold off. To think it survived for centuries in India, only to come to England and be destroyed within a few paltry decades! Truly we live in a wicked world. Parts of Christianity make little sense to me, but I do believe in sin. Men are so willing to desecrate beautiful things. I have never seen the diamond, and now I suppose I never will."

The corners of Holmes's mouth briefly rose. "Do not be too sure of that, sir. You may see it sooner than you imagine."

Tyabji stared at him. "What do you mean?"

"I have reason to believe the thieves may have the diamond delivered to you."

I was rather stupefied myself. "Sherlock, can that possibly be true?"

"Yes." He gazed again at Tyabji. "You took my advice before. Will you take it again?"

"Certainly, Mr. Holmes."

"If a package should be delivered to your house this week, do not open it, but send for me immediately. I—and Inspector Lestrade of Scotland Yard—will come at once."

"Why would anyone send me the diamond?"

Again the corners of his mouth flickered briefly upward. "Because it belongs to you—or rather to the Hindus of Gujarat."

"I would like to believe that is possible, but it does seem unlikely."

I nodded. "I think so too."

"We shall see," Holmes said. "We shall see."

"If it came to me, what if I simply…" Tyabji's voice trailed away.

Holmes stared at him. "What if you simply kept it, you mean? The temptation is great, I know, but I hope you will trust me and do as I ask. If you do not… I cannot explain myself, but if you accept the 'gift,' all might not turn out as you would expect."

Tyabji smiled ironically. "Is charity from thieves thievery? Do two wrongs make a right? I will do as you say, Mr. Holmes. My Christian and my Muslim upbringing may not have an obvious answer for me, but I do have a sense of honor. And you are certainly more experienced than I in these bewildering matters, a worthy guide for a novice like myself."

Holmes nodded. "Thank you."

Sunil had returned with a silver tray bearing a china pitcher and a cup and saucer. He set it down on a small end table, then poured out the hot brown liquid. I could smell both coffee and brandy. Murthwaite managed to raise himself to a mostly upright position, even as he crossed his legs at the ankles and gestured at the wooden arm of the chair. "Set it there." He stared resolutely at the black steaming surface of the liquid, then reached for the cup, lifted it quickly and took a big swallow, slurping loudly as he did so. He lowered the cup at once and drew in his breath, nodding once. "Better." He frowned slightly. "Could use a touch more brandy, though."

"At once, sir," Sunil said.

"No, no—this will do. This will do nicely. Thank you." He looked up at us, his smile more akin to a grimace, then he took another big sip. "I may live after all." His voice was much less hoarse than it had been. "Alice—how is poor Alice?"

I smiled. "She had a headache too."

"Not like mine! Can't have been—can't have been. She stopped round ten, while I… I was just getting starting when I left."

"Where did you go?" I asked.

"A public house, and then a public house, and finally a public house close by. I knew my friend Geoffrey would take me in, even early in the morning." He glanced at Tyabji. "What time was it when I appeared upon your doorstep?"

"A quarter past two. You managed to fall asleep standing and with your eyes open a fraction."

"I don't remember much from last night after the party, only the dim, smoke-filled interiors of the pubs and people laughing and talking."

"You have no alibi, then?" Holmes asked.

Murthwaite smiled. "Probably not. Then, too, I have a double motive for theft: I think the diamond belongs back in India, and I'd like to see Alice free of that particular albatross. I wouldn't have any moral compunction about pinching it, either. Unfortunately, I was in no state to do anything last night. Could have told my accomplices when to strike, I suppose." He winked at us. "Pity I had no accomplices."

He shook his head. "Poor little Alice—of course, I mean little only in a figurative sense. She has three or four inches on me, but I think of her as little compared to that harridan of a sister of hers. I pity that poor husband, that 'James' of Norah. Alice was always the sweet one who could listen to my stories for hours, while even at the age of five or six Norah was proclaiming loudly that she didn't believe a word of it. Didn't believe I'd ever seen a tiger, can you imagine? Last night's dinner was a good one, and I enjoyed talking to Alice, but the high point of the evening was seeing Norah doused with port." A sharp bark of a laugh escaped him, then he coughed once, again, and drank a big sip of coffee. "I wouldn't have missed that for anything—how she had it coming! Ever since they were little, she has bullied Alice. She has all of her father's truculence, while Alice has her mother's sweetness."

He sighed wearily. "All the same, I think I'm getting too old for that kind of drinking. It has been a long time since I have so indulged. Geoffrey, if you're game, after I eat something, we might try a smoke of my special blend again. That mixture with hashish and opium is perfect for calming the gyrating stomach and soothing the battered head."

Tyabji nodded. "Gladly, Jack. And perhaps this time Mr. Holmes might join us."

Holmes smiled. "Not today, I'm afraid. Another time, perhaps."

Murthwaite sighed again. "If you had the need of it that I do, you would not abstain, but you were moderate in your consumption of drink last night. That, in retrospect, seems wise. As I say, I grow too old for such bouts of intemperance. The price one must pay has become painful indeed."

"Come, come, Jack," Tyabji said. "You will live, I assure you."

Murthwaite took a last swallow, finishing the coffee. "I do feel marginally alive now." He glanced at Holmes. "Will the police want to arrest me, Mr. Holmes?"

"I doubt it. They will want to question you further."

"The police told us the diamond had been stolen, but would not give us any details. How did it happen, Mr. Holmes?"

Holmes slid the fingers of one hand between the fingers of the other. "It was taken from Mrs. Bromley's bedroom. She was alone for half an hour or so after the doctor left and before we went up to reclaim the necklace. A hole had been cut in the glass, and the window was open."

Tyabji shook his head. "That must have been one or two floors up from the ground. I suppose they used a ladder."

Murthwaite burst into loud laughter. We all stared at him. "What is so amusing, Jack?" Tyabji asked.

"Sorry. The mere idea of me climbing a ladder last night struck me as funny."

I frowned and glanced at Holmes. "Could they have used a rope?"

He shrugged. "It would be possible."

"But there was nothing upon which to hook a rope."

"A rope or a rope ladder with a grappling hook could conceivably have been thrown up to the protruding window ledge, but I saw no marks there."

Murthwaite was smiling again. "I suppose Bromley was devastated."

"It was quite a shock to him," I said.

"He was going to lock it away, anyway, or so he said. Which I found hard to believe. Of course, last night was different."

Holmes stared closely at him. "How so?"

"Usually he can't seem to keep his eyes off the diamond–at least that was true the other times I was around him when Alice was wearing the jewel. He was always ogling it. Oh, those who are more charitable than me might assume that he couldn't take his eyes off Alice, but I always thought he seemed more in love with the diamond than with her."

"That's ridiculous," I said, "–and unfair. You cannot be in love with an inanimate object, even one as beautiful as a diamond."

Murthwaite was still smiling. "Can't you?" He laughed softly. "Sometimes I think that's the real difference between the rich and the poor, wherever you go. The rich are more in love with jewels and gold and pretty trinkets than with people. Treasure becomes the be-all and the end-all. Nothing else really counts for them."

Tyabji stared closely at Murthwaite. "You are rarely so philosophical, Jack."

"Must be sobering up that does it. They say money is a blessing, but it's always seemed more a curse to me. I've never seen a rich man who could take joy in the simple pleasures of life the way the poor man can. Oh, I don't mean the wretchedly poor—theirs can be a miserable lot. But if you have enough and can be content with that, you are truly blessed. Those at the party last night— those peers with all their houses, their horses and carriages, their wives all decked out like great sailing ships with silken sails and... I'd not trade places with them for all the money in the world." He laughed. "I'd rather be here with you, Geoffrey, and have a smoke, or spend time with my wives and children—in moderation, naturally, all in moderation."

Holmes smiled. "You are indeed a philosopher, Mr. Murthwaite."

"Jack—call me Jack. Everyone does."

"Very well, Jack. Henry and I must be on our way. Remember what I said about that package, Mr. Tyabji."

"I shall, Mr. Holmes—you have my promise on that."

"Good day, then."

It was another balmy, beautiful day outside, about seventy degrees with a few puffy clouds in the blue sky above a line of roof tops. I put on my hat, then covered my mouth and yawned. The lingering headache of the morning was gone, but I felt sleepy and wished I were home. Holmes, on the other hand, seemed more invigorated than ever.

He smiled at me from under the brim of his black top hat. "Morpheus beckons, eh, Henry?" I nodded. "Perhaps a stroll down to the bridge, with a visit to Vauxhall Park along the way, then I must stop at Scotland Yard to check with Lestrade. He told me he would be there later this afternoon."

He set off at a good pace, his stick striking the ground rhythmically, and I followed. The Sunday traffic along South Lambeth Road was much lighter than during the week, none of those heavily laden carts which rumbled along as the draft horses pulled them.

"You surprised me back there," I said. "It is difficult to believe someone would steal a diamond of such value and then, after all that effort, simply give it away. Why would they do such a thing?"

"As I indicated–to return it to its rightful owner."

"Honorable thieves?"

"Yes."

I shook my head. "I can understand none of this."

Holmes gave me a quick sideways glance. "No, you would not. These are dark waters this time, Henry. You and Michelle are far too honest and straightforward to comprehend the depths of iniquity which are involved."

"That sounds grave indeed. Yet, you said the thieves were honorable. How can they be honorable and darkly evil at the same time?"

He inhaled through his nose in what was almost a laugh. "I was not thinking of the thieves, but of other persons involved in this business, persons who I fear are completely lacking in any moral scruples or inhibitions whatsoever. Human life means nothing to them. They are willing to kill anyone who gets in their way without the slightest hesitation."

I felt anxiety stirring low in my chest. "Willing to kill? Whom?"

"Mr. Harter, for one."

"I thought you were not sure his death had anything to do with the Moonstone."

"That was before it was stolen. Now I am certain of the connection."

"But why kill him?"

Holmes's smile was totally without humor. "Because he was too good at his trade."

My head had begun to ache. "I cannot understand any of this. I don't suppose you would like to explain yourself?"

"Not yet, Henry. Also, I shall not at all be surprised if the servant girl Amy turns up in one of the police files for those unknown 'floaters' recovered from the Thames."

I looked up at the blue sky and the clouds and tried to control my fear. "I hope you are finished with this list of victims."

"No, unfortunately not."

"Who else has been killed?"

"No one. *Yet.*"

I groaned. "Who then? Another of the servants? Bromley? Or… Alice?" The fear had returned.

"She was right about the curse, you know. A stone like that has an aura of death, or rather–it is as she said. The thing has been drowned in blood. Perhaps that childhood vision of hers was not merely an idle fantasy. Someone with preternatural senses might well see a cloud of blood around it."

"You have said you don't believe in the supernatural, in ghosts or vampires or werewolves, and yet you speak of a cloud of blood! Is this your idea of a ghastly joke?"

He stared more closely at me, then reached out and grasped my arm. "Easy, Henry. I did not mean to upset you. There is no literal cloud of blood. I was only musing out loud."

"But you think Alice may be in danger?"

His bleak smile returned. "In this case, I trust my intuition absolutely. She is in very grave danger."

"But they have the diamond? Why bother to kill her? What would be the point?"

"Remember those dark waters I mentioned? But calm yourself. All is not lost. I told her I would protect her, and I will."

"Who is it, then? Some blood cult of crazed Indians determined to kill her because she has profaned their sacred stone?"

"No, no—that is still the stuff of melodrama. It is all much more simple than that."

"Not so simple I can fathom it."

"We are back where we started. You cannot fathom it because you are too honorable and decent. Do you hear that?"

I frowned, then became aware of music blaring in the distance.

"How agreeable, a Sunday afternoon concert in the park! Although 'Rule Britannia' is hardly very original. Let us stop and listen for a while."

We entered the park through an opening in the black wrought-iron fence. Along a grassy expanse, people stood in their Sunday best listening to the concert. Many men wore light linen suits of pale beige, brown or gray with straw boaters, while the women had colorful dresses of silk or muslin, their copious skirts ballooning out. The small orchestra was under a bandstand with its white-and-green-painted arches topped by an ornate roof. The players wore red-and-gold military-style jackets, and the light glinted off the bright brass and silver of the trombones, french horns, flutes, trumpets and clarinets. After "Rule Britannia" they played a few brisk marches. The audience clapped loudly after each piece. A small boy in a sailor suit listened attentively, while his smaller brother and sister sat and pulled up handfuls of grass.

Everything was so pleasant, so normal, everyone so much at ease, and yet I felt sick at heart. For once I could understand Alice's dislike of sunshine: given the dark influence of the Moonstone, all this yellowish brightness was deceptive, jarring. I had had more than enough of the Moonstone case and the jewel's curse. I wanted to go home to Michelle and forget all about the miserable business. I tried to tell myself I was being unmanly and simply ridiculous– how could Alice possibly be in danger?–and yet I knew that Holmes's judgment in these matters was unsurpassed. If he thought she was in danger, then she surely was. But he had said he would protect her, and he could be counted on–more than any other man alive, he could be counted on.

The music reached a great brassy crescendo and ceased. The crowd applauded with enthusiasm. The conductor, who sported a pince-nez and a goatee, bowed, and then the players lowered their instruments and began to move about. Holmes turned to me. "I fear my observations have ruined what should have been an agreeable afternoon."

I smiled wanly. "Yes."

"I am sorry, Henry. Come, let us see what Inspector Lestrade has to say, and then you may return to Michelle and, I hope, set aside this business for a few days."

"Until the diamond comes to Tyabji?"

"Exactly. And my best estimate of the day would be Wednesday. Time enough for things to calm a bit, for Lestrade to turn to other cases, for some semblance of normalcy to return."

We walked to the exit of the park and found several cabs waiting nearby. Soon we were crossing Vauxhall Bridge. A big barge stacked with barrels steamed by, making its way through a vast flotilla of small rowing-boats, most with a seated lady and a gentleman at the oars, couples enjoying an idyllic afternoon on the river. When we reached Scotland Yard, Holmes asked the driver to wait for us. As it was a Sunday afternoon, there were few people inside. We went upstairs and down the hall to Lestrade's office, Holmes pausing along the way to give an appreciative nod to Sergeant Cuff's unsmiling portrait. Once again, the huge cut-glass ashtray on the dark-stained desk had been filled with cigarette butts. Lestrade had his jacket off, and he rose to shake our hands.

"Have you discovered anything of note?" Holmes asked.

Lestrade shook his head, then picked up his cigarette case from the table. He was about to offer one to Holmes, then laughed and raised his hand. "I know," he said, "you have your own." Holmes also laughed, then removed the silver case from inside his frock coat. Lestrade lit his cigarette and then Holmes's with a single match.

Lestrade inhaled, then sat back as he let the smoke out. "Not a blasted thing! Dr. Cowen arrived not long after you left. He couldn't manage to wait until noon, so I questioned him. He was adamant that the necklace was on the dresser last night when he left the bedroom, and Mrs. Bromley said the same thing. I went to see the Bartrams, the Alexanders and the Harrisons. All of them had perfect alibis. One of my men, Wilkinson, talked to Tyabji and then tried to question Murthwaite, but he was in such a miserable state from all his drink the night before that he was incoherent. I shall have to seek out Murthwaite myself, but Wilkinson said he doubted a man so drunk could have been party to the crime."

Lestrade leaned back in his chair, extending his arm to flick off some cigarette ash. "The couples reacted as might be expected, except for Lady Bartram, the sister." He shook his head. "What an insufferable shrew! The others were astonished when I told them about the theft, but she was outraged. She warned me that her husband's family had connections with the highest authorities and threatened to have me removed from my position if I did not find the diamond within twenty-four hours. Poor Bartram was embarrassed by her outburst and took me aside as I was leaving to apologize. When I asked the lady if she knew who might have taken the diamond, she thought for a moment, then said it was probably Alice herself."

I shook my head. "There's certainly bad blood between those two. We told you about the port last night."

"Ah, yes." Lestrade smiled wickedly. "How I wish I'd seen that! I also had my men interview every household up and down the street on both sides of the back alleyway. No one saw or heard anything unusual last night. You would think if a ladder long enough to reach that window were used, someone would have noticed it passing by. The thieves would have had to use a cart of some kind. Two men carrying a ladder down the street would have been far too obvious. I must admit, I'm partial to the idea of a rope, although, as you pointed out, there were no marks on the ledge."

Holmes shrugged. "I would not necessarily assume anyone used the window with the hole in it to enter the house."

Lestrade stared at him, then shrugged. "No, perhaps not. All the same, no reason to needlessly complicate things. It all looks rather straightforward to me."

The corners of Holmes's mouth rose in a bittersweet smile.

"Of course, you do not agree. Things need not *always* be more complicated than they appear, Mr. Holmes. I'll wager it was the former servant, Amy, in league with professional thieves. She knew the layout of the house and all the routines. She may have still been in contact with another of the servants. She heard about the upcoming dinner party with the final display of the diamond, so it was now or never. They hoped they might have their opportunity, and they did. Perhaps they used a simple signal like having someone pass by a certain window. Maybe two servants were in on it, possibly Matilda and Susan. Or Amy could have advised her friend Susan to apply for the job, so they would have someone else on the inside."

Holmes was still smiling. "It sounds almost plausible."

Lestrade frowned. "Almost, but not quite, eh? Well, we certainly haven't much to go on. Blast it, much as I hate to admit it, I doubt anyone will ever see the Moonstone again. Odds are that they'll simply chisel it into smaller stones and sell them off that way. Far safer than trying to sell a diamond of that size and notoriety. The pieces would still be worth a fortune."

"Henry and I have just come from Mr. Tyabji. I told him that if anyone delivered a small package that he should contact me immediately. I said that I, in turn, would contact you, and we would come at once. Such a package will most likely contain the Moonstone."

This time Lestrade's scowl was truly grotesque. "*What?* Do you think Tyabji is somehow behind the theft?"

"No, not at all."

"Then why would someone send him the diamond? Is it another band of Indians who have stolen the jewel?"

"That, too, is unlikely."

"Who, then?" Holmes only shrugged. Lestrade shook his head. "You are keeping something from me."

"You must allow me my little secrets, Inspector. All the same, I am not hiding any facts which are not obvious."

"Oh, Lord." He stubbed out his cigarette. "Well, be sure you do notify me if you hear from Tyabji. You had better not go there on your own. No fait accompli this time, no sending for me with the case all neatly wrapped up, all right?"

"I have said I will contact you, and so I shall." Holmes took a last draw on his cigarette, then squashed the butt into the ashtray, even as he stood up. "Oh, and if your men do discover a body in the files that might be that of Amy, let me know at once."

Lestrade regarded him curiously. "She gave someone all the information they needed, and then they got rid of her. I suppose that might make sense. One less person to worry about, one less person to share the loot."

"Good afternoon, Inspector."

"Good afternoon, Mr. Holmes."

Holmes had the cab driver drop me off at my home near Paddington Station, while he went on to Baker Street. I had almost dozed on the last solitary lap of the journey. Before I trudged up the stairs to our sitting room, I pulled my watch from my waistcoat pocket. It was almost four thirty. Michelle was sitting in the purple velvet armchair reading with our large black-and-white cat, the irreverently named Victoria, upon her lap.

"There you are at last!" She set down her book, put down Victoria, then stepped forward, gave me a quick embrace and drew back to look at me. "You do look weary. And very much out of spirits, too."

I smiled. "You know me well enough."

"I suppose no one has found the diamond. It is likely lost forever."

"Sherlock thinks someone will send it to Tyabji."

"Tyabji? But why?"

"He is being mysterious." I drew in my breath, then slowly eased it out.

Michelle touched my face lightly with her fingertips. "What is it? What is wrong?"

"Sherlock also thinks someone may want to harm Alice Bromley."

"Alice? But why?"

"More mysteries."

She shook her head brusquely. "He must be wrong."

"You know better than that."

"Oh, poor Alice. You saw her, did you not? How was she?"

"She felt terrible, as you might imagine after all she had to drink. She apologized for being rude to you." I hesitated, then raised my hand and set it alongside Michelle's face. Her blue eyes stared at me from under her thick red-brown eyebrows. Her hair was up, but done more loosely than usual, a soft wave off to one side. Her mouth was a wide one, her lips very full. "You are so beautiful."

"Am I?"

I leaned forward to kiss her, then drew her closer. She felt so full and solid in my arms. "Oh Henry, I love you."

"And I love you."

"Why can't people just love one another? It is not so very hard, after all, is it?"

"It's not hard loving you. It is easy."

"Yes," she said. I kissed her again, longer this time. "I suppose…" she began. "You must be tired. I tried to wait up for you last night, but you know how good I am at that."

I laughed softly. "You must have lasted five or ten minutes."

"You could have woken me."

"It was after two, and I was truly exhausted."

"And now? Are you truly exhausted?"

"No. Only half exhausted." I kissed her again.

"Let's go upstairs, and I shall try to distract you for a while."

And so she did. Afterwards, I slept for a while, and when I woke I was aware of Michelle's long, smooth body alongside my own.

"Feeling better, sleepy-head?"

"Yes. I'm starving, though."

"Me, too. Why don't we go out for dinner? A light dinner. After that meal last night, I thought I would never want to eat again. They serve a ridiculous amount of food at those formal dinners, and I always feel it is my duty to eat it all."

"You did an impressive job, especially compared to Alice."

"She is a beautiful woman, isn't she?"

"I prefer sturdy redheads, myself."

She laughed, then kissed my shoulder. "All the same, why would her husband...? How could you live with someone and never touch them, never go to bed together?"

I sighed softly. "I don't know. This is the best part of my life."

She raised herself up and kissed me lightly on the mouth. "And mine. Somehow it is the part that matters the most. This is how I can show you how much I love you."

"Yes," I murmured.

We were quiet for a while. Only a single sheet covered us, but the room was warm because we had closed the windows, not wanting passers-by to notice strange cries coming from the upper floor. Our housekeeper and cook, Harriet, had Sunday afternoons off.

"At least Alice isn't like Violet," Michelle said at last. "Her husband is not a brute, and she seemed to have found the experience pleasurable."

I laughed. "Pleasurable would seem something of an understatement in your case. Sometimes I fear for my life."

"Henry, if I am ever too rough, too fierce, you must tell me—promise you will tell me."

I laughed again. "That is the last thing you need worry about. You cannot be too ferocious for me. It makes me feel the same way."

"Good. Sometimes... I do feel I could eat you all up like the bad wolf in the fairy tale."

We lay on our backs, our hands clasped together. "And you," I said, "do you find Charles Bromley handsome?"

"Oh yes, certainly, but all the same... I would never want to be married to someone like him."

"Why not? In many ways, he seems the ideal husband."

"He is too amiable, too eager, too charming. Alice told me he is never angry or impatient. How can you trust a man who is never angry or impatient with you? It is too good to be true."

"We rarely quarrel with one another."

"Yes, but we are occasionally ill-tempered or impatient. I cannot help but wonder... He listens so attentively, as if your every word were important to him, but can he truly be listening all the time? How would that even be possible? Surely all of us get distracted or find certain strands of conversation less interesting than others, and yet he always has the same eager expression."

"He is only being polite, I think."

"Well, it must grow tiresome. It would drive me crazy being married to someone like him. I would want to scream at him or pound him with my fists–anything to get a rise out of him."

I laughed. "I wouldn't want to be pounded by your fists. That would hurt."

She gave my hand a squeeze. "I would never pound you with my fists. Squeeze you to death, perhaps." She rolled over and got on top of me, resting on her elbows. A strand of long red hair fell on the left side of my face, tickling my cheek. "I suppose you must be exhausted. Still, you must earn your supper."

"Slave driver," I murmured. She began to kiss me, and I put my arms around her.

Ten

Monday was another busy day at the clinic, and I actually had a few patients of my own on Tuesday. Wednesday morning I had decided that if I did not hear from Holmes by noon, I would head over to Baker Street. However, just after ten, he burst into my consulting room, a tall, lean figure all in black, the long frock coat swirling about him, his top hat in one hand, his stick in the other.

"Henry, I have a cab waiting—you must come at once if you want to see Mr. Tyabji's parcel opened."

"I most certainly do!" I sprang to my feet, grabbed my coat and followed him through the doorway. I rapped gently twice at Michelle's door, then opened it. She was inside with one of her female patients. "I shall be with Sherlock. I don't know when I shall return."

We went out the front door. Above the red-brick houses across the street, the sky was a uniform gray, and the air was filled with a mist of light drizzle. Holmes grasped the handle of the half-length hansom door and pulled it open. He stepped up, sat and slid over to the other side, making room for me. I sank into the leather seat and closed the door.

"Ready!" Holmes cried to the driver. "And remember, a sovereign for you if you make good time to South Lambeth Road!"

I sank back into the seat as the carriage departed, the driver obviously taking Holmes's encouragement to heart. "So you have heard from Mr. Tyabji?"

"I received a telegram half an hour ago. I left at once, pausing only long enough to send Lestrade a telegram at Scotland Yard, then came to fetch you. Lestrade is closer to the river, but he may be occupied, and the telegram may take some time to make its way to him."

The carriage came to an abrupt halt, making us jerk forward. We heard someone cursing and swearing, then we were off again. We swept past a small man with a huge mustache who shook his fist at us.

"I hope your driver gets us there in one piece."

"Oh, he will. I have employed George before. He knows the streets of London better than most, especially the side routes, which are less likely to be blocked by traffic. He drives fast, but not terribly recklessly."

I laughed. "Only moderately recklessly, I suppose! Have you seen anything of the Bromleys these past two days?"

"I stopped there yesterday. Mr. Bromley, as usual, is worried about his wife, who still seems to be recovering from Saturday night's excess. He told me she seems to alternate between bouts of melancholy and of almost manic excitement, but she seemed perfectly well when I spoke to her. Indeed, her relief at being rid of the diamond is palpable."

Holmes and I both leaned to the right as we swept tightly round a turn. I saw a buxom woman with an umbrella and a dog on a leash shake her head disapprovingly. Holmes stared calmly out at the London streets as they hurtled by. His cheek had a slight flush, and his gray eyes glistened with excitement. His two gloved hands held the top of his stick, which was thrust between his long legs. By the time we crossed Vauxhall Bridge into south London, I felt rather seasick from all our jostling about. South Lambeth Road had fewer men in black top hats and frock coats; there were more dark jackets and bowler hats. Street vendors with their carts were at every corner hawking their wares.

We took a sharp left turn and soon pulled to an abrupt stop before Tyabji's house, a stop which once again jerked us forward. Holmes smiled at me, then pushed open the doors and stepped out into the street. "Very well done, George! Here is your sovereign. Drive about where you will, and let your noble steed cool down– perhaps you may spot a horse trough. Return here in half an hour and wait for us."

The short man perched up top on the driver's seat had a dark scarf wrapped round his throat. He wore a black jacket, leather gloves, and an odd hat with a large brim that kept the rain off his face. "Thank you, Mr. Holmes. We'll be here."

Holmes started quickly for the door, and I followed. "Do you really think we shall be done in half an hour?"

Holmes flashed me a quick smile. "It is one way to ensure that his horse has a rest after its exertions on our behalf."

Sunil was dressed in his usual impeccable black suit accompanied by the red slippers. He gave a slight bow, ushered us in and led us to the sitting room. Tyabji rose from a chair to greet us. He wore a proper British gentleman's dress, including an elegant black frock coat. Close by, however, was Murthwaite, once again in his Indian garb, the light tan linen trousers and tunic with red sash. The red turban hid his bald crown and most of his gray hair. The outfit certainly suited him better than the antique vestments he had worn to the party!

"Ah, Mr. Holmes, Dr. Vernier, how good of you to come so swiftly." Tyabji gestured at a table with elaborately carved legs and latticework, upon which sat a small parcel wrapped in brown paper and tied with string. "This came to my door about an hour and a half ago."

Holmes forehead was creased with concentration. "Who delivered it?"

Tyabji nodded at Sunil, who spoke. "It was not the usual postal man, sir. It was a tall, thin gentleman in a well-tailored tweed suit. He merely said this was for Mr. Tyabji. I asked him to wait and speak with my master, but he shook his head and walked away quickly. I saw him get into a cab waiting down the street."

"Tall, you say? I don't suppose he had a beard?"

"No, sir."

"Very good, thank you."

At that moment, a piercing bell sounded. Sunil glanced at Tyabji, then turned and left the room.

"That is most likely Inspector Lestrade," Holmes said, and indeed, the inspector soon stepped into the sitting room, followed by a constable in his blue uniform and helmet.

Lestrade wore a long overcoat and held his bowler in his hand. He gazed around the room at the exotic furnishings and shook his head. "I wasn't expecting Ali Baba's cave." Holmes introduced him to Tyabji and Murthwaite. He shook their hands. You could tell he was surprised that Murthwaite was an Englishman. At last he turned to the table. "So this is the package? Well, Mr. Holmes, should we make a wager as to whether it contains the diamond? If it does not, we will have wasted the morning."

Holmes smiled. "I am not a betting man, but I would give you odds."

Lestrade smiled back. "But I still would not take the bet! Shall we have a look? Who should do the honors?"

"It was addressed to Mr. Tyabji," Holmes said.

"Right enough." Lestrade turned to him. "Would you go ahead and open it, sir?"

Tyabji undid the string, then removed the brown paper to reveal a rather large matchbox, one with the manufacturer's name on top and a strip of frictional material on the side. The box was slightly swollen in the middle.

Lestrade made a gruff laugh. "It would be genuinely amusing if that contained only matches. Too fat for that, I think. Go ahead and open it."

Tyabji managed to slide it open. A folded piece of paper fell out, and he took up an object wrapped in white tissue paper. He quickly pulled away the paper and held up a large diamond that had to be the Moonstone. "Good Lord," he murmured. "How did you know, Mr. Holmes?"

Lestrade shook his head. "The very question I also have."

"You shall know soon enough." Holmes bent over to pick up the folded piece of paper and opened it. "As I expected." He handed it to Lestrade.

I leaned over to read it. The letters were in large print. *Return the Moonstone to its rightful home in the Indian temple.*

Lestrade made a low whistling sound. "It must have been Indians—it must have been. Who else would possibly have…?" He noticed that Tyabji was glaring at him. "Not you, sir—not you, of course. You would hardly steal it, then alert Sherlock Holmes and myself, and deliver it to yourself. That would make no sense."

Holmes smiled. "We agree on that, Inspector."

Tyabji held up the stone, turned it slightly, letting the light from the windows play upon the facets. "What a lovely thing!" All of us stared at the diamond, taking in its beauty. A small fragment of silver chain remained, only an inch or two. Before, I recalled noticing a yellowish tint to the gem in daylight, but now it appeared absolutely colorless and translucent. Sunil clasped his hands together and bowed slightly to the stone, mumbling something in a foreign tongue.

"What a charming moment! The illustrious Mr. Sherlock Holmes and the illustrious Inspector Lestrade in a rare moment of accord, both agreeing that these Indian fellows could not have stolen the diamond. How inspiring to see the police and the famed detective working together so nice like! Please don't make any sudden movements, gentlemen—you especially, Constable. These revolvers are not for mere show, and my compatriots would have little compunction in using them."

We had all been so transfixed by the diamond that we had not heard the three men enter the room. They stood near the doorway, two tall ones on either side, each holding a revolver, and a shorter one in the middle, who had just spoken. They wore nondescript black overcoats and bowlers, and black masks with cut-out eye holes hid their faces. The shorter man was stout, with a roll of fat showing under his mask. Curiously enough, one of the men had oddly long yellow hair resembling a woman's, which fell to his collar, concealing his ears. However, his broad shoulders and chest resolved any uncertainty as to his sex.

"What's the meaning of this?" Lestrade said sternly.

"Obvious, isn't it? It's a robbery, is what. We've come for the diamond."

"But how did you know to come just now?"

The man laughed. "Tell him, Mr. Holmes."

Holmes was the only one who did not seem in the least bit disturbed by the appearance of the three men. "That is rather obvious, is it not? You must have been watching the house. You waited until you saw that Inspector Lestrade and I had arrived. You must have come in the back door."

The man nodded. "Very good, sir, although as you say, it was obvious. Now if you will be kind enough to set the diamond on that table, and then, please back up against that wall there. By the way, the decor here is most impressive. I wouldn't be surprised if this splendid carpet was one of the flying variety. And I like how the elephant statue there in the corner goes so nicely with those formidable beasts on that wall tapestry."

All of us backed away from the table except the constable. His blue eyes were hard, and despite the leather helmet strap resting in the groove between his lower lip and chin, his jaw had thrust forward. The short man shook his head. "Come now, Constable— you too. My friends would willingly shoot you if need be."

"Do as he says, Williams," Lestrade said. The constable backed away.

"I am obliged to you, Inspector. It is good to see that you value the lives of your men." The three of them slowly advanced, all in a neat line. The revolvers were of a silvery steel with the barrels held at stomach level, and they gave me a queasy feeling in the belly.

The short man picked up the stone and turned it slightly in the light. "It's amazing, all right. Pity. Take a last long look, gentlemen.

You won't be seeing it again." He laughed. "No one will be seeing it, matter of fact."

"You cannot!" Tyabji exclaimed. He took a step forward. There was a bang, an explosive one in the confines of the room, and Tyabji froze.

"Are you all right!" I cried. Tyabji sucked in his breath and nodded. The gunpowder smoke had an acrid smell.

"That was what is known as a warning shot. The next one will be to the body. You'll be able to repair that hole in the lathe and plaster, sir. A lucky thing he didn't damage one of these splendid tapestries." The stout man twisted his hand, swallowing up the diamond in his grasp, then thrust it into his coat pocket. "Yes, it is a pity, although perhaps it's for the best. The stone is about to have a litter of pups, a bunch of babies, each one worth a tidy sum on its own. So you see, the diamond will not truly die. Its descendants will live on, each a monument to its noble sire!"

Holmes gave a sharp laugh. "Please—take the diamond if you must, but spare us the melodramatic language and clumsy metaphors."

The man shook his head. "I'm disappointed in you, sir! I would have thought you might appreciate a bit of poetry from thieves. Downright ungrateful, it seems. However, I assure you, I am finished. There remains one last bit of business, and then we shall leave you—in the cellar, that is. No, no, do not move yet. Let me explain. You will depart in two separate parties, proceeding down the hallway and through the kitchen to the stairway to the cellar. You will descend the stairs. All the while, one of the gunmen will be behind you. Once you are all settled in the cellar, we shall lock the door and leave you. By the way, you will find the cook down below. She has not been harmed, merely bound and gagged.

"Do you understand the procedure? No questions? Very good!

I think the constable, Inspector Lestrade and Mr. Holmes should go first. They are the most dangerous. Remember, if anyone tries anything funny, my men will fire. Your Webley service revolver takes a .455 caliber bullet, a frightfully large piece of lead. In the confines of a narrow hallway, such a bullet might well pass cleanly through two or three men. Detectives you may be, but I'm sure you do not wish to conduct experiments upon the penetrating power of the .455 bullet through human bodies. You may proceed, gentlemen."

Lestrade, Holmes and the constable started for the door. One of the gunmen stepped well back, the barrel of his revolver following them as they crossed the room, then he followed them through the doorway. The short man hummed softly to himself. After two or three minutes, his compatriot shouted, "Next!" in the distance. "Your turn, gentlemen." We started for the door. I eyed the man with the yellow hair nervously. The shade was bizarre, not a natural tint at all. He must be wearing a cheap wig. It almost glowed against his black mask, derby and overcoat collar.

Tyabji and Sunil took the lead, Murthwaite went next, and I followed the three of them down the hallway and into the kitchen. The other gunman stood by the doorway to the cellar. He stepped back and let us pass. As soon as I went down onto the steps, the door slammed shut behind me with a bang. It made me start. I stumbled and nearly knocked over Tyabji. "Sorry," I said.

Lestrade pushed past us, back up the stairs and tried the doorknob. "Damnation," he muttered.

A muted voice said, "Farewell, Inspector. I trust, I pray, we shall not meet again."

Beside me, Holmes shook his head. "There is a man who is certainly in love with the sound of his own voice. I wonder if he has read Dickens. His speech has a certain archaic extravagance."

Tyabji's sigh was a groan. "To have the diamond in my hand at last—and then to lose it in an instant. May the Moonstone's curse fall upon those wretched thieves!"

Murthwaite put his arm on his friend's shoulder. "There, there, Geoffrey—it would have been nothing but trouble. It surely is bad luck. Alice was right about that. I wouldn't wish it on either of you."

Lestrade still stood on the steps. "Let's try to break the door in."

Holmes laughed. "It is solid oak. I would not recommend it. And even if you managed it, they still have their revolvers. Besides, we will never catch them. Doubtless another confederate was waiting with a carriage in the alley. They will have removed their masks and will be joining the busy traffic on South Lambeth Road, soon to be lost in our great metropolis of four million souls. A needle in a haystack would be easier to find."

Lestrade shook his head angrily. "So are we to simply wait down here for the rest of the day? Even if we can't catch them, I don't find this cellar comfortable quarters." The sweep of his hand took in the bare beams, the dust, the cobwebs, and the moldy-looking foundation walls. Two tiny windows let in some gray light.

"Nor do I." Holmes turned. "There is a coal chute in the far corner. The opening is not large, but one of us should be able to squeeze through—far easier than breaking down that particular door."

Sunil, as the smallest and thinnest, was the lucky volunteer whom we hoisted up through the opening. Moments later, he unlocked the cellar door, and we all trooped back upstairs, including the cook, whom we had untied. "They were kind enough to leave the key in the door," Sunil said. This remark prompted a terrible scowl from Inspector Lestrade. He spoke briefly with Tyabji and Murthwaite, then went outside, pausing in the small porch.

"Well, that is the end of the Moonstone," Lestrade said. "Blast it! We almost had it."

"Do not give up, Inspector. I still have my hopes that the Moonstone may be recovered."

"How would that be possible? You said yourself it is lost in the vast metropolis. We certainly don't have a complete list of all the London dealers in illicit gems, one which would allow us to intercept the jewel before it is cut up."

"All the same, I think I know where it may be found."

Lestrade gave him an incredulous look. "Tell me, then—at once."

"Give me a day, and then you will know."

"I grow weary of these games of yours, Mr. Holmes! One of these times I shall have to take you into custody for withholding information from the police."

"And then you will never have your answers. A day only, sir. We shall talk tomorrow afternoon, late, in your office. And I warn you, tomorrow we may have a long night before us."

"You do delight in your little mysteries. Very well. Until tomorrow." With a curt nod, Lestrade strode away, the constable following him. Lestrade went ten paces, then suddenly stopped, turned and came back to the porch. "I forgot to tell you. We may indeed have found the maid Amy amongst the files on the bodies pulled from the Thames."

Holmes's brief smile was pained. "Ah. And I suspect she was found sometime in the month of March."

Lestrade made a furious sort of snort. "How the hell did you know that!"

"I shall tell you. I put an advertisement in the agony columns asking if anyone could help determine the whereabouts of a lost woman named Amy who had disappeared within the last six months. I received a response from a boarding house and went to speak with the landlady. Amy Grant had lived there most of February and vanished the first week of March. She had left behind all her clothing and belongings. The implications were all too clear."

Lestrade shook his head. "The thieves must have got all the information about the household that they needed, and then she was disposable." He gave Holmes an inquisitive look.

Holmes smiled again. "Perhaps."

"Again, good day." The inspector and the constable walked away.

I stared at Holmes. "You actually have all this ugly business figured out?"

"Yes, Henry, I believe so. Come, we must make a brief stop at the Bromleys and let them know what happened with the diamond."

"That is sure to upset the household. Why be so eager to trouble them?"

"I have my reasons. Ah, George has waited for us." He withdrew his watch. "Even though we were over an hour."

The hansom with the stout driver up top and the gray horse was parked nearby. Holmes gave him the Bromleys' address, and we were off again, the horse's hooves clopping on the wet cobblestones, the misty drizzle still surrounding us. I gave a weary sigh. Alice Bromley might like this sort of weather, but I missed the recent sunny days.

"Cheer up, Henry. As I told the inspector, I think the end of this case is very near, probably two days at the outside."

"And yet you will tell us nothing! It is rather annoying."

He shrugged. "Very well, I shall tell you something if it will make you happy. Did you happen to recognize the man with the blond hair holding the revolver?"

"Recognize him!" I laughed. "I certainly did not recognize him. He was wearing a mask and probably a wig, I suspect."

Holmes laughed. "Very good, Henry. But why would he wear a wig?"

I frowned. "How should I know? Please tell me."

Holmes laughed again. "He wanted to hide his ears."

"Hide his ears? Why on earth would he want to hide his ears?"

"Because Watson has made many of my methods known, especially my ability to identify people by the distinctive shapes of their ears."

"Then this was someone you know–someone you would have recognized?"

"Exactly, Henry. Exactly."

"Who, then?"

"You have no idea? His build, his carriage, did not remind you of anyone?"

I scrunched up my forehead. There had been something about his shape, the broad shoulders, his posture. "Now that you mention it… But I can't place him."

Holmes's voice was very soft: "Hodges."

"Hodges! Yes, that would fit, but how can you be certain? There was a physical resemblance, but his ears, his head, were hidden, and he was wearing battered, nondescript clothes we have not seen before."

Holmes nodded. "Yes, yes, he was so careful, so very careful, and yet he forgot one thing–his shoes. I recognized his slightly worn brown boots. Of course, even if he had thought to change his shoes, I would have still been suspicious. He has enormous feet, Henry, a size twelve at least, possibly a thirteen."

"Hodges. I cannot believe it. Then he must have been working with Sabine. The servants were behind the whole thing, after all!"

"That does not necessarily follow."

"It doesn't? Who then?"

"I have given you one fact. That must suffice for today. It should give you something to digest."

We soon arrived at the Bromleys' house in Kensington, and again Holmes asked the driver to wait. We walked through the light rain to the front door, and Holmes pressed the bell. The maid Susan let us in, curtsied, and went to find the master. She quickly returned. "Mr. Bromley and the mistress will be happy to see you in the sitting room."

Bromley was dressed in a frock coat and striped trousers, Alice in one of her pale-blue silks, her hair neatly done up. She looked much better than she had on Sunday morning. Sally was on the settee next to her mistress, and she jumped down, then bounded eagerly toward us. Holmes leaned over to scratch at her head with his long fingers.

"Have you any news for us, Mr. Holmes—good news, perhaps?" Bromley asked eagerly.

"I fear not. In a way, nothing has changed, but the situation appears more grave."

Alice sat up in her chair, her mouth stiffening.

"What is it?" Bromley asked.

"The diamond was sent to Mr. Tyabji. Inspector Lestrade and myself were there when he opened the package. However, three thieves with revolvers entered the room. They locked us in the cellar and made off with the diamond. They said they were going to have it cut into pieces."

Alice made a kind of snort, then a pained sound that was

something between a shriek and a bark of laughter. "They stole it? Oh God, they stole it!" She made a similar sound, this one clearly a laugh. "Oh Lord, I cannot believe it. I am jinxed—or rather the diamond is jinxed, as we knew. It's cursed, it's damned, it—" She laughed again, then shuddered, her face very pale.

I stood up. "Perhaps a swallow of brandy might steady her nerves."

Bromley nodded. "Yes, certainly."

I went to the sideboard and poured from a decanter. I handed the glass to Alice. "Drink this down."

She swallowed it, then half-shivered and coughed. Her cheeks had a bright flush. She moaned once, the kind of sound you make when you have laughed too much. "Well, it's gone, isn't it? That's the point, after all. It is gone. It can no longer torment me. It's gone. I shall never wear it again. Cutting it into pieces must break the curse, mustn't it?" The last was as much a plea as a question.

"Of course it will," Bromley exclaimed. He gave Holmes a hard look. "How could the diamond have possibly been stolen from you and the police?"

"We are vulnerable to bullets, sir, and there were two revolvers pointed at us."

Bromley shook his head. "Incredible. Well, I suppose this is the last of it. We shan't see the Moonstone again."

Holmes regarded him closely. "You seem rather philosophical about it, sir."

"What's the use of ranting and raving? It will not bring the diamond back. And perhaps…" He set his hand on Alice's shoulder. "…we shall finally be left in peace." She laughed at this, and he withdrew his hand.

"By the way," Holmes said, "is Hodges about? I wanted to ask him a question about last Saturday evening."

"No, he is out, amusing himself and running some errands for me. He should be back later this afternoon."

Holmes shrugged. "It was not terribly important. It can wait." His eyes shifted ever so slightly, catching my own.

Alice had put her long, thin white fingers across the lower part of her face. Her eyes had filled with tears, and they ran down onto her hand.

"Alice?" Bromley asked. "Oh, Alice, my dear."

Holmes glanced at me. "Perhaps a bit more brandy, Henry. Could you leave us with her just for a moment, Mr. Bromley. We will not be long. We must be off soon."

Bromley gave him a disapproving look. "Oh very well." He strode out of the room, and Sally followed him. I took the glass and poured a little more brandy. Because of the laudanum, I dare not give her too much. I handed her the glass, as well as a handkerchief.

She wiped her eyes and stared down at the glass. "I hate brandy."

"Have a bit," I said. "It will do you good."

She took a small sip, then inhaled resolutely. "Nothing ever turns out the way I expect. I wish... I wish I were dead."

"You mustn't say such things. That is nonsense. It was only a diamond, after all—and you did not even like it."

She stared up at me. "The diamond has nothing to do with it. I only..." She lowered her gaze. "My life is empty. It is meaningless. One stupid frightful day after another with never..." In the silence that followed, I became aware of the loud regular ticking of the china clock on the mantel.

"There are those that love you. There is your husband."

"He doesn't love me," she murmured.

"Of course he does."

She hardly seemed to hear me. "He never has. I once thought he did. It's because he says it so often that I know it is not true. I think... Regardless of what they say, when someone truly loves you, you can see it in their eyes. I cannot see it in his eyes."

I shook my head. "More nonsense."

"Mrs. Bromley," Holmes said. She raised her faded blue eyes to stare at him. Her blond-white eyebrows barely stood out against her pale skin. Her thin face recalled some street waif, but it also showed an intelligence absent from many women. "You must not give up hope, not yet. Your life may yet change for the better."

"Can that possibly be true?"

"Yes."

"If you will but trust your husband," I said.

Her mouth pulled back in dismay, and Holmes gave me a reproachful look. "Be patient a little longer, madam."

She drew in her breath slowly and nodded.

"What is going on here?" Cowen strode into the room, his imperious and customary frown contorting his thick black eyebrows. His frock coat and black beard were damp, and he held his silk hat in one hand, his medical bag in the other.

"Have you heard the news about the diamond, Dr. Cowen?" Holmes asked.

The question made Cowen's frown waver. "Mr. Bromley told me. So the diamond went to Tyabji and was purportedly stolen from him. No doubt a clever charade to deflect suspicion from the actual thieves. Alice, what is wrong? Are you ill?" His gentleness with her was in striking contrast to his ill temper with us.

"I feel so odd," she whispered. "So strange."

"I think you had best lie down for a while. No further disturbances." His glare swept round at us like the beam from some lighthouse. "You did not...?" He shrugged. "She has had so many shocks lately. Little wonder that what she says often makes little sense. You must not take any of her remarks too seriously."

I nodded. "I think not."

"Well, we shall leave her in your excellent hands, Dr. Cowen," Holmes said. "Good afternoon."

His eyes watched us suspiciously as we departed. Bromley was waiting for us in the hallway. "Is she all right? I tell you, it is one blow after another. I do worry so about her! I sometimes fear..." He shook his head. "Never mind what I fear. Is there any hope, Mr. Holmes, any spark of hope?"

"Oh yes, Mr. Bromley. Oh yes. I expect certain developments within the next twenty-four hours."

Bromley gave him a curious look. "Really? Are you at liberty to explain yourself?"

"I fear not."

Bromley ran his fingers back through his curly brown hair. "Well, I hope next time you will have good news for us."

"Count on it, sir. I shall see you tomorrow, I promise."

Bromley still seemed faintly puzzled. "Good day."

We stepped out onto the front porch. Holmes smiled at me. "A useful visit, Henry. I am certain now."

"About Hodges?"

"About everything."

Eleven

Holmes had asked me to join him for breakfast at Baker Street the next day. I arrived shortly after eight to find him at the small table with two covered silver dishes and a coffee pitcher. "Ah, there you are, Henry." He had a cup of coffee before him, and he took up the pitcher and poured some into another of the blue-and-white cups. "I believe you drink yours black. Now then, Mrs. Hudson has prepared ham and eggs, and curried fowl. Which would you prefer?"

"Ham and eggs. I cannot face curried fowl first thing in the morning."

"No? I enjoy the bite of spice early in the day. It does help wake one." He lifted a dome, revealing a heap of yellow-and-white scrambled eggs with the pink cubes of ham. "Here you are. Help yourself."

I used the silver spoon to heap some onto my plate, and I took a slice of buttered toast. Holmes had dished out some boiled rice, and he topped it with the steaming, brilliant yellow-orange-coated chopped chicken. The smell alone was enough to turn my stomach. He took a spoonful, put it in his mouth, and chewed thoughtfully. "Ah yes, deliciously sharp and pungent." He sat back and took another sip of coffee. He had on a white shirt and collar, a black cravat and waistcoat, but over them wore his battered purple dressing gown. "We must fortify ourselves for the day's activities. It will be a busy one."

I took a big swallow of ham and eggs. "Exactly what are we doing?"

"The sequence of events, if all goes according to plan, will be a visit to Dr. Cowen, a stop at the chemist's, then a visit to, first, Mrs. Bromley, and last, Mr. Bromley."

"But what on earth for? We have already seen these people many times. Except the chemist—what do we need a chemist for?"

Holmes had eagerly laid into the curried fowl, obviously relishing each bite. "Henry, you studied chemistry as part of your education, did you not?"

"What?"

"You heard me right. Chemistry—you studied it?"

"Yes, certainly. It is required for a medical degree."

"As you know, I have a fascination with chemistry." He gestured with the fingers of his right hand toward the corner of the room where several flasks, beakers and tubes sat on a scarred table. "There is such an agreeable precision and rigor to the science. When you combine certain ingredients in the right amounts, the same reaction always occurs. I particularly enjoyed the challenge of trying to determine the nature of a chemical 'unknown.' Some solution was given to us students, and through a process of trial and error, various experiments, we were to determine the exact composition of the unknown. As you might well imagine, I excelled at this sort of problem.

"Well, in our case of the Moonstone, we are dealing with a variety of unknowns, of mysterious components. Some of our personalities are obviously gaseous and volatile–Mrs. Bromley, for example. Dr. Cowen, on the other hand, is unstable and prone to explosive reactions. Today we are going to determine the exact nature of all these unknowns, and, as with chemistry, the endeavor is somewhat hazardous. Combining certain compounds may bring disastrous results–toxic gases or uncontrolled flare-ups. Of course, my analogy only goes so far. I actually think I have figured out the nature of these unknowns, so it is more corroboration which I seek."

"And what have you figured out?"

He laughed, then dabbed at his mouth with his napkin. "Come now, you can hardly expect me to give it all away! You know I have a taste for the dramatic. Besides, you have all the facts at hand."

"Yes, but as usual, I can do nothing with them."

"If I tell you too much, it will also prejudice your reactions. You may give things away."

I shrugged. "I am not good at concealing my feelings, it is true."

We both ate silently for a while, and the coffee began to have its desired effect. Holmes took another helping of the curried fowl. "Mrs. Hudson has outdone herself this morning. You're sure you won't try some? A pity."

He soon finished his second portion, dabbed at his mouth, then sat back contentedly in his chair. "Henry, I should warn you that today you will undoubtedly hear things which will astonish and perplex you, but when we are in company, you absolutely must not question me or say anything to contradict me. Try not to appear too astonished. There will be time enough for questions later, when we are alone. Do you understand?"

"Yes."

"Good." With a flourish he threw his napkin onto the table and stood, raising one arm. "Let our revels now begin!"

The two of us were soon in George's cab on our way to Cowen's residence off Harley Street. The clouds and rain were gone, and the day looked to be a fine one, the freshly washed streets of London all aglow with reflected sunlight. We stepped out of the hansom, went up the steps, and the page let us in and led us to the well-furnished waiting room. An old man with mutton-chop sideburns, a fashion long out of style, sat with *The Times* open before him, while a well-dressed woman sat on the sofa with a small, pale child who was clearly terrified.

Holmes and I found adjoining chairs, and five minutes later, a door opened and Dr. Cowen himself stepped into the room. Clearly irritated, he scowled darkly at us. His full black beard gave his visage a certain sinister air. The child nearby whimpered softly. As usual, Cowen was impeccably dressed in the standard black frock coat, waistcoat and striped trousers, his golden Albert chain forming two arcs from the waistcoat button to the pockets on either side.

"What do you want now?" he asked.

"We need to talk to you," Holmes said.

"Well, I have nothing more to say to you, Mr. Holmes. I am done with your questions and your probing and your impudence."

"Are you, indeed? This is an important matter, one which has to do with the health and well-being of your patient, Mrs. Bromley. You are concerned about her welfare, are you not?"

Cowen stared at him a long while. "You know that I am."

"Then grant us a few more minutes of your valuable time."

He drew in his breath, then released it in a great sigh. "Oh very well–but only a few minutes." He turned to the woman on the sofa. "We shan't be long, Mrs. Bartlett." We followed him into his office, and I closed the door. Again he sat back against the edge of the massive mahogany desk, folding his arms. "Yes?"

Holmes glanced at a chair. "May I sit down?"

You could see Cowen weighing just how rude he wished to be. At last he said, "Yes."

"Thank you." Holmes sat, leaned his stick against the wall and set his top hat on his lap. "I have come to some disturbing conclusions which involve Mrs. Bromley, and I need your advice on how to proceed."

Cowen watched him warily. Light from the window shone on his long sloping forehead and bald crown. He gave a slight nod.

"I shall come directly to the point. It is my belief that Mrs. Bromley herself stole the diamond."

I was so surprised I almost said something, but Holmes gave me a quick warning glance.

Cowen stood up and lowered his hands, forming fists. A look of alarm was immediately replaced by one of truculence. "Is this your idea of a joke? A very cruel and sick joke?"

"Not in the least."

"Such a suggestion is preposterous, simply preposterous."

"I do not think so. It is the only real explanation. Who but her could have signaled to someone from the window at exactly the right time? Are we to believe some thief was lurking about, then by happenstance managed to break through the window just when she and the diamond were left alone? That was always the problem. No, she first staged that incendiary encounter with her sister and her friend, and then when she was alone at last, she alerted her waiting accomplice, probably by signaling with a light."

"But why would she ever do such a thing!"

"You know the answer to that as well as I, Dr. Cowen. Because she was terrified of the jewel. It had cast a dark shadow over her life. She would do anything to be rid of it, anything."

He shook his head resolutely. "I don't believe it for an instant. You are desperate—you are coming up with the wildest and most improbable hypotheses. It is insulting."

"Nevertheless, I am going to have to discuss the possibility with Inspector Lestrade of Scotland Yard. We shall see what…"

"You cannot—*you cannot.*" Cowen raised his clenched fists and shook them. For once, he seemed more dismayed than angry.

"That is what I wanted to discuss with you. Could she tolerate an inquiry—and possibly even a trial? Could she…?"

"No, no," he groaned, even as he shook his head wildly. "You cannot do that to her. You cannot. It—she would never survive such an ordeal. You would kill her—you would… Do you want to destroy her life, to ruin her? Is that what you want?"

"Calm yourself, Dr. Cowen. I assure you, I bear her no ill will. It is simply a matter of justice. If she stole the diamond, she must suffer the consequences."

"How can you mouth such blathering platitudes! A woman's life is at stake here. Could you really do such a thing to her?"

"I must tell the police what I know. It is my duty."

"*Duty.*" Cowen paced to the window and stared out of it. Even with his back to us, you could see the tension in his shoulders, in his arms. His every muscle seemed taut. A sort of muted groan came forth. He turned and came back to Holmes, stood just above him, threateningly. "She would never do such a thing—*never.* The diamond is already hers." He gave a harsh laugh. "What crime would there be in stealing what is already yours? The police would surely mock you."

"Come, come, Dr. Cowen. You surely know of her life-interest in the jewel. It was not truly hers. She stole it to give to Mr. Tyabji so it would be returned to India. That was her way of countering the curse and escaping the fearful burden of the Moonstone."

"But–but–she was asleep when I left–knocked out. The chloral hydrate–she could not have signaled! She was unconscious."

Holmes gave a long weary sigh. "Dr. Cowen, you are letting your feelings run away with you. You must not stretch the truth. You already told me and the police that Mrs. Bromley asked about the jewel just before you left and that you saw it on the dresser. Obviously she was still awake when you left."

"But the chloral hydrate!" This last was like some fevered incantation. He shook his head. "No, no, she could not."

"Come now–it would have taken only a few seconds for her to get out of bed and wave the candle before the window. Possibly she even set the necklace on the window sill. And then she went back to bed and was asleep at once."

"But who is this accomplice?" He laughed. "She knows no one– she is a recluse–she could not possibly…"

Holmes shrugged. "Someone could have helped her recruit accomplices. Perhaps her maid Sabine, or Hodges."

"No, no–they are Bromley's tools–she dislikes them both, especially Sabine."

"Does she now? That is interesting. All the same, I'm sure a clever woman like her could have found someone."

Cowen began to pace again, his arms held stiffly at his sides. "You cannot do this to her. You cannot. You cannot. I won't let you."

"Again, Dr. Cowen, I assure you, there is no malice on my part. She is an exemplary woman in many respects, but…"

He shook his head wildly. "No–stop that–stop that! She did

not do it–I swear she did not do it."

"How can you be so sure?"

Cowen swallowed once, his cheeks and forehead over the black beard paling slightly. "I cannot plead with you? I am willing to beg." His voice was suddenly soft, muted. "You are determined?" The man was so crestfallen, so humbled, that for the first time, I actually felt sorry for him.

"I am." Holmes spoke almost as softly as him.

Cowen drew himself up, even as his broad chest swelled. "She did not do it, Mr. Holmes. It was I. I stole the Moonstone."

"Cowen!" I exclaimed. Again Holmes gave me a warning look. I shook my head in disbelief.

"Is this true?" Holmes asked. "Or is it merely desperation speaking again?"

Cowen smiled bleakly. "Come now, Mr. Holmes. Be logical. You are right about the timing of the theft being the real mystery. There is an easier explanation than Mrs. Bromley signaling someone. She was very nearly asleep when I left the room. I stepped outside, waited a few minutes, then quietly re-entered the room. I knew at once that she would not wake up any time soon. I simply took the Moonstone and put it into my medical bag."

Holmes was frowning. "And the hole in the window?"

Cowen was still smiling. "I came prepared with a glass cutting tool in my bag. I cut the hole in the glass, then opened the window. I also tore the chain from the necklace and dropped it out the window. I then quietly closed the door and left the house with the Moonstone. I told you all not to disturb her for a few moments, time enough to make a theft through the window possible. Come, sir, is this not a more plausible explanation than Mrs. Bromley having found some mysterious unknown accomplices?"

"It would explain why there was no trace of the ladder, no one seen on the street. And the padlock?"

"It was simple to find a key for that lock. I silently opened it before I left."

Holmes nodded. "Another very plausible explanation. However, there is one problem."

Cowen stared at him. "What would that be?"

"Why on earth would a respectable doctor like yourself do such a thing? Why take such a terrible risk? You could be ruined–you could go to prison for years. Why would you do such a thing?"

Cowen swallowed once. "The money. I needed the money."

Holmes laughed softly. "Come now, Dr. Cowen. In that case, you would not have given the Moonstone to Mr. Tyabji. I am not an utter fool. If your story is true, then the reason is obvious enough."

Cowen had begun to pale again. "Is it? Yes, I suppose it is."

"Say it, then, or would you prefer that I do?"

He turned and went back to the desk, sank back against it, his big hands clutching at its edge. "Very well, it is because I care for Mrs. Bromley. I care for her… deeply."

"So deeply you would go to prison for her?"

"Yes. Yes! I could see what the Moonstone was doing to her, how it has made her suffer! She was hardly more than a child when I first met her, and already the wretched thing haunted her, and her mother as well. I saw what the Moonstone did to Charlotte–I saw her gradually become more and more fearful, more and more eccentric, until finally in despair she took her own life. I have seen similar changes in Alice. I thought her marriage might possibly help matters, but it has not. Bromley's cloying solicitude is only an act. Could I stand by and watch another beautiful and sensitive woman go mad and take her own life? I could bear it no longer. I resolved that if any chance arose where I might steal the diamond, I would do so. Fate gave me that chance, and I took it."

Holmes's smile was faintly ironic. "Fate?"

"You care for her that much?" I asked.

Cowen's mouth twisted into a brief smile. "I love her."

"Oh, Lord," I murmured.

Holmes nodded. "Your story makes sense, Dr. Cowen. It is a compelling one. All the same, I shall have to let Inspector Lestrade choose between the two alternatives."

"For God's sake, Mr. Holmes—leave Alice out of this! Do not drag her into this affair. Simply tell Lestrade that I did it, that I have confessed, and I swear…" He stood up resolutely. "I am a gentleman, after all, and my word means a great deal to me. I give you my word of honor, Mr. Holmes, that I was the one who took the Moonstone."

Holmes stared briefly at him, then nodded. "Perhaps, after all, the lady may be left out of this business."

"Oh, thank God! Then some good may come from it. Let the Moonstone's curse fall upon me and me alone."

Holmes slowly stood and grasped the handle of his stick firmly. "I must think this over, Dr. Cowen. Give me a day, and I shall get back to you with my decision."

"You will not go to the police first? You will not say anything about Alice? You must promise me that!"

"You lay a heavy burden of responsibility upon me. Given her fragile nature, I have no desire to have Mrs. Bromley dragged into a courtroom. I shall do nothing to bring charges against her until I consult with you first."

"If someone must pay… I would go to prison for her—I would gladly go."

Holmes shook his head. "Let us hope it does not come to that. I shall see you tomorrow. Oh, and until then, stay away from Mrs. Bromley."

Cowen nodded. His color was returning to normal, and he looked suddenly exhausted. He walked around the desk and collapsed into the leather-backed chair. Briefly he clutched at his forehead, then set down his hand. "Tell the page to fetch Mrs. Bartlett."

Holmes softly closed the door behind us. I spoke to the page, then followed Holmes out into the bright daylight. I shook my head. "You were right after breakfast when you said I would hear things that might surprise me. My God, I would not have believed it! Cowen, of all people. He must be telling the truth."

The corners of Holmes's mouth rose in a typically bittersweet sort of smile. "Do you think so?"

"I do."

"Sometimes what people leave out is just as important as what they reveal."

"What is that supposed to mean!"

"All in good time, Henry. And now we must be off to the chemist's!"

"The chemist's? Why a chemist?"

"Why else? I must have a special concoction prepared."

We took the cab to a chemist's shop on Queen's Gate not far from the Albert Hall and from the Bromleys' home. The store was a well-known one, which took up the corner of the block, on either side in large letters over the windows was SAUNDERS PHARMACY. Inside the large plate-glass windows sat two tiers of long shelves. On top were the tall glass carboys filled with liquids of violet, green, pink and blue, symbols for the illiterate that the chemist resided within. On the lower shelf was a wide assortment of ointments, medicines, poultices, tinctures and the like, many in packages with abundant flowery script extolling the virtues of their contents.

We went through the front door, which made a bell ring. A young man was helping an older woman, while an older man, very tall and emaciated, stood with his big bony hands resting on the countertop. His almost skeletal face contrasted with his abundant gray hair and the mustache which hid his upper lip and spilled well over the corners of his mouth. Behind him were shelves lined with stoppered bottles of all conceivable sizes and shapes, filled with liquids of every imaginable color and shade, a rainbow of pharmacopeia.

Holmes went straight to the tall man. "Mr. Saunders, I believe."

Saunders nodded. The placid blue of his eyes somehow emphasized the fierce intensity of his gaze. "Yes, sir. How may I serve you?"

"My name is Sherlock Holmes. Perhaps you have heard of me?"

Saunders spread his thin fingers apart upon the counter and stood taller. "I thought I recognized you, sir, but I could not be sure. I am well acquainted with your reputation, Mr. Holmes. It is an honor to have so distinguished a personage under my humble roof. Certainly, it is with far more than my usual enthusiasm that I once again ask, how may I serve you?"

"I need to have a special draft prepared in your customary blue laudanum bottle. One of your clients has such a bottle near her bedside, and it must be identical to that one."

"One such as this?" Saunders reached under the counter and withdrew a small bottle with a tan label framed in red, with red print. In large capital letters at the top were LAUDANUM and POISON. Below in smaller print was written the dosage of laudanum for different ages, varying from two drops for a three-month old up to thirty drops for an adult. At the bottom was written SAUNDERS and the address of the store. If one could ignore its potential contents, the bottle itself was actually beautiful, made of pale-blue glass which went from the circular neck to the square sides in a graceful curve, the sides themselves gently rounded. The glass looked so thick that the bottle could probably be dropped without breaking, doubtlessly a safety precaution.

"That is the exact one!" Holmes exclaimed. "Excellent."

Saunders gave him an inquisitive glance. "But you do not want my usual preparation of laudanum, that celebrated formula which is unique to Saunders?"

"I do not, sir. I need a mixture of laudanum and chloral hydrate in a dosage which would render someone completely unconscious for several hours if one were to drink the entire contents of the bottle."

"The entire contents? Not merely a few drops?"

Holmes gave a brusque nod. "Yes, the entire contents. And the challenge for you is to make the dose strong enough to completely knock someone out and yet not so much that it might kill them. This is, as you may well imagine, a matter of life and death. If you have any uncertainty about the dosage, you should err on the lower side."

"Sherlock?" I murmured. He glanced at me and placed his forefinger vertically over his lips.

Saunders had been smiling, but his smile had gradually vanished. "This sounds grave indeed. I would be wary of such a request coming from anyone else but you, Mr. Holmes. I have my suspicions of why you might want such a preparation."

Holmes smiled faintly. "Do you now?"

"I think so. You have come to the right person. There are those in London who are so incompetent that they would blunder and create a mixture that might kill rather than sedate. However, as you must know, I need more information to estimate the precise dosage."

"Of course you do!" Holmes exclaimed. "I already made some inquiries. You are well respected in your profession, but you have just helped reassure me of your knowledge. This would be for a woman weighing about one hundred and twenty pounds who has been taking a regular dosage of laudanum on the order of ten drops a night."

Saunders rubbed at his thin chin with his fingers. "All right, then. The balance should probably be of chloral hydrate, since it has the most immediate effect and causes a deep unconsciousness. The opium will retard breathing and help keep the person asleep even after the chloral hydrate begins to wear off."

"Exactly my thinking," Holmes said.

Saunders shook his head. "You would have made quite a chemist yourself, Mr. Holmes."

Holmes smiled. "It is something of an avocation—more, however, in the sense of chemistry as science rather than chemistry as pharmacology. However, as you may well imagine, I know a great deal about poisons."

"I'll wager you do!"

Holmes raised his hand. "One other thing. The bottle itself should not be completely full. The liquid should only come up to the tops of the letters spelling out 'laudanum' on the label."

"Easily done, sir! We'll just mix up the right amount, and then fill it to the desired height with the flavored solution of alcohol I use. It will not take long at all."

He turned away and began to hum softly to himself. All the many colored bottles on the shelves had labels with the contents written in precise block letters. He took down a huge rounded bottle filled with an amber liquid and pulled off the cork. Still humming, he seized a measuring beaker and carefully poured in some of the amber liquid.

Unable to contain myself, I turned to Holmes and whispered fiercely. "For God's sake, what is this all about?"

Holmes's gray eyes stared coolly at me. "Isn't it obvious? Mr. Saunders understands."

I swallowed once. "You think... you think that Mrs...." He shook his head fiercely, and I realized I must not say Alice's name out loud. "You think she might try to drink down the whole bottle?"

The corners of his mouth flickered briefly upward. "Accidents happen, Henry."

"What do you mean by that?"

"Have you completely forgotten our conversation this morning? I am beginning to think it was a mistake to bring you along. Mr. Saunders hardly knows me, and yet he is willing to trust my judgment."

I drew in my breath and eased it out slowly. "Forgive me. It is only... All this talk of life and death, all these vile potions..." I gestured at all the bottles "...make me uneasy."

Saunders was about to pour from another bottle, this one with a clear liquid, but he paused to give me a withering stare. "Nothing vile about them, sir. They are a blessing to the sick and the infirm."

"I beg your pardon, sir. I meant no insult." Under other circumstances I might have argued with him. As a physician, I knew that the vast majority of all these brews were, at best, harmless. Many were downright dangerous. Opium, cocaine and alcohol were the most common ingredients.

Saunders's long fingers were very dexterous. He took the beaker and carefully poured into the blue bottle, slowing the output at the end, and then twisting the beaker upward. He squatted slightly, getting himself down to eye level with the bottle. "Just to the exact top of the L in laudanum." He stood, put the cork into the bottle and handed it to Holmes. "Will that do, sir?"

Holmes raised the bottle and examined it. "Excellent, Mr. Saunders. Excellent! You are an artist at your trade. And should this potion all be drunk off at bedtime, what exactly would be its effects?"

"The lady would lose consciousness very rapidly. You would be unable to revive her for at least four or five hours. The combination would probably then keep her fast asleep until well into the morning. A certain grogginess would last several hours more."

"Just what I would wish. Thank you, sir. What do I owe you?"

Saunders smiled. "This one is on the house, Mr. Holmes. It is a privilege to assist you in any way. There is, however, one thing."

"And what might that be?"

His blue eyes regarded Holmes. I had never seen a face with such pronounced cheekbones. "Let me know how it turns out. Stop by at your leisure."

"I shall do that, Mr. Saunders. Thank you again. This potion…" he raised the bottle, "…may well save a woman's life."

"I hope so. May I wrap it up for you?"

"No, thank you. I shall just put it in my pocket as is." Holmes thrust the bottle into the right outside pocket of his frock coat. "Good day, sir."

"Good day, Mr. Holmes." His enthusiasm waned when he turned to me. "And you, sir."

We stepped outside, and I shook my head. "I hope you know what you are doing."

He gave a sharp laugh. "I hope so, too." He raised his stick.

"Come, you must set aside all your questions and your doubts for now. It is early yet, and I don't want to go to the Bromleys until this afternoon. Let us enjoy the fine weather. There is time for a walk in Hyde Park, a long lunch, and then our visit."

We went into the park and took a leisurely stroll along the lake, the Serpentine. A few puffy picturesque clouds were in the blue sky, the sunlight glistening on the water, and we saw ducks, swans and geese all gliding along. A pair of huge swans with their long, slender white necks, their black-and-orange beaks, were magnificent. Holmes glanced at them.

"Swans are supposed to be monogamous creatures, Henry. Did you know that?"

"No."

He smiled briefly and ironically. "On the whole, I'll wager they are more faithful than their human counterparts."

"Must you be so cynical?"

"Forgive me. On such a day one should not have such sour thoughts. They are splendid birds, are they not?" He raised his stick and pointed in the direction of the swans. "Mrs. Bromley has something of the same grace and elegance, and certainly a similarly long and slender neck."

We reached the bridge, then turned left to head south out of the park. Holmes knew of a small French restaurant nearby, and he treated me to an excellent lunch. He seemed in exceptionally good spirits, and he obviously did not want to discuss the Bromleys or the Moonstone. I felt preoccupied, and I could not forget the small blue bottle tucked away in his coat pocket.

When we reached the Bromleys' house, Susan opened the door, then gazed forlornly up at Holmes. "Thank goodness, you've come, sir. I'll just fetch the master."

Bromley soon strode toward us, his forehead creased beneath his wildly curling mass of brown hair. "Ah, Mr. Holmes, I left word for you at Baker Street. Thank you for coming so promptly."

"I have not been back to Baker Street since early this morning, so I did not get your message. Has something happened?"

He nodded. "Yes. Alice received this telegram this morning. She is most upset." He raised a piece of paper.

Holmes took it, and I turned and leaned sideways so I could also read. *Accursed woman, because of you the Moonstone is lost forever. You must pay the price for such sacrilege with your own blood. Prepare to meet your doom!*

Holmes shook his head. "Ah, we have returned to our earlier lurid and fantastical Indian melodrama."

"I hardly find this amusing, Mr. Holmes!" Bromley exclaimed. "Alice's Indian at the window was not imaginary, after all. There must be a band of Hindu fanatics after the jewel. Somehow they have learned of its loss, and they blame poor Alice."

"So it would seem. Where is Mrs. Bromley now?"

"Resting in her room."

"Could you have her come down? Tell her I would like to briefly walk with her and discuss the matter."

"I hardly know if she is up to walking."

"Oh, I think she will manage it. Also, I must ask that you remain behind."

He shook his head. "Why don't you trust me, Mr. Holmes? Why all this secrecy?"

"Sometimes women are more forthright when they are alone. Don't worry, Mr. Bromley. We shall have a long chat when we return. I have a few things to tell you."

Bromley frowned, nodded, then left. A few minutes later, Alice came down the hall toward us. Her lips rose in a smile as she saw us. Her hair was bound up loosely, and her face seemed even paler than usual. She wore another of her fashionable blue silks, one that emphasized her slender waist, and her long white fingers grasped the wide brim of a blue hat. Holmes's earlier comparison seemed apt: she had the beauty and elegance of a swan.

"Good day, Mr. Holmes, Dr. Vernier. I am so glad to see you both."

"The pleasure is ours, madam," Holmes said. "Do you feel well enough to walk with us for a while?"

"Oh yes. I feel the need for some fresh air."

"Excellent. Let us proceed, then."

She put on the hat, stuffing some straying strands up into its crown. An abundance of plumes, most likely ostrich feathers dyed blue, swept back from the front. She pulled on a pair of white gloves. "I am ready."

Once we had reached the street, she said, "You saw the telegram?"

"We did."

She laughed softly. "More to fear. I thought I was finally rid of the diamond, that I was past all that."

"All the same," I said, "you seem somewhat calmer than I expected."

She laughed again. "Perhaps it is because it proves I was not imagining anything, after all. The thought that I might be seeing things that did not exist was very disturbing to me. At least I am not mad."

I shook my head. "There was never any question of that."

"And the diamond is still gone—out of my house. I do not have to look at it anymore. I told you how when I once stared into its depths, it seemed to go all red, to be drenched with blood." Despite the warm day, her shoulders rose in a brief shudder. "I no longer have to bear its evil presence near me, no longer have to allow it to touch my skin. That is something for which I am thankful."

Holmes nodded. "I see a certain progress in your thinking, madam. As for that telegram, it is, as you noted, quite tangible, and I shall do my utmost to find those who sent it. All the same, I have something else I wish to discuss with you. Shall we go into the park? Henry and I have already spent some time there this morning, but on such a day one cannot have too much of its spectacular greenery." We were quiet for a few moments as we made our way across the busy Kensington Road and reached the shade of the trees.

Some color had come back into Alice's cheeks. "What did you wish to talk about, Mr. Holmes? I hope—I hope it is not some new misery."

"Not exactly. It concerns the theft of the Moonstone. I think I have worked out the puzzle of who took it."

She came to an abrupt stop, even as her eyes opened very wide. I could see a ripple along her throat as she swallowed. "You have? Who?"

"Dr. Cowen."

"Dr. Cowen!" She stared at him, then shook her head fiercely. "How can you say that?"

"It is the only possibility which makes sense. The problem has always been the short interval during which the thief could have broken in and taken the diamond. How would the person have ever known the exact moment? It makes more sense that the doctor simply put it in his bag and left with the jewel."

"But... but I was in bed, and I saw him leave."

"He waited outside the door until you were asleep, then came back in and took it."

"But the hole—the hole in the window."

"He had a glass cutter in his bag and used it. He also tore the chain off the necklace and dropped it out the window."

She had stopped walking and was staring at Holmes. Her cheeks were growing even pinker. "No, no—impossible—not him. Not him."

"I fear it is so, madam. Again, it is the only explanation which makes sense."

"Have you—have you told the police this?"

"Not yet."

"But what will they do to him?"

"There will be a trial, and most likely he will go to prison."

A sort of moan slipped from her. "No, no—it is not right. Why ever would he take it?"

"Perhaps out of concern for you, madam."

"For me." She looked away. "For me." She covered her mouth with her white hand.

I touched her shoulder lightly. "Are you all right? Perhaps we should sit for a moment."

She began shaking her head, again and again. "No, no. No, no. It is not right. You cannot—promise me you will not tell the police— *please.*" She reached out to grasp Holmes's arm.

"I cannot withhold evidence from the police."

"But in the stories—you do it all the time—you did it with the blue carbuncle! Surely Dr. Cowen is as worthy as that other sniveling thief."

Holmes laughed softly. "That was only a story, a fiction."

"You cannot tell them—you must not."

"I fear I must, madam."

She drew herself up, along with a great lungful of air. "You cannot accuse him. It was I, Mr. Holmes–I took the Moonstone."

Holmes laughed again. "Come now, madam. This is desperation speaking. You could not have taken the Moonstone. You were unconscious."

"I… I had an accomplice. I signaled to them from the window. I waved a candle. I was awake enough to do that, then I went back to bed and fell asleep. How happy I was to know that when I woke up, the diamond would be gone forever!"

Holmes stared gravely at her. "Do you realize what you are saying and the consequences?"

She gave a quick nod. "I do. Surely–surely they wouldn't send me to prison for stealing my own diamond? You must know why I did it, Mr. Holmes! Lord, how I hated the Moonstone! I sent it to Mr. Tyabji. It belonged to the Indians, not to me. My great-great-uncle stole it. Why should I keep the damned thing?"

"And who were your accomplices, madam?"

"I…" She looked out across an expanse of lawn. "My accomplices. I shall not say. I cannot say."

"Come now, it will probably go easier with you if you give me their names."

"No, they must remain nameless. No one need suffer but me. Must you tell the police? The diamond is gone, Mr. Holmes. The thieves will have certainly cut it to pieces by now. It was never truly my family's–we, after all, were the real and original thieves." She smiled fiercely.

"You put me in a difficult position, madam. I shall have to think this over. Say nothing of it to anyone–especially not to your husband."

Her smile was fierce. "Why would I talk to him? It would only distress him, or… he might actually show anger. *Finally*."

"I shall give you a day's respite and decide by tomorrow. I may well resolve to speak with Inspector Lestrade."

The animation that had briefly stirred her was receding. "I hope you will not. Nothing ever works out the way I intend. Maybe I truly am…" She laughed softly. "…cursed." We had turned and started back through the park toward the street of her house. "Cursed… curses… Such a terrible idea–that we cannot control our own destiny, that some outside force larger than ourselves controls everything, a sort of dark counterpoint to God."

"That is only an idea, after all," I said. "It is a fantasy, a trick of the mind. There may or may not be a benevolent God, but surely there is no dark force controlling our existence."

"No?" she murmured.

"Henry is right, madam."

"Is he? Then what is the point of all this useless suffering? Something seems to be mocking me, playing with me."

"You mustn't think that way," I said.

"Listen to him," Holmes said. "Such thoughts are not helpful. "They are only a means of self-torment. You should not indulge in them."

She stared at the carts and carriages traversing Kensington under the bright afternoon sun. Her face seemed so thin and pale under the wide-brimmed blue hat with its enormous plumes. "If only it were that easy." She clenched her teeth tightly, then said, "I should like to be there when they cut the stone. I should like to see the chisel driven into it. I never thought it was beautiful. I am not like other women, I know. I found it ugly, vulgar and ostentatious."

Holmes shook his head. "As you said, madam. It is gone. It is out of your life."

She laughed harshly. "Thank God."

We crossed the street. The bright sun had begun to give me a headache, even though the brim of my top hat cast its shadow over my eyes. I felt a subtle anxiousness constrict my chest, no doubt a reaction to Alice's fears. I had been so certain that Cowen had taken the diamond, and yet Alice's confession also made sense. If he loved her, he would do anything to shield her. My temples began to throb.

Twelve

When we returned to the sitting room, Alice smiled weakly at her husband. He gave her a wary look, then frowned at Holmes.

"Perhaps we might speak with you in the library," Holmes said. "First, however, I need to look briefly in Mrs. Bromley's bedroom. I need to examine the window again."

"You know the way, I believe," Alice said.

"Sabine can accompany you." Bromley turned toward the maid who was seated at the sofa working on some embroidery. "Sabine."

She set down the hoop, then stood. Her dark eyes were cautiously neutral, her full lips clamped tightly together in a straight line. She walked past us, and we turned to follow her.

Holmes paused at the stairway, letting her proceed. He leaned toward me and said softly. "I shall keep her occupied. You must switch the bottles." His hand bumped against mine.

"What?"

"You heard me. Be careful she doesn't see you. Put it in your pocket." With a shake of my head, I took the blue bottle and slipped it into my pocket.

Holmes spoke much louder. "It is as I said. There may be some subtle marks on the window ledge which Lestrade's men missed." To Sabine, he said, "We are coming." He took the steps quickly to catch up with her.

We soon reached the door to Alice's room, and Sabine turned the door handle. "Thank you, mademoiselle," Holmes said. We stepped into the room. The big bed was neatly made, the chenille bedspread with its decorative pattern pulled taut. On the nearby mahogany dresser sat the small blue bottle. Sabine stood near the bed, her eyes still surveying us cautiously. She obviously intended to remain in the room as long as we were there.

"Do you attend your mistress before bedtime?" Holmes asked her.

"Not generally."

"So she usually mixes up her own drops?"

"I believe so. Sometimes Meester Bromley does it, I think, when she is weary."

"I see. I shall only be a minute, Henry. You can remain where you are." He crossed the bedroom and went to the window. The glazier had obviously stopped by, since the glass no longer had the hole in it.

Sabine had folded her arms across her bosom as she watched Holmes, ignoring me. Her hair was so black, the shadows were lost in it. Her ear was small and delicate, her jaw curving down into her rounded chin and full throat. So near to her, I was very much aware of her physical presence and a certain slumbering sexuality. Little wonder Hodges was attracted to her.

Holmes had opened the window and stared down at the

wooden sash. Finally he turned to us. "Mademoiselle, could you tell me something about the stables next door? If you would just have a look."

As she walked forward, her back to me, I quickly snatched up the blue bottle and put it in my left jacket pocket, then set the bottle from my right pocket on the dresser. Drawing in my breath, I walked forward and tried not to weigh the implications of what I had done. My cousin was eccentric and mysterious at times, but in the end, I did trust him. If Alice were suicidal, this could save her life.

"Yes," Holmes said, "the neighbor's stables there to our right. Do you know if the second floor is occupied? Do the grooms and the coachman sleep there?"

"Yes, I believe so."

"Very good. Thank you. I am finished."

We left the bedroom, and Sabine followed us back down to the library. She nodded, then closed the door behind us. Bromley had stood up and come round the big dark rectangular table. "Did you find out anything, Mr. Holmes?"

"No. I fear not."

Bromley shook his head, then pulled out another chair and sank down onto it. "Oh, this whole affair is hopeless, hopeless! We shall never see the diamond again, and now, even though it is gone we have received mysterious threats. Will poor Alice ever be left in peace?" I had not seen him so discouraged before. Holmes said nothing, but only smiled faintly. "Do you find this amusing, Mr. Holmes?" Bromley was indignant.

"Certain aspects, yes. Today two different people have confessed to taking the diamond."

Bromley sprang up. "What? You actually have found the thief?"

"I am not certain."

"Who? Who has confessed?"

"First Dr. Cowen. And then your wife."

"What? Is this some kind of ghastly joke, Mr. Holmes?"

"Not at all. I visited Dr. Cowen this morning, and he told me he took the jewel from your wife's bedroom shortly before he came back downstairs. On our walk just now, Mrs. Bromley claimed that she was the thief, that she had an accomplice whom she signaled from the window and who then took the jewel."

He shook his head wildly. "This is madness–simply madness speaking! She could not have taken the diamond. Hers is the most fearful and timid nature imaginable. To think that she could commit so grave a crime... No, it is not possible. Cowen, on the other hand... That does seem a possibility."

Holmes's ironic smile again pulled at his lips. "Perhaps you might also like to confess to the crime, Mr. Bromley?"

Bromley gave him an incredulous look, then again grew indignant. "I do not find that amusing, Mr. Holmes. Not in the least."

"Forgive me, sir. You must grant a certain absurdity to the situation, but never mind that. You do not believe your wife could have had an accomplice?"

"Never. She hardly goes out at all, does not leave the house alone, and has no friends except Lady Alexander."

"You are forgetting the one obvious possibility."

"Am I? Who might that be?"

"Her maid."

Bromley opened his mouth, then slowly closed it. Something like alarm showed briefly in his eyes. "Sabine would not do such a thing."

"Wouldn't she? Tell me, Mr. Bromley. Do you know of any

reason why your wife might harbor a certain animosity toward her maid?"

Bromley's eyes were fixed on Holmes. He swallowed once, then shook his head. "None. Oh, they are not great friends as sometimes occurs, but I don't think Alice dislikes her. Have you reason to believe otherwise?"

"She named Sabine as her primary accomplice, and there was a certain gleeful defiance in her manner."

By that point in the day, I had finally accustomed myself to Holmes's extraordinary statements appearing from out of nowhere, and I managed to show little reaction.

"Oh, this is all madness—true madness now, and nothing more. I have seen it coming for some time. I have been afraid to say it aloud, but Alice has finally tumbled over the edge. This is some crazed manifestation of her fear and animosity toward the Moonstone. Somehow poor Sabine has also become her scapegoat."

"If Sabine were involved, then Hodges would also be suspect."

"No, no! This is all too much. I have the utmost faith in Hodges. He would never be involved in such a crime. He is far too loyal to me. Besides, the two of them were together with us in the sitting room during the entire time the jewel was stolen. Somehow Alice has taken a dislike to the two of them. I cannot imagine why. Perhaps she is envious in some twisted way of their attachment to one another."

His hands formed fists. "There is another possibility, a worse one. Perhaps... I dread to even say it aloud—it would be yet another sign her sanity is failing. In the past, on a few occasions, there have been outbursts of sudden irrational and completely unjustifiable jealousy. Once after a supper, she claimed I had been far too attentive to Lady Alexander. Alice knows that Lady

Alexander and I are old acquaintances, and somehow she assumed the worst. That was bad enough. Surely she could not imagine that I would so lower myself as to… No, no—impossible. She cannot be that far gone."

"All the same," Holmes said, "I am afraid I shall have to discuss the situation with Inspector Lestrade."

Bromley's dismay was obvious. "Oh God, this has all become a nightmare! Truly the diamond was cursed. Please, Mr. Holmes, I beg of you, do not involve Alice with the police. You said… you said that Dr. Cowen had confessed. Tell the police about that if you must, but do not mention Alice's ravings. I am afraid that, after all, she is a very sick woman. I can think of no other reason why she would drag herself—and the servants—into this dreadful business."

"You put in me in a difficult position, sir. Withholding information from the police is a grave matter."

"But when it is so obviously the product of a sadly stricken mind, surely an exception can be made."

"Perhaps. I shall need a day to think about it. In the meantime, you must say nothing of this to Mrs. Bromley."

I opened my mouth, then closed it. A definite pattern had become obvious. I did not feel quite so bewildered as Bromley, but Holmes had certainly managed to startle me in each of our visits today.

"Absolutely not!" Bromley exclaimed. "That would only be affirming her morbid fantasies. I shall not say a word. But really, Mr. Holmes, you could not actually put a troubled soul like Alice at the mercy of the police and the courts? It would exacerbate her condition. It might kill her. Already…" His eyes suddenly glistened, and he was briefly unable to speak. "I am so worried about her."

"Perhaps not, Mr. Bromley. You shall have my decision tomorrow."

"Thank you, and I trust it will be the right one. You could not be so cruel to her."

"We can see ourselves out. Oh, and should you ever feel you need me, should there be further unexpected developments, feel free to summon me regardless of the hour. Good afternoon, sir."

Bromley sank back down into the chair, and ran his fingers back through his curly hair. He looked desperate. Holmes and I went down the hallway and out the front door. We paused to put on our top hats.

"You have certainly outdone yourself today," I said. "That was dry understatement this morning when you said you might surprise me today. These bizarre conversations are still whirling about in my head. You were not exactly truthful with any of the three."

"No, I was not. But then, none of them was exactly truthful with me."

I stared at him. "None of them?"

"You heard me correctly."

"I don't suppose you would like to explain this whole business to me?"

He laughed softly. "It might take a while. You shall see for yourself soon enough, I believe. By tomorrow at this time, all your questions should be resolved. If not, I shall tell you everything."

"Your breakfast analogy with chemistry was certainly apt. You have put the three compounds together in a test tube, then shaken them well."

"Very good, Henry! And now we shall await the results. I suspect you would like to see this through to the end."

"Of course. I would not miss it."

"Then I suggest you spend the night with me at Baker

Street. I expect a summons very early in the morning from the Bromley household."

I frowned. "Mrs. Bromley. You think she may drink the contents of the entire bottle?"

"I do. We must be ready to leave at once. Your assistance as a physician will be useful. I shall lend you the spare bedroom where Watson once resided. Lestrade will have to make do with the sofa."

"Lestrade is coming, too?"

"Yes, I believe so. I am off to see him now, but you may as well go home. I shall have him bring some of his men along, too—armed, this time. We don't want any more surprises from men with revolvers."

"I don't understand. Why would a poor distracted woman taking poison require the police?"

Holmes's gray eyes grew very cold. "One thing I can tell you, Henry: whatever we are dealing with, it is most certainly not a simple case of attempted suicide by a poor distracted woman."

I stared back at him and felt a sudden tightness in my chest. "I shall know everything by this time tomorrow?"

"You shall."

"Very good. I shall stop by later this evening then and be prepared for a long night."

He smiled. "Excellent, Henry!" He extended his arm, his stick striking the ground. George's hansom was still parked across the street. He took a few steps, then turned to me. "Do try to come alone, Henry—without Michelle, that is."

I opened my mouth to give him my assurances, then hesitated. "I shall try." He resumed walking. "But I can't promise you!"

* * *

Holmes's request and my response were prescient. When I told Michelle about the day's events, she immediately proclaimed that she would gladly accompany me. She assured me that she could return by cab in the morning and meet with her patients, and that losing a little sleep was nothing. I made a few feeble attempts to persuade her otherwise—feeble because I knew she was strong-willed in such matters. Harriet served us dinner, and then, as the weather was still unusually fine, we took a leisurely stroll of about half an hour to Baker Street.

Parked across the street from the door to 221B was a large black enclosed carriage with two horses, a so-called "Black Maria" or police van used to transport several constables or to take trespassers to jail. Sure enough, when we entered Holmes's sitting room, Inspector Lestrade was there. He wore one of his usual impeccable dark suits, and he gave Michelle an appreciative glance and then a slight bow. They had met before. She was much taller than him and of a more robust build. Alongside her, he seemed slim and slight and, with his narrow jaw and mouth, his fervid dark eyes, more weasel-like than ever.

We conversed briefly. Lestrade told us three policemen were in the Black Maria, ready to assist us. He was somewhat frustrated (as was I) that Holmes would not, as they say, lay all his cards on the table. Holmes sat in his favorite chair wearing his purple dressing gown, his legs crossed so that his slender ankle in a black stocking showed, and smoked a pipe with a very long stem. He merely assured us that the facts would soon make themselves clear. Michelle smiled and said we must allow him the dramatic flourishes he so relished.

Michelle and I each had had a very busy day, and we retired at about ten. We looked at the tiny bed, then at one another. It was going to be a tight fit, but Michelle was one of those people who could sleep anywhere. We soon lay huddled together, her back against my chest, my arm curled about her. "This is rather cozy, after all," she murmured. She was asleep at once.

I lay thinking about the day's events, recalling Holmes's conversations with Cowen, Alice and Bromley. And of course, our visit to the chemist. I doubted I would be able to sleep, but I saw before me the long shelf with the tall carboys containing the colored liquids, each glass stopper shaped like a translucent flame. I realized I must be dreaming. A long darkness came.

I remembered the blue bottle, and I saw it as well, the thick glass and the label with the red lettering. LAUDANUM. POISON. SAUNDERS. My breath came and went softly. My hand went down to my jacket pocket, and I felt the square lump which would be the bottle. I saw the other blue bottle sitting on the dresser, and Sabine's figure ahead of me, those voluptuously curving hips, only a thin white shift covering them now, her long black hair spilling down onto the white fabric.

I reached for the bottle, and she turned to look at me. She smiled, and I froze with my hand in my pocket. *Look here,* Holmes said. *Look here at the window.* She turned away. I knew that now was the moment to switch the bottles, but I could not move.

Oh look, Michelle said. *I shall just have a sip.* She was also wearing only a shift, and her long white arm reached out for the blue bottle on the dresser.

I shook my head wildly. *You mustn't—that's the wrong bottle.*

She held it in her hand. *Is it?*

Yes—yes.

Alice took the blue bottle—or was it Michelle? The sudden fear squeezed at my heart, making my breath catch in my throat. *No, no, listen to me, you mustn't drink it.* The counterfeit bottle was still in my pocket. That was the real thing with enough laudanum to easily kill her.

Oh Henry, surely one sip can't hurt.

Poison, I murmured. *Poison. It's poison. And the diamond is poison.*

I'm so thirsty. Michelle turned the bottle in her hand. *Oh look! It doesn't say "poison." It says "drink me."* The tag tied to the bottle neck was as long as the bottle itself.

That must be a mistake, I said.

But it isn't, Alice said. *You'll fit through the door if you drink it down. The rabbit told me so.*

Don't make jokes—you are the wrong Alice.

I think not. She was wearing a child's short-sleeved blue dress with short flaring skirts, along with a white apron and black shoes with straps, just like Alice in the story, but her breasts were almost grotesquely large, and her arms and legs were bare and shapely, a woman's not a girl's.

I groaned. *You're trying to confuse me.*

Drink it down, Alice or Michelle! Drink it—it's good for you. Somehow Bromley had halfway transformed himself into a rabbit. Coming up through his curly brown hair were two enormous white ears, and his jaw protruded out into a button nose, complete with whiskers. He wore a plaid jacket and nothing else, his male anatomy only too obvious, nearly as long as his ears. He might be a rabbit, but he still had hands, one of which held a small gold watch. Standing beside him was a short stocky figure wearing a gigantic top hat, bow tie with polka dots and a checkered suit. After looking hard, I realized it was Hodges, but his body appeared to have been squashed down to half his usual height.

Sabine had put on some clothes. She wore a strange ornamental dress of gold, black and red, cut in a way that left her breasts completely exposed. In one hand she held a stick with a red heart on the end. Her face beneath the black hair was transformed, her pout beyond the capacity of a normal face, and her mouth opened impossibly large. *Drink it!*

My head hurt, and I tried to focus on Michelle. She was still in her white shift, beautiful as ever, the only one who looked exactly normal any longer. *Henry, it's all right.*

The figures wavered for a moment, and then I noticed a matchbox of double or triple the usual size sitting on the dresser alongside the blue bottle. Alice was back in her white shift, her long blond hair dangling down on either side of her thin face. She reached out slowly for the matchbox.

Don't open it. Don't open it.

But it opened itself, and the Moonstone tumbled out. The movement made the facets flash, and a brief red spark flared, the color jarring alongside the blue of the bottle.

Alice laughed softly. *It's poison too.*

Don't eat it, Holmes said. *Don't eat the diamond.*

Yes, yes, Bromley whispered. *Eat the diamond. Swallow it down.*

Michelle's arm slowly straightened, her fingers reaching toward the gem. I struggled to reach her, to pull her back, but I could not seem to move—nor could I even cry out. Her forefinger touched the jewel, and she jerked her hand back, crying out, *It hurts.*

The diamond wavered, then was half as tall as the bottle. Light sparkled off the facets, and with a hazy glowing shudder, it doubled again in size. The red inside had also grown, was like some internal wound that had begun to leak blood into the surrounding tissues of adamant. *How beautiful,* Michelle murmured.

It's not beautiful, I cried.

Alice laughed. *It's cursed. It's cursed. Can't you see?*

The red center continued to swell and began to pulse like a heart, filling a network of crystalline vessels with red.

It cannot be alive. It cannot.

But it was still growing in size, the red inside pulsating, and behind the red organ was some shadowy shape, its evil soul or brain. Clearly it was not a dead mineral lump, but a living being of incredible power. The Moonstone was taller than the blue bottle now, but no, the blue bottle had grown as well, and the red letters spelling POISON were also flashing. There must be enough laudanum in that enormous bottle to kill an entire army.

Before I could stop her, Alice seized the gigantic blue bottle and drank, filling her mouth until she could drink no more, and then the sweet-smelling amber liquid spilled down onto her white shift and turned red. She screamed and collapsed, and then Michelle seized the blue bottle with her big white hands. The diamond sat in the shadows pulsing scarlet and watched.

No—no!

I lunged for Michelle, and then the diamond and the blue bottle were gone.

I was lying on the floor in a dim room, aware that my hip hurt and that I had been having a nightmare. A single candle still flickered on a nearby table. Michelle lurched up and stared at me, only half awake herself. She had let down her hair, but we both still had our clothes on so we would be ready to leave immediately if necessary.

"What is it, Henry? What's wrong?"

I took in a big breath and rubbed at my arm. "I was having a nightmare. I fell out of the bed."

"Are you all right?"

"Yes, I think so. A little sore, perhaps."

"Poor darling. Little wonder! There is hardly any room. You sleep near the wall now, and I'll take the outside. What time is it, anyway?"

I stood up, wincing slightly. I had struck the hard wooden floor between the bed and a small braided rung. My arm and my hip did feel bruised. I picked up my watch and tipped it toward the candle flame. "A quarter to two."

"I was sleeping so hard."

"I had an odd dream that went on and on. You were about to drink some poison. I was trying to stop you."

She extended her stockinged foot and stepped out of the bed. "Go on, against the wall with you. It's my turn to fall out of the bed."

I lay down, and this time she curled up against my back and slipped her hand around to clasp my chest. I sighed and closed my eyes. I was almost asleep when a voice said, "Henry, Michelle, wake up. It is time. We must go at once."

Neither of us was exactly asleep. We sat up and saw Holmes at the doorway, candle in hand. In the halo of the candlelight his thin face looked intense and eager. I doubted he had slept at all.

"What has happened?" Michelle asked.

"Hodges has arrived and asked us to come at once. There has been a terrible accident at the Bromleys." He gave the word "accident" an ironic stress, and the reflection of the candle flame flicked in his eyes.

Michelle stood up first. "What do you mean?"

I gave my head a shake. "She drank all the laudanum."

Holmes nodded. "Exactly. They think she is near death. We know better. When we get there, Henry, I want you to examine her to make sure she is not in any real danger. However, I want you to tell Bromley that there is nothing you can do, that she is dying."

I frowned, and Michelle exclaimed, "Sherlock, that would be an unbelievably cruel trick! Making the poor man think his wife is going to die—it is unconscionable."

Sherlock stood taller, the corners of his mouth pulling outward. "If you want to accompany me, you must trust me and do exactly as I say. If you cannot, you may remain behind. There is no time now for questions or discussion."

I gazed at him. "Very well."

Michelle shook her head. "All right, but I do not have to be happy about it."

Michelle and I both took our shoes and sat on the bed to put them on. We followed Holmes downstairs to the sitting room where Lestrade, Hodges and a constable waited. Hodges was clearly uneasy. "Mr. Bromley will not like this," he said. "There's no need for the police."

"I shall be the judge of that," Lestrade said. "Come along now. We can all ride in the back of the Black Maria." This prospect obviously did not appeal to Hodges, but he had little choice.

We all went down to the street. Two other constables sat up front on top of the Black Maria, one at them holding the reins. Its rear wheels were at least four feet tall, the front ones about half that size. The carriage was, fittingly, painted black and had some small barred windows. The constable swung open the rear doors, and Michelle climbed up the metal stairs first. Hodges hesitated briefly before going up. Soon we were all seated: Holmes, Michelle and I on one side, Lestrade, Hodges and the constable on the other.

The carriage rumbled along the streets, the hooves of the horses making a rhythmic clopping. The interior was dark, but beams of yellow-white light came and went through the windows as we passed street lamps, illuminating one pale face, then another. Hodges's eyes showed a barely repressed energy, and I noticed that his big hands were clutching tightly at his legs. Holmes seemed at ease and oddly content, while Lestrade clearly relished the thrill of the chase. Like me, he probably also wanted this business finished, once and for all. Michelle gave a sleepy yawn, and I gave her hand a squeeze.

Since it was after two in the morning, there was no traffic, and we soon arrived at the Bromleys' townhouse. We climbed down from the van, and Hodges started quickly for the door. Holmes grasped Lestrade's arm and said softly, "Have your biggest man focus all his attention on Hodges. He is to watch him at all times and be ready for trouble."

Lestrade gave a quick nod, then drew aside one of the constables to speak in his ear. Holmes strode forward to catch up with Hodges, and the rest of us followed. Holmes left his top hat and stick in the usual place by the door, and I did the same. Lestrade took off his hat but did not pause. The three constables were at the rear. We went down the hallway to the sitting room. The small maid, Susan, sat in her robe weeping softly, the bottom of her face hidden in a handkerchief. Nearby were Mrs. Carlson and Sabine. The housekeeper looked distraught, but Sabine was stony-faced. Bromley had been pacing, but he spun round. He had on trousers, a white shirt and his shoes.

"Thank God, you..." He faltered at the sight of Lestrade and the constables. "What is this? Why have you brought the police?"

Holmes shrugged. "It is customary in situations such as this."

"But so many? At this hour of the morning?"

"What have you to tell me, Mr. Bromley?"

"We cannot wake her—we cannot wake her!" He sobbed once.

"She must have taken all the laudanum. The bottle is empty." He turned and snatched up a piece of paper. "And I found this!"

Holmes took it and stepped nearer a lamp. Michelle, Lestrade and I gathered round him. The note was in rough block letters, rather than cursive.

I CAN BEAR IT NO LONGER. THE CURSE HAS WON. DR. COWEN AND I STOLE THE MOONSTONE. SABINE HAD NOTHING TO DO WITH IT. I LIED TO MR. HOLMES. THE DOCTOR WAS ONLY TRYING TO HELP ME—THE BLAME IS MINE AND MINE ALONE. GOD FORGIVE ME, BUT I CANNOT FACE A TRIAL AND PRISON. GOODBYE, MY DARLING AND FORGIVE ME, ALICE.

Holmes set down the note, even as his lips twitched briefly outward. He turned to me. "You had better have a look at her, Henry."

I nodded. Tears were streaming from Bromley's face. "I cannot bear to come, to see her like that."

"There is no need," I said.

"Perhaps Sabine could assist you." Bromley glanced at her, and she rose quietly.

Holmes shook his head. "That is not necessary, not necessary at all. The two doctors will suffice. Henry knows the way."

I took a candle and started for the door. Michelle followed. Once we were on the stairs she said, "It does seem so cruel, so unnecessary." I said nothing, although I shared her sentiments. We climbed the two flights of stairs and went down the hallway. Sally stood whimpering softly at the door, and she gazed up at us with a longing look.

"Good girl." I reached down and patted her head. I hesitated before opening the door. "I suppose she can't do any harm." I opened it, and Sally slipped in ahead of us. She bounded up onto the bed, then curled up beside her mistress.

The lamp had been lit, and sure enough, the blue bottle sat on the night table, the cork lying next to it. An involuntary shudder brought my shoulder blades together. I knew she would probably recover, but the thought that she would have willingly drunk all of that was chilling. She lay on her back, her left arm thrown up and outward, her face slumped that same way. The long white fingers of her hand curved gently inward, and her palm had a slight rosy flush, and much of her forearm with the blue veins showed above the lacy sleeve of her gown. I picked up her other hand. It felt cold.

"Alice," I said. "Alice." She did not stir, but I could see her breasts slowly moving beneath the gown as she breathed, and in the hollow of her collarbones the shadow dimmed and darkened with her pulse. I placed my fingers alongside her neck, feeling for the artery. "Her pulse is slow, but strong. I think the chemist knew his trade. The chloral hydrate has done its work. She will be unconscious for a while longer."

"Let me listen to her heart." Michelle took a stethoscope out of my black leather bag, put the earpieces into her ears, and set the bell upon the silk fabric just between Alice's breasts. Between her collarbone and the curve of the gown the shadowy outline of her ribs showed. Michelle frowned thoughtfully, then pulled off the stethoscope. "Yes, slow but strong. The same is true of her breathing. She has obviously been sedated, but she should be all right when it wears off."

Sally gazed up at us and whimpered softly again. I stroked her head and ruffled one ear. "You can stay with her, girl. You watch out for her." I turned to Michelle. "Well, let's go give Bromley the good news."

"You are being ironic."

"Yes."

We trooped back down the stairs. I came into the room and hesitated. Bromley gazed at me, his face twisted with grief. Before I could reflect, I spoke. "I'm afraid there is nothing that can be done. She is dying."

Bromley turned away and sobbed. Michelle glared at Holmes. Lestrade had a wary look of intense concentration. Holmes had told him all about our visits of the day, including the switching of the blue bottles.

Holmes went to the sideboard and poured a glass of brandy. He offered it to Bromley. "Drink this, sir." Bromley nodded, then swallowed it down. He coughed once and drew in a great shuddery breath. "How did you come to find her as you did?"

"I could not sleep, Mr. Holmes. She had behaved so oddly this evening. One moment she was laughing, then crying. I tried to calm her, but she was obviously overwrought and irrational. I told her she should be sure to take enough drops to let her sleep. Little did I think…" His voice trailed off.

Holmes watched him closely. "You did not give her the dose yourself?"

"Of course not! Why do you ask such a thing?"

"Sabine told me sometimes that you give her the medicine when she is weary."

Bromley glanced over at Sabine, then back at Holmes. "Yes, but tonight she was not so much weary as excited. I kissed her goodnight, then sat and smoked two cigars. I went to bed, but I only tossed and turned. Finally, at around one, I thought I would check to make sure she was all right. You... you know what I found." He gave his head a wild shake.

Holmes glanced at the piece of paper. "Odd that she should print her suicide note, rather than writing it in her usual handwriting. Do you have any ideas why that might be so, Mr. Bromley?"

Bromley gave him an incredulous stare. "How can you ask me such a thing at a time like this? I have no idea at all!"

Holmes nodded. "What she writes makes sense. Indeed, I had already come to believe that she and Dr. Cowen worked together to steal the diamond."

"Sherlock?" I said. I wasn't sure I should speak, but it had slipped out.

"Yes, Henry. They were each trying to protect the other, but while neither story in itself made sense, if you merged them, things worked perfectly. The doctor said fate had given him his opportunity, but it was Mrs. Bromley who gave him his opportunity with that spectacularly staged outburst at her sister and Lady Alexander. To make it even more convincing, she actually slapped him. Then she could be sick, which was hardly acting at that point, and they could go up to her room together and be alone for a while.

"He quickly cut the hole in the window, pulled off the chain and tossed it out. The diamond was undoubtedly sitting in his medical bag, even as he gravely told us to leave her alone for a few minutes, thereby proving a gap in time for the fictional thieves to break in. It all makes perfect sense and was quite ingenious. The two of them are very creative. Cowen probably put the diamond in a package and entrusted it to a friend. He would not have told him what it was, only that it was precious. The same friend must have delivered it to Mr. Tyabji."

Lestrade nodded eagerly. "Very good, Mr. Holmes—very good indeed! You have done it again."

"I blame Cowen for this!" Bromley's voice shook.

Holmes turned his slender right hand, then clapped with his left hand once, twice. "Bravo, Mr. Bromley! Bravo! You should really have been on the stage. You missed your true calling in life."

I heard Michelle draw in her breath, and I stared myself in disbelief at Holmes. Lestrade only watched, his eyes all aglitter in the lamplight. Bromley shook his head wildly. "What are you saying! How dare you? How dare you? At such a time..." He sobbed once.

"Come now, sir. That is quite enough of the histrionics. It is nearly three in the morning. We are all tired and out of sorts. There is no need to continue with this bravura performance. You prepared a draft for your wife last night. You poured the entire bottle of laudanum into a glass, probably adding some wine to disguise the fact, then gave it to your wife to drink. I'm certain you had some consoling words for her as you tucked her in."

Bromley's face was red. "That is a lie—a monstrous lie."

"And you also wrote this suicide note."

"I did not!"

"I'm afraid I tricked you, and you have given yourself away. Mrs. Bromley said nothing to me about Sabine being her accomplice. In fact, she said nothing about Sabine whatsoever. I do not actually know if she liked or disliked her. She would not name her accomplices."

The color slowly went out of Bromley's face. "What?"

"You heard me, sir. You heard me well enough."

"She must have... she must have thought that you would... that you would deduce that Sabine was her accomplice. She was—it was a final act of charity. She wanted to protect Sabine from the same sort of madness now directed at me!"

Holmes gave his head a shake. "You are very good at improvising, sir. I have never seen better, but it will not do." He glanced at Lestrade. "Inspector, do you find his explanation very convincing?"

Lestrade was smiling. "No, Mr. Holmes, I do not."

"But—but why would I do such a thing? Why?"

"Well, for one thing, you were weary of having to hide your sordid affair with Sabine from your wife."

Hodges stepped forward, but the constable grasped his arm firmly, and another constable drew nearer. Bromley grew paler still, and a brief glimmer of panic showed in his eyes. "How dare you, sir? How dare you? Everyone knows Hodges and Sabine..."

"That is what you wanted everyone to believe. How convenient that your bedroom, your dressing room, and Hodges's room were all adjoining. Sabine could go into Hodges's room, then make her way to your bedroom. You were, I am afraid, hardly discreet. Amy must have burst in upon the two of you, in *flagrante delicto*, I suspect. You paid her off and had her leave, but she must have demanded a regular payment, and she could not be trusted. Best to be rid of her." He turned to Hodges. "And so you sent your loyal servant..."

Hodges tried to lunge forward, but the two brawny constables restrained him.

"Keep hold of him!" Lestrade exclaimed.

Bromley laughed softly. "You truly think I am a monster, Mr. Holmes. You've constructed this edifice... What can I say?"

"And Susan—she heard you groaning in the library. You told her you had a stomach ache." Holmes laughed. "Have you so little control that...? *The library.* Really, sir! You are obviously one of those men who feels a certain sensual thrill when there is the risk of discovery."

Susan sobbed. "I don't understand!" Her tiny hands were clenched into fists. Sabine was watching Holmes, her dark eyes showing a cold fury.

Holmes turned toward Mrs. Carlson. "There is no reason for you and Susan to remain here. Go to bed." He nodded at Susan. "Take care of the girl, madam." Mrs. Carlson helped Susan to her feet, then led her out of the room.

Bromley's mouth formed a brief bitter smile as he inhaled through his nostrils. He was finally at a loss for words.

"I suspect you must have met Sabine during your time in France. You brought her back with you. It does take genuine audacity to make your mistress your wife's maid."

Bromley stared at Holmes. Something in his face had changed. For the first time, I felt I was seeing the real man. "Do you really think I would kill my wife just for a woman, for a mistress? Is that really much of a motive, after all?"

"It is... part of the motive. There is, of course, the other part."

Bromley drew back slightly, his lips parting.

"Mr. Bromley, you showed me your formidable safe early in this case. I have a request for you, since you alone know the combination. I want you to open it for us."

Bromley winced, then shook his head. "I won't."

"No? But why not?"

"I have my reasons."

"Such as?"

"Damn you—I'll not trade wits with you an instant longer! Leave me alone—get out of my house!"

"It is too late for that now, sir. You summoned us, after all. I think we should all go down the hallway to the library."

"I won't open the safe. I will never open it."

"Regrettable," Holmes said. "Most regrettable, but let us have a look anyway."

Holmes took one candle, Lestrade another. We all started for the door, the two constables each with a hand gripping one of Hodges's arms. Only Sabine would not move. "Come along, mademoiselle," Holmes said.

"I won't."

"You can wait for us locked in the Black Maria if you prefer."

The fury in her eyes had become hatred. She slowly started forward. Michelle gave me a worried look, then stepped nearer to Sabine. We went down the hallway to the library. Holmes took the candle, lifted the glass shade of the lamp, then lit it. He turned up the flame to brighten the room. "By the way, Inspector, there is a drawing room just next to this room. Mrs. Bromley often met there with Dr. Cowen. That is where they must have planned the theft."

Lestrade gave an appreciative nod. "Did they?"

"Yes. And Mr. Bromley often listened to them through the wall using his stethoscope."

Bromley said nothing, but his eyes showed his dismay.

"Did he now, Mr. Holmes? So he knew they were going to steal the diamond. But he did nothing? Why was that?"

"To save my wife!" Bromley exclaimed. "Because I knew the diamond was killing her! I let them take it because I loved her!"

Holmes slowly drew in his breath, then gave a nod. "Yes, your powers of improvisation are unequaled, sir. Will you please open the safe for us now?"

Bromley stood up straight, his fists clenched. "I will not. Never."

"A pity. If I could only open the safe, I think that would

perhaps finish off this case, once and for all."

Bromley had begun to lose color again. Lestrade, on the other hand, was clearly enjoying himself. "How so, Mr. Holmes? How so?"

"Let us see now." Holmes went round the table, grasped the gilded frame of the painting of cows in a field, then set it on the floor. Before him was the square black metal of the safe with its round knob.

Bromley smiled coldly. "You will never break into it. That is impossible. The only way is with the combination, and I am the only one who knows it."

Holmes's lips formed a cold smile. "Are you now?" He seemed to sink slightly, his long fingers spreading apart slightly at his sides. "I believe your birthday is in July, is it not? The second as I recall. Seven left, two right, and then…"

Bromley gave a sharp grunt, then sprang toward Holmes, who struck him square in the jaw. He went down at once. Hodges wrenched himself free of one of the policemen and punched him in the face, even as he struck backwards with his other arm at the other man. The smaller constable brought his truncheon down on Hodges's head. The big man fell onto the library table, then slipped off, taking a chair down with him.

Sabine swept past me, but Michelle had stepped before her. "No—you are not going anywhere." Sabine flew at her, hands extended like claws. Michelle cried out, retreated briefly, then sprang forward and caught the smaller woman in her long arms. The two of them went down onto the floor and rolled about, but Sabine could not break Michelle's grip. Sabine was cursing in French, language worthy of a sailor or dock worker.

"For God's sake!" I cried to Lestrade. "Help me!"

We bent over and managed to pull Sabine away from Michelle

and yank her to her feet. "Get the cuffs, Bradley!" Lestrade shouted. Bradley, the smaller constable, dropped his truncheon and pulled out some handcuffs. Lestrade yelled at me, "Behind her back! Behind her back!" We managed to get her hands behind her, even as she lunged and struggled and cursed us. The constable fastened the handcuffs about her wrists.

"That's enough!" Lestrade shouted at Sabine. "That's enough!" She responded by spitting in his face. He immediately slapped her. That finally seemed to take the fight out of her. "Behave now, or we'll chain your feet as well!"

Michelle stood up and gave me a crooked smile. Across her right cheek were two bloody scratches. "Are you all right?" I asked.

She touched her face. "It stings, and I bruised my elbow." She laughed. "We have both ended up on the floor tonight." She gave Sabine a wary look, her smile fading. "She's much stronger than she looks."

"*Putain!*" Sabine snarled.

Holmes shook his head. "That's rich, coming from you."

Lestrade raised a warning finger to her face. "Mademoiselle, Constable Bradley is an able man with a truncheon. If you cannot behave yourself, he can put you to sleep for an hour or so. The choice is yours." He glanced at his men, then nodded at the prostrate Hodges. "Get some handcuffs on the big one there, as well. We don't want him leaping up and starting something else."

Holmes pulled Bromley to his feet. The man put his hand along his jaw. "I don't feel well," he murmured. He pulled out one of the oaken chairs and collapsed into it.

Holmes eagerly rubbed his long, thin hands together. "Now then, shall we just have that look in the safe?"

Bromley groaned softly.

Holmes turned the knob with his long fingers in four short sharp movements. In the quiet that had settled over the room, we heard a rumbling sort of click. Holmes swung the heavy door open and pulled out a black velvet case about six inches square. He opened the case, withdrew a gem and held it up before the lamp. It dangled from its chain—its original chain.

"*The Moonstone*," I said. "The Moonstone."

"Yes, Henry. The Moonstone."

"But that's impossible. We saw it stolen—we saw it taken. And the chain was missing. How can that one be here?"

"The stone at Tyabji's was a fake, Henry. Bromley had substituted it for the real diamond so that on Saturday night, Mrs. Bromley was wearing the fake. Yesterday afternoon, Lestrade and I made inquiries at Bromley's bank. He accessed a box in the vault the day before the party, then again the Monday afterwards. Mrs. Bromley and the doctor thought they were stealing the Moonstone, but they were mistaken." He glanced down at Bromley. "Weren't they?"

Bromley gazed up at him. At last a long weary laugh slipped from his lips. "Yes."

"A fake," I mumbled. "A fake. But it looked so real."

"It was a very good fake, Henry. Harter was a master jeweler. Unfortunately, his skill ultimately cost him his life. When the news about the Moonstone being stolen came out in the newspapers, as it eventually must, he might have put two and two together and gone to the police to tell them about a fake version of the diamond. Therefore, he—like Amy—had to be eliminated. And so, Bromley's former soldier—his *butcher*—was sent forth again. Harter had done business with Bromley for years, giving him commissions for his referrals. He suspected nothing. He eagerly let Hodges into his shop. Hodges is probably one of those twisted soldiers who develop a certain taste for violence and killing, a craving even. That must have finally gotten him into trouble in India. He probably fled before he could be charged for some vicious crime."

Bromley sighed softly but did not speak.

Lestrade whistled softly. "Two murders. They'll both swing for this."

"And almost a third," Holmes said. "Almost but not quite."

Bromley slowly raised his head. "What do you mean?"

"I mean that I substituted another bottle for the one in your wife's room. It contained enough chloral hydrate and laudanum to render her unconscious, but not to kill her. I'm sure she will confirm in the morning that she had her drops from you and that she did not write that ludicrous suicide note."

Bromley laughed even as he shook his head. "I said once, long ago, eons ago it seems, that I could not hide anything from you, Mr. Holmes. I was not exactly being sincere at the time, but it appears to be true, all the same."

Lestrade was smiling broadly and gave his head an enthusiastic shake. "Masterly, Mr. Holmes, simply masterly!" He turned again to his men. "Get the woman and the bloke on the floor into the van. We'll join you shortly."

"I did nothing!" Sabine cried. "It was the two of them—I am not a murderer—never!"

Bromley laughed softly. Holmes stared at Lestrade. "She's probably telling the truth about that. I'm not sure that she has committed any actual crime."

"She was at least an accessory to attempted murder," Lestrade said.

"I didn't give her the drops—he did! He did!"

"Get them out of here," ordered Lestrade.

Sabine seemed tired out at last. She followed quietly. Two of the men helped get the half-conscious Hodges to his feet. He blinked dully, struggling to focus his eyes. They led him out.

Holmes held the Moonstone up again to the light of the lamp. "It is an incredible diamond. I suspected a fake had been substituted even before the party, and I thought then that the gem was not quite as I remembered it. But I could not be positive. Now I am sure. Look at it. Do you see, Henry? During the day it is yellowish, but now it has a bluish glint."

He was right. Again the diamond seemed to come alive in light, the facets sparkling and playing with the beams, and I could see that interior flaw, a hint of pink or red. Lestrade shook his head. "It is remarkable—absolutely amazing. I have never seen its equal."

"I do not find it so beautiful. It is certainly not worth all the lives it has cost." Michelle's voice was cold.

Holmes stared down at Bromley. He was still slumped in the chair, but his brown eyes were fixed on the diamond. "I should have gotten rid of it, as I planned," he said. "I had found a jeweler who could cut it into smaller stones. I thought I would take it to him, but I brought it back here instead. There is no hurry, I thought. I shall wait until things calm down. Then I shall be rid of it. But I don't think I could have. It is the most beautiful thing I have ever seen. I knew from the first moment I beheld the Moonstone that I must have it. It was…" His smile was bitter. "…love at first sight, all right. I spent considerable time here in the library just staring at it. I know its shape so well, its every facet. To destroy a thing of such beauty! It would have been sacrilege."

Holmes laughed. "*Sacrilege?* Your mind is truly warped."

"Is it? You find it beautiful, too. I can see it in your eyes."

"But it is appreciation only—not mania."

Bromley regarded him, then nodded. "I suppose you are right."

"It must have amused you to watch Cowen and your wife plot to steal the diamond."

Bromley laughed. "It did! That it did. They took all the risk. I knew it would be much easier to steal the fake from Tyabji than to take it from a dinner party where the celebrated Sherlock Holmes would be attending."

"But why did you bother to steal it from Tyabji?" I asked. Bromley only shrugged.

"The Indians would no doubt have had the diamond examined and discovered it was a fraud." Holmes turned again to Bromley. "You overheard Cowen and your wife through the wall, then listened in periodically. She must have begged Cowen for his help, and he could not refuse her."

"Very good, Mr. Holmes—very good indeed! Of course, I always knew Cowen was enamored of her. I wonder if he has ever realized that himself."

"He has," Holmes said.

I stared at Bromley's handsome face. My hands were cold, and I felt slightly nauseated. I had thought I knew him, and yet I knew nothing at all—he was a complete mystery, a blank. "That story you told me about the Latin master and the caning, I suppose that was another of your lies, only a fiction?"

The corners of his lips rose. "Oh, it was a true story, true in all the particulars. However, I was the older boy who poured the ink onto the chair."

"Of course you were. Tell me, did you ever love your wife?" My voice had an odd pitch.

His face was utterly relaxed now, calm. "No. Never."

I put one hand on the table and leaned closer to him. "And Sabine?"

His eyes widened. "Sabine?" He began to laugh in earnest. "Are you serious, Dr. Vernier? Her? Love her? Don't be absurd. That was never about love, but about lust." He gave his head an appreciative shake. "She was incredible. She was insatiable, absolutely insatiable, more even than a man. She could never get enough. I have never seen anything like it. Jane was willing enough—Lady Alexander, she is now—but no one could compare to Sabine. Even the back door was always..."

I lunged forward, grabbed his shirt collar and yanked him upward. "Shut your filthy mouth!" He was surprised. "If you want—if you want to boast and vaunt about your filthy exploits, do it when my wife is not present—do it when I am not present. I will not tolerate it—I will not. Do you understand?" He nodded and I pushed him back down into the chair. I was breathing hard and felt almost dizzy.

Michelle put her hand on my shoulder. "It's all right, Henry. It's all right."

Bromley gave me a brief pained smile, then laughed softly. "Sorry, old man. I meant no harm. I have pretended for so long that... it's hard for me to believe anyone is exactly real, if you know what I mean. In my society, Dr. Vernier, you are a unique specimen. You and your wife. I don't think I've ever met anyone quite like you."

My hands were quivering. "You make me sick."

He shrugged.

"I think you now have all the salient facts of the case," said Holmes to Inspector Lestrade.

"I do, Mr. Holmes. Thank you for availing yourself of my

services. This was truly a case like no other. It was a privilege to be included."

"You are most welcome, Inspector."

"Get up, sir," said Lestrade to Bromley. "We have some other accommodation waiting for you."

Bromley stared at Holmes. "One final question: When did you first suspect me? Did anything in particular give me away?"

"I suspected you from the very first. You were too charming by far, and your story was all too pat, too melodramatic. I knew the Indian was a fake. I suppose it was Hodges at the window. He must have run into the empty stables to remove his turban and make-up. And there was one small detail at our first meeting, one tiny thing which was surely not enough to build an entire case upon, but it planted the seeds of doubt."

"What was that?"

"I asked you what color hair your wife had. You said she was light-haired, and yet a long, fine black hair was twisted about upon your white shirt collar."

"I was a fool to come to you. I thought your reputation must be exaggerated and that I could best you. Your fame would help prove my innocence. I was a fool."

Bromley stood at last, and we all started down the hallway. Michelle had grasped my arm loosely and stayed very close to me. We came to the sitting room. "I don't want to ride with him," I said. "I don't want to be anywhere near the lot of them."

Lestrade gave me a concerned look. "I don't much care for the idea either," Holmes said. "I am not particularly sleepy—too much excitement. Wait here, Henry. I shall just see Mr. Bromley stowed, then join you both."

Michelle and I sat on the couch. I ran my hand back through my hair. "I still cannot believe it. I was so certain about him. He had me completely fooled. I was an idiot."

"He was very charming," Michelle said.

I stared at her. "But you had some doubts?"

She drew in her breath slowly. "I did."

"You and Sherlock could see through him—but not I. Not I."

"What of it, Henry? It was not some moral failing on your part—to the contrary. You could not see through him because you assumed that he was as honorable as you and that a man must love his wife and be true to her."

I let my breath out in a muted laugh. "Yes, I suppose I did."

"Henry—I love you so much." She leaned over and kissed me on the lips. Her fingertips touched my cheeks. "There is nothing wrong with you. Nothing whatsoever."

I sagged against her and took her hand in mine. Holmes soon returned. "I told Lestrade to keep the three of them separate and question them alone. They will turn against each other in an instant and give him all the proof he needs in court." He walked to the sideboard, poured three glasses of brandy, then took two of them to Michelle and me. The third he picked up and slowly sipped. His lips formed a smile that came and went, came and went. "Do you feel better?"

"Yes, I think so."

"You are far too decent a man to fathom the likes of Bromley. I should have prepared you. Perhaps I should have left you out of this."

"I don't know. I really don't know. And if you had told me, I would undoubtedly have given something away."

Holmes downed the glass and put it on the sideboard. He pulled out his watch and flipped open the cover. "Good heavens! After four o'clock. All the same, I am still not sleepy. Would you care for a stroll? It is pleasantly cool outside. The sun will be up soon, and it is almost time for breakfast! I know of a place which opens promptly at five thirty."

"I don't feel particularly hungry," I said.

Michelle stood. She extended her hand to me. "Well, I do. Perhaps a walk will give you an appetite."

"Perhaps." I took her hand, then stood.

Holmes nodded. "I shall join you in a moment. There is one thing I must certainly not forget!"

"What is that?" I asked.

He smiled, his thin face showing genuine amusement. "I left the Moonstone in its case on the table in the library. I shall just put the diamond back in the safe. It will be absolutely secure there. After all, Lestrade and his men did not hear the last four numbers of the combination." He gave a brusque laugh. "Yes, a walk, breakfast, and then we should be back in time to wake Mrs. Bromley and tell her all that has happened."

Thirteen

Some two weeks later, I joined Holmes for breakfast. Dr. Cowen and Alice Bromley were coming to visit around nine o'clock, and they wanted to see the both of us. It was well into August by then, the morning sunny and pleasantly cool, and after we had eaten, Holmes stood before the open bow window, cup and saucer in hand, sipped his coffee, and stared down at the bustling traffic on Baker Street.

"Ah." He turned to me. "Here they come." He drank down the last, then strode to the small table and set down cup and saucer. He pulled off his purple dressing gown, threw it through the open doorway into his bedroom, closed the door, then put on his long black frock coat. When Mrs. Hudson showed in his visitors, his hand swept before him in a graceful pass, as if he were conducting some lyrical melody. "Do come in. Henry and I were expecting you."

Cowen had left his hat, stick and bag near the door. His broad forehead and bald crown gleamed over his thick black eyebrows and full black beard. Alice looked very slim and tall alongside his shorter compact figure in the black frock coat. She wore a pale-blue silk with lace at the collar and sleeves, as well as the blue hat with extravagant ostrich feathers. She smiled at us both, and I noticed the color in her cheeks.

"You look well, Mrs. Bromley," I said.

She smiled at me. "Much better than the last time you saw me, I'll wager."

"Yes, indeed."

Holmes and I had been with her that morning when the chemist's potion had worn off. When we tried to explain what had happened, she had laughed and insisted we must be joking. She seemed muddle-headed and near hysteria. We had sent for Dr. Cowen and, alone with him, had told him everything. His usual surliness had been replaced by incredulity, amazement, and then a grudging sort of gratitude. He had stayed with Alice for most of the day.

"Please sit down," Holmes said. They sat on the settee, each at one end, leaving space between them. Holmes flapped back his coat tails, even as he sat in his favorite chair, while I took another. A half-polite, half-mocking smile played about his mouth. "And what brings you to Baker Street this morning? How may I serve you?"

Cowen drew in his breath. "First of all, I must say that I owe you an apology, Mr. Holmes, and you, Dr. Vernier. My boorish behavior was unforgivable. I was under great duress, and I feared the worst from what I mistakenly saw as your meddling, but that does not excuse my conduct. I hope you will not hold it against me." He did seem genuinely penitent.

"I shall not," Holmes said.

"Nor I," I said.

Holmes made a flourish with his slender hand. "Let us begin anew."

Cowen nodded. "That is what I wish. And besides an apology, I must offer you my most profound appreciation for all that you have done for Alice and me. I never much liked Bromley, but I hardly imagined... Do you think he had always planned to take her life, or was it a spur-of-the-moment scheme?"

Holmes shrugged. "Impossible to say for certain. He had hoped to frighten her into suicide or madness—hence, the Indian face appearing at the library window. The meeting with Tyabji brought things to a head. He said he would put the diamond in a bank vault and arranged that final dinner party, knowing that it must drive you to action. I think he still hoped Mrs. Bromley herself might take care of matters for him. However, when I spoke with him that day and implicated Sabine, implied that Mrs. Bromley might know about their relationship, and threatened to bring in the police, that pushed him over the edge, and he decided he must be rid of her, once and for all."

Alice also nodded. "I, too, wish to thank you both. You have certainly shown yourself worthy of my trust, Mr. Holmes. And you have saved my life. If it were not for you..." Her smile was bittersweet.

"I am happy to have been able to remove the threat hanging over you."

Her smile dwindled. "That is the problem, Mr. Holmes. That is why we have come to see you. The threat is not truly gone."

Holmes gave her a puzzled look. "Your husband will not trouble you again. I think I can promise you that. I have little doubt that he will be convicted and..." He did not say "hanged" aloud, but the word still hovered unspoken in the air.

"It is not my husband that worries me."

"What, then?" I asked.

Holmes raised his hand again. "The Moonstone."

She nodded. "Exactly."

"I gave you the combination. Is the diamond still in the safe, or have you put it in a bank vault?"

Her eyes shifted to Cowen, and he reached into his jacket pocket and removed what had become a familiar sight: a square case of black velvet. Holmes gave his head a quick shake. "I suggest you take it to the bank immediately and leave it there."

"We had another course of action in mind. First of all, however, let me bring you up to date on certain matters." He turned briefly toward Alice. "Alice has had her solicitor initiate divorce proceedings against Charles Bromley. As you may know, in England a divorce can be difficult to obtain, but in this case..." His mouth curved upward briefly, even as he stroked at his beard. "Attempted murder is certainly sufficient grounds. Also..."

He hesitated, lowering his eyes, then raising them again. "I have spoken with Alice and revealed to her something of my true feelings. She has given me hope that after things are more settled and sufficient time has elapsed—a year or two, perhaps—I might pursue a more permanent union with her." Alice gave him a smile that was far more revealing than Cowen's elevated language. "At this point, I remain both her doctor and a trusted friend, but in the future if things should work out as I wish, I shall want to relinquish the former role. I do not approve of doctors trying to care for those persons dearest to them. Who knows?" He rolled his eyes briefly upward. "I might even be willing to entrust her to a woman doctor."

I shook my head, smiling. "Amazing!"

"But just now, the Moonstone still casts a dark shadow over our lives—especially over hers. I do not exactly believe in the supernatural, but an object can still be cursed." He turned to Alice. "Tell them."

"The Moonstone has blighted my life, Mr. Holmes. It killed my mother and my father. It destroyed my husband. And it almost killed me. Can you see the truth of what I say?"

Holmes's gray eyes stared at her, even as he touched his chin with his fingertips. "Yes, I can. Your mother was of a sensitive nature like yourself. The Moonstone drove her to her death. It also fueled your father's anger and mania. And your husband..."

Her expression was grave. "I cannot really blame myself, but if I had not been wearing the Moonstone on that first night so long ago... He was smitten by the diamond–captured–the instant he saw it. Oh, perhaps he once had some little love for me, at the beginning." Her smiled was pained. "I hope so." Holmes and I exchanged a look, and I knew we were both recalling Bromley saying that he had never loved Alice. "All the same, the diamond was what really attracted him, and his fascination finally destroyed him. He wanted to kill me so he could possess it absolutely. I understand now... Whenever I wore it, when he stared at me and smiled, it was never for me–it was always for the Moonstone."

"Perhaps..." I began, but my voice faltered.

"It does not greatly pain me, Dr. Vernier. Not any longer. I think a part of me always knew that he did not really love me. And because of that, I, in turn, could never truly love him. He was always elusive, hollow, with something missing at the core of him. So you see, the Moonstone has brought nothing but death and pain into my life. Perhaps someday I may have children." A slight flush appeared on her cheek. "I hope so! And if I do, could I leave them such a monstrous inheritance of death!" She shook her head savagely. "*Impossible.*"

"What do you want me to do?" Holmes asked.

Cowen replied. "We want you to take the Moonstone to Mr. Tyabji and have him return it to India. We have had another fake diamond made. It will go into a bank vault. Alice will never again wear that fake or even speak of the Moonstone. Her sister and her friends can assume the jewel is safely locked away forever. Someday–I hope in the far distant future–when it is passed on to her child or to her nephew, someone will probably discover that it is a fake, but by then it should not matter."

Alice raised one hand in supplication. "You do understand, Mr. Holmes? You must."

"I do. I am of the same mind as Dr. Cowen. I do not believe in the supernatural, but I believe in accursed objects, and surely near the top of a list of the ill-fated and jinxed, would be the Moonstone. After all you have endured, madam, you would be a fool to keep it near you for a moment longer. Its return to its original owners will probably be the first noble event in its long and bloody history."

Alice smiled even as her eyes filled with tears. "Oh thank you, Mr. Holmes–thank you!"

Cowen was staring at me. "Do you understand, Henry?"

I nodded. "Yes, I do."

Cowen stood up, walked over to Holmes and handed him the velvet case. "I leave this, then, in your care, Mr. Holmes."

Holmes slipped the case into his inside jacket pocket. "Very well. I shall take it to my bank for safekeeping and speak soon with Mr. Tyabji. Might I also include Mr. Murthwaite in the conversation?"

Alice nodded. "Oh yes, Jack can absolutely be trusted."

"Murthwaite is returning to India soon. He and Tyabji can take the Moonstone with them to Gujarat. I shall suggest they employ some trustworthy men to accompany them as guards. So long as no one knows what they are actually carrying, they should be safe enough." He laughed softly. "So many ships pass through the Suez Canal, but the one carrying the most valuable cargo of all will be traveling incognito, so to speak."

"I must get back to my practice," Cowen said. "Thank you again for everything."

Holmes, Alice and I stood up. Alice walked toward Holmes, a radiant smile on her face, her skin aglow. I had never seen her so happy. I think she might have actually kissed him on the cheek, but her big hat with the plumes was in the way. Her pale-blue eyes regarded him, and then her slender hand reached out to squeeze his forearm tightly. He started ever so slightly, then stared back, his smile faintly wary.

"Thank you, Mr. Holmes. Now I am free, totally free, for the first time in my life. The Moonstone is gone, truly gone, along with the curse that has plagued my family for nearly a century. I owe it–and my life–to you." She opened her small handbag and withdrew a folded check. "This is for you."

Holmes glanced at it, and his eyes widened. "Very generous, madam."

"It is nothing. I wish I were really wealthy so I could give you what you truly deserve." She turned, and I caught her hand in my own and pressed it tightly. Again, I was struck by how slender and fragile it seemed compared to Michelle's. "I am happy for you," I said. "I am certain your life will be better now."

"I hope so. It will never be easy–I was not made for an easy life. The doctor and I have talked, and I shall try to gradually reduce the laudanum. Someday I hope to be free of it, as well. But for now I am content just to have the diamond gone. That is enough. By the way, thank your wife for her visit last week. She was most kind. Tell her I am well enough for a long walk in the park."

"So I shall."

After a few parting words, they left us. I glanced at Holmes. "I think this may all work out in the end. Cowen has his rough edges, but he is a decent man, a compassionate one, even. He clearly loves her, he has known her for many years, and he will treat her well."

Holmes shrugged. "Perhaps. Again, you know more about matters of the heart than I do."

I shook my head. "I knew absolutely nothing of Bromley in the end."

"That was different. Villains are my specialty, and Dr. Cowen is clearly not a villain. Nor does he have the wandering eye and the perverse inclinations of his predecessor. I do wish them well. In the meantime, would you like to accompany me for a stroll on this fine morning? We shall go wherever our legs will take us—but first they will take us in the most direct route to the bank, so this…" he patted his hand at his jacket near his heart, "…may be safely stowed in the vault. I shall not rest easy until then."

I felt a slight shiver. "I'll gladly come along, and I must admit, I shall be happy to see it locked up."

He smiled at me, his gray eyes suddenly serious. "So will I, Henry. So will I." He hesitated, then reached inside his jacket. "Let us, however, have one last look." He opened the case and withdrew the diamond, holding it between thumb and forefinger. "Curious. You and I are largely immune to its charms. Oh, we find it beautiful enough, but neither of us would kill for it."

"Certainly not."

His fingers slowly turned the stone, letting light play over it, flashing off the facets. By morning it did have a yellow hue, rather than the blue we had seen at night. "To think it was once a crystalline lump buried in the earth. Some artisan of great skill labored with a chisel and hammer to carve it into this splendid object. And then its long tale of woe and grief began. The curse lies not within the stone, but within the hearts of men. Something in this beautiful thing brings out the worst, a frenzy of desire accompanied by a blood lust. Out of beauty and light comes darkness and brutality." He shook his head. "It may soon be set in Chandra's forehead, but of one thing we can be certain—it will not rest there forever. Someone will steal it again someday, and the whole cycle of bloodshed and retribution will begin again."

I found that I had been unconsciously holding my breath, and I drew in some air. "Put it away. We have seen enough."

He stared at me, his clear gray eyes and aquiline nose so prominent in that thin, pale face. His lips drew back. "You don't think I should take it and have a fake made? Then I might keep it for myself." I gave him a horrified look, and he laughed softly. "A joke, Henry, only a joke." He placed the jewel back in the case, snapped shut the lid, and thrust it into his pocket. "Unlike Mr. Bromley, I can see that Mrs. Bromley is the true treasure, one which he foolishly cast aside."

I gave a relieved sigh. "Yes. After all, the Moonstone cannot warm your bed at night."

"No, indeed." We went to the door. Holmes took his top hat and stick, hesitated only an instant, then raised his stick, brandishing it in the air as he proclaimed, "Once more unto the bank, dear friends!"

I gave him a strange look, and he laughed in earnest. "Forgive me, Henry—and forgive me, Shakespeare. The diamond seems to have a curious effect on me. I assure you I shall be quite recovered once it has been left in the vault."

* * *

On a fine Saturday afternoon in October, Michelle sat in the big purple velvet chair stroking our cat Victoria and sipping her coffee. Victoria was a large mass of long black fur with white whiskers and a white splotch at her throat and on her forehead. Michelle's white fingers stood out against the black fur, and I reflected, not for the first time, that her robust and sturdy hands and feet were quite beautiful. One would not think they could be the objects of amorous thoughts, but I truly loved and desired every inch of her. Her hands were so graceful, so expressive, even when doing simple things like holding a cup and stroking a cat.

She had seen some patients that morning, but she was finished by noon. Exchanging a conspiratorial look, we had given Harriet the afternoon off, which would allow us, provided we closed the windows first, to fall upon each other and express our passions as loudly as we pleased. I had prepared ham and cheese sandwiches for lunch, and afterwards we had gone to our sitting room to drink our coffee. In relief, she had let down her long red hair, shaking it about, and pulled off her "wretched boots," as she called them, and her stockings.

She looked up from the cat at me. "A penny for your thoughts."

"I was savoring the sight of you. And looking forward to the afternoon."

She smiled. "I am also looking forward to the afternoon."

"However, I have a chore I had best get over and done with. I have something for you. A present."

"But it's not my birthday. Why a present?"

"Surely a devoted husband doesn't have to have a reason to give his wife a present."

"I suppose not. What is it?"

"You will see soon enough." I went into our bedroom and

returned with a small package wrapped in brown paper. "It should have ribbons and bows and white paper, but I was never much good at wrapping."

Still smiling, she set down her cup and extended her hand. "Now you have me all excited! I can't wait to see what it is."

I hesitated. "I should perhaps warn you... You need not keep it... if it seems too extravagant..."

"No more of this coyness, Henry! Give it to me." She lifted Victoria with both hands and set her resolutely on the floor, causing a wailful meow. Her hands eagerly slipped off the string and opened up the package. When she saw the large purple velvet case, her forehead creased, her smile fading. "Henry..." Her eyes were faintly puzzled.

"Go ahead. Have a look."

She opened the case, and the white of her eyes showed briefly about the round blue irises. "My God," she murmured. "What have you done?"

"Well, take it out."

She set the case on her lap and raised the necklace by its silver chain. The large blue sapphire at the bottom was surrounded by tiny false diamonds, and above it were four smaller sapphires. The big one was slightly darker, a beautiful deep blue which picked up the color of her eyes.

"Do you like it?" I asked.

Her eyes were fixed on the jewels. "Oh yes, I've never seen anything so beautiful." A smile flickered over her lips, then grew wistful as she stared at me. "But I'm not sure..." She shook her head. "It must have cost a great deal."

I drew in my breath. "Yes."

She bit her lower lip. "Exactly how much?"

"A hundred pounds–which was a bargain."

She groaned. "Oh, I cannot keep such a thing! Wherever did you get the money? Surely–surely you did not borrow it! Oh, Henry, tell me you did not borrow money to buy me jewelry."

"I did not borrow money to buy you jewelry." My tone was somewhat aggrieved.

"How then?"

"Sherlock gave me a hundred and fifty pounds a few weeks ago."

"Whatever for?"

"Adam Selton paid him three hundred pounds for his assistance in the case of the White Worm. Sherlock said I deserved half for my helping Adam, for my removing the obstacle to Adam's marriage."

She smiled. "That does make a certain sense. You were the one Adam finally trusted enough to reveal his secret." Her expression grew grave again. "Oh, Henry, I just don't know. It is so extravagant."

"Would you like to try it on?"

"That might shake what little resolve I have."

I stared at her. "It was to show you how much I love you."

She set down the jewel and case, stood up, curled her hand around the back of my neck and shook her head. "You don't need jewels for that–you show me all the time–especially when..." She turned her head to kiss me.

When we had finished at last, I raised her hands and kissed her knuckles. "I knew you might be reluctant to keep it, but I'm afraid I cannot return it to the shop. Still, if you absolutely do not want it, I'm sure we could find a buyer. I might even be able to get back more than I paid."

"Why can't you return it?"

"I got it almost on a whim. It was from Harter's shop.

Remember Harter, the jeweler who was murdered? He showed me that necklace when Holmes and I visited him. The shop had been shut up for a long time, but I happened by, and they were having a liquidation sale of all his goods. Normally I am not much of a bargainer, but I stuck to my guns. It was actually rather amusing once I had determined a strategy. The salesman told me he wanted three hundred pounds, which I knew was ridiculous. I offered him one hundred and was absolutely unyielding. Three times I left the store. Once he ran down the block and begged me to return. He told me he would accept my offer, then started to quibble once we were back inside. I started for the door again, and he gave up at last, weary of the game."

She laughed. "How brave of you!"

"So you see, there is no harm in trying it on."

"Will your feelings be hurt if I do not keep it?"

I shrugged. "I shall manage."

Again her forehead creased. "Oh, I just don't know. I... I wouldn't want to wear it in society—that I absolutely could not bear. I loathe women who parade about in their jewelry, flaunting it to the world. Often, too... It is not charitable to say so, but there often seems to be an inverse ratio between true beauty and the value of the jewelry."

I laughed. "I have noticed that. But the rule does not hold in your case."

"Oh, Henry." She touched my cheek with her fingertips. "You are so very sweet."

"Actually... It would be safer if you did not wear it in society. I am uneasy about keeping such a necklace in our house, but if no one even knows we have it... I'm sure we could find a good hiding place."

"Why keep it, then?"

I stared at her. "You could wear it for me alone. In the bedroom."

Her cheek slowly flushed. "And little else, I suspect."

"How clever you are." I leaned over and kissed her again. It lasted a long while. She drew away at last, and brushed back the long tresses at the right side of her head. "I suppose there is no harm in giving it a trial run, especially if you cannot simply return it."

"No harm at all."

She smiled at me, and then the bell sounded, shattering the calm of the quiet afternoon. "Oh Lord," I moaned. "Ignore it!"

"Someone might be genuinely ill, Henry. It would be one thing if we were—but at this point, we have no excuse. Let me just look out the window." She walked across the room, raised the sash and quickly looked out down below. "It's Sherlock."

"Let him wait."

"Are you sure?"

"Oh, all right, let's see what he wants. I shall be right back." I left the room and quickly went down the stairs.

I opened the door, but no one was there. I stepped out and looked right, then left. Holmes had swung his stick up over his shoulder and started down the sidewalk. I hesitated only an instant. "Sherlock!"

He turned. "Ah, there you are!" He came back toward me. "I hope…" He smiled at me. "I have received a letter from Mr. Murthwaite this morning. I thought it would interest you and Michelle."

"Murthwaite! Then the Moonstone…"

"It is all in the letter."

"Come in, then. We must see it."

He gave me an amused glance. "I shall not detain you long."

I said nothing, just nodded and ushered him in. I went up the stairs first. On one particular case, Holmes had deduced that a man must have spent the afternoon with his mistress from the slight disorder of his dress and the lingering smell of cheap perfume. He had also proclaimed that the afternoon was a time of day reserved exclusively for expensive harlots and their clientele. I told him that was absolutely not true. He had regarded me thoughtfully, then said he must defer to my greater knowledge. I knew, however, that this particular fact had been filed away in that great brain of his!

Michelle had put on her shoes and bound up her long red hair in an unruly coil, errant strands falling every which way. The necklace and its case were gone. "Sherlock, what a pleasant surprise."

"He has a letter from Mr. Murthwaite," I said.

"Does he now? Have he and Mr. Tyabji returned the diamond, then?"

Holmes withdrew an envelope from his pocket. "You shall read it all for yourselves." He unfolded the pages and handed them to me. I went to the window where the light was better, and Michelle followed. We began to read.

Dear Mr. Holmes and Dr. Vernier,

I thought you would want to know all that has happened with the Moonstone. Geoffrey, his father and I presented it to the Maharajah, who was most grateful. Geoffrey has insisted that Alice receive the thousand pounds he originally promised her for its return. I then spent some time with my wife and sons, but rejoined Geoffrey some days later. We had resolved to once again see the magnificent desolation of Somanatha and its ruined temple. The Maharajah has his hopes of restoring the temple, but they may or may not bear fruit.

In the wild regions of the Kathiawar peninsula where Gondal lies, the population is fanatically devoted to the old Hindu religion—to the ancient worship of Brahma and Vishnu. Two of the most famous shrines of Hindu pilgrimage are contained within the boundaries of Kathiawar. One of them is Dwarka, the birthplace of the god Krishna. The other is that sacred city of Somanatha—sacked, and destroyed as long since as the eleventh century, by Muslim conquerors.

Somanatha was some three days distant, journeying on foot, from the Maharajah's palace.

We had not been long on the road, before we noticed that other people—by twos and threes—appeared to be traveling in the same direction as ourselves. By then, Geoffrey and I had both "gone native" as they say, wearing the linen garments of the locals, as well as turbans. With his head of golden hair hidden, the Indian half of my friend becomes prominent. I know the local language as well as I know my own, and I am lean, worn and brown enough to make it no easy matter to detect my European origin. Thus we could pass muster with the people readily, not as one of themselves, but as strangers from a distant part of their own country.

On the second day, the number of Hindus traveling in our direction had increased to fifties and hundreds. On the third day, the throng had swollen to thousands; all slowly converging to one point—the city of Somanatha. This multitude was on its way to a great religious ceremony, which was to take place on a hill at a little distance from Somanatha. The ceremony was in honor of the god of the

Moon; and it was to be held at night.

The crowd detained us as we drew near to the place of celebration. By the time we reached the hill the moon was high in the heaven. Some higher-caste Hindu friends possessed special privileges which enabled them to gain access to the shrine, and they kindly allowed us to accompany them. When we arrived at the place, we found the shrine hidden from our view by a curtain hung between two magnificent trees. Beneath the trees a flat projection of rock jutted out, and formed a species of natural platform. Below this, we stood, in company with our friends.

Looking back down the hill, the view presented the grandest spectacle of Nature and Man, in combination, that I have ever seen. The lower slopes of the eminence melted imperceptibly into a grassy plain, the place of the meeting of three rivers. On one side, the graceful winding of the waters stretched away, now visible, now hidden by trees, as far as the eye could see. On the other, the waveless ocean slept in the calm of the night. Imagine this lovely scene with tens of thousands of human creatures, all dressed in white, stretching down the sides of the hill, overflowing into the plain, and fringing the nearer banks of the winding rivers. Light this halt of the pilgrims by the wild red flames of torches, streaming up at intervals from every part of the innumerable throng. Imagine the moonlight of the East, pouring in unclouded glory over all—and you will form some idea of the view that met us when we looked forth from the summit of the hill!

A strain of plaintive music, played on stringed instruments, and flutes, recalled our attention to the hidden shrine. Suddenly, a new strain of music, loud and jubilant, began.

The crowd around us shuddered, and pressed together.

The curtain between the trees was drawn aside, and the shrine was disclosed to view.

There, raised high on a throne—seated on his typical antelope, with his four arms stretching towards the four corners of the earth—there, soared above us, dark and awful in the mystic light of heaven, the god of the Moon, Chandra. And there, in the forehead of the deity, gleamed the yellow diamond, whose splendor had shone on me in England, from the bosom of a woman's dress!

Yes, after the lapse of eight centuries, the Moonstone looks forth once more, over the walls of the sacred city in which its story first began. You have lost sight of it in England, I hope forever! So the years pass, and repeat each other; so the same events revolve in the cycles of time. What will be the next adventures of the Moonstone? Who can tell? I for one hope it will rest on the god's forehead for many years to come!

Yours truly,
Jack Murthwaite.

I shook my head. "Amazing. I would not have expected such poetry from Jack. He certainly brings the scene alive."

Michelle nodded. "I would have liked to be there to see the moon rising over all the worshipers."

Holmes took the letter from me, folded it up, and put it back into the envelope. "Certainly this is one of the most satisfying endings to a case that I can recall. Alice Bromley is relieved of the burden of the diamond, and it has returned to its rightful home. As for its next adventures, as Murthwaite puts it, let us hope they will be in the far distant future when we have long absented the scene! I am in a celebratory mood. Would the two of you be my guests for dinner this evening? Fittingly enough for a Vernier and a Doudet, there is a new French restaurant which Mycroft has recommended, and he has a most discriminating palate."

I glanced at Michelle. "Certainly. We would be happy to accompany you."

"Excellent, then. I shall be back here at exactly six." The corners of his mouth flickered upward, his gray eyes fixed on me. "In the meantime, the afternoon is yours to amuse yourselves as you will." He nodded. "I can let myself out."

Once he was gone Michelle stared closely at me. "Do you think he knows?"

"Of course he does. I made the mistake of once telling him that the afternoon was not reserved only for harlots and their clients."

"Oh, yes, I remember. You told me that–and I said, *how could you!* Well, I for one am embarrassed."

"You needn't be. Where were we now? You were about to try on the necklace."

"Yes, and Henry…" She reached out to grasp my hand. "I have been thinking. We can keep it, at least for a while, although if we should ever need the money, we must agree to sell it."

"Oh, certainly."

"Very well." She went to the bureau drawer and took it out.

"Let me help you," I said. "First, however, we cannot have the sapphires resting on mere fabric." She was wearing a favorite worn green muslin dress with a row of buttons down the front. Its tight collar hid the hollow between her collarbones. I undid the top buttons and opened up the dress. "That's better." She gave me a bemused smile. "Stay put." I unfastened the necklace, stepped behind her, kissed the nape of her neck, then reached round to grab one end and bring it around. I re-fastened the clasp, then gently turned her around. "Oh, yes. That is lovely." I pulled down her left sleeve, baring her shoulder, and kissed it.

"I can see where this is leading. So I suppose you want me to model it for you?"

"If you insist."

She touched my cheek with her hand. "Give me a minute, then." She walked away in the direction of the bedroom.

I sighed softly. I sat down, then heaved off one boot, then the other. After a while I stood and went down the hallway to the bedroom door. "Ready?"

"One second. All right."

I opened the door. She had wrapped a sheet around her, leaving one long white arm and her feet bare. Her red hair was unbound again and all astray. "I feel slightly preposterous–like Messalina, or Salome, or another femme fatale in some dreadful overwrought romance."

"I shall be the judge of that, foul temptress."

I stepped forward, took hold of the sheet and tugged at it. She resisted for a moment, then let me pull it away. She raised her hands, then lowered them. "This is embarrassing, all right."

"It is as I thought," I murmured.

"And what was that?"

"That you are more beautiful than any diamonds or sapphires."

She flushed slightly. "Oh, Henry, you are a hopeless romantic! You were never this way when I first knew you. Love has made you delirious."

"No, no–love has made me see exactly how glorious you are. The sapphires do bring out the color of your eyes. They complement one another." I reached out with my fingertips to touch the central blue stone, then let my finger slip off onto her sternum and on down to her waist. I felt her shiver. I shook my head. "Bromley really was a fool. How could any man prefer the beauty of something cold and dead to that of a living, breathing woman?"

"Oh, enough talk, my darling—enough talk! And you must take off your clothes, too." She opened my jacket, yanked off one sleeve, then the other, and we held each other.

We discovered almost immediately, that while the necklace might be enticing in the anticipation, when you actually drew together, the stones were truly hard and almost sharp! We cried out in unison as they dug into our flesh. I quickly turned her, unfastened the clasp, and set the necklace on the night table. Sapphires and diamonds were soon forgotten.

About the Author

S am Siciliano is the author of several novels, including the Titan Sherlock Holmes titles *The Angel of the Opera*, *The Web Weaver*, *The Grimswell Curse* and *The White Worm*. He lives in Vancouver, Washington.